PRAISE FOR THE CHOSEN: *AND I WILL GIVE YOU REST*

And I Will Give You Rest made me weep the same way Jerry's son's *The Chosen* does, which oughta keep tissue stocks rising. Don't say I didn't warn you.

Mark Lowry Singer, humorist

And I Will Give You Rest brings the story of Jesus and his followers to life in a way never before seen. By imagining plausible back stories to well-known characters, Jerry allows us to see ourselves in them and bring our own frailties to Christ and draw closer to him. The streaming series and these novels may very well usher in a global revival of love for Christ and move us to love others as he loves us.

Terry Fator Singing ventriloquist/impressionist
and winner of *America's Got Talent*

If you have ever wondered what it might have been like to have been a friend or family member of the twelve disciples of Jesus, Jerry Jenkins's *And I Will Give You Rest* will transport you into the minds of the early followers of Christ. You will be reminded of their humanity and might even see yourself as you seek to follow the One who still radically changes lives today.

Gary D. Chapman Author of *The Five Love Languages*

A fictional work that expands on Bible stories is successful when it drives you back into the Word of God. And Jerry Jenkins's new novel paints a beautiful behind-the-scenes portrait of the first people whose lives were transformed by Jesus. I was especially moved by the imagined conversation between Jesus and one of his disabled followers who did not receive healing. The words chosen for this poignant dialogue struck home in a deep and powerful way. For like this disciple I, too, have asked my Savior to heal me of chronic pain. And this scene relays the stunning fact that Jesus, in all his love and tenderness, often chooses not to heal people. Why? Well, you'll have to read this novel to find the answer. But keep a tissue on hand; your heart will be moved.

Joni Eareckson Tada Joni and Friends International Disability Center

The stories of Jesus' life and ministry in the New Testament are some of the Bible's most encouraging and illuminating passages. With *And I Will Give You Rest*, Jerry Jenkins has once again provided a gripping story that will point readers back to the beauty of Christ as revealed in Scripture.

Jim Daly President and CEO of Focus on the Family

And I Will Give You Rest connects me again to Jesus. And, oh, what a Savior he is!

Ernie Haase Grammy-nominated tenor and founder of Ernie Haase and Signature Sound

Well, Jerry Jenkins has done it again in his third offering in this series. The depth of emotion he captures in those around Jesus only deepens our understanding of what Jesus goes through in this escalating, tension-filled period of his ministry. We were hooked on page one and left wanting more at the end. If you love watching The Chosen Series, this is a must read.

Al & Phil Robertson Authors & Co-hosts of The Unashamed Podcast

The CHOSEN®

BOOK THREE AND I WILL GIVE YOU REST

JERRY B. JENKINS

FOCUS ON THE FAMILY.

BroadStreet PUBLISHING

And I Will Give You Rest

A Focus on the Family book published by BroadStreet Publishing.

Editors: Larry Weeden and Leilani Squires

Cover design by Michael Harrigan

ISBN 978-1-64607-022-0 (hardcover)

ISBN 978-1-64607-130-2 (paperback)

Library of Congress Cataloging-in-Publication Data can be found at www.loc.gov.

Printed in China

27 26 25 24 23 5 4 3 2 1

To Greg Thornton

Based on *The Chosen,* a multi-season TV show created and directed by Dallas Jenkins and written by Ryan M. Swanson, Dallas Jenkins, and Tyler Thompson.

NOTE

The Chosen was created by lovers of and believers in the Bible and Jesus Christ. Our deepest desire is that you delve into the New Testament Gospels for yourself and discover Jesus.

Contents

Part 4 Clean

Part 5 Intensity in Tent City

Part 6 Why?

"Judge not,
that you be not judged.
For with the judgment you
pronounce you will be judged,
and with the measure you use it
will be measured to you."

MATTHEW 7:1-2

PART 1
Homecoming

Chapter 1

"DON'T CALL ME ABBA"

Capernaum, 24 A.D.

Matthew dreads the day ahead.

A rising star within the Roman Authority under Praetor Quintus, he has seen his sphere of authority expanded. Despite being the youngest tax collector in his hometown, he is now in charge of enforcing penalties for any Jewish citizens delinquent in their tributes to Rome. He's known for his business acumen and the ability to squeeze every last shekel from those in his district. Matthew has quickly learned all the tricks of his trade.

To bolster even his lucrative salary, he pockets anything he can collect in excess of what is actually owed to Rome. When implying a higher obligation to fellow Jews who know better, he suggests that compliance will afford them a break in the future—not in the amount he expects, but perhaps in the time they're allowed to pay it. He carefully manages the resources to keep Rome satisfied while more than doubling his income in the long run.

Such practices have afforded Matthew his mansion in the most exclusive neighborhood in town, not to mention the finest imported apparel, footwear, fragrances, and jewelry. The irony of it all is that he laps up the envy of his fellow citizens, while his very oddness makes him long for invisibility. He knows he misses the subtlety of sarcasm and barbed humor, but he fully understands the contempt hurled his way everywhere he is recognized—it comes in curses and spittle. Matthew cannot remember the last time he was met with a smile. He lives for the hint of admiration that comes from the Romans, who shake their heads at what he is able to weasel out of his own people.

My own people, he thinks. Beyond a few fellow tax collectors, he has no friend among the Jews. They clearly view him as the ultimate turncoat, traitor, financial cudgel. It's not enough that they suffer the iron fist of Rome. No. That fist is thrust by the quirky, baby-faced son of Alphaeus and Elisheba—Jews so devout that for years they called Matthew Levi, convinced he would someday honor the one true God as a priest among his people.

Matthew quickly disabused his parents of that notion as a youngster in Hebrew school. Even then he was vilified by boys his age who could have, should have, been his pals. But he was slighter than most, proved anything but athletic, and ran—when he ran—with a halting, awkward gait. He only watched the others roughhouse, having no interest in soiling his tunic or enduring taunts about his idiosyncrasies.

Even he did not understand his obsession with precision and order. His scrolls, paper, writing instruments, and the like had to be arranged just so before him on the table. His seeming preternatural affinity for numbers and calculations made Matthew what the others called the rabbi's pet. And while they painstakingly memorized the Torah, he was pushed ahead to mathematical classes with older students.

Somehow he understood that, though those his own age were loath to admit it, they had to envy him, even if they did not accept him. Well, he would show them, leave them in the dust. And while his ability to induce the disdain of his compatriots extended to his stellar tax collecting career, he told himself he would trade wealth and status for acceptance any day. Even his devastated parents had to acknowledge his singular achievement, didn't they?

Yet today, as he endures his maddening morning routine, more niggles at the back of his mind than simply hoping to avoid as many scowls and curses from his fellow Jews as possible. Selecting his attire, jewelry, and fragrance requires the usual touching of every piece before settling on the very ones he lands on every day, and all the while he rehearses how he'll handle his diciest task so far.

Today is the day he leaves his tax booth closed and makes the rounds of the homes of those behind in their accounts. He'll take with him the centurion Lucius, one of his own guard's most threatening henchmen. Lucius's mere presence intimidates most into paying up immediately. Scofflaws who might normally attempt to shame Matthew for serving as a lapdog to the Romans tend to hold their tongues when they encounter the soldier.

While overdue collection day is always awkward and exhausting, it can also prove lucrative. Yet nothing about this day appeals to Matthew, for he has scheduled his toughest case first. And for this one, he has assigned Lucius the task of making the approach and the demand on his own. Matthew will look on from within earshot but out of sight.

"I've got this," Lucius tells Matthew. "I love this kind of work."

"Just see that he pays—today."

"Oh, he'll pay, one way or the other."

Matthew shows the soldier the name on his ledger and points out the house. Resplendent in red, Lucius strides to the door, his clanging metal and squeaking leather drawing stares from others in the street. He spreads his feet and bangs loudly four times.

"Coming!"

As the door swings open, the resident's look of curiosity dissolves into a shudder. Before the man can speak, Lucius bellows, "Alphaeus bar Joram?"

"Yes," the man manages, sounding tentative.

"You are twenty days past your deadline for this quarter's tribute. Your collector has transferred your case to the Roman office. Are you able to pay your penalty now?"

Alphaeus has turned ashen. "I—I filed for an extension in the month of—"

"I'll take that as a no. By decree of Quintus, honorable praetor of Capernaum, I must remand you into custody."

Matthew blanches. He had not expected Lucius to leapfrog to such aggression so quickly. Surely Alphaeus will quickly find a way to pay.

"I'm very sorry," Alphaeus says. "I didn't realize—"

Lucius removes a leather strap from his waistbelt. "Turn around!"

That'll do it, Matthew decides.

"Sir," Alphaeus whines, "I didn't realize. May I request an extension of just five days?"

Agonizing now, Matthew hopes against hope Lucius will grant the request. Five days is nothing. It's not as if the man is a criminal.

But Lucius grabs Alphaeus's arm. And from inside comes the plaintive call of a woman. "Alphaeus, who is it?"

Oh, no! Matthew thinks. This is spiraling out of control.

"Everything's fine, Elisheba!" Alphaeus calls out, somehow able to sound more confident than he looks. He whispers to Lucius, "Please, I beg you . . ."

Lucius yanks Alphaeus from the doorway and slams him against the frame.

"Adonai in heaven!" Alphaeus cries.

"Adonai is not here," Lucius barks, beginning to tie Alphaeus's hands behind his back.

It's more than Matthew can stomach, and he quickly approaches. "I can settle this, Lucius. There's actually been a mistake."

Lucius looks shocked. "What do you mean? You told me to—"

"I'm aware, but I've realized the timeline was miscalculated. I will clear it up. Thank you."

"*You* miscalculated? That's never happened!"

"I was given inaccurate information, but now it's being corrected. I will handle this. It would be best for you to go to our next house, and I will meet you at the booth in one hour."

Lucius glares at Alphaeus, shakes his head at Matthew, and trudges away.

Alphaeus narrows his eyes at Matthew. "Are *you* now my—"

"It isn't prudent to discuss this now, Abba. There isn't much time."

"First the shame of your choice—and now you are actually my collector?"

"Matthew?" Elisheba says from the door. "What are you doing here?"

"Your son is our publicanus!" Alphaeus says.

"Matthew, no," she says, covering her mouth.

"He sent a soldier to your home!" Alphaeus adds.

"I'm sorry," Matthew says quickly. "I didn't want you to know. I didn't choose this district."

"You *chose* this job!" Alphaeus shouts. "The Romans never forced you into it. You *chose* to apply. You *chose* to betray—"

"Unlike you, Abba, I chose a secure future." Matthew regrets this as soon as it comes from his mouth.

His mother says, "You are called to trust in Adonai with your whole heart and to lean not on your own understanding."

"I *have* trusted!" Matthew says. "But can you name one thing Adonai has done for our people in a hundred years? Five hundred?"

"A traitor *and* a blasphemer," Alphaeus spits.

Don't they realize I have their fate in my hands? Matthew thinks. "Well," he says, "you owe your government two months' worth of tribute."

Alphaeus presses his lips together. "I will bring in a payment at the end of the week."

"You've missed two payments. I was hoping Lucius would convince you, but I will no longer protect you."

"I don't *want* your protection!"

How can he say this? Well, if that's the way he wants it … "Then you have twenty-four hours, Abba."

"Don't call me Abba."

Elisheba says, "Alphaeus, please …"

Matthew knows he should have seen this coming, but still it stings. "What?"

"Elly," Alphaeus says, "cover the windows and put on your veil. We will sit shiva for seven days."

Sit shiva?

"I have no son," Alphaeus adds as he guides his whimpering wife back inside and slams the door.

Chapter 2

TEARS

The Korazim Plateau
Seven years later

To his knowledge, Matthew's parents have still not forgiven him, let alone accepted him. For all he knows, he remains an orphan in his father's eyes. That's why the words of Jesus, the man to whom Matthew has surrendered his entire life and future, seem to wash over him, bathing every fiber of his soul.

His rabbi and master speaks to a massive throng blanketing the hillside, preaching a sermon the former tax collector feels privileged to have helped him rehearse. He mouths the words right along with his rabbi. "You have heard it was said to those of old, 'You shall not murder, and whoever murders will be liable to judgment.' But I say to you that everyone who is angry with his brother will be liable to judgment."

What is it about this man that allows him to speak with such authority and compassion? It's all Matthew can do to drink it in.

Jesus continues, "So if you are offering your gift at the altar and there remember that your brother has something against you, leave your gift there before the altar and go."

A lump rises in Matthew's throat. Jesus is speaking to healing his past and offering hope for the future.

"First be reconciled to your brother, and then come and offer your gift."

Matthew wonders how the other followers of the Messiah must be responding to this. He cannot take his eyes off Jesus.

Judas has never heard anything like this. He finds himself so taken with Jesus' message, his approach, even his delivery, that it makes Judas's profession pale in comparison. He's never before even dreamt of leaving his and his business partner's lucrative—if not entirely aboveboard—enterprise, but suddenly he feels tempted to cast his lot with this man! *Have I lost my mind?* Jesus' ragged band of followers seem to have nothing. How do they eat? They appear to need new clothes.

"Therefore I tell you, do not be anxious about your life, what you will eat or what you will drink, nor about your body, what you will put on ..."

Is this man speaking directly to Judas, somehow able to read his mind?

"Is not life more than food, and the body more than clothing? Look at the birds of the air: they neither sow nor reap nor gather into barns, and yet your heavenly Father feeds them. Are you not of more value than they?"

Am I not? How Judas longs to be seen in such a way!

Tamar the Egyptian harbors no question about the identity of this teacher. She knows beyond doubt that he is the Messiah, for she has seen him perform miracles. She saw him not only approach and touch a leper, but actually embrace him. And instantly heal him! That's why she prevailed upon friends to take a paralytic friend of their own and lower him through a man's roof to get to Jesus. The rabbi healed him too, even in the face of Pharisees who called him a blasphemer and sinner.

"And which of you by being anxious can add a single hour to his span of life?"

That truism also strikes Andrew, who can't deny he feels anxious about nearly everything, especially since leaving his first rabbi, John the Baptizer, who has wound up in prison. Andrew fears for John's life, for his own brother Simon's life, for Jesus, for himself.

"And why are you anxious about clothing? Consider the lilies of the field, how they grow: they neither toil nor spin, yet I tell you, even Solomon in all his glory was not arrayed as one of these. But if God so clothes the grass of the field, which today is alive and tomorrow is thrown into the oven, will He not much more clothe you, O you of little faith?"

Is Jesus looking at me? Am I a man of little faith?

Mary of Magdala, though delivered, redeemed, and forgiven, can't help despairing over her own lack of faith—not in Jesus; she has no doubts about him. But she still doesn't trust herself. Why could she not keep herself from straying, even after all Jesus had done for her?

"Therefore do not be anxious saying, 'What shall we eat?' or 'What shall we drink?' or 'What shall we wear?' For the Gentiles seek after all these things, and your heavenly Father knows that you need them all. But seek first the kingdom of God and His righteousness, and all these things will be added to you."

That's all I want—the kingdom Jesus speaks of.

The young Pharisee Yussif is nothing if not conflicted, sweating in the sun and listening to this man who has brought nothing but trouble to his mentor and rabbi, Shmuel. But Yussif himself has witnessed things that make him question everything he has been taught. He has seen this preacher perform miracles, or at least accomplish tricks that appear miraculous. And now he speaks with such sureness as if he actually could be the chosen one, the—*no, it can't be possible, can it?*

Yussif challenged Jesus of Nazareth because of things he has said and done, and yet he somehow feels a certain empathy for the man and his followers. What is happening to him? And now is Jesus singling him out? It's one thing to confront a man for claiming to be someone he's not, for working on the sabbath, for daring to forgive sins. But it's another to deny what your eyes have shown you—a woman transformed, and a man healed.

"Judge not, that you be not judged. For with the judgment you pronounce you will be judged, and with the measure you use it will be measured to you. Why do you see the speck that is in your brother's eye but do not notice the log that is in your own eye? Or how can you say to your brother, 'Let me take the speck out of your eye,' when there is the log in your own eye? You hypocrite, first take the log out of your own eye, and then you will see clearly to take the speck out of your brother's eye."

Little James, Nathanael, and Thaddeus have been assigned crowd control, though they are hopelessly outnumbered. Nevertheless, this multitude needs no supervision, for they all seem rapt by the profundities flowing from the sage.

"So whatever you wish that others would do to you, do also to them, for this is the Law and the Prophets."

Matthew notices that Mary of Magdala is a pile of tears, as are several of Jesus' disciples. Mother Mary quietly approaches and whispers, "How's he doing?"

Matthew can barely speak. "Wha—the script?"

Mother Mary nods.

He peeks at his tablet. "The words are the same, but …"

"But now *he's* saying them."

Tears stream down Matthew's cheeks as he listens to all the blessings Jesus bestows on his hearers—plainly leaving out no one.

"Blessed are the poor in spirit, for theirs is the kingdom of heaven.

"Blessed are those who mourn, for they shall be comforted.

"Blessed are the meek, for they shall inherit the earth.

"Blessed are those who hunger and thirst for righteousness, for they shall be satisfied.

"Blessed are the merciful, for they shall receive mercy.

"Blessed are the pure in heart, for they shall see God.

"Blessed are the peacemakers, for they shall be called sons of God.

"Blessed are those who are persecuted for righteousness' sake, for theirs is the kingdom of heaven.

"Blessed are you when others revile you and persecute you and utter all kinds of evil against you falsely on my account. Rejoice and be glad, for your reward is great in heaven, for so they persecuted the prophets who were before you."

Matthew jots in his tablet that this plateau should now be known as The Mount of Blessings. But somehow that feels too pedestrian. In the end, these pronouncements are too deep, too touching, too solemn to be referred to as mere blessings. *Beatitudes,* Matthew decides. Some day, when he writes his comprehensive report of all he has witnessed of Jesus, he will memorialize this place as The Mount of Beatitudes.

Chapter 3

LEAVING

The Mount of Beatitudes

The two Simons—one the former fisherman and the other the former Zealot the rest now refer to as Zee—stand watching, listening. The one Jesus told he would now become a fisher of men finds himself wondering what Zee must think of this teaching. The Zealot brought to the group a unique mix of skills—most designed for hand-to-hand combat when the Jews finally find the wherewithal to stand up to the Romans and overthrow them. There's little call for Zee's abilities now, but Simon still finds him an interesting addition to the mix.

Jesus continues, "You have heard it was said, 'An eye for an eye and a tooth for a tooth.' But I say to you, do not resist the one who is evil. But if anyone slaps you on the right cheek, turn to him the other also. And if anyone would sue you and take your tunic, let him have your cloak as well. And if anyone forces you to go one mile, go with him two miles. Give to the one who begs from you, and do not refuse the one who would borrow from you."

Not far away stands Atticus, a senior member of the *Cohortes Urbanae,* an elite police force established by Caesar Augustus to act as marshals or soldier investigators. He has been following the Nazarene from a distance, surveilling his protégés, and meticulously listening—more so today than ever. Finally this man, this potential threat to Rome, is making public his manifesto. Oh, he's done this before, among his disciples and before small—and sometimes not so small—crowds. But this gathering alone shows the magnitude—and potential—of the vagabond's visibility and popularity.

Atticus wonders if he is the only one among the thousands here who thought to bring sustenance. That is nothing new for him—he always carries at least a piece of fruit. But if this goes on much longer, he's going to need something more substantial. And from the looks of the crowd, everyone is going to need something.

For the moment, however, everyone seems mesmerized by the paradoxes the preacher resorts to when making points it seems no one has raised before. Like this one: "You have heard that it was said, 'You shall love your neighbor and hate your enemy.' But I say to you, love your enemies and pray for those who persecute you, so that you may be sons of your Father who is in heaven. For He makes His sun rise on the evil and on the good, and sends rain on the just and on the unjust."

What in the name of Jupiter, Juno, and Minerva could this Jesus of Nazareth mean by that? *Love my enemies? Pray for them? Not on your life.*

In fact, Atticus suppresses a smile at the very thought of the stir such words might cause. And at how wrong Praetor Quintus is about Jesus. The crowd appears entranced. A man like this could be dangerous. And what a showman! If Atticus didn't know better, he'd say the man's moving casually through the crowd as he speaks appears to be a genuine expression of affection for them. Surely he's grooming them for something, but what? Insurrection? The Nazarene actually strokes the cheeks of some and seems to gaze deep into the eyes of others.

"Your Father knows what you need before you ask Him. Pray then like this: 'Our Father in heaven, hallowed be your name. Your kingdom come, your will be done, on earth as it is in heaven. Give us this day our daily bread, and forgive us our debts as we also have forgiven our debtors. And lead us not into temptation, but deliver us from evil. ...'"

Barnaby, the amputee, leans on his crutch next to Shula, his blind friend. They are accompanied by Zebedee and Salome, the parents of John and Big James, whom Jesus has nicknamed the Sons of Thunder. Barnaby can only imagine their pride in having their sons associated with this miracle-working orator.

Jesus continues, "Do not lay up for yourselves treasures on earth, where moth and rust destroy and where thieves break in and steal, but lay up for yourselves treasures in heaven, where neither moth nor rust destroys and where thieves do not break in and steal. For where your treasure is, there your heart will be also."

Judas is more than intrigued. He's fascinated by this magnetic man who stops strolling and stands firm, his eyes seeming to dance over the colossal gathering. Judas has spent the entirety of his young adult life trying to lay up treasures, as the teacher has so poignantly put it. It's true, his heart is in such treasure. What else is there to devote oneself to? Yet Jesus clearly has these people, all of them, in the palm of his hand.

"Everyone who hears these words of mine and does not do them will be like a foolish man who built his house on the sand. And the rain fell, and the floods came, and the winds blew and beat against that house, and it fell, and great was the fall of it. And everyone then who hears these words of mine and does them will be like a wise man who built his house on the rock. And the rain fell, and the floods came, and the winds blew and beat on that house, but it did not fall, because it had been founded on the rock."

Everyone who hears these words and does not do them, Judas repeats in his mind. What, he wonders, does the man want him to do? Is his quest for riches like a house built on sand? Might he be willing to abandon the idea and follow this rabbi? As soon as he allows the thought, it seems to expand within him, and he knows it's exactly what he wishes to do! There is something so dynamic, so compelling, so otherworldly about Jesus of Nazareth that Judas can think of nothing he'd rather do than follow him, become part of his inner circle.

At the golden hour of the day, though he's among thousands, Yussif feels alone. And he's grateful for that. What might he be tempted to say to Shmuel? Might he camouflage his true thoughts, his misgivings, his—he has to admit, if only to himself—intrigue with the mind-jarring thoughts Jesus has planted? How dumbfounding that he understands exactly what Jesus is trying to say.

The chatter around Yussif proves that others are similarly influenced. "You ever hear anything like that?" one asks another.

"Not with that kind of authority. He spoke with *actual* authority—his own, not from someone else."

"Yes, almost above the Law. Is he a revolutionary?"

The other, noticing Yussif's pharisaical garb, shushes his friend, and they both bow as they pass.

A cripple and a blind woman also pass, reciting lines from Jesus. "'Consider the lilies,' he said!" Barnaby cackles. "'How they neither toil nor spin …'"

"'Yet I tell you,'" Shula adds, "'Solomon in all his glory …'"

Yussif must find solitude, somewhere to think this through. He wants to hear no more, say no more, just ponder. He must get back to his chamber at the Beth Midrash in the synagogue, where he will be uninterrupted and close to the sacred scrolls.

Judas has made up his mind. He's on a mission and must tell his partner—the one with whom he swindled a landowner out of his property and later helped Jesus' disciples negotiate for this place to preach his sermon. Finally, Judas spots him, grinning ear to ear. "Hadad!" he calls out.

"I lost you!" Hadad says. "Did you find those guys?"

"I stood with his followers," Judas says, nodding.

"Could you see the people's faces? I've never seen a crowd so moved. That 'turn the other cheek and lay up treasures in heaven' business was a little naïve, but this man has talent!"

The treasures line was the very one that impressed Judas. "No, I've never seen anything like it."

"Can you imagine him selling for us?"

Selling for us? He thinks this man is a huckster? "Hadad?"

"Why didn't they take up a collection? They could live like kings!"

Of course they could, Judas thinks. *Even a shekel from each family would have resulted in a fortune. But that was hardly the point.* "I'm going to join them," he says.

"You're what?"

"I'm leaving. I quit. I'm going with his followers."

"Where?"

"I don't know. To the ends of the earth."

Hadad stares, looking bemused, as if he can't believe his friend is serious.

"Everywhere this message needs to be heard," Judas adds.

Hadad's smile freezes. "I'll sue you. You can't—"

"I renounce my shares!"

"Then I'll sue *him*!"

Judas shakes his head, eager to be done with this conversation, done with Hadad. "Nothing you could take from him would be of any value to you."

Judas strides away, only to pause and turn at Hadad's question: "What's he got to give you then?"

The younger man just stares. "Good luck, Hadad."

Chapter 4

THE HARD THINGS

The Mount of Beatitudes

One of the most senior Roman centurions, Primi Ordine Gaius sits astride his horse, motionless as the excitedly chattering hordes disperse and mill about. Gaius assigned many men to this event, determined to prevent any issues, such as what happened when a much smaller crowd gathered outside an old fisherman's house in the eastern ghetto. There this same man spoke, appeared to heal a man crippled from birth, and created what Gaius's boss, Praetor Quintus, described as a stampede that delayed Herod's envoy and made the praetor look bad.

Well, it hadn't been anything close to a stampede, but yes, the gathering had grown and blocked the street. And the last thing Gaius needs is any semblance of a repeat of that. Who knows what might happen with a crowd hundreds of times larger?

Gaius told himself he had come this day to superintend his men, but the truth is he was there to see Jesus of Nazareth in action on a larger scale and—admittedly—to perhaps get a peek at how Matthew was doing. Gaius had been the strange little man's personal bodyguard for several years, assigned by the Roman Authority, when Matthew was a tax collector. The primi could not deny that, despite Matthew's eccentric peculiarities, he had developed a fondness for the fellow.

Gaius had once been assigned by Quintus to arrest Jesus and haul him before the praetor for questioning. He'd been accompanied by *Cohortes Urbana* Atticus, whom he considered pompous and condescending—just the type Caesar seemed to select for his private goon squad. It was beyond Gaius why Rome needed such a unit when the centurions were perfectly capable.

Speak of the devil. Here comes the selfsame Atticus in all his smugness. Gaius pretends not to notice him, continuing to gaze at the crowd. In truth, he doesn't want to deal with the man. He wants to ponder all he's seen and heard. It would be unprofessional to admit to anyone that he has been strangely impressed by the Nazarene. As unique and disturbing as were so many of the things Jesus said, they resonate deeply within Gaius, and he needs time to make sense of them.

Atticus steps up beside Gaius's horse. "Well?" he says.

Gaius continues to stare straight ahead. "Hm," he grunts. He doesn't have to look at the *urbana* to sense his all-knowing grin.

"My thoughts exactly," Atticus says. "I'll see you in the morning for our report to Quintus."

"Mm-hm."

"Good chat," Atticus says and adds a maddening chuckle as he strides away.

Judas can barely contain himself. He makes his way toward the curtains, through which Jesus has exited to a makeshift stone stage. And apparently he's not the only one hoping to get a moment with Jesus. People everywhere are asking Jesus' followers if the preacher will return, if he's still nearby, if they can chat with him. Judas calls on his prodigious memory to try and recall the names of the people he has met only briefly. There are the two Simons explaining to people, "Please, the rabbi is very tired," and "He's done for today," and "Thank you for coming."

Three smaller men—Little James, Nathanael, and Thaddeus (he can't remember which of those last two is which)—are starting to untie the draperies and clear the rocks. The bigger James and his brother—the name escapes Judas for the moment—are letting the others know that Jesus has called for a brief meeting in a few minutes. Judas looks past the brothers to where Jesus stands with his mother and a younger woman, the wife of one of the disciples. Knowing he should not impose himself upon the meeting later, Judas decides it's now or never. He gathers himself and tentatively approaches Jesus and the women, hoping the rabbi will at least notice and acknowledge him and he'll get a chance to express what an impact the sermon has had on him.

Jesus looks exhausted, and his mother sits him down and hands him a plate of food. The one disciple's wife stands nearby, holding the blue sash Jesus had worn while speaking. Judas hesitates to interrupt, especially now, but neither does he want to miss his chance. Yet when he starts to make his move, the former tax collector barges in. Judas knows this man, Matthew, from the past. He knows many tax collectors, even thought of applying for such a position once. But he cared too much of what others thought of him. There were other ways to earn a lucrative living.

"I was able to write down many of the new things you said," Matthew says as Jesus' mother and the other woman step aside, "but not all of them."

Between bites, Jesus says, "That's fine. I will say them again. We can discuss them."

"I did recognize some of them from my study of the teachings of Rabbi Hillel."

"Very good, Matthew," Jesus says, sounding weary.

"When you said to be reconciled to your brother, can you elaborate on wh—"

"Matthew, let's discuss this another time, please. I'm very hungry and have some things to discuss with our new friend." Jesus gives Judas a look.

So, he has noticed me. "Oh!" Judas says. "I'm sorry. I can come back."

"No, I'm gathering everyone shortly and would like to speak with you. Matthew, could you please help Big James and John gather the others?"

John, yes, that was the brother's name!

"Right now?" Matthew asks, clearly disappointed.

"Mm-hm."

Matthew hesitates and starts off.

Jesus calls after him, "Thank you for helping me."

Matthew smiles. "Yes, Rabbi."

Jesus pops a bite into his mouth and looks up at Judas as the disciples start moving toward them. "So ..."

"I'm Judas of Kerioth," he says, shaking hands.

"Shalom, Judas. I saw you before I stepped out to talk to the people, and then I noticed you listening very intently during my sermon."

"It was wonderful," Judas says, wishing he could be more articulate.

"Thank you. Nathanael briefly told me about the help you gave and that you might be interested in joining us. He's not easy to impress."

Judas places which one is Nathanael. "I attended Beth Midrash," he gushes, "but my father passed away before I could pursue a rabbi, so I stayed home to work. I would like to follow you."

"You would?"

"Very much! I did attend the House of Study."

Jesus chuckles. "I heard you the first time. I don't require that of my followers. You would actually be one of the few who have. I require only what many rabbis do—that you seek to be like me."

"Of course."

"But that will be much more difficult with me than with other rabbis, I can assure you. Are you ready to do the hard things?"

Hard things? I would do anything! "I believe you are going to change the world. And I want to be part of that. I might not be a soldier in battle, but I have business and financial skills, and I want to use them to grow this ministry far and wide, as fast as possible. So, yes, I am ready to do the hard things."

"We will see. So, I assume you know what *Judas* means, yes?"

"*God be praised.*"

"Yes. With your hands. Will you praise God?"

"Every day."

As the other disciples arrive, Jesus sets his plate aside and stands. "Well, in that case, Judas, follow me."

"Thank you."

"Everyone is here, Rabbi," Big James tells Jesus.

Jesus nods and beckons Judas to stand near him. But before he can speak, the rest begin to clap and smile.

"All right, that's good," Jesus says lightheartedly. "That's enough. First of all, thank you for such a wonderful day. Barnaby! Shula! Come on in! Did you approve of the sermon?"

"A little long," Barnaby teases. "But effective."

Shula elbows Barnaby. "It was wonderful."

Jesus addresses all of them. “You did your part in spreading the word, which is a vital part of our ministry. And let’s especially thank Nathanael, Thad, and Little James for their part in getting the land and putting all this together so quickly. I know you’ll all help them clean up here before you go.”

The others applaud those three.

Jesus adds, “I also have a quick announcement. I know a few of you have met him already, but for those who haven’t, this is Judas of Kerioth. He just asked for me to be his rabbi and to contribute some of his talents to our ministry, a request I was happy to grant. So, let’s please welcome Judas to the group.”

More applause and good wishes.

“Well,” Jesus says at last, “it’s been quite a journey these last several weeks. A lot of good work has been done, and there’s quite a lot more to do in the future. But for now, let’s take some time off to rest. Simon, you especially need to get home.” With a twinkle in his eye, he adds, “After the joy of having you gone wore off, Eden has actually started to miss you. So, you two take a break.”

Jesus motions everyone closer, and they stand with arms around each other’s shoulders. “You all can discuss with each other how to stay in touch so we can get together again soon, but for now, let me pray over you.” As they bow their heads, he says, “The Lord bless you and keep you. The Lord make His face shine on you and be gracious to you. The Lord turn His face to you and give you peace.” He looks up. “I will see you soon. Thank you.”

Judas has just joined them, and now they’re taking a break to rest? Where will these nomads go to do that, and what is he supposed to do in the meantime?

Chapter 5

TIME AWAY

The Mount of Beatitudes

Though everyone else seems to be gathering their belongings and preparing to leave this place, Mary of Magdala wishes she could stay here forever. Her heart is full, and yet she wants more. More of Jesus. More of his love, his compassion, his wisdom, his empathy. She could listen to him until dawn.

She's about to ask her friends if they feel the same. But Tamar, the resplendent, ebony-skinned Egyptian, and Ramah, Thomas's love, appear distracted. Another woman approaches—appearing perhaps ten years older than Jesus. She's dressed in finery, including an elaborate shawl that had to be uncomfortable all day in the heat.

"Excuse me," she says. "You are followers of the teacher, yes?"

"Yes," Mary says. "Shalom."

"May I speak with him?"

Tamar speaks up. "He's about to leave. We all are. It's been a very long day."

The woman removes her shawl and turns it inside out to reveal its blood-orange underside. "I want to give you this."

Mary is astounded. "I-I don't, uh—thank you? What for?" Surely none of the three look as if they have any use for such dazzling attire. Even Tamar's sumptuous clothing has become worn and faded.

"It's an offering," the woman says. "There was no collection taken?"

"He didn't ask for that," Ramah says. "This isn't a way to get to speak to him."

Tamar steps closer, eyes wide. "Is this *shahtoosh*?" She grabs the shawl and holds it up.

Mary has heard of the premium wool made from the neck hair of Himalayan ibex, but she's never seen it.

"From Nepal," the woman says.

"You're donating this to his ministry?" Tamar says, sounding in awe.

"Yes, and there will be more."

"Who are you?" Ramah asks.

"My name is Joanna. And I bring greetings for Jesus from someone, if I could have only a few moments …"

"From whom?" Ramah says.

Joanna appears hesitant but whispers, "I come from Machaerus. I've spoken with John, the Baptizer."

John! Mary flashes the woman a double take. "Andrew!"

Andrew finishes his farewells to Zee and Nathanael and makes his way over, seeming to curiously eye the newcomer.

"She says she's spoken with John—in Machaerus."

He raises his brows. "When? How? You've seen him?"

"My husband works in Herod's court," Joanna says, "so I've had the opportunity to speak with John since he's been—brought in. I was intrigued by his words, and—"

Mary moves to fetch Jesus. He'll want to hear this.

After a full, exhausting day, just when Andrew thought nothing could make it better, now this. "You've spoken to him? Is he okay? What did he say?"

"You're Andrew?"

"Yes!"

"He mentioned you. You were a follower of his."

"Yes. Is he hurt?"

"No. Well, yes, it's not a great place for him to be, and he's upset some important people. But he wanted you especially, Andrew, to know he's in good spirits."

"Can I see him?"

Mary returns and introduces Jesus.

"Of course," Joanna says. "I saw your teaching."

"Hello, Joanna. So, you've spoken with my cousin?"

"Yes, and he's been telling me I need to hear your teachings. When word reached Machaerus about this gathering, they didn't think much of it, but John thought this would be a good opportunity for me."

"Rabbi," Andrew says, "I'd like to visit John."

"Just a moment, Andrew." He turns back to Joanna. "So, what will you report back to him?"

"That I want to support your ministry." She hesitates, growing emotional. "This was a healing day for me, as John said it would be. Thank you."

"I'm glad to hear it."

"John wanted me to tell you he is eager for you to come to Herod at some point. He believes there is uncertainty in the court about him, and he also says they aren't taking you seriously yet. He thinks a strong visit from you soon could resolve both issues. But he also wanted to make it clear he is trusting your timing on 'soon.'"

Jesus smiles. "Of course. Thank you for sharing that. Now, so my student here doesn't grind his teeth into dust, is John even able to receive visitors at the moment?"

"Are you coming to Machaerus?"

"No, I am taking some time alone. But if you were able to somehow arrange for Andrew here to safely visit John …"

Andrew can't hide his eagerness.

Joanna says, "I suppose I could make some arrangements. My men are taking me back in my carriage to Machaerus shortly. You can join me."

"Thank you!" Andrew says. "And thank you, Rabbi."

"You need to rest and to trust, Andrew. But perhaps after seeing John, you will be able to do both."

Andrew hugs Jesus, and they exchange shaloms. As the small group is breaking up, Andrew's brother, Simon, approaches. "What's going on?" he says. "Everything good?"

"We'll leave in a few moments, Andrew," Joanna says and moves away.

"Who is she?" Simon asks.

"I'm going to see John. She knows him from Machaerus."

"What do you mean? This isn't—"

"Rabbi already said yes. She works in Herod's court. Don't worry about me. You need to go home with Eden."

"I can't let you go alone …"

"I'm going to be fine."

"Andrew …"

"Listen, I'm going to be fine! But thank you."

"For what?"

Andrew is suddenly overcome. For all their squabbling, he loves his brother, and there's no one with whom he'd rather be sharing this adventure of a lifetime. "For watching out for me.

For everyone. You always have. You're a great leader, and I don't say it enough. Thank you."

Now Simon looks self-conscious. He smirks and sighs and puts a hand behind Andrew's head. "Say shalom to John for me."

"Really?"

"I mean it," Simon says. "John started all this, introducing you to Jesus." He pulls Andrew's forehead to his. "And you introduced me to him. I thank John, and I thank you." He kisses Andrew on the cheek. "I love you. Shalom."

"I love you. Shalom."

Andrew finds Philip and beckons the newcomer, Judas, to join their conversation. He tells them where he's going and invites them to stay at his place until he returns. "It's small, but we'll manage. Judas, Philip can bring you up to speed in the meantime."

"Give me the directions," Judas says, "and I'll find you. I need to take care of a few things at home first."

Thomas stands alone on the edge of the staging area. Though there were no miracle healings this time, he'll never forget Jesus' turning water into wine at the wedding in Cana. Somehow Thomas sensed he would never be the same, and that has certainly proved true. Now he needs to become more proactive about his intentions with Ramah. As she and Mary and Tamar head his way, he steps forward. "Ramah!"

Ramah leaves the others, who hang back, and comes to him. "So, did you talk to John?"

"Yes, I'll be taken care of. And you're all set with Mary?"

"Yes."

"Good," Thomas says. "I'll stop by tomorrow to check in."

Ramah smiles at him. "I figured you would."

Feeling his way now, Thomas says, "Is after second meal a good time?"

"I'll have to see what my plans are."

I need to slow down! Thomas thinks. "Oh!" he says. "I can come later."

She breaks into a grin. "I'm joking, Thomas."

Whew! "Aah, yes—of course." He hesitates, unsure of what to do or say next. Finally, "Well, shalom."

"Shalom."

He turns to leave.

"Thomas?"

He whirls. "Yes?"

"Maybe come by after *first* meal?"

"Of course! I just didn't want to bother you. We've spent a lot of time together lately."

She smiles. "I know."

Oh … he realizes.

And she adds, "I just hope this time away doesn't become too much, you know, time away."

Just what he wants to hear. "It won't."

"Good," she says. "That's all. Shalom."

Thomas stares as Ramah rejoins Mary and Tamar, then notices Barnaby and Shula off to the side, beaming at him. Barnaby nods and pumps his fist. Thomas chuckles and walks off as if on air.

Chapter 6

JAIRUS

Capernaum synagogue, Beth Midrash

Yussif hardly knows what to do with himself. He has always been able to separate his emotions from his study and training, and Shmuel has drilled into him the absolute discipline of sober reflection on the Scriptures. Above all, he is to cautiously and seriously evaluate anyone's commentary on the Torah.

But he has to admit, something is happening within him. He's seen things, heard things, experienced things, *felt* things—all because of this rogue preacher from Nazareth.

Shmuel privately warned him to discount some of the things Nicodemus himself—the teacher of teachers from Jerusalem—has said about Jesus. It's obvious that Jesus has not dissuaded his own disciples from letting it be known that he is the Messiah. Surely that's blasphemy, punishable to the fullest extent of the Sanhedrin.

Yet, dare he admit it—even to himself—Yussif may lean toward Nicodemus's take on all this. While he hasn't come out and said it, Nicodemus clearly at least allows speculation on the matter, remaining open to the possibility that the vagabond may actually be "of God."

Still robed in his temple garb, having rushed from the hillside where Jesus preached, Yussif settles in at his desk, compelled to write his feelings and impressions. He feverishly attacks a fresh scroll with his quill, rapidly and repeatedly refilling it from an inkwell. Soon, he is astonished to discover he has exhausted the liquid just a few pages in—and at mid-thought. No problem—Niv, the executive administrator of the synagogue, always cheerfully refills the pot for him.

His chair loudly scrapes the stone floor as Yussif pushes back and hurries to Niv's office. There he finds a man in his mid-thirties seeming to meticulously arrange scrolls on shelves against the far wall. "Hello?" Yussif says.

The man turns. "Hello."

"Are you—who are you?"

"I'm Jairus."

"Nice to meet you. I'm Yussif. Uh, is Niv here?"

"Niv was transferred. I'm the new synagogue administrator."

"I had no idea …"

"That he was leaving?"

"No, that I'm apparently so unimportant that no one thought to mention it to me."

Jairus chuckles. "I wouldn't trouble myself, Rabbi Yussif. Take it from someone transferred many times over—the good-byes are the hardest. Niv seems to have kept the news to himself to avoid all that."

"You've been around, then?"

"Kadesh, Joppa, Hebron, and now—"

"The Galilee. Welcome, Jairus. Do you have a family?"

Jairus nods. "A wife and daughter. And, Adonai willing, another child on the way."

"Congratulations!"

"Thank you, Rabbi. And what about your family? I hope to meet them soon."

"My family is in Jerusalem," Yussif says.

"I'm sorry. That must be hard."

Yussif shrugs. "I was uncertain how long I would remain in Capernaum. Moving so often must be difficult as well. Your daughter, how old is she?"

"Twelve. And yes, it is difficult for her. Making friends, you know. For my wife, too, but being new and isolated brings us closer too. And, I assure you, it will not prevent me from doing my duty."

Yussif takes in the office, already much tidier than Niv kept it. "Apparently not. Aah, Jairus, I need ink."

"Ha! You and everyone."

"We're out?"

"Dry, I'm afraid. I put in a request to Jerusalem. Until it arrives, you may want to check with some of your less, um, prolific brethren."

Yussif snorts. "Then I'd have to explain what I'm writing." He can tell he's piqued Jairus's interest, but he has just met the man, so he forges ahead. "I'll use my personal supply." He turns to go.

Jairus calls out, "I enjoy a challenge, Rabbi Yussif."

"That will serve you well here." He turns away again, but Jairus is not through.

"It's one of the reasons I've moved around. I'm known for helping bring order to chaos. Well, maybe I'm overstating it. Order to upheaval? Unusual events?"

Yussif stares, unsure of how much to say. Fortunately, Jairus continues. "Word has spread of unusual events happening in Capernaum."

So, he knows? "That's an apt description," Yussif allows.

"Are you perhaps writing of unusual things?"

Dare I say it? "The most." Yussif is tempted to flee before he says too much, but instead he throws caution to the wind. "Yesterday I witnessed a sermon by a rogue preacher. I haven't slept since. He was brilliant!"

"Intriguing. Is it to be a historical record? A letter? Are you filing charges?"

"No! I don't know what I'm writing yet. Or who I will send it to. I am certain only that I must document what I am seeing."

"Rabbi Yussif, I have a safe that I use. I call it *the cellar.* It's where documents go to cool off. You can't imagine how many times our brothers write something they wish the next morning they had not sent. Other documents remain in the cellar for months. It's locked and—entirely confidential. Does this sound like a place you want to store your document?"

Yussif already likes the new man. "I'll bet those goodbyes were very hard for those you've served with, Jairus."

Chapter 7

HOUSEGUESTS

In and around Capernaum

Simon finds himself walking with an extra bounce in his step, carrying his and Eden's bags from The Mount of Beatitudes toward their home. Once inside, he says, "It's good to be home." He draws her into his arms. "It's even better to be here."

"Aren't you exhausted, Love?" she says, reaching to slow him. "I am, and I was there only today. You've been going non-stop for how long? Months."

"What can I say?" he says. "You bring out the best in me, and I'm just eager to be home, alone, with you."

"I'll be surprised if you don't just collapse into bed and sleep for days."

"All in good time," he says, winking.

"Not to change the subject," Eden says, "but is Jesus always teaching?"

"How do you mean?"

"Well, even after that incredible sermon, he tells you all to scatter and take care of each other until he calls for you again."

Simon shrugs and nods. "And you see a lesson there?"

"I do. He's left it to all of you to figure this out for yourselves. Doesn't he usually give everybody assignments, or ask you or Big James or John to tell the others?"

"Usually."

"I'm just saying I didn't hear him do that today. Many of your new friends left everything, including their homes, to follow him. Where will they go during this break? I mean, you and Big James and John have homes to go to, and of course your brother has his little place. I just wonder about the others."

Simon snorts. "They're big boys. So maybe you're right that it's the rabbi's way of teaching them to figure it out for themselves."

"I hope so."

He sighs and whispers in her ear, "Since your ima moved back to your brothers', I hate the thought of you alone here all day and night." He takes her hand and walks backward, leading her. "But in this moment …"

She laughs, but they both freeze at the sound of a knock. Simon moves to the door to find Nathanael with a knapsack over his shoulder.

"Hi," the young man says.

Eden seems to force excitement as she calls out, "Oh, hello!"

Simon narrows his eyes. "What are you doing here?" he says flatly.

Nathanael smiles. "You look at me like you wanna smash my face with a stone."

That's exactly what I want to do, Simon thinks, but Eden steps in front of him.

"Don't be silly," she says. "Please, come in."

"Sorry," Nathanael says. "I know you probably want to be alone. It's just that I'm not from here, and I heard you might have space."

"Who told you that?" Simon says.

"Of course we do," Eden says.

Simon says, "Andrew has a flat in the east quarter. I can give you directions."

But Nathanael drops his pack and sits down. "I thought about that," he says. "It's just that—"

"Just what?"

"He has just the one bedroom, and Philip and Judas are staying there. They're practically on top of each other, and when Andrew gets back from Jordan, they'll be even more crowded."

"Our place isn't much bigger," Simon says.

"It'll work out," Eden says.

"Would you be opposed to sleeping on the roof?"

"Simon!" Eden says.

Nathanael says, "I—well, it's just that I heard you had an extra room that your mom used to stay in, Eden."

Simon throws his hands up. "Who's telling you these things?"

"Have you eaten, Nathanael?" Eden asks.

Simon glares at her.

"I am starving!" Nathanael says. "Thank you. Oh, man. Seriously, though, don't mind me. Just act like I'm not here. Maybe I *will* go up to the roof." He grabs an apple.

"There's a ladder," Simon says. "Right outside."

"I'm not oblivious," Nathanael adds. "I'll put a pillow over my ears."

Eden gasps.

"Nathanael," Simon says, "you can say whatever you want to on the road with the boys, but in my house, try having a thought you don't say or you'll be sleeping in a fish hold."

Nathanael looks down. "Sorry." He pauses, looking awkward. "You still want me to go up to the roof?"

Simon mouths to Eden, "Yes!" and grabs Nathanael's sack, pulls him out of his chair, and steers him toward the door. He opens it to find Zee with his fist raised, about to knock.

"Oh, I hoped this was the right place."

• • •

John carries the bigger, heavier rucksack as he and Big James make their way home from the sermon on the hillside. "Slow down!"

Big James looks over his shoulder. "You're not eager to get home?"

"Yes, but you're not the one carrying the axe and the tent stakes and the hammer …"

"Shut up and let's switch."

John stops and shrugs the rucksack off his shoulders onto the ground with a thump. James sets his own bag down and hoists the bigger bag, getting his feet under him. "I can see how this could get heavy after a while."

"Why are you in a such a rush anyway?" John says.

"C'mon, you don't know?"

"What?"

"John, all I dream about every night is one thing."

"And I'll bet you're gonna tell me what."

"Ima's cinnamon cakes."

"That sounds about right," John says.

"Like you don't?"

"Um, yeah, no. I don't because there are more important things to think about. The teachings? The sermon we just heard? The miracles? Paralytics walking?"

"I know! It makes me hungry."

"You're sick."

"C'mon," James says. "We're so close."

As they pick up the pace, Thomas appears at the next corner. "You guys going to eat?" he says.

"Thomas!" Big James says.

"Everybody's hungry," John says. "Glad you found the neighborhood."

"Wasn't easy," Thomas says. "Your directions were—what's the word? Bad."

"This was planned?" Big James says.

"Didn't I tell you?" John says. "I guess my mind's been on all the history-making while you've been dreaming about cakes."

"Cakes?" Thomas says. "What kind of cakes?"

Big James shrugs. "Forget it."

"Anyway, yes, I invited him," John says. "I figured a guy from the plains of Sharon—a stranger in a strange place—could do worse than Abba's. He can sleep in that room where Ima dries the herbs."

"Sounds extravagant," Thomas teases.

"Glad to have you," James mutters.

From a half block away comes the shout: "Three disciples of Jesus of Nazareth coming to stay under my roof! A triple blessing!"

"Even Abba knew?" Big James says.

"Thomas and I talked to him at—"

But Zebedee rushes to them and hugs his sons. "Of all the fathers in Capernaum, I must be the most envied!"

"I'd introduce you to Thomas," Big James says, "but it seems you've already met."

"Thomas!" Zebedee shouts. "How about that sermon?"

"Actually, sir," he says, "I have some questions about it."

Zebedee grins. "Somehow I thought you might."

"I tend to overthink things."

John interrupts. "Where's Ima?"

"She ran to the market," Zebedee says. "Realized she was out of cinnamon."

James's face falls. "Out of—?"

"I've got something very important I want to talk to you all about," Thomas says.

"I think I know what it is!" Zebedee says, beaming.

"I definitely think I know," John says.

Big James looks baffled. "What are you guys talking about?"

Thomas smiles as John and his father corral him and walk toward home, James trundling behind.

Chapter 8

THE WOMEN

Mary Magdalene's apartment, Capernaum

Still aglow from Jesus' sermon on the Korazim Plateau, which precious Matthew says should now be referred to as The Mount of Beatitudes, Mary is also excited to have her new friends, Ramah and Tamar, with her. But for how long? She's happy to share her tiny abode and looks forward to their talks. What gives her pause, as they unpack and store bread, grapes, cheese, cucumbers, and other foodstuffs from the market, is that none of the three seem to have any idea how long this break will be before they rejoin Jesus. It's okay, she decides, not to know where he might lead them or what form his ministry might take after their rest period, but it would be helpful to know *when*.

Mary can't shake the feeling that the increasing attention Jesus is drawing from both the Romans and the Pharisees cannot bode well for his safety. She's learning to leave such concerns to him. Her more immediate personal concern is how long her store of food might last, and what she and the other two women are to do when and if it runs out.

"I literally left nothing in my cupboards, because I didn't know when I would be back," she says. "I gave everything to Rivka."

"And we pooled all our money at the market, right?" Ramah says. "We spent our last shekel."

Well, Mary thinks, *we'll deal with poverty and hunger if and when we need to.* Through her window, she spots a familiar figure in the street and steps outside.

"What is it?" Tamar says.

"Matthew?" Mary calls.

He looks sheepish in his now-faded and ragged attire that once looked so regal. He appears unsure. Lost. "Oh," he says. "Uh, hello."

Ramah and Tamar join Mary. "What are you doing here, Matthew?" she asks, not unkindly.

"I didn't know who to—or where to—um, go."

Doesn't know where to go? His mansion could accommodate the entire lot of the disciples. "But you have a house in one of the most beautiful neigh—"

"I gave it away," he says quickly.

"To whom?"

"My parents."

"Have you stopped by their home? Surely, they'll—"

"My father will not allow it."

"But you're his son."

"He says I'm not."

Ramah and Tamar quietly groan.

How sad. Mary doesn't know what to say beyond, "I'm sorry." How she wishes she could take him in, but her little place would offer no privacy, and it wouldn't be appropriate for a man to be there.

"Thank you for listening," Matthew says. "I think perhaps I will make camp. I know how to do it now."

"Are you okay, Matthew?" Ramah says, smiling. She whispers, "I've been where he is."

"I feel confused," he says. "Thank you for asking."

Mary's heart aches for him. "You're doing really well, Matthew. Everything is new, and it's okay to make a mistake."

"Thank you," he says, turning away. "Good night."

Mary leads the others back inside. "He's wonderful. God bless his heart." She changes the subject to keep from bursting into tears. "Well, this isn't really that much food, but we'll manage."

Tamar runs her fingers along the shawl Joanna gave them. "Is it too early to use this?"

"Yes," Ramah says. "We shouldn't have accepted it."

Tamar smiles. "She got to you."

"She was presumptuous," Ramah says.

Mary cocks her head. "Rich people can be like that."

"Believe me, I know," Ramah says. "I used to work in the wedding business."

"Who do you think she was, really?" Tamar asks. "Remember how she struggled with her words?"

"I think she was embarrassed," Mary says, "and didn't want anyone she knew to know she was there. That's what I got from her."

Ramah nods. "She was deceptive."

"But also curious," Tamar says.

Mary is rethinking this. "Maybe she was being cautious, but genuine. She wore silver earrings."

Ramah scowls. "Or it was all talk and we'll never see her again? Fine with me. Giving away *shahtoosh*, the most expensive textile in the world …"

Tamar shrugs. "She tried to help us."

Mary doesn't like where this conversation is going. "Can we eat?" she says. "Let's just eat."

Chapter 9

"SOMETHING JUST FOR YOU"

Herod's palace dungeon, Machaerus, Jordan

Excited but heartbroken for his first rabbi and mentor, Andrew follows Joanna and a king's guard through the torchlit underground halls. The dank, damp, disgusting stench assaults him, and he wonders how anyone—especially John the Baptizer, who's always been an outdoor man—can endure this day and night. Most of the men they pass lie sleeping in their grimy, dilapidated cells. Andrew refrains from holding his nose, but he forces himself to breathe shallowly.

"I can't say I blame you for coming back, ma'am," the grizzled guard whispers. "Few visitors do, but we don't get interesting ones like John down here often. Every day it's something new with the wild man. He's either demanding we pass a message to the king or preaching about a new kingdom. His curses are creative."

As they approach John's cell, Joanna slips the guard a handful of coins and says, almost under her breath, "It would embarrass me if you told anyone about my visit or the new friend I brought along. But hear me: To you and your family it would be devastating. Understand?"

The guard shoots her a you-don't-have-to-threaten-me look. "You were never here," he says, and disappears.

John rises from a corner and rushes to the bars, wide eyes reflecting the flicker of the flames on the corridor walls.

"John!" Andrew says, his voice thick. "Are you all right?"

"What are you doing here?" John says, clearly alarmed at Andrew's putting himself at risk. He looks to Joanna. "Who allowed this?"

"No one," she says. "We must be quick."

John smirks at Andrew. "To answer your question, I'll be fine. I've never slept in a palace before. But what are you doing here?"

"I've been so worried, praying for you every day."

"You've got a new rabbi now. *The* rabbi. Focus on him. And hopefully I'll be able to as well, soon enough." He nods at Joanna. "She came to me in distress after Herod had me arrested. But she didn't come for my sake. She was angry I didn't call out her husband for adultery at the same time I accused Herod. But she is proving an apt pupil." He turns to her. "Did you talk to him?"

"Yes, I told Jesus what you told me."

"Thank you, but that's not as important as what you thought of him."

"I don't know how to describe it," she says.

John nods knowingly. "Like you were grateful for food but hadn't realized you'd been starving?"

"That works."

"Anything new, Andrew?"

"So much."

"Tell me. What did he say?"

"Nothing that made sense to me," Joanna says.

John smiles.

She continues, "Everything upside down: the poor, the grieving, the meek, all elevated somehow."

"Blessed," John says.

"Yes," she says, "and other things reversed. 'Love your enemies'! Who can *love* their enemy?"

"He can," John says. "What else?"

"Bizarre imagery, if you ask me. Something about pearls before pigs, logs in eyes …"

"Yes!" John says.

"Salt," Andrew says, "murder, rain, God feeding the birds, houses on sand—"

"He's almost as strange as you, John," Joanna says.

John sighs. "I wish I were so strange." He steps back and begins to pace. "How many were there?"

"Thousands," she says.

"Wonderful! What else?"

Enough of this, Andrew thinks, fighting tears. How it hurts to see such a beloved mentor here. "John, what do we do about you? How can I help?"

"This is helping me, Andrew. What you're sharing."

"You know what I mean."

John returns to the bars and whispers, "Come here."

Andrew leans in.

"Don't be afraid," John says.

That's what Jesus always says, Andrew thinks. *But I am afraid.* And the tears come.

John continues, "The prophecies of Isaiah: 'He has been sent to proclaim liberty to the captives,' and what?"

"'The opening of the prison to those who are bound,'" Andrew recites.

John nods and smiles. "This prison is nothing now that he's here. Do you believe that?"

"I'm trying."

"Andrew, think. In all he said to those thousands of people, surely there was something just for you—for what you're going through. There always is. What was it?"

Andrew pauses, overcome. How can John be so insightful? He's right, of course. At times it *was* as if Jesus had been speaking directly to him.

"Something that stuck with you," John adds.

"'Don't be anxious.'"

John smiles. "Tell me more."

"'Can you add a single hour to your life by being anxious?'"

"That sounds like him," John says. "What else?"

"'But seek first the kingdom of God and His righteousness.'"

"Even more like him," John says. "So, if you want to help me, Andrew—are you listening?"

Andrew nods.

"If you want to help me, listen to him. Go home and do what he says. That's all I want. Got it?"

"Got it."

"Now let Joanna get you out of here before you join me."

Chapter 10

SET APART

Judas's house

Having been invited to Andrew's flat to stay with him and Philip, the newest member of Jesus' disciples is eager to pack up and get there. Both guys seem to be devout followers of Jesus of Nazareth, and they met when first following the crazy man known as John the Baptizer. Until now, Judas has merely been amused by their tales of the preacher who dared call out the king and his relatives for all manner of riotous living. But the man is also known to wear goatskin and subsist on locusts and honey.

Judas can only shake his head at why anyone would fall for the railings of such a character—until he pieces together that John calls himself a forerunner of Jesus. In fact, he is Jesus' slightly older cousin and insists that he is only a proclaimer of the coming Messiah. Little surprise that all that—especially his diatribes about the infidelities of the king himself—has served to land the baptizer in prison, likely fearing for his life.

Judas finds Andrew intriguing, just from the little he knows of him. The brother of one of the leaders, the one they called Simon, Andrew appears to have an almost fanatical passion about Jesus, but he also retains a deep, loving loyalty to his original rabbi. Indeed, he has gone to Jordan to visit the man in Herod's palace dungeon.

Andrew had left Philip the key to his flat and told both him and Judas he would be back as soon as possible. Judas looks forward to the account of his visit to John, but he is also eager to get to know Philip—who seems wiser than his years. The other disciples clearly revere him, listen to him.

But for now, Judas has his own affairs to get in order. He's dead serious about giving up everything to follow Jesus, whether Hadad believes it or not. Judas knows it sounds foolish, but he no longer needs the house he purchased with an inheritance from his father, and he wants to say goodbye to his married sister who lives not far away.

He doesn't need much. Just clothes, really. Judas stuffs a rucksack and notices the single potted mint in the windowsill, sitting mostly in the shade. He gently slides it fully into the sun. That's how he feels—as if he's mostly lived in darkness till now, finally finding his way into the light.

Judas opens a safe and riffles through several documents. He slips one into a leather portfolio, secures the thin strap, and detours to grab the mint plant on his way out the door.

Judas finds his sister Dvorah at her home, washing clothes in a huge kettle outside, his nieces playing on the ground nearby. He greets them all and sits with her. He gushes all his plans, and she nods, her expression giving away nothing except that she is likely aware of the vagabond preacher he's talking about. How could she not be?

He's eager for her response, but when he finishes, she runs a hand through her hair, avoiding his gaze. "Why do I have a bad feeling about this?" she says.

"That's what you said when I joined the mining company."

"And I was glad to be proved wrong, Judas, but now you're leaving it."

"My life can't be just about money."

She scoffs. "It's never not about money with you."

"I know you think you would have spent Abba's inheritance better than I have," he says.

"I *would* have! That house you invested in has not increased in value."

"That's why I'm here." He sets down the potted plant and pulls the leather folder from his rucksack, untying the strap and producing a document. "I need you to hold something for me. The deed to my house. I don't know when or if I'll be back."

He can tell she's thrown, but she recovers. Scanning the document, she says, "Everyone's been talking about your rabbi, you know."

"What are they saying?"

"Too many things to be true. I heard hundreds of people gathered—"

"Thousands. I didn't realize it at the time, but the day before, I actually helped his disciples secure the site. God was working through me, Dvorah. That's never happened before."

Judas hopes for some modicum of a positive response to that, but all she says is, "How will you make money?"

He shrugs. "I will help with what little they do have. Help find benefactors and supporters. Most rabbis are inefficient, and this is the most important ministry in our people's history. To spread his message and to build something to match the Romans, he'll need my skills."

She sets her jaw. "Judas. This is dangerous."

"Yes."

"Rome doesn't like popular preachers with big followings," she adds. "They put them away."

"I think he's the Messiah. I'm almost sure of it."

She shakes her head. "Many have claimed to be the Messiah. You know what happens to them."

"Always the worst-case scenario with you. Their followers aren't always killed. If he truly is the anointed one, Sister, then he won't get killed. He'll defeat Rome and set us all free."

Dvorah softens. "I don't want to lose you, Judas. You're all I have left in this world."

"You have your husband, your daughters!"

"No, I mean—" Her voice quavers. "You know what I mean. You're the last of our name. If anything happens to you, the line of Iscariot will be broken and our family name forgotten."

He reaches to touch her. "Whatever happens, I believe Adonai has set me apart for some purpose I don't yet know."

Her eyes wet, she leans to hug him, and they press their foreheads together. "Make us proud," she says.

"I will."

"Abba and Ima loved you so much. I love you."

"I love you, too," he says.

She kisses his cheek, and they sit back. "Will you keep Ima's plant alive?" he says.

She nods, clearly overcome. "Now get out of here and go follow your rabbi. I really hope you're right about this."

"I am. You'll see!"

Dvorah follows him to the doorway and calls after him, "You know, bearing a son would be a whole lot easier than upending your whole life to go on a perilous journey!"

"Shalom, shalom, Dvorah."

Chapter 11

THE CELLAR

Capernaum synagogue

What to do? What to do? Yussif finishes the missive intended, perhaps someday, for Rabbi Nicodemus himself. But dare he send it?

No. Not yet. Not today, certainly. He rolls the scroll and stands, suddenly aware of his fatigue. Worn, his body sags, and his vestments are wrinkled from sitting so long. He stretches. Oh, he could just burn the letter and be done with it, not worrying about such things again. But the die has been cast, his course set. Though he has no idea when or if he'll find the courage to send it, Yussif has no intention of trashing the parchment.

He makes his way to Jairus's doorway and waits. The man is so efficient and fastidious that Yussif wants less than anything to interrupt him. Finally, Jairus looks up. "Rabbi Yussif." Clearly he notices the scroll and smiles. "You have something you wish to place in the cellar?"

Jairus's euphemism for *safekeeping* amuses Yussif. "Perhaps to cool it off a while." He shrugs. "It's worth a try." He hands the scroll to Jairus with the salutation showing. It reads TO: RABBI NICODEMUS OF THE JERUSALEM SANHEDRIN. IMPORTANT.

"Very well," Jairus says. "Until I hear further from you, you and I will remain the only souls who shall know about this." He turns the cylinder in his hand. "But, Rabbi, it is unsealed."

Yussif returns his gaze and says evenly, "Yes, Jairus. It is." He can tell from Jairus's look that he understands he's free to read it if he so chooses.

Mary of Magdala's apartment

On his way back from Jordan en route to his own flat in the eastern quarter, Andrew approaches the tiny abode he knows now hosts Ramah and Tamar besides the woman he must speak with. As he stands before the door, pawing the ground with his sandal, an ugly scene plays over and over in his mind. It hasn't been so long ago, and it has haunted him since.

Jesus had been arrested and hauled before Praetor Quintus for questioning, and Andrew had been furious at the rest of Jesus' followers for allowing it. He was determined to chase after Jesus and petition for his release.

"Andrew," John had said, "he didn't ask for your help."

Near tears, Andrew had told him, "He shouldn't have to! I don't recognize any of you."

Even Simon had leaned close and whispered, "Brother, you're not yourself."

Andrew had pushed him away, and then it happened. The younger Mary had said, "Maybe I should come with you. I feel responsible."

Andrew still can hardly believe he had whirled to face her, shouting, "You might *be* responsible! How *could* you leave?"

It had been wrong, flat wrong, to throw her failure in her face. Sure, he had his thoughts and feelings, and he may have even been right. But Mary had been no different from the rest of them, no different from Andrew himself, if truth be told. He was no more immune to falling back into his old ways than she had been. He could just as easily have been the one who needed to be brought back into the fold and seek Jesus' forgiveness. But first things first. He needed Mary's forgiveness.

Usually bold and direct, Andrew finds himself tentative and hesitantly knocks. Mary opens the door, looking confused. "Shalom," she says.

"Shalom. I won't take much time." He peeks past her to be sure neither Ramah nor Tamar is close enough to hear.

"It's fine," Mary says. "Do you need something?"

"I, uh, just wanted to say something, Mary. In Rabbi's sermon, he said to reconcile with someone first before worshiping. And I need to apologize to you."

Her smile is so tender, it wounds him. "You don't owe me—"

"Yes, I do. I said awful things to you because I was scared—something Rabbi also talked about. He talked about a lot of things I've got to work on, actually."

"Me too," Mary says softly.

"But you didn't deserve the things I said to you, and I'm really sorry."

She presses her lips together and cocks her head, as if to thank him.

"So, anyway—that's all."

"I'm sorry," she says, emotion in her voice. "I'm not sure what to say. I think this is the first time anyone has ever said *sorry* to me for anything."

"You don't deserve that either," Andrew says. He endures another awkward pause. "Things are better now, eh?"

"Yes. A lot. Thank you for this."

"Shalom, Mary."

"Shalom."

The outskirts of Capernaum

On the one hand, Matthew is proud of the makeshift camp he has fashioned far enough from the thoroughfare into Capernaum that he is hidden from traffic. On the other, he must have forgotten some step Philip has taught him regarding preparing a comfortable sleep chamber. Living on the road with Jesus has been different enough from the luxurious existence he enjoyed as a tax collector, but he has at least benefitted from the skills of his more-outdoor-oriented compatriots. Yet something they know about building a manageable foundation for their sleeping mats has been lost on him, and he wakens less than rested and with a sore back.

But he has more on his mind this morning than his discomfort. After relieving himself, fashioning a small fire, and brewing himself a hot drink, he prays and tidies the campsite before heading toward his childhood home. He's certain his parents will never move into the palatial estate he has bequeathed them. His father, Alphaeus, made it clear he considers Matthew's largesse the result of blood money he extorted from his own people. And of course that is true, though it makes their estrangement no less painful.

Yet Matthew is growing in his faith and his devotion to the Messiah. He longs to worship Jesus and his Father in heaven, but the rabbi made it clear in his sermon that one is to reconcile with anyone he needs to before worshiping. So how can he qualify if he remains at enmity with his own parents? The next move is his. He knows where to find them.

Confident he is doing the right thing, Matthew still feels more of a burden on his shoulders with every step into town and down the familiar street where he grew up. Can he go through with this? Will he? He has been, for all practical purposes, disowned by his father. And while surely his mother is as pained by this as Matthew is, she too expressed disgust, even hatred, for his life choices.

But what do they think now—now that he has turned his back on his past and is following the man he believes to be the Messiah? How he wishes they would at least sell the estate he has given them and enjoy an easier existence—or give the money to the poor if that makes them feel better.

He cautiously approaches the front door and feels suddenly paralyzed. Can he do this? What will he say? He raises a hand to knock but can't force himself to do it. Just like the time he tried to visit them on Shabbat, he fears he will succumb to fear and retreat. He can only hope neither his father nor his mother has seen him standing there. He should just quietly back away, return to his campsite, and seek wisdom from the Lord.

But before he can move, the air is pierced by barking—loud, excited-sounding yips from the dog Matthew also left his parents. It wags its tail, prances, tries to leap on him. *Perfect,* he thinks. *The man his own family sees as a dog is welcomed home only by one of his own kind.*

"Shush, dog!" he whispers urgently. "Shush!"

The door opens a crack. The moment of truth. At last, Matthew's father appears. Surely he'll slam the door in his face.

But no. He fully opens the door.

"Fath—Alphaeus!"

They stare at each other.

"Son!"

PART 2
Two by Two

Chapter 12

EMPEROR OBVIOUS

Capernaum

Primi Gaius stands alongside *Cohortes Urbana* Atticus, determined not to look directly into his eyes. That would only encourage the man, somehow make him think Gaius gives a kernel of wheat what he thinks or has to say. Is Atticus not aware he is the emperor of the obvious—apparently compelled to explain what others can plainly see? And why is he always eating? Gaius has never seen him without at least a piece of fruit. And now, as the man sits astride a wall overlooking the western city gate, he bears a fragrant loaf of rye bread in his lap.

Dozens of tents and lean-tos lie just outside the gate below, composing their own expansive ersatz town of temporary shelters. Many of the occupants limp around on crutches or canes. Others suffer hacking coughs. And some merely lie on ratty blankets, groaning in the setting sun. Women pull ragged laundry from makeshift clotheslines, while others round up children from their play. It will soon be bedtime. Men bow and rock and chant prayers.

From the corner of his eye, Gaius is aware that Atticus has ripped a chunk of bread from the loaf and tucked it in his cheek. "What do you make of this?" he says, gesturing to the shantytown.

Continuing to stare straight ahead, Gaius wonders at the question. He makes of it what anyone would make of it. It's hardly a mystery. He knows why the people have sojourned here and what they want. Everyone does.

"Primi?" Atticus says, forcing Gaius to turn, just as he tosses him a chunk of bread. Gaius snatches it out of the air but neither thanks Atticus nor tastes it. One of the reasons he remains fit and taut is that he refuses to snack during the day. Two meals a day are sufficient. No more, no less.

"They're here for Jesus of Nazareth," Atticus adds.

Next he'll inform me the sun rises in the east. It's no surprise to Gaius why throngs are attracted to Jesus. The fact is, he himself is glad his assignment puts him in proximity to the preacher. "It's understandable," he offers flatly.

Oh, great, now he has Atticus's attention. "You don't think this poses a problem to the order of the law?"

All Gaius needs is word getting back to Praetor Quintus or, worse, to Caesar, that a primi seems impressed with a rabble-rouser. "Yes, sir," he says. "I only meant I can see why—"

"Quintus is going to come out of his sandals when he sees this."

Determined to remain stoic, Gaius fears his face has betrayed a hint of sadness at that idea. Sure enough, Atticus turns his full awareness on him. "Something going on with you, Primi?"

"No, sir. Fit for duty, sir."

"Good. Secrets—like murders—eventually become known. *Eventually.* Tomorrow you ought to be the one to let Quintus know about this new slum. Come on."

Atticus climbs off the wall and walks away, still chewing. Gaius tosses his bread to the birds.

The next evening

Nathanael walks with Zee around the perimeter of the tent city. The former architect senses that the former Zealot is on edge. Zee has been high strung since he joined the disciples, and Nathanael knows Jesus has been working to soften his edges, mellow him out, make him less rigid and rules-focused. Nathanael finds Zee ironically pharisaical in his own way.

Zee stops suddenly, staring at a couple of pilgrims building a fire. What now? When Zee steps toward them, Nathanael reaches to stop him. "What are you doing?"

"They can't have a fire so close to a canvas structure!" Zee whispers. "It's Capernaum law. Plus, a fire will draw Roman attention and put Jesus at risk."

Zee steps toward the men again, but Nathanael blocks him. "What are you going to do?"

"Tell them no fires."

Nathanael sighs. Some people can learn only from experience. "Have it your way."

"Excuse me!" Zee says to the men.

"There's no room here," one says, clearly misunderstanding Zee's intentions.

"No fires fewer than nine cubits from a canvas structure. It's a hazard. You're going to have to figure something out. We can't have trouble."

"Who's *we*?" the man says.

"Are you one of his disciples?" the other asks.

Pilgrims within earshot approach. “Where is he?” one shouts. “In Capernaum?”

“Who said he’s in Capernaum?” Zee says.

“That’s why we’re all here!” a woman says.

A man says, “When will his next sermon be? We have to hear it. He’s The One, isn’t he?”

Nathanael is amused at Zee’s having to backpedal. “He didn’t say that on the mount,” Zee says.

“But it has to be true,” the woman says.

A man adds, “Why did he not speak of overthrowing Rome?”

Zee turns to Nathanael, who smiles and says, “How’s fire patrol working for you?”

Zee backs away from the people and moves on, Nathanael following. Zee speaks in hushed tones. “These crowds will be difficult to manage.”

“Hard for us, yes,” Nathanael says. “Jesus can handle himself. He wants the crowds.”

“Mm, I don’t know. There are too many people.”

“Too many to go around telling them how to build a dinner fire. You have to pick your battles, my friend.”

Chapter 13

AMENDS

The home of Alphaeus and Elisheba

Matthew can hardly believe it, but he feels as nervous sitting across from his father—his mother standing behind him—as he did when Jesus called him to join his disciples. The difference then was that he had never felt surer of anything in his life. In an instant he made up his mind—well, actually, it felt as if his mind had been made up for him—and wholly turned his back on his former life.

No more tax collecting, no more personal armed Roman bodyguard, no more wealth, no more palatial home in the finest neighborhood. Even Gaius, his guard, told him he'd lost his mind. Oh, there would still be vitriol, curses, epithets, scorn—largely from the Pharisees, but also, he learned quickly, even from his fellow disciples. And why not? He had betrayed them, wronged them, in essence extorted them and made their lives as miserable as any of his other fellow Jews.

Thank God for Philip and Thaddeus and a couple of the others—including the women—who recognized that all of

Jesus' followers had pasts. Perhaps theirs weren't as repulsive as Matthew's had been, but as Philip once told him, "I *was* something else once, too. Once you've met the Messiah, *am* is all that matters." Philip was so wise to remind him often to not allow anyone to define him by his past—by his sins.

Jesus had accepted him, and he could only hope and pray the others would eventually as well. He would do whatever necessary to reconcile with them.

But now here he sits, facing his parents, clutching his ever-present handkerchief, the security blanket he can't do without, especially when he's nervous. And when is he not? His heart is filled to overflowing that his father called him "Son," but Matthew won't try to fool himself: The work of reuniting here has only just begun. He can tell his father is uneasy too, sitting across from him in silence. His mother serves them each a cup of wine.

"This is good," Matthew says, eager to get to the matter at hand but not knowing how to broach the subject. "Thank you."

"Not really," his father says. "Our current batch isn't very good."

How Matthew hates small talk, especially now, especially with the two people he loves more than anyone else on earth. For years he has isolated himself from everyone, and being estranged from his family only made things worse. He literally had no one until Jesus came along. Before that, the only creature who didn't judge and revile him was the dog.

But small talk it is for now. "I've been traveling and haven't had good wine, so this is fine."

His mother brightens. "How *were* your travels? We'd love to hear about them."

She sounds almost sincere, but Matthew is sure she's just trying to avoid awkward silences. What can he say? He'd like to tell them all he's been doing and learning, but not now. He's dying to clear the air. "They were good," he says. "Thank you." But that won't be enough for her. She'll press, he knows.

"Are you sure?" she says. "You've lost weight. Did you eat enough?"

Are we really going to pursue this? He sighs. "I used to eat too much."

"No, you didn't!" she says. "You looked especially healthy when I saw you. I hope you are still—"

"Ellie," Alphaeus says, "he said he was good."

A pause. More embarrassing discomfort. Is Matthew going to have to just blurt things out to get on with it?

"I like your beard," Elisheba says.

"Thank you. I won't shave for a long time."

Matthew catches his mother pleading with her eyes for his father to say something, anything.

Alphaeus says, "How did you handle sleeping outside?"

Does he know I did so even last night? "I'm better at it by now. I'm proficient at making a tent, and I have also learned how to strip bark for dry wood. My friend Philip taught me—"

"You have a friend?" Elisheba asks.

She can't know how painful it is to be reminded that other than a brief time in childhood, when his sister and he got along well, he has never before had a friend—not even one. He doesn't know how to respond but doesn't want to lash out and say, "I just said *my friend Philip,* so obviously I have a friend!"

She's trying. But it's time to force the issue. "Yesterday, my rabbi said that every time we pray to God, we should ask him to forgive our debts."

His father and mother both stiffen, just what he dreaded. But he plunges ahead, though haltingly. "And—I recognize that I owe—quite a debt to you." He's pleased that his last phrase sounds as confident as he feels. Hard as it was to say, he in no way questions the truth of it.

"Matthew," his father says, "you don't owe us any money—"

Matthew stands and paces. He has something to say, and he must get it right. "The debt isn't material. I hurt you, and I hurt our community. And my rabbi also said that before we lay a sacrifice at the altar, if we know a brother has an offense against us, we should leave the sacrifice there and go and be reconciled. Of course, only priests lay gifts at the altar, and you are not my brother, but the example is in some way a metaphor, which I'm learning is—"

"Yes, Matthew," Alphaeus says, "we get it. Move on."

His mother nudges his father.

Matthew continues: "I never understood why I was so—*different* from everyone else. I just wanted a comfortable life."

"You wanted to be better than everybody," his father says.

"Alphaeus—"

"No, Mother, he's right. I felt I deserved it. And I loved affluence because of it. I was comfortable behind the bars of my booth with an armed escort nearby. And comfortable at home behind a gold door. All the while you were scorned at synagogue. You lost your reputation and friends. I shamed our family."

Silence.

"I turned my back on our people. I believed my choices were better for me and more important than my family and faith. That was selfish. Which is wrong. I am sorry. I wish I could take back the harm I caused you. I wish—"

"All right, all right," Alphaeus says. "All right."

Elisheba begins weeping, and Alphaeus reaches for her. "Shh …"

Matthew says, "I will search for something I can do to atone."

"Matthew," his father says, "sit down."

"I prefer to stand."

"Please …"

"I don't deserve the courtesy."

Alphaeus shakes his head. "You're not the only one who must atone."

Matthew drops back into his chair. His mother is obviously now full of joy. He hangs his head, full of emotion. What is his father saying?

"Are you hungry?" Alphaeus asks.

Surprisingly, he is. Matthew nods, and his mother kisses his father before moving to the kitchen. He meets Alphaeus's gaze, as if man to man and not father and son.

"You are correct, Matthew. I lost my business because of you. And we lost our reputation and our friends."

"I know."

"But I had no right to reject you as my son."

The words hit Matthew like a rushing wind.

"God should strike me down for the things I said to you. I was shameful." His father lets the words hang in the air. Then, "Can you forgive me?"

Across the room, his mother sobs.

"I made things only worse," Alphaeus says. "I'm sorry."

"*We're* sorry," his mother adds.

They're apologizing to me? "But what has changed? I sinned—"

"We saw him too, Matthew," his father says. "We heard his sermon."

"He is the teacher you are following?" his mother says.

"Yes. He called me, and I—"

"Then you have already atoned," Alphaeus says. "They were the truest words I've ever heard. Some of them shocking—"

"I know. I wrote it all down."

His mother steps closer. "You are his scribe?"

"Yes."

"You will redeem our family's name," Alphaeus says.

Elisheba says, "He chose *you,* Matthew."

Matthew shakes his head. "To this day, I don't know why."

His mother rushes to him and hugs him as she hasn't in years. As she pulls him in, he lays his kerchief on the table and embraces her too. "You say you always felt different from other people," she says, "and you are. Because you were set apart for something special."

"Thank you."

"Thank you, *Ima,*" she says. "Say it."

"Thank you, Ima."

She hugs him tighter and pulls away. "Alphaeus."

"What?"

"Forgive him."

"I did!"

"No, you didn't. It must be said."

Alphaeus sighs and chuckles as he stands. Alphaeus extends his hand, and Matthew shakes it. "I forgive you, Son."

"Thank you."

"Thank you, *Abba,*" she says.

"Abba," Matthew says.

They pause to wipe tears.

His mother says, "How long are you in Capernaum?"

"I don't know. But as long as I'm here, I promise I'll make amends."

"You have," she says.

Alphaeus raises a brow. "We've rented out your old room for years."

"It's all right, Abba, Ima. I've gotten used to sleeping on the ground."

"Hey!" Alphaeus says. "Aah-ha! Wait right here."

He returns a moment later, looking triumphant. "I'm glad I didn't throw this away." He opens his palm to reveal Matthew's house key, given to him on Matthew's behalf by Gaius.

Matthew recoils. "I will never live in that home again."

"So, give it away," Alphaeus says, winking at his wife. "Tear it down. Burn it if you want."

"Why would I do that?"

Alphaeus shrugs as he drops the key into Matthew's hand. "You'll find something to do with it. Till then, you can have any floor in it."

Chapter 14

REDRAW

The Roman Authority, Capernaum

Gaius can't help but suspect Atticus of some ulterior motive for allowing him to inform Praetor Quintus of the shantytown outside the western gate. Atticus has always seemed the sort who enjoys needling the praetor with bad news. But it *is* the primi's job to keep his boss informed. And he's learned that Quintus appreciates straight talk—no hemming and hawing.

But as Gaius and Atticus sweep past the receiving desk and the guard who has clearly learned the futility of trying to make the *Cohortes Urbana* wait and be announced, Quintus can be heard even in the foyer.

"And *you*!" he rails. "What color does that look like to you?"

After a mumbled, timid response, Quintus is on the attack again. "Is it supposed to look like that? Drink it! Drink it!"

Atticus appears to stifle a laugh and nods for Gaius to follow him into Quintus's office. Just as they enter, Quintus throws a clay cup against the wall while a cowering underling—obviously a Roman engineer—kneels at his feet. Atticus affects a huge, innocent-looking grin. "Quintus! My old friend! Oh, are you busy?"

Quintus leans into the engineer. "Fix. The. Water. Fix it! If I see another drop of sewage in my water, I will personally drown you in it, I swear to Apollo. Octavius, you will gargle sewage."

"Vivid," Atticus says. "I think he gets it. You did get that, right? He's gonna drown you in … well, you know."

Octavius, head still down, addresses the praetor. "I will find the breach, Dominus."

While Quintus bores into the engineer with a death stare, Gaius says, "I will oversee the project."

"You do that," Quintus says, then turns back to the engineer. "Brown water make you deaf? Go! Do it now!"

The man rushes away, and Atticus takes a seat, smirking. Gaius remains at attention.

"You can watch the talent leave their bodies when they arrive from Rome," Quintus says. "You can keep time by it."

Atticus nods. "Good help is hard to f—"

"It's these people!" Quintus says. "This land. It's going to force me to do something drastic."

"Like work?" Atticus says.

"I'm capable of anything. Hail Caesar." Quintus plops into his desk chair. "What do you want?"

Atticus looks to Gaius.

"Um, yes, Praetor. A camp has sprung up just beyond the western perimeter of the city."

"So, send them on their way."

Gaius looks to Atticus, who ignores him, cleaning his fingernails.

"They're pilgrims, Dominus," Gaius says.

"Pilgrims to what?"

"To *whom*. … Jesus of Nazareth."

"Ugh!"

"He delivered a sermon on the Korazim Pla—"

"Stop. He delivered it? You're just telling me now?"

Atticus reengages. "And then he's building a hut. And now he's relieving himself. Quintus, neither Gaius nor I have enough hours in a day to inform you of everything this man—"

"Don't speak for the men in my command," Quintus says. "Please. This feels a little more significant than relieving himself. Gaius, what was said?"

What was said? Though Gaius found the sermon riveting, almost hypnotic, and probably could have recited much of it—especially the poignant paradoxes—the less Quintus knows, the better. "It sounded like any other sermon, Dominus."

Atticus shoots Gaius a double take.

"Is that what *you* heard, *Cohortes*?" Quintus says.

"Well," Atticus says, "I haven't heard many sermons." He shrugs. "Lengthy instructions about, what was it, something about animal hooves, always read right to left. You know, Jewish stuff."

Gaius is stunned at Atticus's lie.

Quintus looks puzzled. "If it was so boring, why didn't the pilgrims stay on the plateau? Did Jesus lead them here?"

"No, Dominus," Gaius says. "No one knows where Jesus is now. But many of his followers reside in the city."

Quintus cocks his head. "Was our former tax collector there?"

Gaius finds himself suddenly protective of Matthew, but when Atticus nods, he can't deny it. "Matthew. Yes."

"Well," Quintus says, "who cares anyway? Just get rid of them."

Get rid of them? "Dominus?"

"Pack them up!" Quintus says. "Force them out. We are still Rome!"

"Or," Atticus says, "you could turn them into revenue."

This plainly catches Quintus's attention. "How?"

"Redraw the city boundary to encompass the squatters."

"But they're not on our census."

"All the better for you. They're not paying taxes wherever they've come from, which means other praetors'—"

"—Ledgers are down," Quintus says, as if warming to the idea. "I get it."

Gaius feels the need to rein this in before it gets out of hand. "The pilgrims have been peaceful to this point. I can't say how they'll respond to being taxed."

"You'd better get some rest then, Gaius. My plan is to redraw the city lines, and fast. We're behind this month."

"It's a good plan," Atticus says, "but you do have to consider Pilate."

"Stop being coy," Quintus says. "What do you mean?"

"As you know, Pilate is always concerned with order."

"Of course."

"But he's been under some pressure not to overuse force to achieve it."

"From Caesar? Hail."

Atticus nods.

"Fine," Quintus continues. "Gaius, I need you to do your job without leaving marks." He looks to Atticus. "Happy now?"

"I'll be headed to Jerusalem soon."

"Aah," Quintus says. "Delightful place."

"I owe Pilate a visit," Atticus says.

Quintus's face falls.

"Lots to catch up on," Atticus adds, standing and heading for the door.

Quintus's smile freezes, and the color drains from his face. "Wonderful."

Chapter 15

THE ANNOUNCEMENT

The home of Zebedee and Salome

So, this is the place, Thomas thinks, peeking at the ceiling where the beautiful Tamar and her friends were said to have lowered their paralytic friend through the roof to be healed by Jesus. He knows it has to be true—there were many witnesses, after all. But the skeptic in him so wishes he had been here for that. What must it have been like for a man crippled from birth? But even the Pharisees buzzed about it, tried to charge the rabbi with claiming to be God for not only healing the man (with some sort of a trick, they say), but for also presuming to forgive the man's sins!

Thomas can't deny the patchwork Big James and John's father has applied to the ceiling. Something happened up there for sure. Meanwhile, Thomas feels strangely warmed in this tiny, cozy kitchen where the brothers' mother has laid out a cornucopia of delights—various chewables and spices. Thomas can't make sense of the mocking the other two disciple brothers—Simon and Andrew—have tormented Big James and John with about their mother's cooking. They've not really been mean-spirited, but neither have they hidden their disdain for her culinary skills. Maybe it's just the way men tease each other, but Simon claims he actually lets her main dishes pass by when he visits.

If her actual cooking is anything like what she has chosen for Thomas and her sons and husband to snack on, he can't imagine ever declining to try it. And having been in the catering business, he knows prepared food.

Thomas enjoys John's talking with his mouth full, suggesting to his mother that she might sew little pouches inside his and Big James's and even Thomas's belts, where they could store raisins for their travels. "An emergency stash!" John says.

Salome appears embarrassed by the flattery as Big James pours it on. "I spent so many nights dreaming about your little squares, Ima! The cinnamon and fig ones."

"So good!" John adds.

Apparently that's all the encouragement she needs. "I will load you three boys up like pack mules. You will never go hungry on the road again."

Zebedee produces a small vial and excitedly hands it to Thomas. "Taste this!"

Thomas squints. "What is it?"

Zebedee grins. "Do you think I would poison you, our guest?"

Thomas sniffs it. "Olive oil."

"Go on!" Zebedee says.

Thomas pours a little onto his tongue and savors it. He nods. "Really good."

Zebedee exults to Salome, "And he knows flavor! From the wine business!"

"What's the point, Father?" John says.

"I made it!"

Thomas passes the vial to John, who takes a sip.

Zebedee continues, "I traded one of the guys at the dock for a little press. I can make only a few vials at a time."

"For what?" Big James says.

"It's a ceremonial press," his father says, then whispers, "but it's also delicious."

Salome smiles. "Your abba is very good at making oil."

"I love doing it."

John passes the vial to Big James, who tips it bottoms up. "There's none left!"

Thomas blurts, "I think I'm gonna ask Ramah to marry me."

Everyone in the kitchen falls silent, staring.

Zebedee shouts, "I knew it!"

John claps Thomas on the back. "Atta boy!"

Big James wraps Thomas in a bear hug. "You're gonna make a fine husband!"

"I'd marry you," John deadpans.

Salome beams as the men heap more congratulations.

Zebedee asks, "Do your and Ramah's fathers know each other?"

Thomas hesitates. He so loves this home because he didn't enjoy the same, but he hates to douse the happy conversation now. "My father is dead."

Zebedee's smile fades. "I'm sorry to hear that."

"May he rest in peace," Salome says.

"Got an older brother?" Zebedee says.

"No."

"Then who can arrange?" Big James says.

"Her father is aware of my intentions."

"It's not unheard of," Zebedee says. "Samson chose his own wife."

John smirks. "Not exactly the model Israelite, Father."

Thomas cocks his head. "David chose Abigail."

"Also not the best example," Big James says.

"Boys," Salome weighs in, "give the man a chance."

"Have you spoken with your rabbi about this?" Zebedee says.

"The next time we see him, I'll share my intention. I've searched my heart and know it's right. Jesus will make it work."

Chapter 16

"STUDYING"

Simon's house, dusk

Eden has prevailed upon Simon to not make Nathanael or Zee sleep on the roof. They'll stay where her ima had stayed. They're talking in there now as she stands in the kitchen, gleefully kneading dough for the second meal of the day—for all four of them. Of course she looked forward to time alone with Simon, but no one promised this new life would be easy.

Simon slips up behind her, wrapping his arms around her waist and resting his chin on her shoulder. How she's missed his touch. "Are you going to be here the whole time I'm doing this?" she asks.

"Yes," he whispers.

"Good," she says, smiling.

Nathanael's and Zee's voices rise as they argue about something. "Boys!" Simon hollers, and they both immediately call out their apologies.

Eden turns to gaze at Simon, amused and impressed. "You've trained them."

"Your cooking is a powerful incentive." He turns and talks louder so Nathanael and Zee can hear him. "If they want to eat, they will stay in their room quietly!"

"We're quiet now," Nathanael says.

"Sorry," Zee says.

"Won't they get bored?" Eden says.

"They both have much to study," Simon says.

She faces him. "And you don't?"

"Of course I do," he says, "but I think you could help me."

"Oh, really?"

"Yes. Yes, let's study …" He takes her hand and leads her out of the kitchen toward their bedroom. "I have much to learn."

Eden follows, laughing.

Chapter 17

FOLLOWED

Tent city, Capernaum, evening

Gaius is doing his duty. He always does. But patrolling the edge of this shantytown with a young centurion named Julius makes him wonder what's become of his career. Always the idealist, he became a Roman guard out of a sense of patriotism and a commitment to justice. He's largely enjoyed his role till now. What is the point of tormenting these pilgrims? They have enough trouble already or they wouldn't be flocking to follow Jesus wherever he goes.

At first, Gaius was as suspicious of the preacher as Praetor Quintus was. But after arresting him, being aware of what many considered his miracles, and then hearing him preach, Gaius doesn't understand the fear and opposition. The man *is* engaging, and he can be profound. But a revolutionary? His pronouncing blessings on the disenfranchised and his pearls of paradoxical advice—the poor being rich, enemies being loved, the great serving the least of men—well, the only thing revolutionary about the man is how authoritative he sounds. Atticus sees him as a threat. Quintus hopes he doesn't have to kill him. Gaius is merely intrigued.

Yes, the man has the potential and the charisma to draw and impress—even motivate—the masses. But to what end? Certainly not a revolt. It sounds as if all he is calling for is a change of hearts. Of God or not of God, what's the harm? Why all the fuss? His own people, especially the Pharisees, see him as a blasphemer, so not all the Jews are enamored with him. How influential can he be?

Well, this crowd is infatuated with Jesus, that's for sure. Everywhere Gaius looks, more shelters are erected. One small gaggle secures the last tent post of their makeshift dwelling and gathers around a fire, passing each other a jug from which they fill their cups.

Julius confronts them. "Is that a fermented liquid?"

"What?" a pilgrim slurs. "This?"

"No wine on public property! Only in your private home or a tavern."

"This *is* my home."

"Primi?" Julius says.

"Let them drink it," Gaius says.

Julius stares at him, hesitating and looking puzzled.

Gaius shakes his head, bored with it all. "So, he should duck inside, drink it, and come back out? What difference will that make?"

Julius appears frustrated, defeated. "Yes, Primi."

Gaius moves on. Julius catches up. "How are we going to redraw the city limits when they keep arriving in such numbers? You'll have to do it over and over to encompass them all."

My thoughts exactly.

"Gaius?"

"I heard you, Julius. I think tonight my time would be better spent elsewhere. You finish the rounds, enforce protocol—patiently—and give me a full report in the morning."

Town square, Capernaum, night

Zee remains in shape from daily workouts and is constantly on the alert. While Jesus has made it clear he doesn't expect the former Zealot to use his prodigious physical combat skills in his new position, Zee cannot turn off his keen sense of awareness. If and when Jesus—or any of Zee's new friends—is threatened, he wants to be the one who anticipates danger and is prepared to deal with it.

Even on a routine errand as a guest in Simon and Eden's home, fetching a bucket of water for them from the city well, he scans the area, sniffs the air, listens for anything out of the ordinary. He senses something is up as he lowers his vessel with a pulley, but he can't put his finger on what it is. Too quiet? One of the shadowy figures on the street out of place? Zee doesn't know, but he's ready for anything.

As he carries the water through the streets, the city somehow feels more barren than it should be, even at this time of night. Why? Does he hear something behind him? Should he make it obvious, turn menacingly, scare off any threat? That would be no fun. If someone means him harm, bring it on. But to be sure, he cuts through an alley. When he emerges, determined to regulate his breathing so his pulse and respiration don't drown out what he needs to hear, he stops still and watches.

Moving on, Zee turns a corner, drops his bucket, and runs. Not so fast that he'll outpace any attacker, but fast enough to force whoever it is to race to keep up. And sure enough, he hears footsteps. No question now, someone is pursuing him. He presses his lips together, breathing evenly through his nose, actually fighting a grin. If he looks cowardly, so be it. He knows where to hide, not to evade danger but to invite it. He ducks down another alley and quickly climbs a drainpipe, edging along a roof, and peering into the darkness. A shadow moves. Something falls and crashes. Zee runs to the edge and leaps to another rooftop. Then another. He leans over a wall to examine the dark street.

"Lose something?" A voice from behind. Someone as stealthy as he. Zee fights a kneejerk reaction, not even flinching. He turns to find Atticus on the roof, a finger to his lips, Zee's bucket in his other hand. "Shh …"

"What do you want?" Zee says flatly.

"I'm just hunting." Atticus unfurls his tunic to reveal his weapon.

"Hunting what?"

"You were behind a plot to murder the Roman magistrate in Jerusalem."

Zee holds his gaze. "And you were there in the desert, at the gates of the city. Why did you let me get into Jerusalem in the first place?"

"You know."

"You thought you were good enough to stop me?"

Atticus shrugs. "I liked my chances. But we'll never know. Something unexpected happened."

All Zee knew was that he had soon lost the man, and when he saw him again at the failed assassination attempt, Zee's own brother had just been healed. "A miracle," Zee says.

"If you say so. What is he, Simon?"

Zee bristles at the reference to Jesus.

"Relax, Zealot," Atticus says, "or whatever you are now. I'm just interested in what happens next."

"So, if I walk away right now, you're not going to put a knife in my back?"

"I could have done that anywhere," Atticus says.

"How do you know I won't kill *you*?"

"Because your weapon is at the bottom of the Jordan. Right where he put it. So, there's that."

How can he know that? How long has this guy been watching him?

"That does leave you defenseless, though," Atticus continues. "And that's bad for you."

"But—"

"I didn't chase you up here, Simon. But someone did. You left some dangerous men in the lurch."

True, he had abandoned his Zealot compatriots, but it couldn't be helped. He assumed a day of reckoning lay in his future. "The Order is here?"

"Are you surprised?"

Zee shakes his head. "They won't quit."

"Well, one of us has to make them."

That's true. The last thing he wants is Zealots becoming threats to Jesus. He'll have to lure his pursuers away. "I'm leaving Capernaum for a while," Zee says.

"They had better follow. If they stay in Capernaum, I'll be forced to clean up your mess. I can't have Zealots in a Roman town."

"Others will come for me."

"Now you're getting it," Atticus says. "Who knows? Maybe they'll see your Messiah and come to believe." He laughs. "But believe what?"

"We, his disciples, are zealous too, man."

"Then what are you doing on a rooftop, chatting with a Roman?"

Atticus lays a hand on Zee's shoulder. He recoils.

"Sorry," Atticus says. "You *were* a Zealot. Now you're a traitor. And you're right. They won't stop."

Simon and Eden's home, night

Finally alone, the couple sit holding each other before a crackling fire. Simon could be happy staying right here for days.

Eden breaks the silence. "I can't believe I have you back."

He finds that bittersweet, because he knows that she knows as well as he does that this is temporary. "I don't believe you don't believe," he says. "Here I am. Where I'll always be." *Even when I'm not here physically,* he thinks.

"When you were gone this time, I had moments of feeling ..."

"Of feeling what?"

"Lost. I don't know what to call those feelings."

"What did they feel like?"

"I was angry. Sad—"

"Oh, Love, you know I'm with Jesus. We both are. You remember what he told you ..."

"I'll always remember that. It's what gets me through the days."

"He sees you."

"I know," she says. "I think of that moment so often. But sometimes, in the memory, I forget what his face looks like."

"What do you mean?"

"Haven't you ever been separated from someone and you can't recall their face after a while?"

"Do you forget my face?"

She gives him a look and laughs as if he's being selfish, childish. Which he knows he is. But she also has wonder in her eyes. She sinks into him. "I don't forget your face. Things are so good now."

"We just have to spend more time together, you know? I think Jesus has work to do here." Meaning they can stay put for a while. *A man can dream.* "I've been thinking about—our family."

Eden shrugs. "Ima is healthy, my brothers are fishing—"

"No, *our* family."

She looks at him, eyes wide.

"It's time," he says.

She throws her arms around him, clearly overcome.

Chapter 18

LOVE IS LOVE

Mary of Magdala's apartment

Until now, Mary has given little thought to the hardships that have emerged from following Jesus. They seem like mere bumps in the road, short detours, minor inconveniences. The privilege of knowing him, hearing him, watching him perform miracles, or observing him simply show limitless compassion to everyone outweighs occasional hunger pangs or soreness from sleeping in new and strange places. And that he forgave her yet again, after having redeemed her …

Being home for a while has been a treat, sleeping in her own bed and getting to know Tamar and Ramah better. But it hasn't all been rosy. She looks forward to taking Matthew up on his offer to move the three of them into his former mansion, where they'll be safest and can find ways to help support Jesus and the disciples monetarily. Now they busy themselves packing.

"We are really low on food," Tamar says, emptying the last cupboard. "And money."

"We'll be in Matthew's former home by Erev Shabbat," Mary says.

"Friday, yes," Ramah says. "Where will Matthew stay?"

"I hope with his family," Mary says. "He wants a fresh start."

"You understand all about that," Tamar says, causing Mary to wince. Ramah glances at her, obviously having caught the uncharacteristic insensitivity on the part of the beautiful Egyptian.

Mary changes the subject. "In any case, with no food, we'll have less to carry."

"Money is still low," Tamar says.

And before she can curb her tongue, Mary says, "Well—you could—sell some of your jewelry."

Tamar freezes and lays a hand on her ornate necklace. "It's just that—they're all very personal."

Ramah scoffs. "Every single piece?"

"I said *all,*" Tamar says flatly.

Ramah looks again to Mary, who looks away. Ramah won't let it go. "We've each given up some of our personal lives to follow Jesus."

That's for sure, Mary thinks. "I gave up a name."

That creates an awkward silence. Have the women been living too close together for too long? Mary appreciates Ramah's immediately trying to put a positive spin on things. "But we each gained so much," she says. "Thomas says Zebedee is making olive oil now and that maybe we could be part of turning it into a business."

"I wonder," Mary says, "if it could be sold as anointing oil."

"Holy anointing oil is very specific," Ramah says. "It's laid out in the Books of Moses."

"Oh!" Mary says. "It's not just olive oil?" Then it hits her. "Wait, you've studied through Moses?"

"You talked to Thomas?" Tamar says.

Ramah fails to keep from smiling, but Mary notices she ignores Tamar's question. "Well," Ramah says, "it is oil. But there are spices mixed in. We use some of them in our wines—cinnamon, cassia, and some other things. We would buy it from the same vendors the priests do."

"Thomas would know where to get them," Mary says.

Tamar smirks. "I think Thomas has other things on his mind."

Ramah nods. "The ministry *is* demanding."

Mary pretends not to know what Tamar is driving at and wonders if Ramah is doing the same.

"Don't misunderstand, Ramah," Tamar says. "Thomas is a dedicated student."

"And a hard worker," Mary adds, teasing. She thinks Ramah is playing dumb.

"Yes," Ramah says. "A very hard worker. And smart. And very dedicated."

"Maybe a little distracted," Tamar presses.

"What are you saying, Tamar?" Ramah asks.

"All right," Mary says, "let's all stop dancing around this and call it what it is."

"*Thank* you," Tamar says.

Mary continues, "His dedication to you was obvious the moment I saw you both at the wedding, Ramah."

"I was *very* stressed at that wedding."

"Mm, but it wasn't a 'concerned for your stress' look I noticed. Well, it was, but—"

"You're in love with him," Tamar says.

"That's not how it works with our people," Ramah says. "You're a Gentile; you don't understand. Love comes from marriage."

"Jew, Gentile," Tamar says. "Love is love."

"But Tamar," Mary says, "in our culture, marriages are arranged by fathers. That's all she's saying."

Tamar winces.

Mary adds, "Where you come from, do people—"

"I'd rather not talk about where I come from," Tamar says, "if that's okay with you."

"Of course." Mary turns to Ramah. "Thomas's feelings toward you are as plain as day."

"Painfully obvious," Tamar says.

"What we are asking," Mary says, "is whether you *want* to …"

Ramah hesitates. "It is complicated with my father, and considering our circumstances, this wouldn't be traditional. But yes. If my father approved, I would be very fortunate."

Tamar appears to study her. "That's a Jewish way of saying you love him and would be excited, yes?"

Ramah stares at her, then at Mary. She nods and smiles, and the three laugh together.

Chapter 19

EVERY DIRECTION

Simon and Eden's home, Capernaum

Simon is giddy with anticipation. Jesus has finally spread the word that all should reassemble, and right here. This, Simon knows, is where the rabbi will lay out the plans for his ministry in this town. Oh, he knows there will be more traveling in the future. But being able to work from home, venture out during the day with Jesus, and spend nights at home with his wife, well, what could be better?

Simon is curious, however, why Eden is the only female here, in and out of their crammed living room serving food and drinks to all the disciples. Mother Mary has returned to her home, and maybe Jesus has already communicated with Mary, Tamar, and Ramah.

When everyone is settled and silent, Jesus says, "I'm sure by now most of you are aware of the tent village rapidly growing west of Capernaum."

Most of you? Simon thinks. Everyone knows, which is confirmed with nods all around.

Jesus continues, "Those are people who followed us from the Mount and who are now waiting to hear more. Their numbers grow by the day, as does the suspicion of Rome. Zee informs me that some members of his former order have even journeyed here."

"It would appear we were building an army, Teacher," Andrew says.

"I suppose that's one way to look at it," Jesus says. "The other way to look at it is my way."

"The correct way, you mean," Simon says.

Jesus chuckles. "Yes, Simon." He pauses. "Those people are like those in regions all over. They are not an army. Not now. They are in need of rescue. And you are going to help me rescue them."

Now you're talking, Simon thinks. And Zee must agree, as he pounds his fist and leans forward.

Nothing eludes Jesus. "Different kind of rescue, Zee. It is not sustainable for me to do all the preaching, all the healing, and all the ministering. I called you here today—and thank you, Eden, for looking after us—because our ministry will only grow. And we want it to grow till the end of the age. There will be more followers, and like those not here, they will all have roles and responsibilities. Most will become disciples, students. But I have chosen you twelve as my apostles."

Even Eden seems to know how monumental this is. She stops in mid-stride, and Simon holds his breath. No one makes a sound until Big James asks, "You're sending us?"

Matthew breaks in, "An apostle is the same as a messenger, one who—"

"I know what it means, Matthew," Big James says. "That's why I'm asking."

"You are my leaders," Jesus says. "And for the mission I have for you, it's best that you spread out and not be concentrated in one place."

Uh-oh, Simon thinks, and he notices Eden is rapt as well.

"I don't understand," Andrew says.

Jesus sighs. "I'm going to go home to Nazareth for a time, and while I'm there, I am sending you out in every direction, two by two, to our people only."

The room falls dead silent. Simon tries to tell himself he misheard. The others have to feel the same.

Thomas blurts, "Every direction, Rabbi?"

"Yes," Jesus says, "but not to the Gentiles yet. That will come in time, but for now to the lost sheep of the House of Israel. Just as Joshua led the twelve tribes to take the Promised Land, you will proclaim as you go, 'The kingdom of heaven is at hand.' And while you are on this mission, you will heal the sick and lame by anointing them with oil. And you will cast out demons."

Simon is about to burst, and Eden for the moment has made herself scarce.

Jesus scans the room. "Why are you all looking at me like that?"

Matthew cocks his head. "Could you just repeat that one more time?"

"I am sending you out, two by two, proclaiming as you go, 'The kingdom of heaven is at hand.' You will heal the sick, cast out demons—"

Simon's eyes dart to where Eden had been standing. "How soon are we talking about here, Rabbi?"

"There's that word again," Jesus says with a twinkle. "We will get to that, Simon."

"Heal the sick ..." Philip says.

Little James looks flabbergasted.

"Cast out demons?" Thaddeus says.

"While you're on this mission," Jesus says, "I grant you this authority. Someday you will have it all the time."

"Was there a ceremony I missed?" Nathanael asks.

"This is it," Jesus says.

"I don't feel any different."

"I don't need you to feel anything to do great things."

John speaks up. "With all due respect, Rabbi, we've only just begun as students. We're not nearly qualified. Why would you need us for this work?"

"He doesn't need us," Zee says. "He wants us."

"Very good, Zee. John, if I needed religious leaders and qualified students for my ministry, I wouldn't have chosen—well, you get the point."

Philip says, "Can we go back to the healing the sick thing for a second?"

"You will take nothing for your journey except a staff. No bread, no bag, no money. Not even Salome's food."

John and Big James raise their eyebrows.

"Wear sandals," Jesus continues, "but don't bring an extra tunic."

"Not even a change of clothes?" Little James says.

Matthew shakes his head. "Even the wandering Cynic philosophers carry a second tunic."

"Yes, and I'd like to distinguish you from the Cynics. They carry beggars' bags for people to put gold and silver coins in, and you will not do that. You received without paying. Now give without pay."

Simon can tell everyone is as restless and fearful as he is.

"Whatever town or village you enter, find out who is worthy in it and stay at their home until you depart. And if anyone will not receive you or listen to your words, shake off the dust from your feet when you leave that house or town. Don't waste your time."

Thaddeus raises his hand. "You said if anyone will not listen to our words. What words exactly? What are we supposed to teach?"

"Anything you've ever heard from me."

"I've heard only the one sermon," Judas says.

"You heard the best one anyway," Nathanael says, then catches himself and turns to Jesus. "I mean, don't get me wrong—they're all good."

"That message wasn't just for all the thousands there," Jesus says. "It was for all those who will hear it from now until the end of the age. How will they know it, you ask? Good question, thanks for asking. You will tell them. And the areas you're going to are areas I will soon go to, so you are preparing the way for my arrival and helping ensure more are ready to hear the good news. The miracles you'll perform on God's authority will prove my ministry."

Big James says, "Suppose we have a bad streak, where several towns in a row reject us, maybe for days. How are we to eat?"

Of course Big James would ask that, Simon thinks.

"And what if it gets bad," Andrew says, "like it has for your cousin John?"

"Listen carefully, all of you," Jesus says. "Do not fear those who kill the body but cannot kill the soul."

"So, you're saying we could die," John says.

"There will come a time when this becomes far more difficult. When persecution is an ever-present part of your ministry, you will follow in my footsteps and learn what it actually means to give up your life. I have more to teach you about that. In the meantime, this journey will not come to that."

"Rabbi," Thomas says, "I have a concern. You said you are sending us out two by two."

"Yes. The women will stay here in Capernaum and begin to support the ministry financially. They will also minister to the tent city, and Zebedee agreed to be responsible for their safety. Matthew has selflessly donated the use of his previous home, which will serve as the new place for them to stay."

Nathanael looks flummoxed. "I still can't understand. We're supposed to go out there, no defenses, no food, no shelter—just go out into strange lands—"

"He said not to be afraid," Andrew says.

"Fear's not something you just stop, Andrew," Thomas says.

"I'm going with Zee then," Nathanael says.

Zee says, "I may be the most at risk of all of us."

"Great," Nathanael says.

"Whatever happened to *trust*?" Thaddeus says.

Simon has heard enough. "Everybody calm down! If you have a real question, ask one at a time."

"I have a question," Judas says.

"That was fast," Simon says.

"It's more a concern, actually. I know I'm new, but Rabbi, I'd like to return to what you were saying about not bringing food or clothes and relying on those we minister to. Forgive me, but we cannot rely on everyone equally. I've developed some ideas for ways we can generate income to sustain our ministry in a reliable way."

"I appreciate that, Judas," Jesus says. "But for this journey, at least, I want you to learn how to rely fully on your Father in heaven, as well as on those around you and those you will serve. For food, Big James. And for your life, John. This is what it means to follow. And to lead."

Judas nods, but Simon thinks he doesn't look convinced. And Simon has his own concern. "Teacher, even if not for this journey, now would be a good time to assign someone to manage the few resources we do have, or anything we bring back."

"Do you have someone in mind?" Jesus says.

"I nominate Matthew," Philip says. "He's obviously the most experienced."

"Believe it or not," Simon says, "I agree that would be prudent." He's aware of all the surprised looks.

"I'm sorry," Matthew says, "but I am not comfortable dealing with money again. I formally decline."

John snorts. "A simple *no* would have been fine."

"Then no! I nominate Judas. His experience would serve us better."

"I accept," Judas says. "I would love to be helpful."

Simon looks to Jesus, who nods.

"Done," Simon says.

Chapter 20

THE ASSIGNMENTS

Simon and Eden's home

Simon can read his wife by her body language. No one seems to need anything, so she stands at the edge of the room, expressionless but plainly listening. Simon dreads what's coming.

"All right," Jesus says, appearing to take them all in at a glance. His eyes stop on Simon. "Simon and Judas, north to Caesarea Philippi."

His heart sinks, and he steals a glance at Eden. Sad. Sober.

"Andrew and Philip, east to Naveh. Nathanael and Thad, south to Perea. John and Thomas, southwest to Joppa."

Simon's mind is full. He's eager to commiserate with Eden, but he also notices that John appears pleased with his traveling partner and that his brother, Big James, looks hurt, perhaps that John would be so excited about going with someone other than him.

"Big James and Little James—"

"Wait!" Simon says. "For real?" *Such a big man with such a little man …*

"Come on," Jesus says. "They can make it a thing. Humor disarms people. West to the Plains of Sharon. Matthew and Zee—"

The room goes quiet again. Matthew swallows hard. Zee looks around. "What?" he says.

Simon leans close to Jesus and whispers, "Rabbi, are you sure about that? A Zealot and a—you know …?"

Jesus looks to Zee. "All the way down to Jericho. Yes, I know it's near Samaria. You'll be fine. Zee, everyone is reacting to the notion of you traveling with a tax collector."

Zee flinches, then doesn't move. "What?"

"We have not told you," Jesus says, "about Matthew's former occupation."

"He's a tax collector?"

"He's no more of a tax collector than you are a Zealot. Not one of you is what you once were. Remember that, all of you. And Zee, you and Matthew will be able to remember that better than anyone. I'm confident the two of you will be able to do and say great things *because* of your pasts. I know I can count on you."

Zee nods, but Simon thinks that he, like Judas, remains not fully sold on this whole idea.

"You all have a lot to take in," Jesus says. "Take a day to handle what you need to …" He glances at Simon and nods toward Eden. Simon can tell she's trying not to cry.

"Some final details will come tomorrow," Jesus adds. "I'll have Simon spread the word. Shalom."

As everyone stands and mills about, chatting, Simon finds Eden has moved to the kitchen, putting food away. "This doesn't change our family plans. I don't have to be—"

"Not now."

"I can talk to Rabbi. He can shorten my trip."

"Do *not* say anything to him. I will be fine. I just need a minute." Her voice catches, and she hurries away.

Proud, Simon thinks. *We've both been so proud that Jesus chose me to follow him.* That truth had seemed to so fill Eden that the very novelty of it had made her strong in the early going. But it has become hard. Reality is setting in. Simon knows well that she needs more than a minute. But then what? What can he say or do to make this easier, or, short of that, bearable?

Across the room, Thomas determines to approach Jesus. He pushes through the pack. "Rabbi?"

"Yes, Thomas."

"I am—I thank you for believing in me."

"Of course. I do."

"It's just that I wanted to ask—well, I wanted your blessing to ask—" He steels himself. "For Ramah's hand."

Thomas can feel Jesus' gaze, forcing him to lift his chin. "Did you hear in what direction I am sending you?"

"Southwest, but . . ." *Aah, so that's it.* "Kafni is to the southwest."

Jesus nods. "You will complete your mission with John. Afterward, you may visit Kafni as the second part of your mission."

"Really?"

"Last I heard, Kafni was not a believer. Maybe while you make a pitch for yourself, you can put in a good word for me."

He thinks of everything! Thomas thinks. *He misses nothing!* Thomas can't help himself. He throws his arms around the rabbi, then hustles away.

Little James has been watching Thomas and Jesus from across the room. When they separate, Jesus makes his way to the door and heads out. Little James rushes, limping to catch up. "Master?"

"Yes, Little James."

"Can I please have a moment?"

"Of course."

He pauses and exhales. How to begin? "I, uh, I'm not always confident to speak, but …"

"Slow to speak," Jesus says. "That's a very good quality."

"I want to ask you a question."

"Please."

"You're sending us out with the ability to heal the sick and lame, yes? That's what you said."

"Yes."

"You're telling me I have the ability to heal?"

Jesus nods and smiles.

He must know what's coming, Little James thinks. *Of course he does!* "Please forgive me, but—it's hard to imagine, with my—condition—which you haven't healed …"

"Do you want to be healed?"

"If that's possible—of course."

Jesus' compassionate smile overwhelms Little James. "I think you've seen enough to know it's possible."

Of course I have! But dare he be so bold as to ask? Yes! "Then why haven't you?"

"Because I trust you."

Because he trusts *me? Trusts me with what?*

"Little James, precious Little James, I need you to listen to me very carefully. Because what I'm going to say defines your whole life to this point and will define the rest of your life. Do you understand?"

Little James nods, but he isn't so sure. Still, he believes Jesus will make it plain, as he always does.

"In the Father's will, I could heal you. Right now. And you'd have a good story to tell, yes?"

"Yes. That you do miracles."

"Yes, and that's a good story. But there are already many who can tell that story, and there will be hundreds more. But think of the story *you* have, especially on this journey to come, if I *don't* heal you."

Little James loses the battle to hide his befuddlement.

"This is what I trust you with," Jesus continues. "To know how to proclaim that you still praise God in spite of this, to know how to focus on all that matters so much more than the body. To show people how you can be patient with your suffering here on earth because you know you will spend eternity with no suffering. Not everyone can understand that. How many people do you think the Father and I trust with this? Not many."

"But the others are so much more—"

"So much more what?"

"I don't know. Stronger. Better at this."

Jesus narrows his eyes at Little James. "I love you," he says, "but I don't want to hear that again."

The last thing Little James wants is to offend the master. "It's easy to recite the song of David that I'm fearfully and wonderfully made. But it doesn't make it easier for me, especially in this group, to feel like less of a burden."

"A burden?" Jesus says. "First of all, it's far easier for me to deal with your slow walking than it is to deal with Simon's temper—trust me."

Little James laughs.

"Are you fast?" Jesus continues. "Do you look impressive when you walk? No, but those are the things the Father doesn't care about. You're going to do more for me than most people could ever dream. So many people need healing in order to believe in me, or they need healing because their hearts are so sick. That doesn't apply to you! And many are healed, or not healed, because the Father in heaven has a certain plan for them that may be a mystery. And remember what Job said: 'The Lord gives, and the Lord takes away' …"

Little James recites the rest with him: "'… blessed be the name of the Lord.'"

"Little James, when you pass from this earth and meet your Father in heaven, as Isaiah promises, you will leap like a deer. Your reward will be great."

Little James feels filled to overflowing.

Jesus puts his hands on Little James's shoulders. "Hold on a little longer. And when you see yourself finding true strength because of your weakness, and when you do great things in my name in spite of all of this, your impact will last for generations. Do you understand?"

Overcome, James manages to nod. "Thank you, Master."

"A man like you, healing others … I can't wait to hear your stories when you return. Shalom."

"Shalom."

"Remember, you *will* be healed. It's only a matter of time."

Chapter 21

THE GOLDEN DOOR

Capernaum, evening

Matthew once walked this street daily. This had been his neighborhood. Everyone knew who lived in these palatial homes, and part of him enjoyed that they knew. But he was also forced to find his incognito transport the rest of the way to his tax booth in the town square, because so many who recognized him chose to spit at him, curse him, or rail on him for choosing to turn on his own people.

Beyond a block or two of likeminded neighbors—other tax collectors and wealthy businessmen who appreciated anyone who knew how to earn a shekel—Matthew faced the commoners. Jews who worked sunup to sundown to keep a modest roof over their heads and enough bread and lentils on the table to feed their families were less than impressed with Matthew's success—for it came at their expense.

He had felt safe only inside the golden door of his lavishly appointed home or inside his locked tax booth with his armed Roman guard nearby. Those who waited in line, trying to remain current with their tributes to Caesar or desperately trying to eke out of Matthew a modicum of grace—or time—had to at least pretend to show him deference. It didn't pay them to spit at or curse him. He held all the cards.

Matthew's mind is full of memories as he approaches his former manor—unable to forget pretending not to see the obscene gestures, hear the epithets, or acknowledge the spittle on his way to his ride to work—or rushing to the safety on the other side of the golden door at the end of the day. Now, as he passes the same citizenry as in the past, he half expects the same taunts and torment he endured for so many years.

But the faces he passes seem not to even recognize him. It hasn't been that long since he lived here and made their lives miserable. Yet now they tussle with another tax collector and a different Roman guard. Matthew wears the same raiment he did back then, but the road and the life of a nomad have dulled the sheen of his garments, left them in tatters. No, he doesn't look like a tax collector anymore or like anyone who belongs in this district.

Somehow, being able to traverse this area unmolested gives him a sense of momentum—almost confidence. Almost. He no longer trudges along with his head down and shoulders slumped. He raises his chin, turns a corner, and comes face to face with the golden door. If he expected a rush of warm reminiscences or some longing to return to the comforts of this place, he's pleased to feel none of that. He can't deny there have been times, in the crude camps he and his new compatriots fashion in out-of-the-way spots in the wilderness, when he thought back to the relaxing softness of the bed he had imported for this place.

But his new life, his new obsession, overcomes any desire to return here. That's why he bequeathed the place to his parents—though, to his knowledge, they never even visited to take a peek. That lack of curiosity stuns but also pleases him. They are consistent, he can certainly give them that. They believe he treated himself to this estate and its luxurious furnishings with blood money from his own people, and thus Alphaeus and Elisheba have zero interest in such spoils. Now he shares their disdain for the whole idea.

Yet, if this valuable piece of real estate can be used in any way to further the ministry of his rabbi, to somehow contribute to the mission of ushering in the kingdom of God, what could be better than that?

Funny, Matthew thinks, that he still feels compelled to wonder whether he fully locked the place the last time he left it. For years he had fought the urge to lock the door, unlock it, and lock it again—not just once but three times. Surely he did that when he left it for good. But now he can't help himself. Some things never change. Before inserting the key, he tries the knob—just to see. Of course it's locked. How could it not be?

He steps back to take in the breadth of the estate, the gate from bottom to top and to the house beyond. Such melancholy memories. Had the opulence and all the amenities he enjoyed really made up for his ostracization from his countrymen and, worse, the estrangement from his own family? Not hardly.

Now who is that at the opposite end of the street? Can it be? Yes! It's Gaius! They stare at each other, and Matthew is the first to blink. "Hello, Gaius."

Always maintaining his dignified role, the primi centurion nods, lips pressed together. They approach each other in the faint light from street torches. "Hi, Matthew. Er, uh, shalom."

Matthew tries to hide his amusement over Gaius's attempt to sound Jewish and colloquial, but in the end he can't stifle a chuckle.

Gaius looks wounded. "Did I say it wrong?"

"No! I just—I didn't expect to see you."

"Yeah, well, I'm stationed here."

A primi assigned to my old house? Matthew thinks. *What's this?* He doesn't know what to say, and apparently neither does Gaius.

The soldier looks embarrassed, uneasy. "Are you moving back in, Matthew?"

"No, no. I can't live here now."

Gaius looks surprised. "Nobody wants the best house on the block?"

"It will be used for the ministry."

"By friends of yours?"

Friends? Matthew would sure like to think so. "I suppose they are my friends, yes. I doubt the neighbors will like it."

Gaius straightens. "As long as order is kept … And if they're friends of yours, I'll make sure—well, we patrol the area regularly. For your safety and for the general peace."

Matthew realizes how much he's missed the man. "Are you well?"

"Never better," Gaius says. "Yourself?"

Simon and Andrew emerge from the alley. Gaius tenses. Thaddeus and Little James approach from the opposite direction. They all look curious, concerned. This is the centurion who arrested Jesus.

"It's okay, Gaius," Matthew says quickly. "They're just here to eat. Many of us will be leaving Capernaum for missionary work."

"For how long?"

"We don't kn—it will be dangerous." As the four other disciples draw closer and the rest appear—gawking at the size of the house—Matthew says, "I must go now."

"Trust your wits, Matthew," Gaius says. "I'll see you around."

Matthew realizes he is the only one watching as Gaius strides away. The others appear focused and solemn. Matthew assumes they're wondering—as he is—whether this will be the last time they're all together. He produces the key. "Welcome to the home I don't live in anymore."

Simon and Andrew chuckle and shake their heads. "Only Matthew," Simon mutters, stepping before him, palm outstretched. Matthew drops the key into it. He knows that when they enter, the others will gawk at pieces of furniture purchased and shipped from faraway lands, each costing more than half their year's wages in their past lives. But Simon is apparently not ready to enter the mansion just yet. He addresses them all, and Matthew is struck that they all seem to easily defer to him—even Big James and John.

"Can I say the hard part first?" Simon begins, and they all seem to come to attention in the courtyard. "This could be the last time we're all together—for a while."

"What's the easy part?" Big James says.

"Who said there was an easy part?" Simon says, making Big James smile. "I just held my wife as she tried to accept the idea that I will be the one making Pharisees and Romans upset the way Jesus does now. It scares her."

"But not you?" Andrew says.

"Of course it does."

"The unknowns are overwhelming," Judas says.

Thaddeus says, "Are we ready?"

"I'm terrified," Nathanael says.

"I am not afraid," Zee says.

A hush falls over them until Simon says, "Except for Zee, who is never afraid of anything."

Matthew feels as if the tension has been broken a bit.

Simon turns to Philip. "You've done this kind of thing before. Any thoughts?"

"Well, I did a little preaching for the baptizer, but we didn't do anything quite like this. All I can tell you is, yes, it's scary when powerful people are upset with you. But it's worth it."

"This is what we signed up for," John says. "We might not have known it at the time, but we go where he sends us."

Simon nods. "Master has told us what to do, and we've seen how he does it. So, we have what we need and, whoever you go with, let's stay strong together. I'm sure he put us with our partners for a reason. Let's make the most of it. Now, let's gather around. Come in. Stand next to your partner."

Matthew looks for Zee, just as Simon pulls the man close. Though he whispers, Matthew can hear him. "Will you, as a former Zealot, be okay with a former tax collector? I probably couldn't do it myself, but Master knows you're a better man than I am. Can I trust you?"

Zee looks at Matthew, then back at Simon, and nods gravely.

"Matthew," Simon says, "you'll be fine." He puts his hands on the shoulders of Zee on his one side and Judas on his other, urging the whole group to do the same. "Come on, all of us. Matthew, I know you hate it, but you too."

Matthew hesitates as the others form a circle, arms around each other's shoulders. Zee reaches for him with his free hand and draws him in. With the ring complete, Simon says, "When I was with Eden, a psalm of David came to mind. The one when he fled from Absalom, his own son. I shared it with Eden as a reminder, because she was fearful. I think we need it too." He closes his eyes. "'O Lord, how many are my foes! Many are rising against me; many are saying of my soul, there is no salvation for him in God.'"

Judas and Andrew join in the recitation. "'I cried aloud to the Lord, and He answered me from His holy hill.'"

One by one the others join in until all, even Matthew, are quoting the psalm together. "'I lay down and slept. I woke again, for the Lord sustained me. I will not be afraid of many thousands of people who have set themselves against me all around.

"'Arise, O Lord, save me, O my God, for You strike all my enemies on the cheek. You break the teeth of the wicked. Salvation belongs to the Lord—Your blessing be on Your people.'"

PART 3
"Physician, Heal Yourself"

Chapter 22

THE BOX

Nazareth, dusk

Naturally preoccupied with his disciples and how they will fare—not only with their assignments, but also with each other—Jesus finds himself at peace with the decision to house the women at Matthew's former mansion. He smiles remembering the meal so many of them enjoyed there the day Matthew chose to obey his call to follow him. Though it ended in a confrontation with two intrusive Pharisees, the food had proved plentiful and delicious, and the banter warming. But the size of that place and its extravagant accoutrements! Mary of Magdala, Ramah, and Tamar will rattle around in it.

How he loves the ones he has chosen! And yet he also enjoys his occasional solitude. It seems strange that for all his years on earth, everything he owns is in the broad backpack strapped to his shoulders. Though weary from preaching, teaching, and discipling, Jesus picks up the pace as he enters the city gate. Odd, the mangy dog that's hung out here for years is nowhere to be seen.

But his destination takes precedence, and it's not just his humble childhood home that draws him. It's his beloved mother and his four brothers. She knows he is coming and will holler for him to simply come in, but what fun would that be? Let her wonder if the one knocking might be someone else.

He raps on the door.

"Oh! I'm coming! If it's you, come in, but I'm coming!"

He chuckles and waits in silence. Finally, the door swings open, and she kisses the Mezuzah and rushes to him. "Oh, yes, it's you! *L'shana tova!*"

"Yes, it will be a good year, Ima!"

She embraces him, and he lifts her off the ground, as has become his custom, and lets her pull him inside. They both kiss the Mezuzah, and she says, "Why didn't you just come in? You know you can just come in! Did you have a good journey? You look tired. You're hungry, yes? We'll sit and eat."

Jesus notices only two cups of wine and two plates on the table as he washes his feet near the door. His mother approaches the oven. "Just set your bag down there. Then we'll eat and you can go to bed. I'm sure you're exhausted. The *challah* is hot and ready. Your timing is perfect. Did you have a good journey?"

"Yes, it was fine. The brown dog was not at the gate. Did something happen?"

"He died several months ago. Sit, sit."

"Aah, I figured. I don't think I've walked through that gate in ten years without seeing him nearby being ignored by everyone."

As she brings the bread from the oven, Jesus quickly washes his hands and whispers, "Blessed are You, Lord our God, King of the Universe, who has sanctified us through Your commandments and has commanded us concerning the washing of hands."

"The bread is not perfectly round," his mother says. "I've never been able to do it perfect, but the raisins cooked in nicely."

"Ima, you know I don't like raisins."

"And you know I'm going to do it for a sweet new year anyway, so hush."

She lowers her head, and they recite together, "Blessed are You, Lord our God, King of the Universe, who has kept us alive and sustained us and brought us to this holiday season."

As they break the bread and eat, Jesus says, "So, no Jude or James or—?"

She purses her lips. "Well, your brothers felt it best to celebrate in Sepphoris while you were here. Just to avoid conflict."

"I understand."

"I think it's just hard for them, especially with so many people here excited to see you tomorrow. Everyone has been hearing about what you've been doing, the signs and wonders, and you know how the boys feel about all that."

"I understand."

"But we'll have a lovely time. How is the bread?"

"It's wonderful. Even with the raisins."

"So—tell me about how your students are doing. Each one of them. I need to know what to pray for."

"Well, we don't have time for all of them. I'm heading to bed soon."

"Fine," she says, smiling. "Tell me about your five favorites."

He laughs. "I don't have favorites. You know that."

"Of course you do. Admit it."

"You tell me *your* favorites of my group."

"The women!" she announces.

"Ha! That was fast."

"And the one they call Zee, because he'll protect you."

"Really? Anyone else?"

"I'm teasing! I love them all. Is anyone troubling you? What about Andrew? How's he doing? He wasn't doing well when I was with them."

"He's fine, actually. Our boy John set him straight. They're all doing well right now. I have the boys on missionary journeys to our people, performing signs and wonders of their own. Well, not their own, but—"

"I know what you mean," she says. "And the women?"

"They're in Capernaum, helping James and John's father with a new olive oil business that will also support the ministry."

"And Thomas and Ramah?"

"What about them?"

She gives him a look, as if to say, "Really?"

"How did you know anything was going on?"

"I have eyes, haven't I? I saw they were in love at the wedding. I thought we should just have their ceremony after Asher and Sarah's. Will he ask for her father's blessing?"

"Yes."

"Do you bless it?"

"I would love to see them betrothed. They are both faithful followers."

"What about Simon? He's your leader, yes?"

"He is. Or at least he will be. He's still a bit of a wild animal, but I have plans to refine him."

"I can't wait," she says, then leans back. "So—are you ready for tomorrow? So many have told me they can't wait to see you. And guess who is in town?"

"I couldn't tell you."

"Lazarus and his sisters. They got in today and figured it was a good opportunity to see you."

"Really? That's wonderful. I haven't seen Laz in a while."

Mother Mary is suddenly transported back nearly three decades to when she and Lazarus's mother were trying to teach their infant sons to walk. In her gauzy memory, toys dot the floor, and she remembers urging Jesus to stand up. Her friend is encouraging her own son.

Mary bites her lip at the recollection, as that was when her husband entered and gleefully grabbed Jesus and tossed him into the air.

"I'm exhausted," Jesus says now. "I need to get to bed. But I need the box while I'm here, Ima. Where do you keep it?"

"Now?"

"Mm-hm."

"You're sure this is your last time here before—"

He nods. "I believe my time is coming."

It pains him to see her countenance cloud over. "I don't know that I'm ready," she says.

"I know how you feel," he says. "But I do the—"

And she finishes the line for him: "'—will of Him who sent me.' But does it have to be so soon? Are you sure?"

"If not now ..." he says.

She looks away. Finally, she murmurs, "I miss your father the most during celebrations. He had so much fun. It'll be a fun day tomorrow. The box is near your bed. I'll clean up. You go on."

"I can help you."

He can tell she's fighting tears. "No, I've got it. I'll be fine."

When she stands, Jesus stands quickly and reaches for her. He draws her close and kisses her head. "*Laylah tov,* Ima."

"Good night, my beloved son."

He takes his backpack to his room, which of course looks so much smaller than he remembers. The box is next to his bed. It contains a donkey bridle Jesus soberly examines before slipping it into his backpack.

Chapter 23

OLD FRIENDS

Nazareth, the next day

Mother Mary ponders many memories of celebrating holidays in this very field as she proudly enters the festive area with her eldest son. She and Jesus carry covered baskets of food and make their way through clusters of revelers lounging at tables or sitting on the ground, eating what they've brought from home or bought from vendors in crude booths or at rickety tables.

She loves the music, the dancing, the delightful squeals of children entertained by a juggler. In the field beyond, men play Trigon—standing in triangles and trying to simultaneously toss and catch three balls while another keeps score, taking pebbles from a bag and arranging them on the ground for each drop or bad throw.

Mary is warmed by the merriment and even the noise. Rosh Hashanah or Yom Teruah is, after all, to be a "day of shouting" or blasting the shofar to celebrate the new year. She just hopes all keep in mind that at its core, it's about much more than just the calendar. It is the first of the Jewish High Holy Days, according to the Scriptures.

Jesus says, "I don't know how long ago was my last Rosh Hashanah in Nazareth."

"Four years," she says quickly.

He chuckles. "But who's keeping track, hm?"

"We may be poor," she says, "but we celebrate better than those other towns you've been in."

"I don't deny it," he says. "It's good to be home."

"Mary! Jesus!"

Here comes Dinah, the mother of the groom at the wedding in Cana, and her husband, Rafi.

"Dinah!" Mary shouts. "I didn't know you'd be here!"

"We decided to make the trip just yesterday," Dinah says as they embrace.

"Correction," Rafi says, obviously pretending frustration. "*Dinah* decided to make the trip. I had little choice in the matter."

"Oh, hush," Dinah says.

Jesus and Rafi shake hands, and the men nod to the women. "I didn't know you'd be here, Jesus," Dinah says. "I apologize …"

"For what?"

"You'll get questions about the wedding," Rafi says. "No doubt."

"I've told some people about what happened," Dinah says, "though a few had already heard."

Rafi adds, "Don't be surprised if some folks run out of wine on purpose just to see what you'll do."

"Oh," Jesus says, "that was a special occasion, so—"

"I know, I know," Dinah says. "Oh, it's so good to see you both."

From behind, Jesus feels an arm wrap around him and a hand covers his eyes. "I was wondering when this was coming," he says and deftly slips out of the grip. He whirls to face Lazarus. They kiss each other on the cheek and embrace.

Jesus turns to Lazarus's sisters. Martha is not much younger than he and Lazarus, but Mary, now in her teens, looks much different from when he last saw her. "Good to see you both," he says. "It's been a while."

They both nod and whisper "Shalom," embracing Jesus' mother.

Dinah hustles the older Mary away, saying she has reserved a spot and telling Rafi to bring Jesus' food. "We'll set it up there."

Jesus is impressed that Dinah must have sensed that he and his old friends were eager to catch up. "Thanks, Rafi," he says. "We'll be along."

When it's just Jesus and the three siblings, Lazarus says, "So many things to talk about. You're here for how long?"

"Not long. Had to grab some things from home. Wanted to see Ima, celebrate a bit, go to the service."

"Well, now that we're here, maybe you can stay a little longer. We're staying in a great place. You should stop by."

"Maybe."

"You look good! The rabbi role appears to be treating you well. Still, no home though, huh?"

"I have what I need."

Lazarus turns to his sisters. "Years ago, I tried to get him to join me in the business in Bethany. Turned me down. Just wanted to be a craftsman—well, first a craftsman, then a rabbi."

"Your brother didn't need me, obviously," Jesus tells them.

"But we would have had so much fun!" Lazarus says.

"True," Jesus says.

"I'll give you credit, though," Lazarus says. "You never wavered. You did what you set out to do, and becoming a rabbi without all the schooling most receive … Amazing."

Jesus smiles.

Young Mary speaks up. "Are you really performing miracles?"

"Mary!" Martha says.

"I'm just asking."

Lazarus says, "Forgive Mary for being—well, for being Mary. As is her custom, she says what we only think. *Is* what we're hearing true?"

"Depends on what you're hearing and from whom."

"I'm hearing you've turned water to wine," Lazarus says. "Healed hundreds in places like Syria. Preached some sermon to thousands that many are still talking about. You made a bunch of friends in Samaria—which we'll have to talk about—and a bunch of enemies in places we actually like. And not unimportant enemies. Am I missing anything?"

"Not bad," Jesus says with a smirk.

"C'mon," Lazarus says. "I know everyone and hear everything, you know that."

"So, it's true?" Mary says.

"You're the greatest rabbi who ever lived?" Lazarus asks.

"Well, there's more work to be done."

Lazarus laughs. "Still with the humility. I love it."

Mary speaks up again. "We're also hearing that some are saying, and you're not denying—"

"Mary," Martha says, "not now."

"I *do* want to ask," Lazarus says, "and we can do this privately, if—" He turns as a man and his wife, both in their fifties, approach. "Rabbi Benjamin! Leah! Shalom!"

"Shalom, Lazarus," the woman says. "Girls, Jesus, welcome home!"

"Good to see you, Leah," Jesus says, shaking Rabbi Benjamin's hand. "It's been a while."

"Jesus," the rabbi says, gripping his hand limply and looking as if he'd like to say it hasn't been long enough.

"Well," Leah says, "many here are very excited that you're visiting. So much being said …"

"I was just telling him that," Lazarus says. "Everyone is talking about Nazareth's big success story, and they don't mean me anymore! So, what are *you* hearing, Leah?"

Chapter 24

RUMORS

Jesus rolls his eyes but also listens carefully as the rebbetzin answers with relish. "All kinds of rumors," Leah says. "That you're becoming quite a popular rabbi. Some saw you speak to thousands and even perform signs and wonders. Gossip comes with it, of course. Hannah even told me you claimed to be the Messiah. I told her, 'Not the humble Jesus I know.' But here, have some apples and honey. You're skin and bones."

At the rabbi's wife's mention of the word *Messiah,* Lazarus and his sisters look at Jesus. He silences them with a subtle look as Leah thrusts a plate before him. "May this first day of *Tishrei* be as sweet as this food."

"For you as well," Jesus says, dipping a slice of apple into the honey. "Apples and honey," he prays silently. "We did well on both of those, didn't we?"

He finds himself bemused at Lazarus as his old friend continues to stir the pot by needling the cleric. "Rabbi Benjamin, with all the excitement about Jesus being here, wouldn't he be the perfect man to read the Scripture and share the instruction at tonight's service?"

The rabbi narrows his eyes and hesitates. His wife blurts, "Oh, that's a great idea! Ben, you were telling me you hadn't yet prepared for—"

"Well, I was planning this afternoon to—"

"Jesus is a rabbi now," Lazarus presses.

"Yes. I'm aware."

"I know he wasn't your favorite student, and I know he didn't go to Beth Midrash and that he teaches in his own way, but—"

"All right, Lazarus," Jesus says. "He understands."

"We celebrate the creation of the world today," Rabbi Benjamin says, "and that's fine. But tonight Rosh Hoshana is more serious."

"Yes," Lazarus says, "you've never loved the fun stuff beforehand. But as much as we love your interpretations, Rabbi, it would be lovely for everyone to see how much Jesus learned from your teachings. It might encourage the children to pursue a similar path, yes? Jesus, what do you think?"

"I would be happy to, but only if Rabbi Benjamin is comfortable."

"I suppose," the rabbi says, "there could be value in hearing what Yahweh has been revealing to you from the Scriptures."

"Then it's settled!" Lazarus says. "So wise and humble of you, Rabbi Benjamin. Everyone will appreciate it. Jesus, can you come up with something impactful on short notice?"

"We'll see."

"Can't wait," Lazarus says. "All right, I've got to get this man into a Trigon game and get him some more food. We'll see you tonight."

As they part and trade shaloms, Jesus notes that the rabbi's is mumbled. Mary and Martha head off to find the others, and

Jesus leans in to Lazarus. "You're still causing trouble with the rabbi, and I'm still getting blamed."

"Aah, you love seeing him annoyed as much as I do. Come on, let's get in a quick game."

Now here, Jesus thinks, is one reason he has laid aside his divine omniscience. Knowing people's hearts makes him eternally empathetic to the tormented, but he would never use such supernatural knowledge for trivial things like games. What would be the point? Knowing where a ball would be thrown and at what speed and angle would allow him to easily catch it, and knowing the precise reflexes of the recipient would tell him at what speed to toss it. In the flesh, he is no more or less athletically gifted than any other man, so it wouldn't be right to take advantage of his otherworldly gifts for anything but the work of his Father's kingdom.

Jesus has never considered equality with God something to be used for his own advantage and is happy to play the game as a mere mortal. As they approach the other players, one of whom is Rafi, Lazarus greets them and says, "I hate to break up the fun, but it's time for me to start embarrassing you. And for us all to embarrass Jesus."

The men chuckle and exchange greetings. Rafi's opponent, Aaron, says that their third rival, John, "is playing awful and will soon lose. He has four drops or bad throws already. Rafi has three. I have two."

Lazarus suggests that he'll substitute for Rafi and that Jesus will replace Aaron. "And I'll still win."

Aaron asks Jesus, "Have you gotten any better since last time?"

"I don't know."

"You don't know?"

"I haven't played since last time."

Jesus notices Aaron's shoulders slump.

"Come on," Lazarus says, "this won't take long. I'll win fast for Rafi, and we'll be on our way."

Aaron tells Jesus, "At least throw fast. John just needs to drop one more and it's over."

"No promises," Jesus says.

In unison the players count down from three and toss their ball to the left hand of the person next to them. Immediately, Jesus drops his.

"That didn't take long," Lazarus says. "Now you have three, the same as me."

Aaron shakes his head.

"All right," Jesus says. "It's been a while. I've got it. Let's go."

They count down again and toss. Jesus catches a couple before flinging one wide to Lazarus. "That's a no-reach!" Lazarus says. "And one more for you. Now you and John both have four."

"I apologize, Aaron," Jesus says. "Maybe we should have refused Laz's offer."

"It's fine," Aaron says, chuckling. "Just focus. Maybe you can get John on this one and get second place. Lazarus has clearly been practicing."

"Practice?" Lazarus says, cackling. "Don't need it. Let's go. Three, four, four. Here we play."

They begin throwing again, and Jesus does better but finally drops the ball again, losing the game. Lazarus and Rafi cheer, and all the players shake hands. "Sorry, Aaron," Jesus says. "Not my strength."

"Clearly," Lazarus says, smiling. "But all of you, don't be late for tonight's service. Jesus is handling the reading and interpretation. *That's* his strength. This game was just to humble him beforehand."

Lazarus throws his arm around Jesus as they move away.

"Well," Jesus says, "thanks for that. I trust it was satisfying for you."

"We've still got a lot to talk about, and I expect some answers from you by tonight about all that's been going on."

"Be careful what you ask for."

Chapter 25

I AM

The Nazareth synagogue

Jesus knows virtually everyone in the crowded temple he grew up in. It seems all those he reunited with during the festival have shown up to hear him speak. On the one hand, it pains him that his own brothers have chosen to be away while he's in town. On the other, he's relieved that they won't witness what he is about to incite.

He has conferred with Rabbi Benjamin on which scroll he'd like to reference, and the priest admits, "My wife insists that I show grace in introducing you."

"I appreciate that, sir. I know you can't pretend to be featuring one of your star pupils."

"Be that as it may …"

Jesus sits next to Lazarus. His mother sits across the way in the women's section with Dinah and the others.

The rabbi steps to the lectern. "Blessed are You, Lord our God, king of the universe, Who has kept us alive and sustained us for another year. Who bestows kindness, restores, and redeems.

Praise to You, Adonai our God, Sovereign over creation, Who has chosen us from all the peoples.

"May Your blessings be upon all who seek You earnestly. Bring joy to Your land and gladness to Your city. In Your mercy, bestow on us a prosperous year, a bountiful harvest, and the promised arrival of Meshiach, Your anointed one, the Son of David."

The congregation says, "Amen."

Rabbi Benjamin nods to the bearer of the shofar, who commences with a long blast, the *tekiah,* on the ram's horn. He follows with three short blasts, the *shevarim*; nine staccato blasts, the *teruah*; and one very long blast, the *tekiah gedolah.*

The congregation cheers.

"And now," the rabbi continues, "for the reading and interpretation, we have with us our own Jesus bar Joseph. He was one of my students in Torah class, and we've heard reports—some of them very positive—of his rabbinic journeys. Jesus?"

Leah nods at her husband and smiles as Jesus stands and receives a scroll from an attendant.

"Thank you, Rabbi Benjamin. It's not easy to share in front of Nazareth's preeminent rabbi, but I'll do my best. If I misread any words or say anything you disapprove of, I'm sure I don't need to worry about you speaking up."

Everyone laughs.

"A reading from the scroll of the prophet Isaiah." Jesus pauses, falling serious. He looks at the congregants and back down as they lean in. He reads, "'The spirit of the Lord God is upon me, because the Lord has anointed me to bring good news to the poor.'" At this he looks up again, and he continues doing this throughout the reading, as if to refer to them specifically as he comes to each descriptor.

"'He has sent me to heal the brokenhearted, to proclaim liberty to the captives, recovery of sight to the blind, and the opening of the prison to those who are bound.'" He pauses yet again. "'To proclaim the year of the Lord's favor.'"

Jesus stops, rerolls the scroll, and holds it out to the clearly confused attendant, who hesitates before taking it. Jesus sits on a small chair behind the lectern, aware of all the stares. "The fulfillment of this Scripture, as you have heard it, is today. This is the year of the Lord's favor, a year of jubilee, and the poor, brokenhearted, and captive—and the blind—are offered redemption. Here. Now."

The room has gone deathly silent until Lazarus calls out, "We're with you! Keep going! Not bad for a carpenter's son, yes?"

"Especially Joseph," Rafi teases, "may he rest in peace."

Many chuckle at this, but Rabbi Benjamin is plainly not amused. "Jesus," he says, "please explain why you stopped the reading before Isaiah spoke of the day of vengeance of our God. Especially during a time of such oppression."

"The day of vengeance is in the future," Jesus says. "I'm not here for vengeance. I'm here for salvation."

"*You're* here for salvation?" Rabbi Benjamin asks. "What are you saying?"

Jesus catches Lazarus's intense stare.

"You know what I'm saying. And this year of jubilee, this year of the Lord's favor, is not about the release of financial debts. I'm here to provide relief from spiritual debt."

"We're the chosen seed of Abraham," Rabbi Benjamin says, sounding enraged. "We don't have spiritual debt."

"Jesus?"

"Yes, Aaron."

"We've been hearing about the signs and wonders, and now this. Are you claiming to be more than a rabbi? More than even the baptizer?"

The whole crowd looks ready to burst, especially Lazarus. Jesus says, "No doubt one of you will quote to me the proverb, 'Physician, heal yourself.' And you'll say, 'What we've heard you did in Capernaum and Syria, do here in your hometown.' Yes?"

"Why not?" Aaron says.

"I get it," Jesus says. "I'm the clumsy teenager you saw years ago. A few of you got a glimpse of that today. Laz here would be more believable as a prophet. It's always easier to accept hard truth and especially greatness from strangers than from those you know well. This is an important truth: 'No prophet is without honor, except in his hometown.'"

Rabbi Benjamin says, "Prophet? Be careful what you call yourself."

"This should be easy to prove," Aaron says. "Dinah and Rafi, you say you saw the miracle, yes?"

"Yes," Rafi says. "But he didn't claim *this*."

"A true prophet from Yahweh," Rabbi Benjamin says, "would not deny his own people signs and wonders."

"Listen carefully," Jesus says. "When great famine hit Israel in the days of Elijah, there were many widows, yes? And we know how much the Father cares about His chosen people, especially widows. But Elijah was sent to none of them. He was sent to a widow in Sidon, in Zarephath. A Gentile woman. And Martha, what happened?"

"She gave up her last flour and oil for one more cake and gave it to Elijah."

"Why would she do that?" Jesus asks.

"Elijah told her the Lord said to."

"Yes, he said the Lord would make her flour and oil never run out. And she *believed*. A pagan Gentile in a pagan land, but she was hungry enough to need God and obey, and so God used Elijah to multiply her food.

"And what about Elisha and Naaman? There were many lepers in Israel during this time, but none of them were cleansed. Only Naaman, a Gentile, a Syrian soldier, an enemy of the Lord's people. He was so desperate that he trusted Elisha and was cleansed of his leprosy."

Jesus scans the room. Rabbi Benjamin is clearly seething. Rafi and Dinah look ill. Even Jesus' mother looks concerned, as do Lazarus's sisters. Lazarus appears to be studying the others.

It's time for Jesus to be crystal clear. "You may be the chosen seed of Abraham," he says. "You may be the people of the covenants. But that is not what brings you my salvation. If you cannot accept that you are spiritually poor and captive, in the same way that a Gentile widow and a Syrian leper recognized their need ..." He pauses. "If you do not realize you need a year of the Lord's favor, I cannot save you."

Several men stand, including Aaron, who shouts, "Who do you think you are?"

The rabbi's wife cries out, "This is what Hannah talked about! That he even called himself the Messiah!"

Rabbi Benjamin leaps to his feet and approaches Jesus, who remains calmly seated. "Are you claiming to be the Messiah, or are you merely claiming to speak for the Lord as a prophet?"

"Yes."

"You are a false prophet!"

Mother Mary covers her mouth. Lazarus stands and steps between Jesus and the rabbi. "Whoa, Jesus," he says. "That's quite a thing to say. Maybe we should—"

"Lazarus!" Aaron says. "You're his friend. You can't be involved. You know what the Law of Moses says."

"We're all his friends, Aaron. We can't say things like this."

"Jesus," Rabbi Benjamin says, "stand up at once."

Jesus stands.

"Rabbi, please," Lazarus says. "Rafi, come with Jesus and me. We'll leave, and you all can continue the service."

Rafi looks stricken. "Rabbi Benjamin has charged him with false prophecy, and I cannot argue it."

"You said you saw the miracle!" Lazarus says.

"I did, but now he's saying only he can save us."

"He didn't use those words."

Jesus says, "It's what I meant."

The crowd gasps, and Lazarus tells Jesus, "You're not helping."

Rafi says, "He's saying we are not Yahweh's chosen."

"No," Lazarus says, "he didn't say—"

Rabbi Benjamin breaks in, quoting a book of Moses: "'But the prophet who presumes to speak a word in my name that I have not commanded him to speak, that same prophet shall die.'"

"Rabbi," Lazarus says, "I beg of you …"

"Lazarus," Jesus says, and shakes his head. "It's fine."

"But they're going to—"

Jesus pulls Lazarus close and whispers, "It is not my time. Assure my mother I will be okay. Yes?"

Lazarus nods but looks terrified as Rabbi Benjamin waves over another priest and more men.

"Jesus," Rabbi Benjamin announces, "if you do not renounce your words, we will have no choice but to follow the Law of Moses."

It seems as if everyone is looking to Jesus and praying he will disavow what he's said. But he says, "I *am* the Law of Moses."

Chapter 26

NOT TODAY

So, this is what it will be like for me in the end, Jesus thinks. *Led away even with friends nearby.*

Rafi, Aaron, and the other priest grab Jesus and pull him away. His mother yells, "No!" and runs toward him, but Lazarus lunges for her and holds her as she struggles and calls out for her son. Lazarus whispers in her ear. She appears to be barely breathing until Jesus catches her eye and offers a nod and a slight smile.

It's dusk now as Rabbi Benjamin leads the procession of men hauling Jesus through town. Jesus can tell how conflicted some are who have known him all his life. They could never have imagined they would one day volunteer to take part in his demise. As others on the street notice what's going on and begin to follow, the gaggle leads him to a cliff on the edge of Nazareth. They press him toward the edge.

"Jesus bar Joseph," Rabbi Benjamin announces, "because you have repeatedly prophesied falsely and have offered no denial or renouncement of your blasphemous claims, there is no need for a trial. Do you stand by all you have said?"

"I believe I was clear."

"Your father," the rabbi continues, "may he rest in peace, was a righteous man. Your mother is a good woman. We take no pleasure in the shame you are bringing to their names, nor the grief this will bring upon Mary. But according to the Law of Moses, whose life and words you have spat upon today, your sentence is death."

Rabbi Benjamin steps aside and looks to Rafi and Aaron, signaling them to do what they have to do and push him over the edge.

The men stare at each other as if this is easier said than done. Rafi looks pleadingly to the other priest, who solemnly nods. Rafi looks to Jesus, and he and Aaron step toward him.

When Jesus doesn't even flinch but in fact moves toward Rafi, the man looks startled and stops, as does Aaron.

"Rafi," Jesus says. "Aaron. Rabbi Benjamin." He pauses. "This isn't going to happen. Not today." And he simply walks past them and through the crowd as everyone looks at each other, apparently hoping someone will do something.

Evening

Alone now, Jesus reaches a familiar clearing. A stone covers the opening to his earthly father's resting place. The gravesite is overgrown, definitely not manicured. Deeply saddened by melancholy memories, Jesus recalls his father's workshop as a six-year-old.

Young Jesus sits on a stool and painstakingly sounds out each word from a sacred scroll. As Joseph works, he patiently coaxes the boy through the passage until Jesus is able to piece together, "'He has sent me to heal the brokenhearted.' What does that mean, Father?"

"A heart that is broken, but not the heart in your chest. It's that part of you that makes you happy or sad. A broken heart is sad or hurt. A brokenhearted person is someone who needs help. Keep going."

"'To proclaim liberty.'"

"Good. Here, quick, hold this for me."

"I can help?"

"Yes, come. You need to learn to do this well." He hands Jesus a hammer. "In our family, we can drive a nail in all the way with one swing. *Maybe* two. I'll allow you two on your first try." He holds the nail in place. "Now, someday you won't be doing carpentry like me …"

"Why, Abba?"

"You'll be a craftsman, working with stone and other materials, not just wood."

"Why, Abba?"

"Because there's not much wood around here. This is a place of rock and stone. I picked the wrong business, ha! All right, here we go. Remember, you don't use your whole arm to swing." He exaggeratedly demonstrates the wrong way. "Just use the bottom half of your arm. Swing from your elbow for more control. I will hold the nail. Ready?"

"What if I hit your hand?"

"Oh, you have talent like your abba. You'll be fine. Go ahead."

The boy slowly practices twice, seriously concentrating. Jesus swings hard and comes down flush on the nail. To his horror, his father screams and rears back, holding his hand, making Jesus cry out. But Joseph quickly bursts into laughter.

"Just joking! That was great! Look."

The nail is halfway in, but Jesus is still recovering from the scare. Joseph pulls him in for a hug, still chortling. "I'm sorry, but I couldn't help it. Okay, I have something special I want to show you. Go get that box over there in the corner."

Jesus fetches it and brings it to Joseph.

"Listen carefully, yes?"

Jesus nods.

Joseph opens the box. "This is a mule's bit and bridle. You've seen these before, but this is special. Thousands of years ago, when our people were finally set free from slavery in Egypt, as they were leaving, one of our ancestors of the tribe of Judah used this very bit and bridle to lead his mule, laden with supplies."

Young Jesus notices his mother leaning against the door frame, listening, smiling.

Joseph continues, "Of course the mule eventually died, and everything else was lost in the wilderness. But this bridle was in his hand when he escaped, so he kept it. The men in our family have handed it down to each other for thirty generations as a remembrance of our bondage, but more importantly our being led to the Promised Land.

"It's old, and it's not beautiful, but my father handed it to me to own like I'm handing it to you. We always joked, 'Who knows? Maybe one of us will need it one day.' I don't suppose you will bear a son, so maybe it will end its journey with you. But I can't leave this earth without passing it on."

Jesus stares at it, mesmerized. "Thank you, Abba."

His father leans in close. "I know I'm not your father in the same way your friends' fathers are theirs. We've talked about this. But the privilege, and the blessing, of stewarding your life here on earth for the short time I was granted is the greatest gift I could ask for. And I pray I have done right by you."

• • •

"Jesus! I thought I might find you here."

"Hi, Ima. Hello, Laz."

"Where did they take you?" she says. "I was so scared."

"I said I would be fine. It's not that time yet."

She hugs him.

Lazarus hands him his backpack. "It's got everything, plus some food."

Jesus quickly opens it and pulls out the bridle, relieved the precious heirloom is still there.

"Well," Lazarus says, "what happened today was interesting. I suppose that explains quite a bit. Didn't want to tell me before today?"

"It wasn't time."

"We going to get a chance to talk about it more anytime soon?"

Jesus nods.

"Great. Well, let me know."

"Don't worry."

Jesus turns to his mother. "I had to say what I said today. I know it was frightening, but even they must hear it."

"I know."

Jesus turns back to the tomb. "I wanted to see it one last time. I'm not welcome back here. Obviously."

"Next Rosh Hashanah," Lazarus says, "come to Bethany."

"Ima, you should leave for a bit as well. Let things calm down."

"Mary and Martha would love to have you stay with us," Lazarus says.

They fall silent a moment. Then Jesus says, "There's no turning back. Not after today."

"I know," Mother Mary says.

"What's the bridle for?" Lazarus says.

"You'll know soon enough," Jesus says.

"Soon," Mary says, woe in her voice.

"Soon," Jesus says.

PART 4
Clean

Chapter 27

SENT

Judea

Throughout the entire region, the disciples have been assigned tasks in various towns and hamlets, Jesus assuring them that the needs they're to address will quickly become apparent. When the citizenry gets wind of who these men are, they ask for Jesus, of course, but they also desperately hope for something, anything, from his students.

In Joppa, paired with John, Thomas wonders what he has gotten himself into. They've been invited into a shabby hut by an extended family who appear to have nothing. A grandfather and grandmother hold each other, looking hopeful but terrified. Nearby, the parents of a young boy, about eight, sit with their arms around him as they all stare at John. He's kneeling before their blind teenage daughter with her head in his hands. Her pupils are milky.

Thomas pulls a small vial of oil from his bag, which Jesus instructed him to use for such occasions. He so wants to believe it has some magical power and will make some difference, but how can it? This makes no sense. And yet he has seen Jesus turn water to wine, heal the sick … Thomas forces himself to obey, despite his lack of faith. Quivering, he gently anoints the girl's forehead with oil.

John covers her eyes and whispers, "May Adonai Almighty, *El Roi,* the God who sees me, restore to you—vision."

That's it? Thomas wonders. *It can't possibly be that simple.*

John removes his hand, and the girl blinks.

What's this?

Her pupils have turned a beautiful hazel! She blinks again and squints and breaks into tears. Thomas finds himself weeping as well, shedding tears of shock as much as joy. John is crying too, and the entire family falls into an elated mass of hugs and tears.

John looks as astonished as Thomas feels.

In a Decapolis garden, a small group of Jewish families—and Philip—listens intently as Andrew preaches. He desperately tries to remember what he's heard Jesus say. Why the master even dreamed Andrew could preach like him is unfathomable. All he can do is trust the material—the truths Jesus espouses. Maybe his amateurish delivery will prevail if reality is declared. At the very least, Andrew feels compassion for these people and wants that to come through.

As lovingly as he can, he says, "You are probably inclined to love your neighbor and hate your enemy, right?"

They nod, and Philip flashes him a smile of encouragement, as if to say, "Keep going. Get to the *love your enemies* part." And so, Andrew plunges ahead as children climb all over Philip as if he's their favorite uncle.

A Roman priest in his forties carrying a *lituus*, a curved wand, pushes his way through the crowd, followed by a teenage apprentice. He's clearly an augur, a religious official charged with analyzing natural signs—usually involving the activity of birds, trying to determine divine approval or disapproval of what's going on. As Andrew moves on to "Do not be anxious about your lives, what you will eat or drink," he wonders what this augur makes of what he's hearing and what he plans to do with that stick he's holding.

In a residential backyard in Perea, Nathanael and Thaddeus stand before many who appear sick or lame. Nathanael preaches, gesturing toward the sky and announcing that "Jesus is the one whose ministry we are proving here today."

Thaddeus covers the ears of a deaf woman in her twenties and prays. He releases his hands and she starts, her eyes filling. She rushes to her father, who rejoices with her and wraps Thaddeus in a hug.

In Caesarea Philippi, Hellenists—Greek speakers who are not Greek—gather around an augur who has placed a bird on a pedestal. As Simon and Judas look on, he slices the bird open and spreads out its innards, praying to the Roman gods for wisdom.

Simon signals Judas to join him in trying to pull the Jews away so he can preach to them. "You must reject the things of this world and focus on the coming kingdom!" he says. "The Messiah is here, and the God of Abraham wants your attention and worship!"

On a grassy knoll in Ptolemais, Big James feels for his partner, Little James. They've agreed that Big James will preach to the crowd, which includes a crippled man, while Little James will attempt to demonstrate the power of God by performing a healing. *This has to be hard,* Big James thinks, *when Little James himself has not been healed.*

Nonetheless, Big James does his part, speaking boldly and with his natural good humor, explaining how the Messiah they have anticipated for so long is here "and will soon come to this very town! My associate here will prove to you the power and lordship of the master we serve."

Little James approaches the lame man, gently places his hand on the man's hip, and prays. He takes the man's cane and urges him to test the leg. Soon he's jumping and laughing with his friends, who slap him on the back and hoist him up and down.

Big James can tell that Little James is genuinely moved. He hugs his partner and lifts him off the ground.

In Jericho, a father in his fifties rushes Zee and Matthew toward his home, with his wife close behind. When they reach the door, he warns the disciples to tread carefully and shakily unlocks it. Matthew is scared and shoots Zee a look, but Zee is all business.

As the door opens, Matthew is relieved to see nothing amiss in the low light. But then he hears movement, shuffling, and spots a coiled form in the far corner. It's a man in his thirties, clearly possessed. Matthew freezes, but Zee rushes in. As the man growls, Matthew and the man's parents leap back.

Zee grabs the man, who violently resists, and finally subdues him. His mother cries out and covers her mouth. Zee motions for Matthew, breaking him from his daze. He digs through his bag for a vial of oil and hurries to Zee's side. While the former Zealot holds the man's head, Matthew anoints him at the hairline, whispering a psalm. Zee crosses the man's arms in front of him and restrains him in a hug.

Matthew knows what he is to do next, but he hesitates. He's never done this before, though he's seen Jesus do it. He forces himself to shout, "Out!"

The man gradually stops shuddering, peering at the disciples in wonder as Zee gently wipes his mouth. The parents envelop their son as Zee slings an arm around Matthew, who's fighting to stay on his feet. *That just happened.*

Chapter 28

SLUDGE

The Capernaum synagogue

Zebedee sits in the back of the men's section with his sons, Big James and John, and their fellow disciple Nathanael. Since all the boys have been back, Zebedee and Salome—smiling at him from the women's section—have been regaled by the stories of their exploits. Apparently John and Thomas have worked together swimmingly, preaching in tandem, playing off each other—the precise, scholarly-sounding Thomas nearly matching the zeal of the former fisherman.

An augur and his apprentice, along with some angry Gentiles, threw Philip and Andrew out of the Decapolis—which didn't seem to bother them in the least. They reported shaking the dust from their sandals and moving on.

Just that morning, before synagogue, Nathanael told of his and Thaddeus's experience with a sick old woman in a Perea home. "I did the preaching, and Thad healed her by anointing her head with oil. It reminded me of Simon and Andrew's story of Jesus' healing Simon's mother-in-law right here in town."

Simon and Judas saw similar success in Caesarea Philippi, where Simon prayed over a demon-possessed woman and Judas cast it out.

Zebedee especially enjoys Big James's tales of his and Little James's preaching and healing in Ptolemais. He also loves hearing Zee's accounts of Matthew's preaching by peeking at his notes from Jesus' sermon. "He was clearly not comfortable," Zee had said. "But he didn't hold back, either."

Yet now, as the service commences, Zebedee senses something is off. Off with his own sons. He has many memories of the boys as youngsters, sitting in this very spot and having to discipline them to keep them quiet and still. Now, even though they're grown men, all of a sudden they're sitting like choir boys? And when the Torah cantillations begin, they're from Leviticus! Surely Big James and John won't be able to sit somberly through this. Jesus' nicknaming them the Sons of Thunder was perfect, so what's this?

Zebedee notices shoulders drooping throughout the congregation as Rabbi Josiah continues his less-than-inspiring reading: "And whoever touches the body of the one with the discharge shall wash his clothes and bathe himself in water and be unclean until the evening." That kind of passage never failed to elicit something funny from the boys, and, sure enough, John surreptitiously edges slightly away from James. Despite watching for the reaction, Zebedee observes nothing from James.

The rabbi continues: "And if the one with the discharge spits on someone who is clean, then he shall wash his clothes and bathe himself in water and be unclean until the evening."

Zebedee is still peeking. Still nothing.

"And any saddle on which the one with the discharge rides shall be unclean. And whoever touches anything that was under him shall be unclean until the evening …"

As the rabbi drones on, Zebedee can't take any more. He leans over and whispers, "What's the matter with you two?"

"… And whoever carries such things shall wash his clothes and bathe himself in water and be unclean until the evening."

Zebedee says, "What else happened on your missions? Why are you sitting so still?"

"In temple?" James says. "You taught us to!"

"You usually fidget and chat when he goes on like this."

John gives Zebedee a look. "You admonish us for being quiet in temple?"

"This isn't exactly one of Torah's best. Years from now, no one will claim, 'Oh, yes, I was there for the pronouncement on washing.'"

"Abba!" John says.

Zebedee shakes his head. "I'm on to you two. Something's up."

Suddenly the entire congregation appears to turn as one at sounds from outside.

Yussif, who has been trying to maintain at least a look of rapt interest in this difficult passage, is grateful for a reason to leave his seat. He must investigate this for Rabbi Josiah's sake, mustn't he?

"Where was I?" the rabbi says as Yussif tiptoes out. "Oh, yes, the ritual cleansing …"

Yussif reaches the cobblestone courtyard with a capsule-shaped cistern in its center. A servant at the head of a restless queue of outsiders sifts slimy residue from his bucket. He and the rest grumble, irritated at this slowdown at the water source.

Yussif approaches and says, "People, please! Rabbi Josiah is reading from Leviticus."

The servant says, "The cistern—"

"The cistern is closed!" bellows a Roman soldier, accompanied by an engineer.

"What's the meaning of this?" Yussif asks.

"Sludge!" the servant says. "Look." He scoops a palm full of sediment from his pail.

The engineer gags as he pushes his way toward Yussif. "A tunnel that feeds the cistern has ruptured and is overflowing into a sewage line, contaminating the water."

"Probably from the weight of these filthy people," the soldier says.

"They are pilgrims," Yussif says, surprised at his own courage. "We did not invite them, but they are here, and they are peaceful. What is to be done now?"

The Roman soldier looks down on him. "If you were enterprising, you'd drag everybody out of your meeting hall and set to work fixing this."

"This is a sacred synagogue, and we are worshipping."

"Which is what I thought you'd say. So that leaves it to Rome to fix your cistern."

Yussif sighs. "When?"

The engineer says, "Well, your *honorable* praetor is adamant that the work be done this instant. But despite his *benevolence,* he's overlooked the realities of the supply chain. And so, this will be fixed when the materials arrive from Rome."

Rome? Yussif thinks. "That could take weeks!"

"Unless …" the engineer says.

"… Unless we get the materials ourselves."

"Your temple seems well-financed."

"Looks can be deceiving," Yussif says. "What do we need?"

Chapter 29

DISCRETION

Capernaum synagogue, the next day

Yussif needs to see Jairus. It's been a while, but if he's going to get to the bottom of the cistern issue, he must move on it. The new man has already proved a paragon of efficiency and will undoubtedly be able to help. But when he reaches the man's office, he finds Jairus sitting at an uncharacteristically cluttered table, apparently deep in concentration. He seems to be comparing documents and reading intently. Yussif waits until he lifts his head.

"Hello, Jairus. It's been too long."

"Aah, Rabbi Yussif!" he says, rising quickly and pulling the door shut. "Please—"

Taken aback by this sudden flash of hospitality, not to mention the messy desk, Yussif asks, "Is everything all right?"

"I've been meaning to talk with you for some time, but seeing as how you've now come to me, I presume you have pressing business. How may I assist you?"

Yussif smiles. Such formality. "I do appreciate your sense of order, Jairus."

Jairus sighs and smiles. "I have one job, Rabbi."

"I need parchment and a courier."

Jairus retrieves a sheet of parchment from a cabinet. "And to where will the courier be traveling?"

"Jerusalem. There's a problem with our cistern."

Jairus looks shocked. "No one informed me. Clean water is essential to our purification ritual."

"I'm requisitioning materials for its repair."

"That will have to go through our budget—"

"It's taken care of. Paid in full."

Jairus raises a brow. "Dare I ask . . . ?"

"I've taken care of it," Yussif says. But off Jairus's look of skepticism he adds, "My family is in construction in Jerusalem. We own the stone quarry, and we manufacture bricks."

"Impressive."

Maybe, Yussif thinks. *But no one else must know.* "Discretion, Jairus."

"On my life."

"Now then," Yussif says, "what did you want to see *me* about?"

Jairus takes a deep breath, as if carefully considering his words. "I received a request for a detailed report on the sermon Jesus of Nazareth preached on the Korazim Plateau."

"From whom?"

"Rabbi Shmuel."

Yussif shrugs, but Jairus adds, "And stamped by Rabbi Shammai himself."

Yussif is speechless, his mind racing.

"Far be it from me," Jairus continues, "to tell you how to conduct your affairs, Rabbi, but—"

"Mm-hm," Yussif says, deep in thought.

"They must not know about your letter."

Yussif at last realizes what Jairus is saying—and what he must be studying. "You read it?"

"Not at first. But by now I've pored over it every day for almost a month. What you have written of that sermon and your encounters with him and his followers—well, Jesus is a very new thing, Rabbi. Do you stand behind every word?"

"Jairus, please …"

"Oh, I don't mean to question your trustworthiness. I'm asking—"

"I know what you're asking." Yussif wrestles with all the implications—with his faith, his life's work, everything. He decides to be diplomatic, even with this new friend and confidant. "You must be able to tell that I was emotional when I wrote that. I was reeling! I-I drew conclusions about Jesus that couldn't possibly—"

"Couldn't they?" Jairus says.

Yussif narrows his eyes at the man, wondering …

"Now I feel it as well, Rabbi," Jairus continues. "I am reeling too. I have spent the past month comparing his sermon to Torah and rereading the prophecies. I even tracked down Rabbi Shmuel's own account of the healing of the paralytic. Sometimes knowing more is not helpful."

"I am sorry if my report has sown doubt."

"No! Jesus of Nazareth is not the problem. I see light, Rabbi! Torah spells out the coming of this man. Only dogma and tradition paint a picture of a military figure. If everything you're saying is true, do you know what this means?"

Of course he knows what it means. It means that Jesus, despite his not being one who would overthrow the Roman government, as so many Jews want to believe of the Messiah, seems to fit all the criteria the Scriptures lay out about the chosen one. "Jairus, be careful."

"But it's more than just that he's a great new rabbi," Jairus says. "You leaders and the Sanhedrin members might be so close to it that you're not seeing the bigger view. He could very well be—no, I would sooner be unborn than return to when I was ignorant of your letter's contents."

"You understand the consequences of what you're saying . . ."

"Of course I do," Jairus says. "It's why I feel this way, and I mean what I say. I think you meant it as well. And Nicodemus?"

Yussif nods. "Now you understand my dilemma."

Jairus presses his lips together as if carefully choosing his next words. "I love our people," he says at last. "But I am leery of what the order may do. Rabbi Shmuel is requesting this information on behalf of Rabbi Shammai, the majority leader of the Sanhedrin. It will not be received with understanding."

"What do you think I should do?"

"I've already been too bold," Jairus says. "But if you're asking—"

"I am."

"I would send as diluted a version as you possibly can."

"We agree then," Yussif says. "The Sanhedrin need know nothing specific of the sermon. Now, just so we're clear, you realize that knowing the account I submit is inaccurate makes you complicit."

Jairus appears to hesitate but finally nods. "Discretion, please," he says.

"On my life."

Yussif smiles and Jairus chuckles, but the rabbi knows they have entered into a pact from which there is no return.

Chapter 30

THE REUNION

Capernaum countryside

Simon is eager to get home. How long he can stay, he's not sure, but any time with Eden refreshes him in every way. His mission with Judas was thrilling—seeing God work through both of them, just as Jesus had predicted. And getting to know the new guy, that was interesting too. Simon had always considered himself as much a businessman as a fisherman, though admittedly his most creative enterprising idea had also nearly been the end of him. But Judas, now there is a man who knows business—finances, selling, entrepreneurship, everything. There's much he can learn from the man.

And Judas has suggested everyone get together tomorrow, somewhere convenient to all—which means at Simon's home. It doesn't have to be a long meeting, he hopes, because naturally he wants as much alone time with Eden as he can get. Surely she'll be open to that. She loves all these guys.

As he passes the well at the edge of town, Simon is struck by the long lines of people waiting in the sun for their turn. Have the other sources of water dried up in Capernaum? The citizens look exhausted, sweating, eager to get their water and get back home. Two women are tending a third, who appears doubled over with heat exhaustion. Simon considers stopping to help, but they seem to have the situation in hand.

Knowing Eden isn't expecting him for several more hours will make this reunion all the sweeter. He'll creep inside, quietly wash his feet, and try to surprise her. Though he won't likely be home long, right now he's hungry, not to mention pining for Eden's touch.

Eden has rearranged the furniture and is in the final stages of cleaning the house in anticipation of Simon's evening arrival, yearning desperately for all the activity to somehow overcome her deep sorrow. So far, nothing has worked. It's bad enough that he's been away so long and won't be home until dark, but she long ago steeled herself for that and fully supports his following—or in this case, obeying—the Messiah. That doesn't make it easier, especially now. Maybe if she busies herself by kneading some dough for a fresh loaf of bread before finishing her housework … It's worth a try.

Fighting tears, she's far into the process when she's frightened by a deep voice, right behind her, demanding, "Where is your husband?"

Eden shrieks and whirls to strike, only to discover it's Simon! "Oh! What are you doing?"

He wraps his arms around her waist and lifts her, laughing. "Were you ready to fight?"

"Oh, you can't do that! Don't do that again! I can barely breathe!" He sets her down, and she reaches for another hug. "You're lucky I missed you," she says. "I could be angry, you scaring me like that."

"I missed you, Love."

She pulls back to face him. "I'm sorry it's a bit of a mess still. I wasn't expecting you till tonight."

"Oh, I don't care. You know that."

Actually, she does know, but she wishes he *did* care. He steps to the counter and starts scarfing down any bits of food he can reach. "I definitely missed this. I'm starving."

"Did you not eat well?"

With his mouth full, he says, "We traveled way too much for the amount of food we got."

"So—notice anything different?"

"About what?"

Is he teasing, like when he pretended to not remember the details of their wedding day? "The house," she says.

"There's something different?"

He's serious! "The table," she says. "It's normally there, but I moved it here to create a little more room. I moved the dresser so more light would come in. And Ima gave me some of her cloths to put on that wall."

"Those weren't there before?"

"What do you mean? Of course not. I got them while you were gone."

Simon shrugs and mutters, "Hmm."

Despite everything she loves about this man, this exasperates her. "You didn't notice anything different? You live in this house."

"I'm sorry. I'm exhausted. It looks great."

Too late, she thinks, but maybe she should cut him some slack. "Should you take a nap today when I go to market?"

"I was hoping to, actually." He reaches for her again. "If I can get a little sleep, I'll be refreshed for dinner and then—early bedtime?" He kisses her on the cheek and steps toward the bedroom.

"A nap now?" she says.

"Is now not good?"

Well, you just got home, she thinks. "Um, no. It's fine. I was hoping we—never mind. It's fine. I'll go now."

"Oh, yeah," Simon says, "with all the boys coming back in, Judas is suggesting we all come by here tomorrow." He points at the counter and her dough. "Do you have more bread than this?"

"Tomorrow? You just got back."

"Yeah, we just want to connect a bit, talk about the journeys, and they wanted to meet here. Which is annoying, but it's been a while since we've all seen each other."

"Yes, I know." *It's been a while since you and I have seen each other too.*

"I won't let them stay long or anything. This is just the best spot to gather. So, is there more?"

"More what?"

"Bread. For when they come."

Eden hesitates, gathers herself. There's more she needs to say, but she bites her tongue. "I can make more. I'll just stop by the well for water."

"Aah, thank you. They'll appreciate that. You make the best bread."

The flattery falls flat. As he steps toward her, she turns to leave. "Have a nice nap."

"Love you!" he says. "So glad to be home."

"Love you," she says on her way out, knowing it sounds halfhearted.

Outside, she locks the door and hoists her shoulder pole, an empty bucket on either end.

"Excuse me."

Eden turns to find a woman limping toward her, bent under the weight on her back—two buckets bound together with a washboard and two bags of laundry. "Yes?"

"Do you have any clothes you need washed?"

"I don't," Eden says kindly. "Well, I do, but I'm on my way to fetch water to do them myself."

"I see."

"But thank you."

"I charge a fair price," the woman says. "And your garments come back like new."

"I believe they would," Eden says, then has a thought. "Would you like to join me?"

The woman looks startled, perhaps even stumped. She clearly wasn't expecting this. She doesn't appear the type who gets invited places. "I may not be good company," she says.

This amuses Eden. "What an interesting thing to say. I think most people don't know that about themselves."

"They're probably just as strange as me, you mean," the woman says.

"Or just as lovely."

The woman seems to consider this.

"I've never seen you before," Eden says.

"I'm not from here."

"Where are you from?"

"Caesarea Philippi. You going to the well outside of town?"

Eden nods. "I heard the cistern is broken."

"You don't want to go to that well. Yesterday I saw lines of people waiting for hours in the hot sun."

"What choice do we have?"

"I know of a secret spring north of town."

"Would you take me to it?" Eden asks.

"I just said I would."

Eden is tickled. This woman is not good with people.

Chapter 31

THE SCARE

Jairus's home

Jairus's pregnant wife, Michal, sautés onions and garlic in olive oil during the middle of the day. Her twelve-year-old daughter, Nili, stands on a step stool next to her, stirring the pan. "You're very good at this," Michal says.

"Thank you, Ima."

"Smells good, doesn't it?"

Nili sniffs the concoction just as the front door opens. "Abba!" She steps down and rushes to give him a hug. Jairus accepts her with open arms.

He's certainly not home this early, Michal thinks.

"A question of prophecy has come up," he explains. "I need one of my scrolls. I can stay only a moment."

"One of the rabbis needs you to bail him out?" Michal teases.

He purses his lips and seems to force a smile, then disappears into his study.

"Let's keep stirring, Nili. Can't let the onion burn."

When Michal takes the pan off the flame and sets it aside, Nili moves her step stool before a table and begins measuring out spices. She uses a knife to level off the top of a spoonful of cumin, holding it right in front of her eyes to be sure before handing it to her mother.

"Perfect," Michal says, finding her daughter's earnest work adorable. "But it can be rounded."

Nili drops the spoon and goes ashen.

"Don't be like that, Nili. Do it however you want. I'm just trying to teach—"

But the girl looks suddenly ill. "My tummy hurts." Her knees buckle.

Michal drops everything, lunging to catch her. "Nili! Wh—"

"I don't feel good."

"Jairus! Jairus!"

Michal is on the floor with Nili as Jairus hurries to them. "What's happened?"

"We were just cooking. Nili was measuring cumin."

Jairus picks up Nili. "Come on. Let's lie down." He places her in her bed, and Michal appreciates his attempt to reassure her with a look. But her breathing sounds erratic. "Stay there, hon," he adds.

"I will."

Jairus whispers to Michal, "I'm going to get the doctor."

• • •

Eden slows herself to follow the limping woman toward the spring. "Thank you for doing this. I—I don't know your name. I'm Eden."

"Veronica."

"It was very kind of you to tell me of this place. Most people would have kept it a secret."

"I don't like secrets."

Well, so much for trying to compliment you, Eden thinks. "Everybody has secrets." In fact, she has her own.

The woman turns to face her with a dour look. "If people know something that could help me, I wouldn't want them to withhold it. So why would I do the same?"

Eden is lost in thought. She has a secret she needs to tell Simon, but the timing hasn't been right yet. "Sure," she says.

"Not that it's done me any good," the woman says.

"What do you mean?"

"Forget it. Here we are."

Veronica pushes through some brush to reveal a glorious spring in a natural clearing. She gestures. "You'll want to—"

"I know how to wash clothes," Eden says, lowering a bucket into the water as Veronica sets down all her stuff. "I didn't mean to snap at you," Eden adds. "There's a lot going on in my life."

"I understand," Veronica says, not looking up from her work.

"No, I was wrong. I'm sorry."

Veronica shrugs and kneels downstream, pushing her first load into the water.

Eden sets her full bucket in the clearing and returns to the spring with her second. "How does your husband like Capernaum?" she asks.

"I am not married," Veronica says.

"You're not—but you've traveled so far …" She squints at Veronica's wash bundle, garments sodden with blood. Eden is quickly overcome and holds her breath.

Chapter 32

THE BUSINESS

Matthew's former mansion, morning

Mary of Magdala can't help but be saddened by the tenor of her conversations with Tamar and Ramah. She had been so excited by the prospect of their living together, working together, following Jesus together. But with the familiarity has come a measure of contempt. It's not right, she knows, but she's at a loss. Maybe if she tries to play mediator and responds to any anger or frustration with a soft word … Or perhaps, now alone briefly with Tamar, she can raise the issue. But already, Tamar has an opinion.

"I'm grateful to Matthew for letting us live here," Tamar says, looking around. "But if there's one thing this house has confirmed for me, it's that having money is not the same as having taste."

That sounds like gossip, but Mary wants to give Tamar the benefit of the doubt. "What do you mean?"

"The turn of the leg on this table, and the foot style. That was a brief trend five years ago."

"Maybe he bought it five years ago."

"And this rug. This aggressive orange pattern raises the heartbeat. No wonder he's anxious all the time."

Mary's determination to act as a calming influence fades as she feels compelled to defend poor Matthew. "He's not anxious because of a rug. What's your point?"

"I just don't know how much we'll get auctioning these things off."

"Auction?" Mary says.

"The ministry needs financing," Tamar says. "We cannot rely solely on alms."

"Well," Mary says, "we did mention the possibility of selling your jewelry."

"I told you, this is not just jewelry. It's my family story. Every piece belonged to one of my ancestors. I carry their lives with me on my body."

"I'm sorry, Tamar," Mary says, "I'm trying to be sensitive. But honestly, that sounds a little pagan. Or like animism, which you may want to consider shedding now that you're with us."

"It's not animism. It's honor. You have no idea what I've been through."

"Do you know what I've been through?"

"I've heard rumors." She pauses, regret on her face. "I'm sorry."

"I do have a past, Tamar. A past. As for the question of money, we should just leave it to Judas, the keeper of the purse."

There's a knock at the door, and Tamar moves to answer it.

"Please let it be Jesus," Mary whispers.

"Zebedee!" Tamar says. "Shalom. You know, I realized the other day that I've never apologized to you about your roof."

"Oh, don't give it another thought. Jesus told you, 'Your faith is beautiful,' eh? Do you ladies have a moment?"

"Of course."

Zebedee steps in, a vial in his hand. "I've pressed a batch of olive oil. Will you give me your honest opinions? Tell me what you taste in it."

Mary takes a careful sip. She fights a grimace and tries to be diplomatic. "Hmm."

"What kind of an *Hmm* was that?" Zebedee says.

"I need a minute to think of the right word."

"Tamar?" Zebedee says.

She nearly empties the vial into her mouth and puts a hand to her chest. Passing the vial off to Mary, she rushes out the door and spits the oil onto the stoop.

"What?" Zebedee says. "What is it? What's wrong?"

Catching her breath, Tamar says, "I am the daughter of one of the seven princes of my people. The olive tree originated in Ethiopia and then spread to the rest of the nations."

Mary furrows her brow. "You're certain the olive tree originated in Ethiopia?"

Tamar races on. "I have lived in Egypt, Nubia, and Anatolia and have sampled the finest oils of each."

"And?" Zebedee says. "What do you think?

Tamar appears to try to be gentle. "It's—rancid."

"Tamar!" Mary says.

"No," Zebedee says, "it's okay. I need you both to be honest. You only do me harm by flattery. Mary, I know I can count on you to tell me the truth too."

Mary hates to offend, but he's right. "Mold," she says. "Something between—black pepper and—vinegar."

"But look at this," Tamar says, pulling a looking glass off the wall and shaking onto it the last of the oil from the vial. "It has been expertly racked and purged. See the clarity? Not a trace of solid matter."

"Thank you," Zebedee says, "but what can be done about the taste?"

"That depends on the olives," Tamar says. "Were the olives light green or dark green?"

"Dark, because they're the cheapest, and they produce more oil."

"But with less flavor," Tamar says. "The lighter the color, the less oil it will produce, but more flavor. The lighter the brighter. Did you buy a press?"

"I leased one, along with the donkey that pulls the crushing stone."

"What about the olives?"

"I buy them wholesale from the owner of a grove."

"A reputable grove?"

"I think so. I mean—I think."

"Zebedee," Tamar says, "could you arrange an introduction to the owner?"

"Of the grove or the press?"

"Both," she says.

"Tamar," Mary says, "what are you—"

"That woman, Joanna," Tamar says, "from Herod's court—the one who got Andrew into the prison to see the baptizer. She gave a large donation to the ministry and urged us to find a way to multiply it if we could."

"This would go to my business?" Zebedee says.

"For the ministry," Mary says.

"Yes," Tamar says, "but the profit from the oil business is how we will multiply her gift. We could work with you, Zebedee, to grow it."

Mary says, "You'll need to speak with Judas. He'll have to be on board."

"Well," Tamar says, "where is he?"

"Andrew's flat, I think," Mary says.

"What are we waiting for?" Zebedee says. "Let's go!"

It turns out that Judas is more than on board. He has plenty of ideas, including that Zebedee must get some solid experience, regardless of what that takes. Days later, the old fisherman is at the Capernaum docks with the boat that has served him so well for so long.

"She's seaworthy," Zebedee tells a potential buyer. "Inspect her from every angle. The holds are fast, the sails are true."

"I don't have to inspect it to know your word is your bond, Zeb."

"So, we have a deal?"

"Yes, but I don't understand. You're the best fisherman in town. And now you're becoming an apprentice to a mediocre olive vendor?"

"I met a man who is no man."

"Yes, yes, Jesus the Nazarene, you told me. He wants you to give up your business now?"

"What am I working for? I have food to eat. I own my home. My wife is true."

"We own nothing under Rome."

"I own nothing *above* Rome," Zebedee says. "That's what I want to work for. I will make the best anointing oil this side of the Sinai."

"I believe you," the man says, reaching into his belt. "Let's get this over with."

Chapter 33

TENSION

Simon's home

As the rest of the disciples begin arriving, Eden tries to subdue her resentment. She needs time alone with Simon, time to talk, time to think. But he seems no more interested in that than in being sure they're ready for their guests.

She knows it's unhealthy to seethe. Her relationship with Simon has always been based on love, playfulness, even flirting. Little has made her so fulfilled as locking eyes with him, teasing, smiling. Yet now that's the last thing in the world she cares to do. Eden tries to distract herself and hide her true feelings with all the busyness of hosting such a large group. On the one hand, she doesn't want Simon to notice that she's emotionally distant from him just now. On the other, she wants it obvious, in his face. Her inner pot is bubbling, she knows, and is in danger of boiling over.

She's sobered, however, as she cordially greets each man, putting on her best face for them. Though today they may be one of the major contributors to her frustration, it isn't their fault.

Simon could have, should have, precluded this. He's their leader, after all. Whether that's been formally established by Jesus or not, everyone knows it, can see it. Why couldn't he tell them he needed a few days with his beloved before committing to one more obligation with all of them—and here of all places?

To Eden, the other disciples look like soldiers returning from battle. No more youthful, innocent faces. Some look haunted. Others hardened. All have been changed. She counts eleven—who's missing?

As they drag chairs together and fill her humble place, they begin talking, even without any announcement or ground rules. John is immersed in an account from his assignment. "… and in an instant, just like that, her eyes went from gray to hazel. Thomas and I had never seen anything like it."

"Neither had she," Judas quips.

While crushing soaked chickpeas for a bread dip, Eden looks for Thomas's reaction, but it's he who is missing. *Hmm.*

"Her parents burst into tears," John continues.

"What a shame," Andrew says, "that the first thing she had to see with her new eyes was you."

"Traumatizing," Big James says, and Eden can't help but smile. These guys …

Simon stands next to her, pouring water into cups. She's struck that he's not involved in the banter as he would normally be. Maybe he's getting the picture that something's up with her. "Do you need any help with that?" he asks.

"No," she says. Flat. Cold.

He whispers, "Has something been bothering you lately?"

"No."

The repartee among the boys grows louder. "Turns out Andrew is truly a bold preacher," Philip says. It's obvious he's serious, and Andrew looks self-conscious.

"I'd like to think we made a difference," he says.

Thaddeus says, "You were in the Decapolis with Gentiles?"

"Gentiles and Hellenistic Jews," Philip says. "They hated us almost as much as they hate each other."

"The Gentiles kicked us out," Andrew says. "I think they thought we were helping start a war."

Little James says, "Simon, are you proud of your brother?"

When Simon doesn't respond, Eden nudges him. "Simon …"

"Sorry, what?"

"I said you must be proud of your brother," Little James says.

"Of course I am."

Thaddeus asks Big James how things went in Ptolemais.

"It was fine. We preached. We did what Jesus gave us the power to do."

Nathanael snorts. "You sound as enthusiastic as a Sadducee with a toothache."

"He didn't give us power, though," Andrew says. "Right?"

"He worked through us," Judas says.

Andrew says, "Right."

But Big James looks conflicted. "I just don't know if this was a good idea," he says.

Now the men are talking over each other, most questioning Big James.

"Not a good idea?"

"What are you saying?"

"We just raised more fuss," he says. "This is all going to create more headaches. More crowds. More scrutiny."

"What," Judas says, "you want to slow Jesus down?"

"James is just mad at me," John says. "He's annoyed I've gotten close to Thomas, and because Jesus once called me 'beloved.'"

All eyes turn to Big James. "I felt that way before we left, yes. But I don't care about that now. Tell them what you said to me before."

"Tell them yourself," John says. "You're the one struggling with it."

Big James hesitates, and Eden can hear her own heartbeat. Finally he says, "By using us as vessels, Jesus gave us power but no understanding."

Some stare at him. Others look away. Eden wishes there were a way to cut the tension. Matthew breaks the silence. "I also struggled to understand."

John nods. "We healed people, yes, but still felt overwhelmed."

"But did he *require* understanding?" Nathanael asks. "This all seems to be more about what we were doing."

"Easy for you to say," Big James says, "you and Thaddeus going door to door in Cana. Jesus is *known* in Cana. They probably invited you into their homes."

To Eden, Thad and Nathanael look caught. "I'll go on harder missions," Nathanael says.

"Nathanael is right," Judas says. "Jesus never said anything about understanding. And this was temporary anyway."

"Sometimes when I was preaching," Little James says, "I could feel Jesus giving me the words."

Several seem to agree.

"I said things I don't even fully comprehend or live by," Big James says. "I felt like a fraud."

"I felt the same way," Andrew says, "but it didn't bother me."

"I felt powerful," John says, "like I could do anything."

"I did too," Philip says, "but that seems dangerous if it left us feeling like *that*."

"Why?" John asks.

"Because he's the Messiah, John," Philip says.

"And none of us is the Messiah," Zee says.

Eden has heard enough and can't stop herself. "Instead of arguing about it," she says, "you could just ask Jesus about it when he gets back."

Everyone falls silent, apparently surprised by her chiming in. She's surprised herself. Women don't speak in synagogue, and she's certainly not a disciple.

"That's actually a very good idea," Matthew says.

"But who can say when he'll be back?" Thaddeus says.

"Soon," they all seem to say together.

"The most imprecise word," Philip says.

"So, some of it was confusing, James," his brother says. "Can you live with that until we get understanding?"

"You're the one who brought it up to me, John!"

"Understanding or not," Simon says at last, "you're all hungry. I think that's the real problem."

"Food is not the solution to this," Big James says.

"Do you have a better one?" Simon says. "My wife has practically given up her home for us."

There's a flicker of the Simon Eden loves.

"I don't mean disrespect," Big James says. "Eden, I'm s—"

"Everyone, please!" Eden says, "I took no offense. Now come, eat."

She sets out the bread, and the men gather around the table. Nathanael taps Andrew on the shoulder. "I have to sit next to Little James."

"Why?"

"I want to know what happened to Big James on the road that turned him into this!"

As the rest continue their discussion, Eden scoops onto a plate the hummus she has made of the chickpeas. Andrew whispers, "Eden, is everything all right?"

"I'm fine," she says, forcing a smile and moving on to serve the others. Simon is dropping bread onto people's plates, and Eden sees Andrew stop him, obviously asking him the same question. Getting no response, he says, "Simon?"

Simon and Eden return to the counter. He says something that barely registers with her and leans in to kiss her cheek. She not-so-subtly dodges it and realizes Andrew is watching.

Chapter 34

BLOOD

Capernaum countryside

Eden lugs her laundry toward the spring Veronica has shown her. Despite the friction at home, she can still find a degree of joy in serving the men who follow Jesus. They've been displaced, spread out, crowded in together wherever they've landed, and she's happy to do their washes for them. But something is going to have to give with Simon. She's felt justified in giving him the cold shoulder, but she also knows it's unfair for her to make him wonder what's wrong.

That it's not obvious to him contributes to her exasperation. But it's his very impetuousness that drew her to him in the first place. She can't expect him to be perfect. And yet he's been so insensitive since his return.

As she reaches the spring, Eden finds her new friend—or sort of friend, she can't be sure—appearing to painfully do her own laundry. "Shalom, Veronica!"

The woman looks up. Without so much as a shalom, she says, "Your house isn't empty anymore."

"What?"

"Those look like men's tunics."

"My husband and his friends returned home." Eden plunges various clothes into the water.

"The perfect place," Veronica says.

"I assure you there's nothing perfect about my place—or about me."

"I meant Eden," Veronica says. "The garden."

This makes Eden rise from her work and study Veronica. "What brought you here from Caesarea Philippi?"

"The preacher. Came to hear him on the mount."

"Of course."

"Surely you were there …"

"Yes. Yes, I—I was." Eden suddenly realizes she is not practicing what Jesus preached.

"What? You didn't like what you heard?"

"I did," Eden says. "It's just that a lot has happened since then." But she doesn't want to talk about it. "It must have been a hard journey for you, Veronica, with your—ah—"

"With my what?"

"Just the—I don't know—your limp."

"My limbs are fine. I've been—"

Eden can tell the woman is as uncomfortable as she is, and she wishes she hadn't said anything. She notices that Veronica is bleeding. The woman covers the spot, but Eden remembers her bloody laundry from last time and notices more of the same now. The poor woman.

"How long have you been bl—"

"Twelve years."

"You mean days, right?"

"I mean years."

"Twelve! How is that possible?"

"It's a rare disease."

"How have you stayed alive?"

"It just leaves me weak."

"This is why you're unmarried?"

"I'm un-everything. I haven't seen my parents in years. They won't allow me in the house. You'd better keep your distance. If you touch any of it, you'll be ritually unclean and unable to touch your husband for seven days."

"Oh, I assure you, I haven't been touching my husband." Eden regrets this immediately and feels she has betrayed Simon by saying it.

Veronica's brows rise, and the women continue to wash in silence. Finally, she speaks. "There's no cure for my ailment. I spent all my money on doctors, and they made it only worse. No hope there."

How sad, Eden thinks. "So, what do you do with no hope?"

"I haven't lost *all* hope. I'm just saying there's no cure from *doctors.* But there could be another way I haven't tried yet."

Chapter 35

TAKE IT BACK

Capernaum synagogue

Jairus is just outside his office, instructing a young student to fetch him two buckets of good water and deliver them to his house. He shoos the man off as he notices Yussif walking by, and he invites him in.

"What's wrong?" Yussif says. "You look—"

"There's an emergency at home. I have to leave again soon."

"I'm sorry! Can I help in any way?"

"The water situation is urgent. The doctor believes our daughter may be ill because of the water. And, not to be indelicate, but every woman who has her time of the month will have a problem. We can't wait for the cistern to be repaired."

"What can I do?"

"See that every able-bodied student brings water from the rural well, springs—the Jordan if need be."

"Done. Anything else?"

Jairus hesitates. "I'm frightened."

"Of course you are."

"Rabbi, am I being punished by God for believing in this Nazarene?"

Yussif looks stricken. "If you are, I have done this to you. Forgive me, Jairus! It's not too late for us to stop investigating and just take it all back."

"No," Jairus says. "Taking it back would not change what I believe."

"But—"

"I must go now."

The Jerusalem temple

Biting his lip, Shmuel paces an inner chamber with Yanni on his heels. They watch from the wings as Shammai and his coterie of Pharisee devotees enter the Sanhedrin and approach the pulpit. The attending judges rise.

Shammai bows slightly and begins, "Av Bet Dien. Honored President Shimon, distinguished judges …" They all nod, and he continues: "I hereby propose a new decree that would extend to the four corners of the land of Israel and to any Diaspora living beyond our borders. A scourge of false prophecy has bedeviled our people and is diluting our faith, jeopardizing our credibility, and besmirching our reputation. This. Must. Stop.

"Any preacher espousing teaching not supported by known and respected rabbis, and *especially* anyone invoking the messianic title 'Son of Man' from the prophet Daniel, shall be reported immediately to regional Sanhedrin judges. If one is unrepentant, the high priest alone will adjudicate. All those in favor?"

More than eighty percent of the hands go up, but Shmuel notices Nicodemus's seat is vacant. Shmuel looks skyward and whispers, "Praise Adonai." Yanni beams.

Shmuel sidles up to one of Shammai's sycophants and asks quietly, "So, what now?"

"What now? Listen to the applause. We won the day. Great work."

As the man strides off, Shmuel hurries to follow. "Work?" he says. "There hasn't been work yet. Can we detain the Nazarene? I'd hoped this was the final step to recognizing Jesus as dangerous."

"Rabbi Shammai's speech is the victory."

Feeling dismissed, Shmuel says, "This is all political?"

"Not entirely. Now there's an edict."

"What good is an edict?"

"It's almost as good as a law."

"But we can't do anything?"

"We can wait."

"Wait?"

"Shmuel, if this Jesus is as much a threat as you say, we will hear about it. Eventually."

Shmuel trudges back to Yanni, who, having heard none of this conversation, continues to celebrate.

Tent city, Capernaum

Veronica carries a folded load of laundry to one of the makeshift shelters and announces herself. Though weak and fatigued and eager to find somewhere to simply take a nap, delivering her pristine work remains one of her few tiny pleasures. Receiving payment and often a compliment is frequently the only bright spot in her day.

She hands the man his clothes and is warmed to hear, "Faster than I expected."

"As I promised," she says. "Thorough and swift."

He presses a few coins into her hand, just as she feels blood trickling down her ankle. She moves to quickly cover it, but too late. The man gasps and flings the clothes into her face. "Unclean! You deceitful woman!"

Veronica stumbles and falls to the ground, knowing he believes he has touched a menstruating woman. As she struggles to rise, she cries out, "I'm sorry! I—you don't underst—"

"Now I'm unclean until sundown!"

Through tears, Veronica says, "I'm sure that will be very difficult for you, sir."

"Get away! You are not to be in the street or among us!"

Parents all around pull children into their tents and fasten the flaps, as if she is a monster. The man backs into his place. "Shame! Sarah, I'll be back at evening. I must wash myself in the sea."

Chapter 36

THE VISIT

Simon's home

Simon lies in bed, back-to-back with Eden. He can tell from her breathing that she's still awake. *What is going on?* He stares out the window into the moonlight. This will be the last night, he decides, that he will go to bed without knowing what has her so frigid.

Simon thought they were in this thing together. It hasn't been easy, he knows, for either of them. But hasn't it all been worth it for the joy of following the Messiah? Without the bliss he's always relished with Eden, even having been chosen by Jesus has lost its luster. How will he even sleep now? *Tomorrow,* he promises himself.

But the next day, Eden appears no more willing to talk than she had the day before. Simon busies himself with chores that have piled up in his absence. He's tweaking this, fixing that, hoping she'll see that he's trying. He wants to make their home as secure as he can for her in his absence, but there's no way he's leaving again without resolving whatever has come between them.

Early in the evening, Simon can endure the tension no longer. Eden has made herself scarce most of the day, somehow finding a way to be in a room far from him, no matter where he is. But now she has finally gotten to the leftover dishes from the gathering the day before. He approaches and leans back against the counter, arms crossed. "There's obviously something bothering you," he says. "But you're not bleeding. It's not that time."

"Please don't talk to me about things like that, Simon."

"What *can* I talk to you about?"

Silence.

"I know I've made a lot of mistakes," he says. "So, if it's my fault, I will apologize. But I have to know what I've done."

She pauses and lets out a huge sigh, then turns to leave. "Maybe it's what you haven't done, Simon. I'm going for a walk."

He follows. "There, that's a start. What haven't I done? I'll do it three times over."

"I don't want to be the one to have to tell you," she says, reaching the door. "If you know me—"

The door opens, and Jesus says, "Good evening!"

With him stand five friends: Big James, Zee, Mary Magdalene, Tamar, and Andrew. Eden quickly covers her head and wipes her face as they enter.

"Evening," Simon says.

"Just *evening*?" Jesus says. "Without *good*?"

"You might say that."

"Have you all eaten dinner?" Eden says. "What can I get you to drink?"

From outside come the rustle of footsteps as a crush of pilgrims arrives, obviously from the tent city. "He's in there!" one says. "I saw him go in!"

"Bolt it," Big James says. "Fast."

Zee hauls up the wood beam and secures it.

"Is Jesus of Nazareth in there?"

"Are you teaching?"

The window fills with pilgrims jockeying for position. Big James and Zee gently push them back. "Please be respectful of his privacy. Patience, please."

"When will the next miracle be?"

Simon shakes his head. "So, this is what it's going to be like now?"

"Simon!" Andrew says.

Mary lightly touches Andrew's arm.

"Like what, Simon?" Jesus asks.

"I'm sorry, Master. It's just upsetting that after a long journey, my house is no longer my home. It's a meeting place, a forum."

"A house cannot have many functions?" Jesus says.

Simon wheels around and storms toward the back door. Andrew follows. "Brother!"

But Jesus seizes Andrew by the arm. "Let him go. Simon needs to work out some things by himself."

Eden lowers her head and presses both palms on the counter. Mary lays a hand on her shoulder.

Plodding the streets in the darkness, Simon has no idea where he's going. Instinctively he's drawn toward the aroma of the sea, but as he rounds a corner into the city courtyard where the wreckage of the cistern lies, a familiar face approaches—Gaius, out of uniform and clearly off duty.

"What're you looking at?" Gaius says.

"Sorry, I've just never seen you without a sword."

"I'm armed," Gaius says, exposing a dagger at his waist. "And I still hold authority."

"I wasn't questioning."

"The only time I see you anymore is on the heels of that exasperating preacher."

"At the moment I'm finding it a little exasperating myself."

"You're in good company for once."

"I didn't mean that," Simon says. "I'm just tired."

"Well, then, good evening."

Gaius makes a move to leave, but Simon continues. "This cistern is the problem. Long walks to the well …"

"You're on a roll tonight," Gaius says. "My boss just told me the same thing."

"Are you going to fix it?"

"Are *you*?" Gaius says.

"I mean no offense," Simon says. "Isn't it, uh, what do you call it—a civic matter?"

"Quintus doesn't want to pay for it."

"Then I would say we're at an impasse," Simon says, idly picking up a stray length of rope from the wreckage of the cistern. "Seems like the theme of the night." He absently starts tying a series of knots.

"What theme?" Gaius says.

"It's nothing."

Gaius seems to study Simon. "What are you doing out here at this hour?"

"Am I being detained?"

"You're being questioned."

"And if I don't answer, you'll arrest me?"

"I've arrested people for less."

"I was on a walk, officer."

"*Primi*."

"I was on a walk, Primi."

Gaius chuckles and takes a seat next to Simon. He pulls out a flask and takes a sip, wincing. "What's *impasse* mean?"

"It's like a road that's blocked."

"Like you're stuck? Because you can't undo something you did?"

Gaius is clearly referring to Simon's decision to give up his career to follow Jesus. But Simon's mind is on what's happening at home. "No, it's because I don't know what I can't undo that I did in the past." He blinks. "That was a mouthful, I know."

Gaius offers him the flask.

"Sorry, I can't drink, um, from a vessel that's been—"

Gaius shakes his head. "You Jews. Your rules make your lives very complicated."

"Us Jews? Jesus will undo some of that. He reminds us what we live for."

"They say he performs miracles, right? Or what appear to be miracles? Why doesn't he just miraculously fix this cistern?"

"You'd have to ask him that."

"How about you ask him for me?"

"I'm not inclined to speak with him at the moment," Simon says.

"I can relate to that," Gaius says, taking a sip. "Not wanting to talk with the boss, I mean. Quintus is ready to burn down the town. Since you're back, does it mean Jesus is here in Capernaum too?"

"You don't think I'd tell *you*, do you?"

"You'd better hope to your god that Quintus doesn't find out. I do know that Matthew's back."

"My other favorite person."

"I get that," Gaius says. "But twenty denarii says you'll end up liking him."

"I don't gamble anymore, and I don't take advantage of Romans."

"Why dislike Matthew? I mean, besides the tax thing."

"Why are you so interested in us?" Simon says.

"Are you kidding? You're my job. Are you blind? The city is overrun with pilgrims because of your teacher. If I were you, I'd lie low at home for a while."

"I don't particularly want to be in my home."

"Haven't you just come back fr—? Hey, if you don't want to be home and you want to distract Quintus from looking for Jesus, you could fix this cistern."

"With who?" Simon says. "With what?"

"The temple will be getting materials within a day. And you seem the sort who needs to be doing something with his hands."

"That's a lot of work."

"I could, uh, oversee the labor," Gaius says.

"You're drunk. Sir."

"Maybe a little, but you need something to do. Don't think I haven't noticed you tying about eight knots."

"If you were a seafaring military man, you'd know that these are—"

Gaius takes the rope and ties one of the complicated knots Simon just tied and hands it back.

Shocked, Simon says, "How'd you do that?"

"My grandfather was a sailor. Taught me all of them."

"All?"

"All the ones you just did."

Simon tosses him the rope. "Double Dragon."

"I don't know the names," Gaius says. "Is that the one with the two …" He effortlessly ties it.

Simon lets out a laugh. "Turn Hook."

"That sounds dangerous. I'll just tie 'em, and you can tell me what they're called."

"Double Stopper."

Again, success. Gaius ties another.

"*That's* the Snake in the Hole," Simon says. "Wow."

Gaius laughs and tosses the rope back to Simon. "Be here in the morning. I'll check with the temple administrator about the materials. If this trouble of yours at home has anything to do with the wife, all I can suggest is that you get used to saying five words: You. Are. Right. I'm. Sorry."

Jairus's home

Michal hangs a frying pan and wipes the counter. She pours boiling water into a cup, spoons in some powder, and stirs. She sits, removes her head covering, and rubs her neck, then her pregnant belly. As she lifts her cup toward her lips and absorbs its calming aroma, she senses the house is too quiet. "Jairus? Have you checked on Nili?"

"Not in a while."

She grabs a lamp and makes her way to Nili's room, listening carefully to the girl's labored breathing.

"Jairus!"

PART 5

Intensity in Tent City

Chapter 37

THE LOSS

Capernaum, night
Two weeks earlier

Eden feels strange all day, to the point where she nearly tells her mother, Dasha, that she fears something is wrong. But she's new to this pregnancy thing and doesn't want to unnecessarily worry Ima. Whatever it is will likely fade and pass, though she does admit to her mother that she's abnormally exhausted and goes to bed earlier than usual.

Despite her fatigue, she can never go to bed alone without thinking of Simon and praying for him—wherever Jesus' latest assignment has taken him. To her great relief, she then quickly drifts off and sleeps soundly until she hears a nearby watchman call out, "Third watch!" So, she's slept from just after dark until midnight. Now, if she can fall back to sleep and not rise till dawn …

But searing pain attacks Eden, making her sit straight up and cry out. She quickly covers her mouth, praying she hasn't roused Ima in the next room. But her mother has apparently been on the alert and soon appears in the doorway, oil lamp in hand. "What is it, dear heart?"

"Nothing, I'm fine. Sorry to have dist—oh! Oh, Ima!"

Her mother approaches. "Eden! You're bleeding!"

Eden cradles her abdomen, rocking, moaning. "Can you fetch the doctor?"

"I dare not leave you! I'll get a neighbor to go for him."

But as Dasha turns to leave, Eden shrieks. "Ima, something's happening! Help me!"

Her mother sets down the lamp and lifts the hem of her daughter's nightclothes. "Eden, can you stand, walk?"

"I don't know!"

"We mustn't waste any time. I need to get you to the doctor now!"

"I can make it!"

Her mother helps her out of bed, supports her with an arm around her waist, and grabs the lamp with her free hand. They set out, moving as quickly as Eden dares. "God, help me!"

Fortunately, the doctor is only a couple of streets away. Eden is failing, feeling faint, and leaving a trail of blood.

"I hope I'm doing the right thing," her mother says.

"Just get me there!"

Eden's mother raps loudly on the door as both women call out for help. From inside, a woman says, "Udi!"

"I hear it," a man says.

"That doesn't sound good."

"It's never good at this time of the night. I'm getting up."

The doctor opens the door, eyes wide as Eden slumps in her mother's arms. They work together to get her inside and onto a table. As his wife lights lamps, the doctor labors with towels, blankets, cloths. "There's too much blood. I need more—"

"I've nothing more left to stop the flow," his wife says.

"Pull the sheets off the bed!"

Eden fades in and out of consciousness, senses the chaos, catches glimpses of her mother's terrified look, the doctor's wife running, returning, thrusting bundled sheets to her husband.

"Doctor!" Eden's mother says. "I think she's passing out!"

"Just keep breathing," he says. "Big breaths."

"Is she going to be okay?"

"I don't know. Give her water!"

Eden's mother pours a cup of water onto Eden's forehead and into her hair, smoothing it and stroking her. She lifts her head and tries to get her to drink. "Stay with us! Stay with us!"

The doctor tells his wife to press down on her stomach to contract the womb. "There," he says. "There, that's it."

But Eden screeches and struggles to sit up, sobbing. "Did I lose my baby?"

Her mother's pained expression tells her the truth, and Eden dissolves, shaking, devastated. Dasha holds her daughter's hand and head and whispers, "It's all right, little girl," and it strikes Eden that she hasn't called her that since childhood. Sobbing herself now, Dasha adds, "You're going to be all right. I'm here."

Chapter 38

ARRANGEMENTS

Jairus's home, night
Two weeks later

Death and only slightly lesser disappointments have long been the bane of Dr. Udi, but whatever has been going on with the contaminated water lately leaves him spent and depressed. Hardly a day goes by that doesn't include some emergency. Where he used to enjoy welcoming the occasional patient into his home for a variety of successful treatments, now he is summoned frequently and finds himself on the run to someone's home—praying he will get there in time to provide relief.

At least an employee of the local synagogue can pay for his services—not that anyone's inability to do so has ever stopped him. He became a doctor to help people, not to get rich—and it's a good thing. During times of scarcity, when he and his wife have to scramble to put bread on the table themselves, he's still warmed by the thought of providing necessary services.

But even though being called to this house—where the husband and father is an administrator at the synagogue—should result in a paying customer, the doctor worries they may have summoned him too late. As he examines the twelve-year-old, a girl named Nili who appears much younger due to her paleness and lack of appetite, he doesn't like what he finds. Her limbs feel weak and limp, and she's struggling to breathe. He sandwiches her chest, front and back, between his palms. Her heartbeat is faint, her breathing feeble and raspy.

Her parents stand close behind him, peering over his shoulder. The father was straight-faced when he roused the doctor, clearly trying to remain stoic. The mother, Michal, looked petrified when he arrived. "It took everything just to get her breathing again," she whispers.

The doctor had administered the best elixirs he knew for rejuvenating the heart and lungs. Now he carefully lays her back down and stands, pursing his lips.

"So?" Michal says.

How do I tell them? "I'm sorry," he says.

"What do you mean?"

"Her heart has weakened and is not responding. I don't believe I can do any more."

The mother pushes past him and reaches for her daughter. "No! Nili, please! Please, child, just breathe."

"Jairus?" the doctor says quietly.

Jairus just stares. Finally, he says, "Yes?"

Udi beckons him with a nod to follow him from the room. In the hall he whispers, "I know this is painful, but I believe it's time to make arrangements. I'm afraid she won't make it much longer."

"Of course. Yes."

"You know the tradition. Rabbi Judah says even the poorest man in Israel should not hire fewer than two flutes and one professional wailing woman. If you simply tell me how many flutes and how many mourners you can afford, I will make the arrangements for you."

"No."

"Jairus, I'm sorry, but—"

"Please don't make any arrangement until she dies. I will be back soon."

Hurting parents are all very much alike, the doctor decides. Jairus strides off with a purpose, looking belligerent. He marches outside and doesn't even shut the door.

Chapter 39

AN EFFORT

Simon's home, morning

Eden busies herself in the kitchen, slicing vegetables, as Simon dresses. He appears, cinching his belt, slipping into sandals, grabbing a knapsack. He reaches around her to take an apple, then tries to wrap a piece of bread in a kerchief. She can't help but notice he fails to completely secure his food, which means it'll likely grow dry and stale before he gets to it. Normally she would wrap his lunch for him, but she's not appearing eager to help him with anything these days, and he's noticed.

Simon has said something about working on the city cistern—which doesn't sound like a specialty of his, though she's grateful someone is on it. He grabs his bag of tools and heads for the door, plainly not interested in a farewell kiss because she hasn't responded well to such lately. But suddenly he stops and turns to face her, forcing her to look up from her work.

"Whatever it is," he says, "you are right. And I'm sorry."

"Whatever it is?" she says, with a slight shake of her head.

"Yes."

Eden shakes her head and turns back to her work. He stands there a moment and finally slogs out, head down.

Chapter 40

LEGACY

Zebedee's house, Capernaum

John loves being home. His parents have always been fun, and though he and big brother James still squabble like youngsters, there's no one he'd rather be with. Salome is working at the counter, and John grabs food as soon as she's finished preparing it.

Big James enters, yawning. "Morning, Ima," he says.

"How did you sleep?" she asks.

"Much better! More room to stretch out. Nice to wake up without Thomas's feet in my face, now that he's gone."

"You could have reversed," John says, "and slept with your feet toward the door like Thomas and I did."

"But then I'd have to wake up to his face and morning breath."

"Boys," Salome says, "don't start."

John says, "And he still claims he's not jealous of my trip with Thomas."

Zebedee breezes in. "Any word from Thomas?"

"Abba," John says, "he left only yesterday. He's probably not even made it to Tel-Dor yet."

"Ah, of course. His intended, Ramah, she makes wine, right?"

"Made," James says. "I don't know what she does now. I think she's learning to read."

"She's still a vintner," John says, "even when she's not making wine."

"That's right," Zebedee says. "She ran a business that required making things that taste good. She's got a great palate. Is she an honest woman?"

"What in heaven's name?" Salome says.

"How about Mary and Tamar?" Zebedee says. "Do you find them trustworthy?"

"They follow Jesus," James says. "That's enough. Say, is this, whatever it is you're doing, becoming more than just a hobby?"

"Yeah," John says, "you've been spending a lot of time …"

"And money," James adds.

Salome stops what she's doing and gives Zebedee a knowing glance.

"I sold the boat!" Zebedee says, grinning.

"What!" John says. "Why did you do that?"

"Fishing is hard work! It was always hard. But now the merchants are up earlier and earlier."

"Is it because we left?" James says.

"Boys," Zebedee says, beckoning them close and putting his hands on their shoulders. "My father fished his whole life and taught me to fish. He raised six kids, went to temple two times a week, and died waiting for the Messiah." He grows emotional. "Then I took over and turned his boat into a fleet, raised you boys, fed a hundred families, went to temple, and waited for the Messiah till I was old."

"You're not old," John says.

"My legacy was waiting for the Messiah as much as it was fishing. I fished only to make ends meet until you got your *real* jobs. Your whole lives led to this. He chose *you*! Now I'm free to try something new too, right?"

John finds James has the same idea he does, and they both hug their father. "Yes."

"Wish me luck," Zebedee says, strapping on his money belt.

John asks where he's going.

"I'm going to buy an olive grove! Can you believe it?"

Chapter 41

A DIFFERENT DOCTOR

Capernaum countryside road, morning

Nathanael considers Zee fascinating and has since he first met him. Imagine a real-life Zealot who has chosen to follow a man of peace! Zee still seems to bubble with hyper-acute rage, as if looking for action. And strong? While Nathanael struggles with his yoke containing two full buckets of water from the remote well, Zee strides along, his yoke bouncing in rhythm.

Nathanael can't stifle his curiosity or his tongue. "Let me ask you something, Zee. Now that you're no longer a Zealot, do you still feel murderous?"

Zee stops and turns to face Nathanael, and his buckets stop bobbing. "Your capacity to say anything that comes to mind, at any time, is astonishing."

C'mon, Nathanael thinks, *everyone knows a true Zealot is trained for combat, for assassination, for killing.* "I don't say *anything* that comes to mind. I just say what I think everyone else is already thinking. I have strange thoughts all the time. I don't share those."

Zee, appearing stupefied, seems to search Nathanael's eyes.

"Like right now," Nathanael adds.

"Say what's on your mind then."

"Well, I don't want you to kill me."

"That's the strange thought?"

"No."

Zee appears annoyed, as if he's given up trying to figure out Nathanael. They continue walking a few paces, and Nathanael decides to explain himself. "I asked about your murderous tendencies because I saw Simon with a Roman officer yesterday."

"He was being questioned?"

"No. In fact, it looked like they were just having a chat."

"Simon would never betray us," Zee says.

"I know—but it was strange to see him with a Roman. I mean, they attack us. And tax us."

"And men like Matthew used to collect those taxes. But you've seen what Jesus does to—" Zee stops abruptly and stares. He unshoulders his yoke and approaches a trail of blood.

"Don't touch it," Nathanael says, "or you'll be uncl—"

"I know." Zee crouches and looks closely. "It's fresh." He follows the trail across the road. Nathanael sets down his burden and follows cautiously at a distance until Zee reaches a thicket, then he catches up. Zee pushes through the brush, seeming to deftly follow the blood trail as a dog would.

They come upon a woman lying under a bush, a mess of her belongings strewn about her. Zee crouches close. Nathanael asks, "Is she dead?"

Zee signals for silence, but too late.

"Who are you?" the woman says.

"What's happened?" Zee asks. "Did someone hurt you?"

"I'm not hurt."

"You need a doctor," Zee says. "Does your head feel light? Can you see clearly?"

"Listen," she says, "you don't have to help me—"

"Nathanael," Zee says, "go into town and get a doctor."

"No!" the woman cries. "Don't. I spent all my money on doctors."

Nathanael grabs Zee's arm. "Maybe *he* could help."

"Not now. Master has not been out to the public." In truth, Nathanael has no more idea exactly where Jesus is than Zee does.

"What are you talking about?" the woman says.

"We are followers of a rabbi," Nathanael says. "A very special one. A different kind of doctor."

"No," she says. "Different kinds of doctors make things only worse."

"She doesn't want this," Zee says. "And it's not safe for him right now."

Zee's right, Nathanael knows. "We're sorry. Shalom."

As they move away, the woman sits up, looking alert and intent. "Wait! This rabbi of yours, you say he's special?"

"The most," Nathanael says.

"Is he the man who healed a paralytic man at the Pool of Bethesda?"

Zee smiles. "And so many more."

"You *know* him?" she says.

"We are his followers," Nathanael says.

The woman bites her lip, and tears roll. "Where is he now?"

Nathanael shoots Zee an uncertain glance.

"I won't talk to him until I'm clean, of course," she says, "but I just need a moment. And if he's the holy man they say he is, I don't need to waste his time. I could just touch his garment."

"That's a superstition," Nathanael says.

"Maybe with other holy men," she says. "But I'm not talking about them. I'm talking about him. I've heard what he can do, and I listened to his sermon. I'm talking about him. *His* garment."

"I understand," Zee says.

"Please!" she says. "I've been shunned by my family, banned from the synagogue. I have no one. I've come all this way and have been waiting so long to meet him."

Nathanael gives Zee another look, then says to her, "You could help us look for him."

The woman nods, plainly excited, and quickly gathers her things.

Chapter 42

NEGOTIATING

Capernaum countryside

Mary is still trying to decide what to make of Tamar, the radiant, ebony Egyptian. The woman clearly knows her own mind and isn't afraid to express herself, and Mary has learned that a person's strength can also sometimes manifest as her weakness. The forthrightness that made Tamar so bold as to direct her companions to burrow through Zebedee's roof and lower their paralyzed friend to where Jesus could heal him also sometimes makes her come across as brash.

Still, Mary considers Tamar a dear sister and plainly devoted to Jesus. And she certainly knows her stuff about olives and olive trees and oil. It's great to have her along, with Zebedee and Judas, as the four of them tour a yellow, dying olive tree grove they have just purchased from a man now standing off to the side, counting the money Judas has paid him.

"It's funny," Judas whispers to the others. "I've never bought land to use for anything. Only to sell it again."

"Were you feeling sentimental when you negotiated the price?" Tamar asks, her gentle way—Mary decides—of needling Judas.

"We got a pretty good deal," Judas says. "Considering the size with the trees and all."

"Dying trees," Mary says.

"Are they?" Judas says.

"They're pitiful!" Tamar says.

"If the trees are bad," he says, "then why did we do this?"

"It's within the budget we set," Mary says. "And we're going to make the most of it."

"It's exciting!" Zebedee says. "Isn't it?"

"We need answers," Tamar says. She turns to the seller. "You! Hey!"

"Tamar!" Mary says.

"Why are these trees dying?"

"It's my abba," the man says. "He's sick. He didn't tend to them."

"See?" Zebedee says. "The land's fine. Just needs caring for."

Judas asks the seller, "Why didn't *you* do it?"

"I was away. I got married."

"But you know how to grow olives?" Judas presses.

He nods. "I grew up in this field."

Judas nods at Zebedee. "How much to teach him?"

"What are you doing, Judas?" Mary says.

"Well," the seller says, "I have to look after my father. But I could stay on until next harvest—for seventy percent."

"Ha!" Judas says. "Thanks anyway."

"Fifty," the man says. "But I'll work only one day a week for that."

"Thirty percent," Judas says, "two days a week, and we don't pay if I have to replant—say, any more than five of these trees."

"Deal," the man says, and walks away.

"What just happened?" Zebedee says.

"Looks like you have a boss," Tamar says.

"I have a boss?" Zebedee says.

Capernaum courtyard

Simon has to admit he feels conspicuous, working shoulder to shoulder with a Roman on the cistern. But someone has to get it fixed, and no one else stepped up. He and Gaius use a lever and pulley to hoist a heavy stone into place above the tunnel.

"On my count," Gaius says. "One, two, three!"

Simon mirrors Gaius as he pushes with all his might until the block finally drops into place. They both whoop and shake hands with a smack, the bigger man making Simon's hand sting. "Oh, Styx!" Gaius says. "Were you not supposed to touch me?"

"That may be true, actually," Simon says.

They sit next to each other, panting and dusting off their hands. "Don't you refer to us as dogs or something?" Gaius asks.

"You call *us* dogs. Among other things. Rats. Vermin."

"Well, you wouldn't drink from my flask last night. Acted like I'd offered to kiss you or something."

"Kissing or drinking from the same vessel is not the same as working together to solve a public health crisis that affects both of our communities."

Simon pulls out his canteen, and Gaius grabs his own. "So, we are allowed to—"

Simon hesitantly clinks his canteen with Gaius's and whispers, "Blessed are You, Lord our God, King of the universe, who creates the fruit of the vine." Gaius rolls his eyes as they both drink. Simon stares at the clouds. "It didn't work, by the way," he says.

"What's that?"

"Telling her she was right."

"Did you mean it?" Gaius says. "Or were you just saying it to placate her? There's an art to this sort of thing."

"How could I mean it? I don't even know what's wrong! I tried to sound sincere."

"Simon, it doesn't work if you don't know what you're conceding, no matter how sincere. Is there another woman?"

"No."

"Are the kids all right?"

"We don't have kids yet."

"Hmm. Well, you shouldn't be taking marriage advice from me anyway, that's for sure."

"You offered it!"

"I just meant that line has worked for me, many times." Gaius stands. "Come on. Let's get back to it." He holds out a hand. "Shovel."

Simon tosses him one, and as they work, Simon says, "What about you? You have kids?"

"Two. Well, I should say two children in the house. My son and a servant boy the same age. They're friends."

Simon shakes his head. "Child slavery," he teases. "And you wonder why our people find you distasteful."

"His mother worked for us. She died giving birth, so we're raising him as our own. Is that so barbaric? His options would have been far worse, I assure you."

"Yes, your merciful kindness is dazzling. You deserve a medal."

Gaius shovels a scoop of gravel at Simon's shins.

"It was just a joke!" Simon says.

"It's not funny! Don't make light of my situation."

"Situation?"

"Just shovel."

"Fine, I went too far."

Gaius appears to be working with a vengeance. "I don't want a *medal.* I want—"

"What?"

"Let's just keep going, Simon. Maybe we can have this cleared by lunch. We're going to need a mason for reassembly. You know one?"

"I might."

But Simon remains captivated by something inscrutable going on with Gaius.

Chapter 43

THE SEARCH

Capernaum synagogue

As Yussif passes Jairus's office, he notices him frantically riffling through scrolls, clearly in distress. "Jairus, are you all right?"

"I don't have time for your pity."

My pity? "What?"

"It's my daughter, Nili. She had a horrible episode in the night, and she's dying. I'm trying to find information on healing and—"

"You daughter is dy—"

"Yes, but—"

"Adonai in heaven!"

"Take me to him, Yussif. You know who I mean." Jairus grabs him by the collar. "I need him *now*!"

"I don't know where he is."

"You have an idea. You know people who know."

The very thought of this terrifies Yussif, yet he longs to help. "His men often don't even know where he is. But I will take you to them."

They rush from the synagogue, Yussif explaining that he'll start with Andrew.

"You're sure he's the one to ask?" Jairus says.

"I'm not. But his brother is one of their leaders, and I saw Andrew with Jesus at Matthew's house once, and at the house of Zebedee, the father of two other followers of his."

Yussif pounds on the door. "Andrew, son of Jonah! This is an emergency! Open up!"

"On temple authority!" Jairus shouts. "Immediately!"

"Andrew!" Yussif roars. "Are you there?"

The door opens.

"Who are you?" Yussif says.

"I'm Judas," a young man says. "I'm new here."

"I'm the Capernaum temple ruler," Jairus says. "I need to speak with Andrew's rabbi."

"He's my rabbi too," Judas says.

"Take me to him."

"I don't know where he is. And even if I did, I wouldn't be at liberty to—"

Judas tries to shut the door, but Jairus slams his palm against it and speaks slowly and firmly. "My daughter, her name is Nili, is twelve years old with beautiful eyes. But they're shut right now, yet not forever. It can't be forever. Do you hear me?"

"I'm very sorry," Judas says.

"If there is blood in your veins, man, you must help me!"

Judas appears to consider this. Finally, he says, "All I can say is that you might consider asking Andrew's brother." He points east.

Matthew's former home

Mary of Magdala is working with Ramah and Tamar, assessing some drapes for auction. Thaddeus barrels in, breathless. "He's back!"

"At Simon's?" Mary says.

"Just this morning."

They all run.

Simon's home

Eden, still at her wits' end with Simon yet wishing he were here, sets a plate before Jesus as he sits with Matthew, Andrew, Little James, and Philip. The others have already eaten, but Jesus has said he is hungry. "And now to the breaking of my fast. Thank you, Eden!"

"Of course," she says, and means it. *What a privilege!*

Little James says, "You fasted while you were away?"

"No, just overnight. Eight hours. Eden, these pickled cucumbers are magnificent."

Eden leans over the counter, lips pursed, choking back her emotions.

"I've been meaning to ask you about fasting," Philip says.

"Something I am very happy not to be doing right now," Jesus says.

"Your cousin John required us to fast at regular intervals," Philip says. "He said the sacrifice of fasting is integral to any serious commitment to God. And you've never once asked us to. I mean, there was that time on Shabbat when we ate the heads of grain in the wheat field, but we were just hungry. That wasn't intentional fasting."

"What are you getting at?" Jesus asks.

"The Pharisees fast all the time."

"And make a big scene out of it," Andrew says. "Even disfiguring their faces."

"If it's such a big deal to them," Philip says, "and they find out we don't do it, don't you think they might, I don't know, use that against us?"

Jesus says, "Can the wedding guests mourn as long as the bridegroom is with them? The days will come when the bridegroom is taken away from them, and then they will fast."

"Taken away?" Matthew says.

"Hold that thought, Matthew," Jesus says. "Philip, when you fasted before, what did you pray for?"

"Your arrival."

"Right," Andrew says, "so what would be the point now?"

"Exactly," Jesus says. "Eden, are you fermenting any wine right at the moment?"

That he has addressed her throws Eden, but how she loves being included in the conversation, despite all that's going on. "Uh, yes, in the back room."

"Little James," Jesus says, "please take down that empty wineskin."

"Ooh," Philip says, "I feel a lesson coming."

"Eden," Jesus says, "the last time you checked on the wine, what was it doing?"

"What it always does at this stage. Sort of bubbling, popping out little plumes of air."

"James," Jesus says, "how does that wineskin feel?"

"Stiff. Not very flexible."

"So, if Eden were to put her new wine into that, what would happen?"

"The old leather can't stretch anymore," Philip says.

"The new wine would keep expanding," Matthew says, "and it would explode."

Jesus says, "New wine must be put into fresh wineskins."

"I'll be the first to admit it," Andrew says. "I don't get it."

Jesus says, "The ways of the kingdom I am bringing into this world will not fit into the old containers or frameworks."

Interesting, Eden thinks, noticing that Philip too is beaming. *He must be starting to get it too.*

"Being revolutionary is fun," Philip says.

Outside

Yussif struggles to keep up with Jairus, who seems to be walking as fast as he can. Far in the distance, at an intersection, Yussif spots Nathanael and an athletic-looking man leading a woman who is limping behind them. "You!" he calls out. The woman cowers, but it's Nathanael Yussif is addressing. "I have seen you with Simon, son of Jonah! Where is your rabbi?"

"I'm sorry?" Nathanael says.

"Take us to him at once!" Jairus shouts.

"I don't know you."

"You know *me*!" Yussif says. "I came to your brothers in Jotapata to warn them—"

"That was you?"

"I took a risk to help you then. We mean no harm to Jesus now." He looks up to see a disciple of Jesus and three women rushing into a home. "Those are his followers." He breaks into a run toward the house, Jairus right behind him and Nathanael and the other man trailing. The poor, limping woman is painstakingly failing to keep up.

Simon's home

Eden welcomes Thaddeus, Mary, Ramah, and Tamar, and as they take their seats, Jesus continues: "So John made you fast, as he preached a message of repentance, and you will again fast when I'm gone. But as I am here, preaching a message of salvation, now is not the time."

Little James says, "I still want to know what you mean by *gone*."

"What have we missed?" Ramah says.

Eden starts as two Pharisees burst through the door without so much as a knock. Jesus and the disciples quickly stand. "Shalom, Rabbi," one says, and tells the other, "This is him."

"Shalom, Yussif," Jesus says.

The other approaches Jesus and drops to his knees. "I know you," he says.

"Do you?" Jesus reaches for him. "Stand with me."

"Yes. I've heard and I've read accounts from, aah, someone I trust. You do miracles, yes? You are a healer?"

"Of more than just physical maladies," Jesus says. "Yes."

"Please. My daughter is dying."

"I'm so sorry."

"But come and lay your hand on her, and she will live."

"It's all right, Zee." Jesus turns back to Jairus. "You haven't met me, yet you have this much faith that I can heal your daughter?"

Jairus places his hand over his heart. "I know you. Please!"

Jesus looks deep into his eyes and nods. "Take me to her."

Eden looks on in wonder, feeling betrayed that Jesus wasn't there when her baby needed healing.

Chapter 44

ONE TOUCH

Capernaum courtyard

Simon enjoys sweating in the sun, even if it is with a Roman. He's already weary of Gaius's cracks about Judaism, but he *is* impressed with the man's work ethic. No one ever doubted such in a fisherman, but many of Simon's compatriots speculated on how easy it might have been to be a centurion in a gaudy red outfit astride a mighty steed. It's good to know Gaius could shed his helmet and weapon and wield a shovel, swing a hammer, or handle a trowel.

As the two men kneel and lean over the edge of the walls of the cistern, working to coat them with lime plaster, Simon breaks the silence. "You have a religion?"

"Who, me?" Gaius says.

"You Romans. You have gods, festivals, no?"

"Oh, sure. But not anything like you. Just parties mostly."

"We have parties too," Simon says.

"From what I can tell, they don't look as fun as ours."

"Depends on your definition of parties," Simon says. "Another thing we have is prophecies."

"So I'm told."

"And I'm beginning to think I'm living in one."

"What, with that preacher?"

"No, with this cistern. Our prophet Jeremiah said, 'My people have committed two evils. They have forsaken Me, the fountain of living waters, and hewed out cisterns for themselves, broken cisterns that can hold no water.'"

"Sounds like a riddle," Gaius says.

"You'd make a good Jew. We love riddles. We call them metaphors."

"So have you?"

"Have we what?"

"Forsaken your god of water," Gaius says. "It sounds like your god identifies as a source of water, and the broken cisterns are a sign that you've turned your back on him."

"We have only one God. Of water, fire, wind, and everything else."

"Efficient," Gaius says. "Maybe a little boring."

"It's a lot easier than having a pantheon of gods."

"They're not so hard to keep track of. Jupiter, Juno, Mars, Mercury, Neptune, Venus, Apollo, Diana—"

"All right! Stop! I'm exhausted already. And you have to sacrifice to all of them?"

"That depends on what we want. Safe travel? Mercury. Victory in war? Mars. Fertility? Juno."

"A big catch of fish?"

"Neptune."

"Peace in a relationship?"

"Vesta," Gaius says. "Goddess of hearth and home."

"What's going on?" Simon says as people start rushing by in waves.

"Where are you going?" Gaius demands of one.

"The preacher!" a passerby Simon recognizes as Barnaby says. "They say he's going to perform a miracle! You should be there!"

Simon drops his trowel and leaps to his feet, finding John and Big James amid the fray. "What is this?"

"We don't know any more than you do," Big James says, not breaking stride.

"Come on!" John says.

Simon joins them as Gaius puts on his helmet and straps on his sword.

Jesus' trek to Jairus's house has become chaotic, the very thing Gaius has been charged with avoiding by Praetor Quintus himself. Crowds press around Jesus, reaching for him, shouting questions, demanding explanations.

Zee works feverishly with Thaddeus and Philip to keep the throng at bay. The three women—Mary, Ramah, and Tamar—appear to be struggling to keep up, but they're quickly overwhelmed by the clawing pilgrims.

Matthew hangs back with Little James to stay with Eden. "There are too many people," he says. "Where's Simon?"

"Something I've been asking myself a lot lately," Eden says.

Little James appears concerned with what she's said before he's knocked to the ground by a rushing pilgrim.

"Little James!" Matthew cries out, rushing to help him up.

But he's nearly already standing again. "I'm fine. It's all right. An accident."

Up ahead of Jesus, Zee tries to make space for Veronica as she hobbles among the crowd. But then he locks eyes with an armed Zealot. At a time like this, he wishes he had kept his knife. Veronica stumbles and falls. Zee moves to help her, staying alert for his enemy, prepared to defend himself with only his hands and feet. He scans the crowd again, but the Zealot is gone. *Trained well,* Zee thinks.

Veronica is on her feet again, and Zee is struck by her focus, her singular mind and purpose. She gathers herself and calls out, "Teacher!"

Zee knows there's no way Jesus has heard her. No one has in this din. She keeps shuffling along, appearing determined not to let the miracle worker pass and leave her behind. But suddenly she stops, presses her knees together, and hunches forward. "No, no, no!" It's clear she's bleeding again and trying to stop it. Her eyes dart everywhere, likely terrified someone will notice. "Please," she moans. "No. Not now."

Jesus and the crowd pass her, and Zee can tell she's ready to shout again. But she gathers her clothes around her, apparently frantic to hide any hint of blood. "One thread," she whines. "One thread … Just the fringe. One touch."

Zee is relieved to see Simon, John, and Big James force their way through to join him and Nathanael, Thaddeus, and Philip to surround Jesus. Still on the lookout for the armed Zealot, Zee notices the Roman Primi Gaius standing at the edge of the crowd, observing. It's as if he's decided not to intervene—yet.

Veronica reaches out, but the man from the tent city—the one who had called her unclean when she tried to deliver his clothes—blocks her path and shouts, "You! I know you! Get away from him!"

"No! No! Stop it! Please!"

The man grabs Yussif, who is trying to keep up with Jesus. "Rabbi, this woman bleeds! She is unclean! We removed her—"

"Please!" Veronica wails. "Please! I promise I won't touch him. I just need to—"

"Woman, please," Yussif says. "We can help you, but not now."

"No, no, no, please, just a moment, just his garment!"

As she presses forward, Yussif backs away from her, hands raised. Zee sees her dive between Big James and Thaddeus. She swipes at Jesus and falls, brushing his cloak as it trails behind him. Veronica lands on the ground with a thud.

Jesus stops and shudders, as if—it seems to Zee—he's been punched in the stomach. The entire crowd immediately falls silent, all eyes on him.

"What's wrong?" Simon asks. "What's happened?"

"Who touched me?" Jesus says.

Who touched you? Zee thinks. *What kind of question is that?* At his feet, Veronica looks transformed, her face luminous. From under her dress she pulls a large cloth. It's spotless. She whimpers and smiles.

"Everyone back!" John shouts.

"I asked a question!" Jesus says. "Who touched me?"

"Master," Simon says, "the crowds are pressing in all around you, and you ask who touched you? They *all* have."

"Someone touched me. Power has gone out from me." Jesus addresses the crowd. "Whoever touched me, come forward!"

Yussif steps toward Jesus. "Teacher—"

"It was me," Veronica says from her knees, and murmurs ripple through the crowd. "Only the fringe of your garment, I promise. You are not unclean."

"Why my garment?"

Weeping, she says, "I'm sorry. I know I should have asked. But if you touched me, it would make you unclean according to the Law. I was sick—for twelve years. I bled, and no one could stop it." The crowd gasps and pulls back. "I believed if I could just touch a piece of your clothing—and I was right. I was right. Thank you."

"Who told you I could heal?"

She appears barely able to get the words out. "A man from the pool."

My brother! Zee realizes.

"And he was right," she says. "The blood has ceased."

Jesus kneels and gazes into her eyes. "My daughter."

She shakes her head. "I'm no one's daughter anymore."

"Look up."

She peeks up at him.

"Yes, you are," he says. "Daughter."

She bursts into tears.

"It wasn't my piece of clothing that healed you."

"But it was instant. I felt it right away."

"I know. But it wasn't this. It was your faith."

Yussif steps close again. "Teacher, she was bleeding so long. We can take her to—"

"She is clean," Jesus says. He whispers to Veronica, "You have blessed me today. I know, my daughter—I know it has been a fight for you for so long. You must be so—"

"Exhausted," she says.

"Now go in peace. Your faith has made you well. I wish I could stay longer, but I have some business to attend to. Someone else has faith like yours." He cups her face. "I'm glad we found each other."

He stands and addresses the crowd. "Please! I promise I will speak to all of you soon. And my students and I will care for your needs. But right now, there is something very important that I must do, and I kindly ask you to let me go so I can take care of this urgent issue. I promise I will see you, but right now is not possible. Thank you for your understanding."

As the crowd begins to disperse, Jesus tells Zee, "You stay back and help them back to their tents. And please, be kind to them." He turns. "Nathanael, Thad, and Philip, make sure no one bothers her. Simon, Big James, John, come with us."

Yussif follows them.

Gaius, still in his work clothes, studies the crowd as they flow past him on either side.

As the assigned disciples stand guard on either side of Veronica, Mary of Magdala rushes to kneel beside her. "Do you have everything you need?"

"I could use a knife," the woman says.

"A what?"

Veronica whispers in her ear, whereupon Mary says, "Philip, could we borrow your knife?"

"My knife?"

"Please …"

"Sure."

Chapter 45

LITTLE LAMB

Capernaum street

Despite his exhaustion after teaching the disciples and healing the woman, Jesus returns to the matter at hand—the man who has expressed such belief and faith, even though his daughter is dying. The rest of the crowd has huddled behind Jesus and the synagogue official, who has introduced himself as Jairus. They're quickly joined by Big James, John, and Simon. Jesus notices Yussif not far behind.

Jairus says, "Looks like I indeed came to the right man."

Jesus smiles. "Between you and her, it's been quite a big day of faith. How far are we going?"

"It's just up ahead," Jairus says, then stops. "Do you hear that?"

Flutes and wailing. And a priest approaches Jesus, his jaw set.

"No!" Jairus says. "What is this?"

"Jairus," the priest says, "while you were gone—"

"No! Why am I hearing mourners and flutes? I said not to do that! She was sick, but—"

"Your daughter passed away, Jairus. We had to act quickly and make arrangements ..."

"No, no! I was getting the teacher! He was going to heal her! He—"

"I know who you are," the priest says, looking down his nose at Jesus. He turns back to Jairus. "Let's not trouble him anymore. Michal is with Nili's body."

Jesus closes his eyes, then looks up.

"No!" Jairus says, voice quavering. "I was getting Jesus! I went as fast as I could. I—"

Jesus places a hand on Jairus's shoulder and looks deep into his eyes. "Don't be afraid. Only believe. She will be well."

"Jairus," the priest says, "let's go in." He turns to Jesus. "Please stay here. We will—"

"She will be well," Jesus tells the priest, nudging Jairus into the house, followed by Big James, John, Simon, and even Yussif. They come upon two flute players performing a dirge as two women wail and repeat, "Nili! Nili!"

"All of you," Jesus says, "stop it."

One of the flute players stops, looking baffled.

"I said stop!" Jesus says, and the noise ceases. "What are you doing?"

One of the wailers points upstairs. "There's a girl—"

The other says, "She's dead."

"Go away," Jesus says, "for she isn't dead but sleeping."

The mourners fall silent, then break out into laughter. The priest enters and demands, "What is all this laughing?"

"He said she's only asleep," one of the flautists says.

"What a cruel thing to say," a wailing woman adds.

John steps up. "Do you know who you're talking to?"

"If you were a member of the family," the priest tells Jesus, "I'd invite you to see just how dead she is. What are you, a necromancer? Shame on you for saying such a ridiculous thing."

"Everyone out," Jesus says.

Everyone stares, but no one moves. "You heard him!" Jairus says.

"Boys," Jesus says, "take everyone outside."

The disciples approach the mourners, one of whom says, "We were paid to play—"

Simon digs a thumb under the man's shoulder blade, rendering him helpless as he hustles out, the others following quickly.

The solemn priest confronts Jesus again. "You listen to me right now—"

Jesus looks to Yussif, who puts his arm around the man and says, "Come. Let's give them a moment."

Jesus, his three closest disciples, and Jairus reach Nili's bedroom and find the girl lying still, a blanket covering her face, her mother kneeling near the foot of the bed, weeping. Michal stands and faces them. "Where were you, Jairus?"

"I was finding this man."

"She's dead, and you were gone! Why would you just leave us like this?"

He grabs her arm as Jesus moves past them. "Trust me!" Jairus says. "Please trust me. And trust him."

"For what? She's—"

Jesus lifts the sheet from Nili and takes her hand. Again he closes his eyes and then looks to heaven. Finally, he whispers in her ear, "Little lamb, arise."

Nili opens her eyes, sits up, and looks around. Jairus and Michal rush to her as she stands.

"Everyone in this room, please listen carefully to me," Jesus says. "Simon, James, John, Jairus, Michal—and Nili—none of you are to say a word about this to anyone under any circumstances. Do I make myself clear? *No one.* Not even to the others."

Simon, John, and Big James say in unison, "Yes, Rabbi."

"It is not time yet for the commotion that will result," Jesus says, "and none of you need the attention. Not all of it will be good."

Jairus, clearly overcome, says, "Whatever you command, we will do."

"Nili," Jesus says, "you must be hungry."

She nods.

Jesus reaches the door as Michal steps up to him, wiping her eyes. "How can I thank you? I don't understand what you've done, but—"

"You're welcome. Let's get Nili something to eat first, yes?"

She laughs through her tears and takes Nili by the hand. As Jesus starts to follow them out, Jairus says, "Thank you. I don't know what to say other than that."

"Thank you for your faith," Jesus says. "I pray more in the synagogue will share it."

Chapter 46

SWIMMING

Capernaum alley

Veronica is so full of joy she can barely contain herself. She presses her back against the wall of a building and slides down to sit. With Philip's knife, she slices through the ropes that have for twelve years bound all the absorbent materials so crucial for her condition. The construct has been her only means of hiding her ailment, and even it didn't always hold.

Dare she hope that she can now cut away from her knees the cumbersome layers of ridiculous robes with which she has had to cover herself for so long? Yes, she decides. Jesus would not have healed her only temporarily. She feels whole. She feels young. And when she hacks through the material, Veronica can only gape at miraculously healthy legs. She gathers up all the extraneous remnants. Rising, she goes looking for somewhere to dump it all.

Perfect. A blacksmith shop bears a roaring cauldron that will incinerate and obliterate her former necessities. With a flourish, she stuffs everything into it and, with long-awaited finality, tosses the rope apparatus atop it all and watches the flames lick and then devour every trace of her past.

Now, what to do and where to go? Little strikes her as more inviting than the Sea of Galilee itself. How long has it been since she has frolicked in the water with no worry of exposing her terrible secret or ruining her accoutrements? As the last vestiges of her previous life smolder, she heads toward the water. Veronica feels lithe and limber, enjoying every step of freedom. Freedom from shame. Freedom from fetters.

She walks faster and faster, finally breaking into a sprint—something she had never hoped to do again—and finds herself laughing and crying, feeling the grass with her bare feet. At last she reaches the sandy shore and sheds her outer layer of clothing as she dashes into the water, rolling, roiling, relishing a body no longer hunched, squeezed, or curled in upon itself.

Finally, Veronica turns onto her back and basks in the sunshine sparkling off the water. This, she decides, must be a taste of heaven on earth.

Outside Jairus's house, the priest steps before Jesus and the three disciples as all his other followers and the women look on. Even the Roman, Gaius, watches from a few paces away.

"I don't know what may or may not have happened in there," the priest says, "but did you touch a corpse?"

"Go see for yourself," Jesus says.

"I've also been told you touched a woman who was bleeding."

"She wasn't bleeding anymore."

"How could you know for sure?"

Jesus notices Mary Magdalene's and Tamar's looks of disgust.

Simon says, "Are we really having this conversation?"

"You have no right to question him," John says.

The priest is focused on Jesus. "You and anyone you have touched are ceremonially unclean until sundown and must carry out the rituals of purification."

Jesus eyes the man. "What are your intentions if that doesn't happen?"

"I'll report you to the Sanhedrin."

Jesus scans his entourage, which includes Simon, John, and Big James. "Who among you has touched either me or the woman who was formerly bleeding?"

One by one, they slowly raise their hands.

"Come with me," Jesus says, "and let's get the others."

They leave the priest agape.

Moments later they reach the Sea of Galilee, where Jesus espies Veronica floating on her back. "You there!" he calls out, wading in with everyone else right behind him.

Veronica bolts upright and stands in the shallow water. "Oh, no! Did I make you unclean? Did the priest send you?"

"He thinks he did," Jesus says. "We just wanted to go for a swim."

"The joke's on him," Simon says.

"We wanted to find you, Veronica," Mary says.

"To see how you're doing," Jesus adds.

"Thank you! I-I know I disturbed you."

"It was a welcome disturbance," Jesus says. "My favorite kind."

Big James shoves John under the water. Simon joins the fray as the three tussle, laughing.

"If you'll excuse me, Veronica," Jesus says, "I can't miss this." He swims toward the splashing as the rest of the men join in.

Mary and Tamar stay with Veronica, pressing in close to her. "Twelve years," Tamar says. "How did you survive?"

"It's a long story."

"Good stories usually are," Mary says.

As the men leap on each other's shoulders for a chicken fight and the women remain with Veronica, Eden watches from the shore, grief-stricken and deep in thought, a tear rolling down her cheek.

PART 6
Why?

Chapter 47

STRATEGIC ACQUAINTANCES

A forest clearing, pre-dawn

A yellow serpent slithers in the grass past clusters of sleeping disciples and pauses before the last man, Simon. Finally it creeps into the woodland, where Jesus kneels on all fours, his forehead pressed to the ground, fists clenched, praying. Jesus raises a fist and slams the ground.

The serpent closes in and stops. And Jesus turns to face the snake.

A mansion bedroom, early morning

Realizing the snake was just a dream, Claudia bolts upright, gasping in her lush four-poster bed, draped in finery and appointed with plush pillows. She wipes moisture from her forehead and remembers the days when she dreamt of residing in such luxury. So much for childish dreams and prayers to the gods. She got more than she bargained for when she won the heart of the young governor—his idiosyncrasies, his ego, his politics, his incessant maneuvering to be noticed by Rome.

But what has awakened her? A wail. An animal? She rises, pulls a shawl over her shoulders, and steps out onto a broad balcony. The howl, she now realizes, was human and came from the courtyard below, where a fourth crucifix lies on the ground next to three already standing. A man hangs on each, bloody and dying. The one being pinned to the fourth rails and shrieks as hammered spikes tear the flesh of his hands and feet. Roman guards bark at him to keep quiet. Not a view Claudia would advertise, were she trying to sell the estate.

"You'll catch your death out there," her husband says from their dressing room.

"Four more, Pontius?" she says. "And so early in the morning?"

He laces his sandals and pads out. "What time of day is ideal for dying? I'm a governor, not a philosopher."

"It's excessive," she says. "The people already resent you, and Tiberius will be loath to hear of another insurrection."

"Four convicted revolutionaries," Pontius says in the genteel manner Claudia wishes he would reserve for his subjects. "Jewish Zealots, Darling. Leave the governing to me, hm? Go back to bed."

"I haven't been sleeping well."

"Then amuse yourself. Go pick some flowers."

"Where are you going?" she asks.

"I have a date."

She raises a brow. "Oh?"

"An old friend."

"You don't have friends."

"I do so!"

"You have valuable contacts, people you find useful. Strategic acquaintances."

He smiles as if proud of her for understanding the game. He turns to the mirror and drapes a laurel on his head. "Maybe *you* should be governor."

Claudia turns back toward the bed, watching as he clamps above his biceps a gold armlet—shaped and stamped with the snake from her dream.

Chapter 48

SHARPENING IRON

The shore of the Sea of Galilee, midday

Despite all he has learned and how he feels he has grown since following Jesus—largely, he knows, by being forced to interact with his fellow disciples and the women—Matthew remains frustrated. Oh, he has good days, days when the things Jesus tells the disciples make sense. Days when Jesus patiently explains things to him alone. Days when Mary of Magdala flashes that warm smile and treats him as a treasured friend. And days when he feels privileged to spend any time at all with Philip, the one who actually seems to get him.

Today, however, he's looking for Zee, with whom he has been paired again. It's been good to get to know the former Zealot, though *former* doesn't always seem the best descriptor of the man. Zee remains obsessed with staying in shape, honing his body, being prepared for anything. He seems a bubbling mix of alertness and what? Eagerness. Matthew is convinced Zee would love any excuse to use every skill he has mastered.

Zee seems to have accepted Matthew, though he probably bites his tongue to keep from raising the issue of how he could have ever been a dirty, rotten scum of a tax collector. *But there I go,* Matthew thinks, *putting words in his mouth.*

Matthew finds Zee with his back to several of their compatriots, all sitting and working feverishly on weapons, of all things. This is right up Zee's alley, but Matthew is puzzled. As Big James sharpens an axe, John sharpens a dagger, and Little James and Thaddeus each polish a sword. If he didn't know better, Matthew would think Simon looks hungover as he grinds the tip of a spear. He must not be sleeping well—something on his mind.

Philip sharpens what looks like one of Eden's chopping knives. Nathanael strops a straight razor on a piece of leather, while Andrew affixes an arrowhead to a thin, wooden shaft.

Matthew has to ask. "What are you all doing?"

But they ignore him as if he's asked a stupid question, probably wondering what it looks like they're doing. "You know," Nathanael says, "John and Thomas healed a blind person."

"I'd love to do it again," John says.

So, Matthew realizes, they're implying he's blind. So, he tries again, a little louder. "I can see you're sharpening weapons. But why?"

Nathanael responds. "Some of us are worried, Matthew. Things are becoming serious. More people have heard. You were there when he healed the bleeding woman."

"Of course. I wrote it all down. But I did not see what happened in the house."

"I said I would give you the details later," John says.

"I just don't want you to forg—"

"I won't forget," John says.

"Crowds were pressing in," Big James says. "A hobbling woman was able to grab him."

"Only the fringe of his garment, James," Philip says.

"The power went out of him without his consent," James says.

"It looked like he was gut punched," Thaddeus says.

"He didn't say it hurt," Little James says.

"No, it just looked like it," Nathanael says. "If we'd had blades, we could have hurt her."

"We might have had to," Zee says, still facing the other way and sharpening his own weapon.

"Well," Big James says, glaring at his brother, "one of us *did* have a blade. He just neglected to use it."

"I was distracted!" John says. "You know I don't do well in crowds."

"So, what if he did have a blade?" Nathanael says. "We can't just stab people who get close to Jesus."

John glares at Big James and throws his sharpening rock to the ground.

"Aah, the irony," Simon says. "As iron sharpens iron …"

"Don't you dare finish that sentence," John says, but Matthew has already finished it in his mind. … *so one person sharpens another.*

"Nathanael has a point," Philip says. "If we had kept the crowd at bay, that poor woman would not have been healed."

Still not looking up from his work, Zee says, "I assessed that he was in no real danger."

"Jesus just wanted to know who touched him," Little James says.

"He praised her faith," Philip says. "He called her 'Daughter.'"

"Philip," Simon says, "is that one of Eden's knives?"

"Yeah."

Thaddeus says, "I don't think all this worrying about protecting Jesus is necessary."

"You just—asked her for it?" Simon says.

"Yeah," Philip says. "She mentioned it hadn't been sharpened in a long time."

Simon glowers at him.

John laughs. "I understand, Simon. You've been busy, what with all the time you spend with your Roman."

His Roman? Matthew thinks.

"Gaius puts his sandals on one foot at a time," Simon says. "Just like you and me."

"Gaius?" Matthew says.

"Yes," Simon says. "We're fixing the cistern. Maybe these ingrates would rather keep trekking to the old well."

"Gaius is not an evil man," Matthew says, knowing him better than anyone here.

"Oh, wonderful," John says. "Now we have two devoted fans of a terrorist."

Matthew can't let this go on. "He has been ruthless, yes. But he is not like other Romans I have met."

Big James weighs in. "Associating with him could hurt our reputation with the pilgrims in the tent city."

"We have a reputation?" Little James asks.

Philip says, "Reputation has never seemed a priority of Jesus.'"

Matthew remains frustrated, distracted, stuck on a conundrum. "If you're all sharpening weapons, should I be too?"

"But Matthew," Simon says, "you have the sharpest weapon of all."

Matthew wonders if he's being made light of again.

"His wit?" John says.

"His mind," Simon says. "And your pen, Matthew. You could always poke somebody in the eye with it in a pinch."

"I could not do that," Matthew says, knowing he has missed something here.

"I'll show you," Simon says, picking up a rusty blade.

Nathanael approaches Zee, who is still working on his dagger. Zee says, "If you need something sharpened, leave it there."

"Tell me about the one you're sharpening," Nathanael says, knowing the story of Jesus' having tossed Zee's Zealot-issued weapon into the river.

"This is a dagger," Zee says.

"Why don't you sharpen a kitchen knife? Or a utility knife? Or an axe?"

"A dagger is more of a weapon, Nathanael."

"You could turn my prayer cap into a weapon, Zee. Why did you choose a dagger?"

Zee stops working and appears to scan the others—who continue to talk amongst themselves. He sighs. "I'm not sure I can trust you with information."

Can't trust me? Nathanael locks eyes with him. "Fine. How about Little James?" He beckons him. As they pass, Nathanael whispers, "See what you can find out. Zee trusts you."

Little James enjoys being needed. His own physical challenges limit his contributions to the group, but if he can be of service through personal diplomacy …

"What's going on, Zee?" he asks.

"Members of the Order have tracked me to Capernaum."

"Dangerous men?"

"Lethal."

"So, tell Jesus."

Zee pauses. "Did you hear me? These men train for a lifetime to do one thing—kill. Jesus cannot be involved."

"But you don't solve problems with a dagger anymore, Zee."

"I will not put Jesus in danger."

"Why not let *him* decide that?"

But before Zee can answer, Little James whirls at the sound of Simon's voice. "Zebedee is doing *what*?" he says.

"He's buying an olive grove," John says. "Judas and the women are there with him."

"What does he want with an olive grove?"

"Our abba is getting out of fishing," Big James says. "He wants to press oil."

"Wait," Simon says. "So, Zebedee is done fishing?"

Big James smiles at him. "Why do you care?"

Chapter 49

DRESSED DOWN

Roman Authority headquarters, Praetor Quintus's office

Gaius feels bred for military service. His strict upbringing imbued in him the realities of the chain of command, of duty, loyalty, service without question, honor, and especially obedience to superiors. As he has matured, however, and moved up the ranks, he has gained confidence in himself, in his own intellect and reasoning. Though he still understands that his very life depends on subordinating himself to his boss, he allows himself to second guess the man—at least silently.

It becomes crystal clear within the first minute of his audience with the praetor that Gaius has been summoned not for any plaudit or recognition for, say, his part in working on the broken cistern. No, he's here as a fall guy to take in the teeth whatever it is Quintus wants to rant about. The boss doesn't even acknowledge the primi's presence. He just stares out the window and finishes an obnoxiously large goblet of wine in one gulp, then clears his throat.

But when Quintus says nothing, Gaius feels obligated to open the conversation, such as it is, to at least let the man know he's there. "Dominus?" he says.

"Do you have brothers, Gaius?" Quintus asks suddenly.

"Yes, sir. One."

"You're Germanic and have only one?"

So, we Germans are known for our fertility? Gaius bites his tongue and sits. "Yes."

"Older or younger?"

"What?"

"Your brother! You know I could have you drawn and quartered for not answering me the first time."

"Younger," Gaius says, hoping his frustration is not evident. Of course he knows Quintus could slay him on the spot for any real or perceived slight. He doesn't need to be reminded every time he's in the man's presence. How he'd enjoy working for someone he admires.

Quintus begins lighting several candles. "Did your little brother ever tell on you if you broke a dish, stole a piece of fruit, did something with a girl?"

"I don't often reminisce, but yes."

"Atticus is meeting with Pilate in Jerusalem, and he's telling on me—like a meddling little brother. He's there right now, slandering our oversight of Capernaum."

Our oversight? Gaius thinks. *Now it's ours?*

Quintus continues. "I need Pilate's endorsement if I'm ever going to get another promotion."

"Your record speaks for itself, Dominus," he says, aiming for the perfect matter-of-fact tone with only a hint of flattery.

"You have utterly failed me in the tent city!"

Oh, here we go, Gaius thinks. *If this man would ever move his tail beyond his office and see what we're dealing with out there, maybe* … But again, Gaius thinks of his family, his future. "I will do better," he says, gritting his teeth.

"You haven't enforced the ordinances I suggested, and worst of all, those people have no money! Zero! No one works. They're waiting around for a spectacle from the preacher, who, I might add, I thought we were done with. And it costs money to jail them, so—"

"How can I make it right?"

"You could kill Jesus of Nazareth! Make a public display of it so they have no reason to stay any longer."

Gaius grimaces, hoping Quintus doesn't notice.

Quintus rails on. "But then they will revolt, and it will get bloody. And I hate the wailing." He shivers. "I do hate the death wailing. I don't know how Pilate endures it. Anyway, we're not savages. Let's get rid of tent city."

All right, Gaius thinks, *now this is too much. Get rid of it?* "Wha—how can I do that?"

Quintus approaches one of the candles. "Gaius! Use your imagination! If you see a damaged home …" He licks his fingers and pinches out the flame. "Tell them it's not up to code and tear it down. You see somebody who's sick …" He pinches out another. "Arrest them for spreading pestilence. Somebody selling wares …" He pinches out yet another. "Tell them they don't have permission and shut them down. Put out the fires, Gaius! Until it becomes too cold, too dark, and too miserable to stay."

Gaius neither responds nor nods. In the shadowy darkness, he levels a look of contempt at Quintus.

"Primi?" Quintus says.

Gaius covers quickly. "I know what I must do, Dominus."

Chapter 50

MESSY

Andrew's home, night

Though he sometimes misses the bond with his brother, Simon—the camaraderie they have shared since childhood—Andrew enjoys his own place and getting to know some of the other disciples. Simon has gravitated into a leadership role with Jesus' entourage—no surprise to Andrew—and he gets enough time with him, he supposes.

In truth, he wouldn't mind a little alone time. In a way it's been fun having Philip sleeping across the room and Judas a few more feet away. But Andrew's place is not really suitable for more than one inhabitant. If or when he marries, he'll have to move.

Such are Andrew's thoughts as Philip's rhythmic breathing lulls him to sleep. He's not sure how long he's been out when he's roused by someone crashing to the floor between the beds. "Who's that? Who's there?"

"What?" Philip says.

"Andrew! Philip!" the man says. "It's me! Leander!"

"Who?" Andrew says.

The man moves into a beam of moonlight, revealing a Greek, maybe thirty years old. He raises his hands as if to show he's no danger, but he's wielding a knife. "It's me! Leander from Naveh!"

"Whoa!" Philip shouts. "Take it easy!"

"Drop your knife," Judas says from the doorway, his own knife in hand.

The young man drops his knife as if it's hot. "Oh, I forgot I had this. There you go. Sorry."

"What is happening?" Philip says.

"Who are you?" Andrew says.

"You guys remember me, right? I led you out of the city when the council said you had to go."

"Leander?" Philip says.

"Yes!"

"Why didn't you just knock?" Andrew says. "You could've gotten yourself ki—"

"I did! But I didn't want to shout."

"Why?" Judas says.

"No one can know I'm here."

"What's happened?" Philip says.

"The Decapolis is up in arms because of you."

"What're you talking about?" Andrew says. "We didn't even go to any cities in the Decapolis."

"People from there overheard you in Naveh, like me, and not everyone took it as well as I did."

"Took what?"

"Your preaching! The consequences of your mission were disastrous."

"Consequences?"

"The Decapolis is mostly Hellenist, but it's really a melting pot. Jews, Romans, Seleucids, Arabians—"

"Sounds messy," Judas says.

"It is. It's barely holding together. Your preaching set the town on fire—well, not literally, but you know what I mean."

"I don't understand," Philip says. "We were there to preach only to Jews."

"It doesn't matter who you were there for," Leander says. "Greeks overheard you, a few Jews kept sharing what you said, and before you know it, some Greeks quit worshiping Olympian gods or even reading the auspices."

"That superstition of getting signs from birds?" Andrew says.

"Exactly, and that's a big deal. Demeaning tradition makes people angry, so they turned against the Jews. Now the Jews have closed ranks and are sending Hellenists and sympathizers out of their communities."

"Oh, man!" Judas says. "You two really turned the place upside down."

"You said your teaching was interrupted," Leander says. "Incomplete ..."

"Not by choice," Philip says. "We were sent away."

"But what you *did* say has spread to the cities in the Decapolis, so now all the tension we have in Naveh has boiled up everywhere. In the whole area."

"New wineskins," Philip says, "bursting the old—just like Jesus said."

"People want to know more," Leander says. "They're hungry for the words of your rabbi."

"That was an isolated mission," Andrew says. "We were sent two by two for only a specific time, to strengthen and unify our people."

"Your mission can't be over," Leander says. "It's brother against brother out there. Is that what you meant for us?"

"Of course not," Andrew says.

"Then come back and finish what you started."

Andrew looks to Philip, then to Judas and finally back to Leander. "Next time, knock louder."

Chapter 51

THE CONFRONTATION

Matthew's former mansion

Mary of Magdala sits at the kitchen table, writing. She's trying to keep her mind on her letter to Ramah, wondering how the young woman is doing. Thomas's intended has left to try to rendezvous with Thomas at her father Kafni's home in the hopes of helping put the older man's mind at ease. She and Thomas have agreed that it will require a united front to persuade him to surrender her hand in marriage to a man he is not sure about.

When Tamar enters with a cheerful "Mary!" the Magdalene tries to be cordial. Tamar is smiling, bearing a bowl of olives in one hand and a bowl of grapes in the other. But Mary and Tamar's relationship has felt strained of late, and Mary is not sure what to do about it. It's not in her to fake the affection she once had for the beautiful Egyptian. Their cultures are so different, and Tamar has proved herself more outspoken and opinionated than Mary is comfortable with.

Mary returns her greeting by barely looking up and saying, “Hey.”

There can be no doubt Tamar senses her coolness. She appears to busy herself by setting down the bowls and helping herself to an olive. She grimaces. “Ugh! We’ve been swindled.” She spits out the olive and tosses it out the door.

Mary continues writing and murmurs, “Hmm?”

“The olives. They’re disgusting.”

“We already knew that. We’re working on it.”

Tamar pops a grape into her mouth. “It doesn’t make sense. If the soil is bad, why are the grapes so good?”

Mary wonders why they’re discussing this. “We bought an olive grove, not a vineyard.” She senses Tamar still staring at her. Mary continues to write, trying to ignore Tamar, but apparently, she will not be dismissed.

Tamar announces, “We need to speak with grape growers. The best in the upper Galilee.”

Mary is clearly not going to be left alone. She looks up from her work. “Why?”

“Because they know what they’re doing. They know the soil.”

Can this woman not take a hint? Mary says, “I’ll ask Ramah when she returns, okay? She must have curated grapes from this region for her wines.”

Tamar appears to pout. “What are you doing that’s so important?”

“I’m writing Ramah.” *If you must know.*

“I thought you were bookkeeping.”

“Judas keeps the books.”

Tamar takes another grape and idly sits at the other end of the table. Mary can feel her focus. She keeps writing until Tamar blurts, “Are we okay?”

Are we really going to do this? Mary wonders. She sighs and takes in Tamar. She hesitates. *Okay, here goes.* "I thought you were rude to Zebedee."

"At the oil tasting?"

"Yes."

"I didn't mean to be." She pauses. "But I believed he was asking our opinion."

"Well, you gave it. I don't think I've ever heard a woman speak to an elder like that."

Tamar appears sobered. "What else?"

"What do you mean?"

Tamar gives her a "Really?" look.

Mary feels cornered. There is more, but she doesn't really want to get into it. "Tamar, please …"

"It's fine," Tamar says. "I don't have to know what it is about me. But I have the right to be concerned when it comes to our work. This business is our contribution to the ministry."

"We have more to contribute than just supporting it financially."

"You're right," Tamar says. "You always know what to say. You even correct the boys when they fight."

"Why are you bringing the boys into this?"

"Is it because I can't read or write?"

"No!"

"Then what?"

Mary can't believe she's being pushed like this. "I—what do you—do you really want to—" She gathers herself. Tamar is right. There is more. Mary leaves her pen in the inkwell and sighs. As Tamar's eyes bore into her, Mary comes clean. "You pushed your way to the front of the crowd, you tore the roof off a house and proclaimed, for all to hear, 'I know you can do this.' And the first words out of Jesus' mouth to you were, 'Your faith is beautiful.' Tamar! Do you know where Jesus found me? In a bar. Drunk. Possessed." This has gushed from her in a torrent, hardly something she planned to say. She sits back. "I pray every day I'll never be anywhere without him again. But you? You just—like it here. That must be nice."

Tamar appears stunned. "You resent how Jesus met us?" she whispers.

"Of course not. No. It's just that—and I'm sorry to say this—I think we should be more humble. I'm doing everything I can, day after day. And I-I'm afraid I'm still broken. I worry I will never be enough."

Tamar looks pained and leans forward, her eyes pleading. "Mary! You are amazing! Can't you see it?"

"I don't think we're supposed to see it. I can't imagine doing what you do. I struggle to understand your entitlement. Where is your curiosity? You don't even know the pain of our people, our ways. You just show up and you do everything loudly and boldly and right. You do everything right!"

"Well," Tamar says, clearly taken aback. "I *am* sorry."

"Please don't apologize—"

"No, I mean I am sorry for the shame and regret that you feel. Truly, it must be very painful. But Jesus forgave you. Yet you choose to hold onto it."

The last thing Mary wants is for Tamar, of all people, to be right about this. But she is. Mary can't deny it.

And Tamar continues. "Just because I'm not Jewish doesn't mean I don't know pain." Her voice grows husky. "You don't know what it cost me to get here." She reaches behind her neck and unclasps her ornate, amber-beaded necklace.

"What are you doing?"

Tamar holds the enormous piece in front of her, giving Mary a full view of it. "What do you see?"

"I don't understand—"

"There, between the beads. What do you see?"

"A stain. Is that—dried—"

"Blood," Tamar says. "I come from a war-torn country. My brother and I went on a trip to unearth minerals for the family business, and when we returned, our entire village had been wiped out by a rival clan. Including my father and my mother."

Mary is overcome. "Oh, no."

"This necklace, passed down through generations—that I didn't want to sell for just oats—still has my mother's blood on it."

Tamar, weeping, begins refastening it around her neck but struggles with the clasp. Mary wipes her own tears and rushes to her. "May I?" She gently reaches to help. "Please."

Mary quietly connects the clasp as Tamar sobs. Still behind her, smoothing out Tamar's hair, she says softly, "I lost my father suddenly, too. And the thing he left me to remember him by, I-I tore up and threw away."

Tamar shakes her head. "I should have told you sooner."

Mary struggles for words. "I judged your strength against my weakness. Pitied myself." She peeks over Tamar's shoulder to face her. "Forgive me?"

Tamar smiles through her tears and nods.

Mary says, "I'd do well to have some of what you have." She moves next to Tamar. They sit in silence a moment. "My head is spinning," she says at last. "I don't know the right thing to say."

Tamar gives her a knowing look. "Finally."

This makes them both laugh.

Mary says, "I appreciate how hard you've worked on the olive grove." Tamar nods, and Mary is grateful the air has seemed to settle between them. She adds, "And you're right. We don't need to ask Ramah who the best grape growers are in this region."

"What about the soil?"

Mary smiles. "You know my past. You think I don't know the best vineyard in town?"

Tamar chuckles.

"It's just outside town," Mary says. "A nice walk."

Tamar nods. "We could use some fresh air." She reaches for Mary's hand. "Are you okay with going?"

"Let's do it."

As they stand to leave, Tamar says, "Mary, I could use some of what you have, too. Maybe not the shame, but the gratitude."

Chapter 52

RENDEZVOUS

A field outside Jerusalem

Atticus slows his horse to a trot, then halts in a field. He watches and listens, caution paramount in his job. No discernable threats, but in the distance stands a tent supported by four gilded posts and surrounded by half a dozen guards. He rolls his eyes. Just like the governor to establish a lavish, though makeshift, stronghold for a one-on-one meeting. Atticus spurs his horse.

Pontius Pilate sits reading in a slightly reclined folding chair before the tent. His guards' horses water nearby. He laughs at what he's reading, knowing his appointment will be here soon. The man is never late. Presently two guards shift into defensive position, hands on the hilts of their swords. A third advances. "A man on horseback, Governor."

He ditches the parchment, ignores the guard, stands, and flashes Atticus a self-satisfied smile as he approaches. "Did I do it?" Pontius crows.

"What?" Atticus says. "Announce your position to any opportunist who happens by?"

Pontius raises both arms in victory. "Yes! I wondered how I could annoy a red-bottomed old man. All it took was six men and this stupid tent."

A guard collects Atticus's horse as he dismounts. He laughs in spite of himself. He doesn't want to like Pontius the Pompous, but he does, and how much surprises him each time. "You've done it again. Well done."

"You know how easy I am to amuse," the governor says.

"Definitely not. I'm surprised there's no wine or women."

"I don't drink wine for the effect, and I'm married. So there. But I admit I was reading *Miles Gloriosus* by Plautus. Do you know it? It's hilarious."

"About the vainglorious swaggering braggart soldier," Atticus says.

"Yes!"

"What are you saying?" Atticus says, affecting a stern look. Pilate searches his face, but Atticus remains stolid. "I had you!" Atticus says, breaking into a grin.

"You did not!"

"I did."

"Yes, you had me! That was good. Why are you charming, Atticus? Haven't you been undercover for a year? It's been a year since I've seen you!"

"I've had a foil the last few months."

"Some prostitute in the Decapolis?"

"Far less charming, I'm afraid. The praetor in Upper Galilee, though he slips occasionally and claims the whole of Israel."

"I'll kill him!" Pilate says with a grin. "Wait, Galilee does well."

"Yeah, don't kill him."

"Let me think—his name is Quintus. Revenues are strong. He was reprimanded for use of force after putting down an uprising last year."

"That's him," Atticus says. "And he would be all too honored by your recital. He's the kind of man who wants to be remembered."

"We are very different then. My problem with the reprimand is that I have been reprimanded for *my* use of force. If word spreads that he's heavy-handed and under my command, I'll have to be even less forceful. How was the repartee?"

"I tormented him—for you, Governor."

"Just for me?" Pontius laughs. "I don't believe it, but thank you. What I really want to know is what landed you in Capernaum. From the top. Please, I've got all afternoon for this."

"Really?"

"No. About ten more minutes."

"I'll be fast."

Chapter 53

THE SOLUTION

Matthew's former house

Mary is pleased beyond measure but also amazed at how she has bonded with Tamar since their clearing of the air. She had been taken with the Egyptian when they first met, and she and Ramah and Tamar had gotten along famously for a time. Living together had—naturally, she assumed—injected minor irritations into their relationship. But soon, real resentment had set in—over things none of the three seemed fully aware of.

With Ramah off to help Thomas finally settle things with her father so they could be betrothed, that left Mary and Tamar to their own devices. Until they finally got everything on the table, Mary had nearly given up hope for their friendship.

But now—now things are different. It was a lesson, she decides, in how truth heals. How truth can, as she has heard Jesus say, set one free. Indeed, Mary now feels an affection for Tamar that supersedes even what they had enjoyed in the past, and she feels the same from Tamar.

Now they work together in harmony, and it gives Mary joy.

They're hard at work scooping wood ash into a bucket and adding liquid. They're also commiserating on what this is doing to their garments and how they should have worn aprons. When Zebedee enters, Tamar says cheerily, "We have been waiting for you! There's so much to do."

"To do?" he says.

"We solved the olive problem," Mary says, adding vinegar to the mix.

"I thought it was just the way the oil was made that upset you," he says. "There was a problem with the olives themselves? Other than being too dark?"

"It was terrible," Tamar says. "They taste like sour milk and wet hay."

Mary chuckles and says, "We knew it had to be something to do with the soil."

"So," Tamar says, "Mary introduced me to grape vendors in this region she used to know back at The Hammer."

That appears to give Zebedee pause. "Uh, are these good men, Mary?"

"Not really," she says. "But they know the ground."

"And they told us ways to improve the quality of the soil in the grove we purchased," Tamar says. "First we add wood ash to the topsoil near the roots."

Mary says, "So, we need you to go to each of the disciples' houses and have them bring their ashes here. And tell them to go around town offering to clean out people's woodburning stoves."

"*All* the disciples? I'm not sure I have the authority. What if Jesus needs them?"

"No one has seen him since the healing," Mary says. "We're just trying to be productive with the time we have while we wait."

"But," Tamar says, "he did give his blessing on purchasing the olive grove so we could support him out of our own means."

Zebedee points to the concoction they've blended in the bucket. "What is that?"

"Water, vinegar, and pine needles," Tamar says. "The grape people said it will make the trees sing."

"They said it's like magic," Mary says. "But not sinful."

"That's an important detail," Zebedee says.

"Oh, and one more thing," Tamar says, "sulphur. They said to add it to the wood ash."

"So, we need you to go to the market," Mary says, "and buy as much as they have available. And if that's a lot, maybe have one of the boys help you carry it back. Probably Big James."

"I'm not sure I have the cash to buy up all the sulphur the vendors have available."

"Joanna sent more money," Tamar says. "Judas put it in the safe upstairs."

"I'll get it for you, Zebedee," Mary says, snatching the key and heading for the stairs.

Tamar has always been amused by Zebedee. She continues to work while he waits. "If James and John had been as enthusiastic and hard-working as you two," he says, "I'd be retired and living in a mansion."

Tamar nods but determines to pretend she doesn't get it.

"You know," he says, "because I'd be rich. From catching so many fish, hm?" He chuckles. "It's a joke, Tamar."

She nods again. He looks puzzled at her response. Such a precious man.

Meanwhile, Mary unlocks the safe upstairs. She finds stacks of coins and puts one stack in a pouch. But she also discovers a small box containing what appears to be an old tzitzit in it—Jewish prayer tassels. Strange. Why would Matthew keep them in a safe, and was he ever devout enough to wear them?

• • •

Guards begin to disassemble Pontius's tent as the governor and Atticus conclude their business. It's obvious Pilate is deep in thought, but Atticus is eager to raise a new issue. "The camp outside Capernaum's walls grows by the day."

"What, with people hoping to see the peaceful preacher?"

"Peaceful and magnetic. I think Quintus is out of his depth."

Pontius removes his elaborate headgear and faces the sun, eyes closed. He takes a deep breath. "They say this is a backwater, you know? A bad assignment. A punishment even."

"Guess we're in the same cell then," Atticus says.

"Oh, I'm content. I'd rather not rule a warring nation in important times. I like the sea and the people. They're poetic and complicated. Except Caiaphas. Horrible, horrible man."

"For a moment there you almost sounded like a holy man yourself."

"I wish. I can't see ten cubits in front of my face most days. I just want peace. I want the people to get what they want. For Rome to be sated."

"Sometimes," Atticus says, "peace takes a war."

"Aah, military man. Right. I do thank you for the intelligence, Atticus. And I trust you. If the peaceful preacher or his movement ever becomes something I need to know about, I will need your counsel. And I will listen. Unlike Quintus, I understand your concerns. Until then, learn all you can."

Tent city

Zee has disguised himself, his face filthy under a hooded tunic as he sits near a fire, pretending to mend a water bucket. In truth, he's focused on the Zealot from his former order—the one he had seen in the crowd when Jesus healed the woman with the issue of blood.

In the midst of chatter, smoke, and pilgrims engaged in all manner of enterprise, Zee squints past a row of tents to where the man blends in with the crowd. Three men moving past block his view for a second, and the Zealot disappears. Not good. Zee surreptitiously tries to reacquire his target.

Suddenly, emerging from a tent, the man fixes his eyes on Zee, smirking. Neither blinks. Zee quickly makes his way to the end of the row of tents where another Zealot, this one long-haired, stands in his path. The man pushes his tunic aside to reveal a sica dagger. Part of Zee welcomes this—combat he can't ignore—but he thinks better of it. He whirls to find yet another Zealot blocking his path.

Chapter 54

INTERRUPTED

Simon's home

Eden doesn't know how much longer she can go without having it out with Simon. Part of her is tempted to waver from her determination to make him see his offense. After all, there's no way he could have known what she's suffered. It doesn't seem fair to charge him with insensitivity over something of which he had zero knowledge.

But she's emitted so many signals that something is bothering her! Why can't he see it's more than just some minor frustration? He's made several lame attempts to ask her what's wrong, but he seems so preoccupied with everything else that he has no clue. Eden's driving herself mad justifying her coldness while also seeing things from his perspective. Still, the weight is coming down on the side of her venting, letting him have it.

Nothing will ever dampen her pride in Simon's recognizing the Messiah and wholeheartedly following him. She even knew he would obsess over his calling, the way he always has over anything he puts his mind to—including some of his shortsighted schemes. Yet that's what makes him a natural leader. Of course it's also what can make him blind and deaf and mute at times, most maddeningly when it comes to her. Isn't the contrast between how she's treating him now starkly different enough from her usual flirty, romantic approach? Why, oh why, can he not see how deeply hurt she is?

And why can't she simply spell it out for him?

For the second meal of the day, she has prepared a simple soup with bread. For some reason she has outdone herself with the preparations, and she doesn't even know why. Is this the time she opens up? Might it be the night he forces the issue? Or has she simply needed the diversion of working hard at a mundane task to try to maintain her sanity? And all this tension comes in the midst of a grief so deep she couldn't have imagined it before it overwhelmed her.

What she needs more than anything right now is the best of Simon, the epitome of what drew her to him in the first place. She knows they'll get there again somewhere down the road, but it had better be soon.

He's trying. Trying so hard. It's easy to tell. Subtlety is not Simon's gift. They're sitting, eating, and she's avoiding his eyes. Funny, she thinks, what still reaches her in her despair and frustration with him. Like right now, how fetching he looks. He's always had that spark, that twinkle, and that manliness despite his modest stature. She's long been proud to be seen on his arm, to be known as his choice. He's certainly hers. But once the door is opened to her crisis, she's going to make him suffer before she lets him back in.

The sound of their spoons, even their breaking of bread, assaults her ears in the otherwise silence. Simon seems to make a show of swallowing a large spoonful, pausing, cocking his head, smiling. "This soup is really good!"

Oh, for the love... "Thank you," she says.

"What's in it?"

"Carrots. Vegetable stock. Olive oil. You've had it before."

"No, but today—today it's a beautiful thing. Fit for kings, this soup. And the bread! What is this on the top?"

"You know what it is."

"I see that it's thyme and sesame seeds, but what's this red spice?"

"Sumac. Salome gave it to me."

"It's almost tart, like lemon. Sweetness."

Eden shrugs. She'd rather they argue and raise their voices than converse like cordial party guests.

"But not sweeter than you," Simon says.

Pitiful, she thinks. *He's trying so hard, but ...* She rests her spoon in the bowl and looks up at him. *Is this the night? Should I tell him now?*

An urgent knock at the door.

"Simon, are you home?"

It's John's voice. Simon winks at Eden. "What if I just don't respond?"

"Well, the lamps in the windows are lit."

"Simon!" Big James now. "It's urgent!"

Simon sighs and tosses his napkin on the table. "Coming! Stop your pounding!" He opens the door and says, "I'd love it if you guys could make this quick."

John says, "Two men from Judea are demanding to see Jesus."

"Welcome to Capernaum," Simon says. "Everyone's demanding to see Jesus. Tell them we don't know where he is, because that's the truth." He starts to shut the door. "Have a good night."

Big James holds the door open. "They claim to be disciples of John the Baptizer and that they bear an important message—*from* John."

Simon is nonplussed. "Why wouldn't he have sent it with Andrew when that woman from Herod's court—aah—"

"Joanna," John says.

"Right, when she snuck him into the prison?"

"That was over a month ago," John adds. "They say it can't wait."

"But they could be spies," Big James says. "From any of the Four Philosophies, or even Rome."

"So, send Philip or Andrew to verify their identities," Simon says. "They'll know if they're comrades or not."

"What universe are you living in, Simon?" John says. "Andrew and Philip are gone."

"You didn't know?" James says.

"I'm not my brother's keeper."

"Except when you want to be," John says. "And then it's the Code of Hammurabi."

"Yeah, like I'm as rigid as ancient Babylonian laws. Take the log out of your eye, John. Don't think I haven't noticed the thing between you two lately."

"Well, we're here now," John says, "working together to find a solution."

"So where did Philip and Andrew go?"

"Back to the Decapolis for some reason," Big James says. "Judas knows more details, but right now we need you to come and see if these guys can prove they actually know Andrew."

"I'm in the middle of dinner with my wife. Tell them to wait till morning."

"But what if the message is a threat?" Big James says. "From Herod."

"It can't wait till morning," John says.

"Oh, but John—it can and it will."

He shuts the door and says, "You see, dear? I can say no to work, too."

But she's left the table, and the bedroom door is closed. It'll be another night on the roof for him.

The next morning, Big James and John lead Simon through Capernaum. From a side street, two young men appear and introduce themselves as Avner and Nadab. Avner says, "Simon bar Jonah! These brothers were right to question our identity."

Nadab adds, "Strict edicts are coming out of Jerusalem about false prophecy. Your suspicion is warranted."

And my suspicion remains, Simon thinks. "True or false, Andrew is a fine dancer."

The men laugh. "False!" Nadab says.

"Absolutely the worst," Avner adds.

Maybe anyone could know that, Simon thinks. "True or false, when Andrew relieves himself, he wretches and gags at the smell."

"We wouldn't know," Nadab says. "He always goes so far into the wilderness because he's shy about that sort of—"

"Mm-hm," Simon says.

"Nice!" Big James says. "Trick question."

Simon remains all business. "The baptizer is in a maximum-security prison that does not permit visitors. How is it you got a message from him?"

"A woman from Herod's court," Avner says. "Joanna—"

"All right, I believe you. What's the message?"

Avner and Nadab exchange glances, and Simon wonders why they look so uncomfortable.

Chapter 55

UNARMED

Tent city

Gaius knows he appears to be casually strolling, but any pilgrim with a brain should know he's actually patrolling on high alert. Who are these odd people, and what do they expect from a vagabond preacher? Life was certainly easier and simpler when Gaius merely loathed the Jews at will. He hadn't even paused to consider why he knew without doubt that this race consisted of dogs, worthy of his disgust.

The primi has never admitted to anyone—beyond a veiled implication to Matthew's parents—that he somehow became at least empathetic to the pitiful little tax collector everyone else hated so much. Gaius himself came to think his own soft spot for the man as some sort of a strange one-off, a temporary letdown of his emotional guard. Maybe he just decided that Matthew had enough enemies among his own people that he didn't need a Roman guard despising him as well. Admittedly, Gaius found certain character traits in the man, well, endearing. *That* he must never admit to a living soul.

But now his view of the Jews has been further compromised by his exposure to the bizarre former fisherman. He had known Simon—more so than even his brother, Andrew—as an enterprising sort, dangerously blurring the lines between obeying and flouting the law. He is bright, no question. But Gaius had felt justified feeling revulsion, especially when Simon abruptly retired from his life on the Galilee to follow the Nazarene.

Yet working side by side with him on the cistern, reluctantly at first, revealed a side of the man he never expected. He still thinks the Jews strange and that they follow lists of seemingly unending and severely rigid rules—some of which are real head-scratchers—but Simon somehow proves to be less a weirdo than Gaius expects. His work ethic cannot be questioned, nor his intellect.

And then following that crowd, seeing what appeared to be the healing of a very sick woman, and witnessing the fear on the part of the Jewish clergy over what was rumored to have happened with the little girl in the home of the synagogue administrator, well …

For some mysterious reason, all these things work together to give Gaius an entirely different view of the pilgrims in this makeshift city. Yes, it was certainly easier and simpler when he could just revile them. But something is going on. They have enough enemies, like the praetor himself, who want them either extinguished or expelled. As for Gaius, he is nothing if not intrigued by them. Maybe that's not the best attitude for a primi, he decides, but he can't deny it.

His inclination when he comes upon a damaged tent that exposes a half dozen cold and hungry-looking pilgrims inside is to stop and help them, but how would that look? He studies an old man with a wracking cough but forces himself to move on. What is happening to him? He must admit his conscience is working overtime.

Two women argue in the distance. He watches to be sure things don't escalate. He passes a man trying to reassemble his disintegrating makeshift tent and again finds himself tempted to help.

Gaius idly picks up a piece of rope and ties a quick knot, smiling at the recollection of his conversations and work with Simon. And an idea comes to him. But before he moves away, he notices a feeble old man trying to carry one end of a wood structure with cooking pots dangling from it. The man startles when Gaius approaches, but the primi just bids him good morning and takes his place, helping move the frame into position over a fire. "All is well," he tells the man.

Not far away, Zee prepares himself for combat. He breathes deeply, prays, and then kneels and lowers his hood to fully reveal his identity to his pursuers—as if there had been any doubt who he was. The lead Zealot and the two who have blocked his path—one with long hair and the other squat—chuckle and shake their heads. They have to be impressed by his fearlessness.

He follows their gazes down the path on the other side of the tents from his position where a Roman soldier strolls, taking his time, talking to various pilgrims while remaining conspicuous in his brilliant red uniform. This creates a stalemate, because Zee knows the Zealots won't dare start anything with the guard so close.

Zee whispers to the lead man, "I recognize you from the Order."

"Mine will be the last face you see," the Zealot says.

"I suppose you could kill me," Zee says, careful to exhibit not an iota of concern. "But my rabbi's will be the face that awaits me in heaven."

"Is that why you turned traitor?"

"I joined the Order to fight for the Messiah's coming. And he is here, brothers."

"It was chilly last night," Gaius says, and Zee and the Zealots turn at the sound of his voice. "It looks like your tent is damaged." The pilgrims look unsure how to respond to kindness from a Roman. Gaius looks self-conscious. "Do you need a hand?"

Zee tells the Zealot, "And the kingdom of heaven is at hand."

The Zealot makes a show of scanning the entirety of tent city. "Looks like no kingdom I've ever been promised." He spits.

"The Messiah is not what we thought, brothers," Zee says. He rises from his knees. The Zealots feel for the daggers at their waists. "I have bet my life on it." He pulls back his tunic to reveal no weapon. "I have given up the sica and our way of life to follow the Christ, after I witnessed the healing of my brother."

The Zealots exchange looks, as if they're listening but not about to back off—for now.

Capernaum street

Simon can hardly believe the question for Jesus that John's disciples have posed. "That's it?" he says. "*That's* what you want me to ask him?"

"Yes," Avner says.

"We'll pass it along."

"I'm sorry," Nadab says, "but how soon can we expect a response?"

"How soon?" Simon says. "Let me tell you something about that word *soon*—"

A pilgrim rushes past with a little girl in his arms.

John follows.

"What's going on?" Simon says.

"You want your answer?" John says. "He's back."

Simon, the Sons of Thunder, and Nadab and Avner race toward tent city.

Does it get better than this? Simon wonders. Whenever Jesus appears, things happen. Simon had had no idea what following Jesus would mean. He simply knew he had no choice. And now he would trade his new life for nothing. He wants peace with his beloved Eden, of course. But even she—regardless what's going on with her—will be eager to hear all about what's happening.

Chapter 56

THE BAPTIZER'S QUESTION

Tent city

Simon wishes he were faster, giving his all to keep up with the others. But when they skid to a stop at the edge of a crowd around Jesus, he espies Zee nearby with what appear to be three Zealots. Nathanael and Thaddeus gently shepherd a hunched old woman, nearly doubled over. Her face is a mask of pain. Thaddeus summons Jesus.

The master gently embraces her and rests a palm on her back. She gasps as she slowly straightens to her full height. Clearly overwhelmed, she collapses into Jesus' arms, and the crowd erupts in cheers.

Simon catches a glimpse of Gaius, his face a mask of confusion and wonder as Jesus' attention appears drawn to a woman supporting an older man. Simon can only hope the Roman will see something for himself this time.

The old man's dangling foot is plainly gangrenous and appears about to fall off.

"Please!" the woman cries out. "The doctors say the only remedy is to amputate!"

Jesus tenderly takes the foot in hand. "Well now," he says, "this does not look good at all."

Simon sees near the city gate the same scowling, strict priest who had accosted Jesus at Jairus's house.

Jesus merely blows on the man's leg, and the man starts dancing. Avner and Nadab stare wide-eyed as the man throws himself into Jesus' arms.

Simon notices Barnaby with Shula and moves to him. "What's going on? How long has he been here?"

"Not long," Barnaby says. "As soon as he showed up, he was surrounded. He's safe. He'll be all ri—"

Jesus gently kisses the eyelids of a young boy as onlookers hold their breath. The boy's eyes flutter open, and his face lights up. The boy's mother cups his face in her hands and shouts, "Blessed be Adonai! The teacher has healed my son's blindness!"

Simon tells the plainly overcome disciples of John, "Let's get you closer. *Soon* might be now." He says to Big James and John, "Let's get the baptizer's question answered."

As they push through the crowd, they find Jesus with a man bearing a chalkboard hanging from twine around his neck. He is writing desperately on it in Hebrew. "I know," Jesus says.

Gaius muscles his way closer, appearing to watch intently. Meanwhile, Jairus and Yussif arrive at the city gate and pass the priest.

Jesus asks Nathanael for his knife and slices the twine, the man's chalkboard clanking to the ground. Jesus places his hands on the man's neck. The man appears to gnaw on his tongue, extends it, and then opens his mouth wide. "I've never said anything with my own voice," he manages.

Jesus smiles. "Where would you like to start?"

The man clutches Jesus' tunic. "Blessed are you, Lord our God, King of the universe …"

Jesus pulls him close. "Let's save those big titles for a little later."

"Master," Simon says, nudging Avner and Nadab closer.

"Yes," Jesus says. "Who do we have here?"

"Two of your cousin's disciples," John says. "Avner and Nadab."

"Jesus of Nazareth," Avner breathes.

"That name I respond to readily, though I'll not be returning to Nazareth in this lifetime."

"The baptizer has an urgent question for you," Simon says and notices the scowling priest pushing his way through the crowd.

"As for you, Nadab," Jesus says, "I recognize you from the day John introduced me to Simon's brother, Andrew."

Nadab quotes John, "'Behold the Lamb of God who takes away the sin of the world.'"

"Yes, good memory. My cousin can get excited."

Simon notices Yussif's eyes darting toward the priest and worries things could get hairy.

"What is it John wants to know?" Jesus says.

Avner looks to Simon, then seems to scan the crowd. "Simon brought us in haste. This isn't appropriate here. We can talk later."

"Simon?" Jesus says.

"I think now is actually the perfect time," Simon says.

Jesus addresses the crowd. "Which of you has experienced John the Baptizer in any way?"

Many nod, raise their hands, call out, "Me!"

"I know some of you rejected John," Jesus says. "But some of you accepted his message. He has had a profound impact on so many in this region, and these are two of his disciples. Let's welcome them."

At a smattering of applause, Avner and Nadab look nervous, but Simon is pleased at the building tension.

Jesus continues, "Some of you may know that John is currently imprisoned by Herod in Machaerus. I think it would be very instructive for us to hear what is on his mind in the midst of such a challenge."

Avner leans in to Jesus. "It's a volatile question that might be better asked privately."

With a peek at Simon, Jesus whispers to Avner, "It's fine. This is healthy."

Avner clears his throat, hesitating. "He sent us to ask you if you are really the one who is to come …" Now whispering, "Or should we look for someone else?"

Simon is thrilled when Jesus announces, "For those who couldn't hear, John the Baptizer, my cousin who has prepared the way for me, is questioning whether I'm the Messiah, or if maybe we should keep waiting."

The crowd has gone deathly silent.

"John is getting impatient, yes?" Jesus asks Avner and Nadab. "It's one of his quirks."

"He didn't add details," Nadab says. "He just sent us with the question."

"Hmm."

Avner adds, "He *has* been in prison a long time."

"Word reached us," Nadab says, "about what happened in Nazareth. That you said the Spirit of the Lord is upon you to proclaim liberty to the captives."

"If you're here to free prisoners," Avner says, "why then does he remain? He rightfully wonders why you would allow his entire ministry to be halted by an imposter king."

"Proclaiming liberty to the captives," Jesus says, "can mean more than just freeing inmates. People suffer many types of captivity."

"Is that what we're supposed to tell him?" Nadab says.

"No, that's just for you."

"We heard our former comrades, Andrew and Philip, have gone to the Decapolis," Avner says. "Is that where you're planning to overthrow Rome?"

Simon notices Gaius, the priest, and the Zealots edge closer.

"I have something in mind for the Decapolis," Jesus says, "and it will be revolutionary, but probably not in the way you're thinking."

Nadab sounds impatient but respectful. "What are we supposed to report back?"

Simon hears Yussif whisper, "Careful, careful …"

Jesus says, "Go and tell John what you have heard and seen. The blind receive sight, the lame walk, lepers are cleansed, the mute speak. And the poor have good news preached to them." He pauses, and Simon catches his glance at the scowling priest. "And blessed is the one who is not offended by me."

"I will always be offended by blasphemy!" the priest cries out. "As should all of you!"

Simon points to Jairus. "You saw what happened to his daughter! You know this isn't blasphemy!"

Jesus gestures to Simon to quiet him.

"I did *not* see what happened!" the priest says. "Your supposed rabbi disrespected me as a holy man—another sign of his evil spirit. And I also don't know any of the details that happened. But I know he is hiding something! And I cannot stand here and allow you all to be deceived by his sorcery, even if I am the only one willing to protect you!" He glares at Yussif.

Jesus turns to Avner and Nadab. "Go. Relay to my cousin what you have seen and heard here today. Add to that that the dead are raised as well. And tell John I love him."

As Avner and Nadab nod and turn silently to leave, the crowd parts for them, looking uncertain.

Jesus addresses them. "Did my response to the baptizer's disciples sound to any of you like a rebuke?"

"Yes," Nathanael says.

"I can always count on you, Nathanael," Jesus says. "Many of you were baptized by John. I myself was. You heard how strong he was, how passionately he believed. And yet now even he has questions. When you went into the wilderness to see him, did you find a reed shaken by the wind? Someone in fine clothing like those in kings' courts? Or did you find a prophet?"

The crowd responds, "A prophet!"

"A prophet, yes," Jesus says, "and I tell you that John is whom Isaiah and Malachi spoke of. What did they say, Big James?"

"'Behold, I send my messenger before you, who will prepare your way before you.'"

"Yes! This should tell you something. Among those born of women, none is greater than John. Yet even he has questions."

"Another demon-possessed blasphemer," the priest says. "And you call him great. He called *your* religious leaders, *your* men of God, vipers! Well, Jesus, are you going to say something?"

"His silence is his response," Simon says.

Jesus turns again to the crowd. "And here's what is so wonderful. None are greater than John here on earth, but in the kingdom of God, the one who is the *least* is greater even than he. And John himself would say the same. Please listen carefully and do not waste this moment. Hear the truth I have for you:

The kingdom of God is at hand, yet so many in this generation are missing it. Do not miss it!

"Those of you who've rejected John's message of repentance, and those who are now rejecting mine, you remind me of the children in the marketplace who play games while the adults are busy. And you know how they pretend to be adults in a wedding or even at a funeral. You are like the children who refuse to play, whether it's a happy or sad game, no matter what it is. And like in Aesop's fable written half a millennium ago, the others say, 'We played the flute for you, and you did not sing. We sang a dirge, and you did not weep.'"

Jesus faces the priest. "You and those in your order say John has a demon because he lived in the wilderness, preaching repentance while refusing bread and drink. And now the Son of Man comes preaching salvation while eating and drinking and dancing—" He turns to Yussif. "—And I'm called a glutton and drunkard, a friend of tax collectors and sinners. It does not matter what is put in front of you. You will reject it."

Jesus turns to the crowd. "Beware of this! Wisdom means nothing if it's not acted upon. Wisdom is justified by all her works." He looks directly at the three Zealots. "As you see what is happening to those around you, as you see the lives changed by repentance and salvation, do not ignore the evidence of the kingdom of God! Woe to you if you do not receive it."

The strict priest appears about to launch into another rant, but Jairus clears his throat and strikes a tone of formal authority. "Uh, pardon! I'd like to remind everyone that Praetor Quintus has imposed a limit on outdoor public gatherings of twenty-five or more people in the latter part of the day. Judging by the location of the sun, we are all at risk of detainment."

"The man is right," Gaius announces. "All of you return to your homes and shelters immediately." The crowd protests, but Gaius adds, "I said immediately!"

"Let's return to our homes!" Yussif calls out. "It's all right."

Simon, Big James, and John hustle Jesus away.

"I will report all of this!" the priest shouts. "You are deceiving—"

Gaius draws his sword and advances on the priest. "I said, 'Go home.'"

Now only Zee and the three Zealots remain. "Do you understand now?" Zee asks the lead man.

"I understand very little of what I just heard and even less of what I saw."

"The Messiah does not need our daggers," Zee says.

Long Hair says, "Maybe you've forgotten what the Order stands for, but we have not."

The lead man says, "Enough! Are you blind? He is not a traitor."

"You could join me," Zee says.

"I'll find my own way. But I'll return to the Order with the truth, that you, Simon the Sicarius, are dead."

Chapter 57

"IT'S TIME"

Capernaum side street

Simon leads Big James, John, and Jesus around a corner to an empty, quiet spot. He tells Jesus, "I can never decide what's more fun, watching you perform miracles or watching the reactions."

John nods. "The miracles are better when Pharisees are around."

"All right," James says. "We need to get you to a new place, Rabbi. Do you have a camp, or do you want to stay at Simon's again? Probably best if it's a new place, maybe with Andrew …"

Barnaby emerges from an alley, Shula's hand on his shoulder as he leads her along, then pauses.

"Who is it?" she says. "Why did we stop?"

"It's him."

"Barnaby," she says, "we don't need to bother—"

"Shula," Jesus says, "it's fine. Thank you for bringing Barnaby here for a healing of his leg."

She chuckles, but Barnaby says, "No, I brought *her* here. She's the one who—"

"I know, Barnaby."

"Aah," Barnaby says, laughing. "Of course you do." He gestures toward her. "Please. She won't ask."

Jesus steps close to her. "Shula. Are you afraid to ask for healing?"

She lowers her head. "Yes."

"Do you have faith that I can heal you?"

"Of course."

"Then why haven't you asked?"

"You have so much to do, Rabbi. So many people who need you more. I am used to this."

"Shula," Jesus says. "Look at me."

"Look at you?" she says, smiling. "I can't see you anyway."

"I want to see your face."

She lifts her head.

"You and Barnaby have been so kind and lovely since I first met you. You've shown such strong faith, even though you haven't experienced a miracle."

Shula's voice is thick with emotion. "You redeemed my friend. Mary's miracle was so clear to me that I didn't need sight."

"I know," Jesus says. "You see better than most in this region. But, since your friend here won't leave me alone—" He winks at Barnaby and lays a hand over Shula's eyes, the other cradling her neck.

She draws in a quick breath, and as Jesus pulls his hands away, her eyes are closed tight. She covers them and weeps.

Shula gasps. Barnaby leans in. "Well? Did it work?"

"It's been so long, I'm afraid to look."

Jesus gently lowers her hands. "It's time, Shula."

She opens her eyes, and Simon beams to see they're no longer clouded. She huffs again, blinks, squints, lets out a whimper, and covers her mouth.

"Well?" Barnaby repeats. "Did it—"

"Yes, Barnaby, it worked. I can see you're not as handsome as you said."

Barnaby yells and laughs and hugs Jesus, tears streaming.

"Oh, my," she says, "I didn't remember everything being so bright!"

"How long has it been?" John says.

"Over ten years." She looks to Jesus. "Thank you, thank you." She hugs him, and Jesus smiles.

She turns to Barnaby. "Thank *you* too, friend." He wipes a tear, and Shula turns again to Jesus. "What about him?"

"No, I'm fine," Barnaby says. "This was about you. Some other time maybe."

Jesus lays a hand on Barnaby's shoulder. "We'll see. You are a true friend." He steps back and addresses the others. "We all must get home. Barnaby, she'll still need you to walk her. It's getting late. Shalom, shalom."

But before Shula and Barnaby move away, Jesus reaches for Shula's staff. "I don't think you need this anymore."

"No," she says, laughing.

As she and Barnaby walk away, Simon notices Jesus' smirk.

"Wait a minute—" Barnaby calls out.

"There it is," Jesus says.

"My leg!" Barnaby stomps and takes a normal step, then whirls around. "Did you—?"

"Of course he did, Barnaby," Shula says. "Who else?"

Barnaby squeals and runs to hug Jesus again, lifting him off the ground and nearly bowling him over. "Thank you, thank you, thank you!"

"You're welcome, Barnaby. Now take Shula to her home. You can do it faster than usual tonight, eh?"

As they hurry away cackling, Jesus turns to Simon and the brothers. "No Pharisees around for this one."

"Still," Simon says, "just as fun."

"Agreed," Jesus says, his eyes full.

Chapter 58

UNFAIR

While the Sons of Thunder rush Jesus off to who knows where, Simon sprints for home in the darkness. Giddy, he can barely contain himself, giggling as he wheezes and puffs, eager to tell Eden everything. She'll be dumbfounded!

He bursts into the house, calling her name. "Where are you? Come here for a second! You remember Shula? Never mind, I'll tell you later. Anyway, so the guys did turn out to be Andrew's old friends."

She appears from the other room in a robe, wrapping her wet hair in a towel.

He continues as he removes his sandals. "So, I used questions only someone who truly knows my brother would know, and it worked! Suddenly Jesus was in the square, healing all these people, and he even recognized John's disciples. They wanted to know if he was the real thing, which was crazy, given everything they'd just seen. And so he—"

"I lost the baby."

Simon can't breathe. "What?"

"You didn't know."

"Say that again."

"Our baby."

"You were with child? We—?"

"You were gone when I found out."

"No, no, no. No, this isn't—"

"—and you were gone when I miscarried."

"Were you working too hard?"

"No! And that's not what causes these things."

"Why didn't you tell me?"

"Because I didn't want to distract you or make you regret your choice. Because what could be more important than—? I thought I could just keep it to myself, but I didn't know the hurt would go on so long."

"Eden! This happened weeks ago, and you didn't tell me?"

"See? I was right. Look how you're handling this."

"I have a right to grieve my own child!" he says.

"I know. I know. There's no right answer."

"The right answer would have been to tell your husband!"

She stares. "Are you mad that it happened or that I didn't handle it the way you wanted?"

"I'm not mad."

"You're *furious*! I can see it."

"I'm furious? You were acting like I'd done something wrong. I had no idea what had happened. I even took marriage advice from a Roman! What did I do wrong?"

"You didn't do anything, Simon!"

"What?"

"You did nothing. You asked *nothing*. You came home after being gone and you didn't even ask me how I was. You didn't offer to help with anything. You just took a nap."

"You *told* me to!"

"Yes, because I'm considerate of you and was trying to show love to you while I was in pain. But I didn't think you'd rush to bed and then have the boys over the next day."

"*You* said I should take a nap. Am I supposed to read your mind?"

"Well, you seemed happy to read my body. It might have been nice for you to try to read my mind."

"That's not fair. You know that."

"I know it's not fair. I know I wasn't always right. I know, I know, I know. But I was a little distracted from losing my own—" She gently weeps.

He bites his tongue. Finally, "You're upset I was on a mission."

"You're putting words in my mouth."

"Maybe, but weren't they in your head?"

"Don't ask me that. You can't ask me—"

"I'm sorry," Simon says, in truth never sorrier for anything in his life. "I'm sorry for everything. He should never have called me."

"That," Eden says, "is exactly what I was afraid of."

"On a stupid mission to Caesarea with Judas."

"Leave Jesus out of this! This is between us, Simon. It's not his problem."

Simon paces. "He created the universe, Eden," he mutters.

"It was our idea to start a family," she says. "Don't take it out on him."

"If it's not his problem, whose is it?" Simon can no longer stand and drops to his knees. Eden crouches and takes him into her arms.

"You're the one comforting me now?"

"I've had a lot more time with it," she says.

"Why did this happen? I don't understand. Why, why, why, why?"

"You're asking the wrong person."

He collapses, and they hold one another.

PART 7
Danger

Chapter 59

PURIM

Jairus's house, evening

Jairus has always found it interesting that he can juggle two things in his mind at once. As he reads the story of Esther to his mother-in-law; his wife, Michal; his daughter, Nili; and his six-year-old niece, Yaeli, he does his best to communicate all the emotion and drama the festival tradition calls for. But at the same time, he's exulting over the miraculous resurrection of Nili. Will it ever leave his consciousness? He can't imagine that, and it's fine with him. Having the Messiah himself bring back to life your own loved one—what could be better than that?

He reads with melodramatic exaggeration, "'… And the king arose in his wrath from the wine drinking and went into the palace garden, but Haman—'" And here Jairus's rapt listeners stomp and hiss and pound the table. "'—stayed to beg for his life from Queen Esther, for he saw that harm was determined against him by the king. And the king returned from the palace garden to the place where they were drinking wine, as Haman—'" More stomping and hissing and pounding. "'—was falling on the couch where Esther was. And the king said, "Will he even assault the queen in my presence, in my own house?"'"

Zebedee's house, at the same time

Zebedee reads the same story to his own Purim festival audience of his wife, Salome; his sons, James and John; and their guests, Shula and Barnaby. Zeb's voice is full of humor and pathos. "'... This was on the thirteenth day of the month of Adar, and on the fourteenth day they rested and made that a day of feasting and gladness.'"

Here the guests rattle noisemakers, and Zebedee breaks into song: "'Therefore the Jews of the villages hold the fourteenth day of the month of Adar as a day of gladness and feasting, as a holiday.'"

Barnaby shouts, "*L'Chaim!*" and all raise their cups and chime in, "Aye!"

Jairus's house

The family ascends to the rooftop, carrying goblets, playing a tambourine, and cheering. Jairus scans the neighborhood, where other families are doing the same, some in the street. Revelers dance, play music, sing, cheer, and eat.

Jairus and Michal lead a toast to the festival before Jairus notices little Yaeli staring at something across the way and, apparently, mimicking what she sees. She frowns, cocks her head, kicks the roof ledge, stomps in a circle. She runs her hands through her hair, then grabs an empty wooden box and raises it over her head, clearly planning to slam it to the floor.

Jairus rushes to stop her at the last second. "No, no, no, Yaeli! What are you doing?"

From across the away comes a crash, and dust rises from a huge clay pot Simon has smashed to the ground from his own rooftop. He screams in obvious agony and frustration.

"I was just trying to celebrate like that man," Yaeli says.

But Jairus knows Simon is not celebrating at all. He's rarely seen a man so angry. As he guides Yaeli back toward the others, he watches Simon trudge down off his rooftop and has to wonder what has him so incensed. The man's rage is such a contrast to the revelry everywhere else that Jairus hopes he can somehow find out what's going on with Simon.

Chapter 60

CARNAGE

Galilean countryside, late afternoon

Philip tries to keep up with Andrew but should know better. He's heard Andrew tease his own brother about how much faster he is. Philip lowers his head and tries to accelerate even more. The fact is, he's tortured by what he's seen and experienced.

Andrew hollers over his shoulder, "Are you dragging your feet?"

"I'm not."

"Every time I look, you're a few cubits farther behind than before!"

"I'm thinking," Philip says, panting. "And my thoughts make my body heavy."

"Then stop thinking and walk!"

"After what we just saw?"

"All the more reason to move. Don't make this difficult."

"You think the situation among those Gentiles isn't difficult?"

"Of course it is. But walking doesn't have to be."

Philip stubs his toe on a rock and goes down. "Hades!"

"Or maybe it does," Andrew mutters. He stops and turns back for Philip, who limps to a large outcropping, where he sits. "You're bleeding."

"Oh, thank you, doctor! I know what blood looks like."

"Oh, wow," Andrew says, "you've torn the nail clean off."

"You go on ahead. I was slowing you down anyway."

Andrew laughs and opens his rucksack. "Are you suggesting you'll stay behind and die?"

Philip shrugs, wondering what the option is.

"Come on," Andrew says, tearing a rag into strips. "We're almost home." He wraps the wound as Philip fights to keep from crying out.

"Just perfect," Philip says.

"What now?"

"Blood. Carnage. A fitting end to our trip to the Decapolis."

"No one was bleeding."

"Not from their skin," Philip says. "But the whole town was torn apart, just like my toe. And all because of our teaching."

"Hold here—" Philip yelps when Andrew applies pressure to the wound. "You're the one who was supposed to be made for this."

"I thought I *was*. That's what's so—"

"John caused controversy all the time," Andrew says.

"Yes, but among the Jews! We caused a multinational crisis on the verge of erupting into violence, maybe even war. We might have blood on our hands! People might die because of us!"

"Blood on our hands?" Andrew says. "That's a bit much."

"We failed in our mission, Andrew! Messiah gave us his words, and we didn't deliver. If that doesn't upset you, then maybe it should."

"You need a walking stick."

Andrew heads off to find one, and Philip calls after him, "As long as home is only a mile more! Otherwise, I'm done for!"

Chapter 61

CHALLENGED

Andrew's flat, dusk

A Purim tradition, Judas thinks. So Little James has told him. So, while he's alone and has time, Judas sits packing tiny satchels of foodstuffs for the poor—dates and slices of pita bread.

Andrew and Philip come stumbling through the door, the latter hobbling.

"Oh!" Judas says. "Welcome back."

Philip says, "At least one person is happy to see us."

Judas cocks his head and wonders what that means.

"He's a different Philip right now," Andrew says.

"For good reason!" Philip says.

"Why? What happened?"

"Judas," Andrew says, pointing. "What are these?"

"Food for the homeless."

"Purim!" Andrew says. "I had completely forgotten."

Philip shouts, "How can we talk about holidays right now?"

"What do you mean?" Judas asks, a look of realization coming over him. "What happened in the Decapolis?"

"Our teaching," Philip says, "made a mess."

"Not intentionally," Andrew says, rummaging through a cabinet. "We preached the words of Jesus, and some took issue. Where's the vinegar?"

"Bottom shelf," Judas says. "I rearranged them. The way you organized things was very inefficient."

"The Decapolis is in a meltdown, Judas," Philip mutters, "and you're rearranging cabinets?"

"Philip!" Andrew says. "What's gotten into you? How could he have known?"

"Why do you need vinegar?" Judas says.

"To disinfect his wound," Andrew says.

"So it doesn't spread through my mortal body and kill me?"

"Actually, yes!"

Andrew pours the vinegar directly onto Philip's toe, making him howl.

"You still haven't told me what you did to the Decapolis," Judas says.

"Not what we *did*," Philips says. "What we said."

"To try and smooth things over?" Judas says.

"Sometimes," Andrew says, "people respond better to stories than to teaching, so …"

"A parable!" Judas says. "Oh, good! Which one?"

"The banquet."

"Aah! I love a banquet."

Andrew and Philip trade a look, and Philip shakes his head. "You might as well just tell him what happened."

"Yes! I'd love to hear it."

"Thank you, Philip," Andrew says with a sneer. "Well, Judas, it's directly from Jesus, so it's perfect—don't misunderstand."

"Okay … But what?"

"In fact, I think Jesus perhaps shares it when he wants a challenge."

"Were you challenged?"

"Oh, yes!" Andrew says.

"Challenged is fair, yeah," Philip says.

"So," Andrew says, "it goes like this: A rich man throws a big party, a great banquet he wants lots of people to come to. So, he sends his servant to those invited to tell them it's time to come. But all of them make excuses. The first says, 'I have bought a field and need to look it over.' Another says, 'I have bought five oxen and must go examine them.' Another says, 'I have married, and so I cannot come.'"

Judas says, "Those sound like perfectly legitimate reasons."

Andrew looks incredulous, exasperated. "Even our own people heckle, Philip."

"Someone in the crowd said the same thing," Philip mutters.

"So, anyway," Andrew says, "the servant comes and reports these things to his master. This angers the master, so he tells the servant to go into the city and invite the poor and crippled and blind and lame."

"So, he does that," Philip says, "and they come, but there's still room for more, so the master tells the servant to go to the highways and hedges and compel more people to come 'that my house may be filled.'"

Judas isn't sure what he thinks of this story. "You told that to a mixed crowd?"

"Mostly," Philip says. "I mean, we thought they were Jewish. We did not know the extent to which the crowd was mixed."

"So," Judas says, appearing to stifle a grin, "the go-out-and-find-some-leftovers did not exactly go over well?"

"Well, it should have," Andrew says. "God wants everyone to come to the party."

Philip adds, "The master said, 'I want my whole house filled. Everyone's invited.'"

"Okay," Judas says, "so tell me if I have this right. The Jews understood you to mean that Jesus was calling for Gentiles, and the Gentiles thought you were referring to them as second class. And then the conservatives, who base their lives on Jeremiah, would have heard you saying the original guests who didn't want to attend would miss the party. And those better versed in Isaiah—'… Behold, I am doing a new thing'—were probably emboldened, except that Gentiles were there."

Philip and Andrew trade looks. "Yeah," Andrew says, "that's about right."

"How did you know that?" Philip says.

"I was a businessman. My job was to know people, and I met all kinds."

"It was demoralizing," Andrew says.

"Maybe you're overstating your role in it," Judas says.

Philip shakes his head. "Would people be brawling in the streets of the Decapolis if we'd not preached there?"

"Brawling!" Judas says. "Boys, it's way too early for war. We've got to be smarter."

Judas is startled when Nathanael bursts in, shouting "*Chag Purim sameach!*" His smile fades when no one responds. "Happy Purim!" he tries. "Or not happy. Come on, it's a holiday, not shiva."

"We didn't exactly fix things in the Decapolis," Andrew says.

"So," Nathanael says, "talk to Jesus about it."

"I was just about to suggest that," Judas says.

"What happened to your foot?" Nathanael says.

Philip lets out a muffled groan as if the last thing he wants to do is discuss his wound yet again.

"We'll go see Jesus first thing in the morning," Andrew says. "So, how often does Philip get like this?"

"About twice a year," Nathanael says. "I just keep my distance."

"I'm sitting right here."

"We know."

Chapter 62

THE RETURN

Matthew's former home

It still strikes Matthew as strange to visit the house he used to live in and feel like a guest. Nothing about the place appeals to him or even tempts him anymore. He's happy to be following and serving Jesus along with his fellow disciples and the women, even as he sits across the table from Tamar, who carefully weighs small scoops of ground cinnamon while he reviews the new land deed. "This is very well-written," he says.

Tamar glances up. "I'll just have to trust you on that."

"You cannot read?" he says, vaguely aware that perhaps he should be more delicate in his responses, as Philip and a few of the others have been trying to teach him. But he finds himself plunging ahead. "That must be very limiting."

"It wasn't my choice," she says flatly, and Matthew senses her discomfort. He wants to fix it but isn't sure how.

"You could learn," he says brightly. "You're very intelligent."

Maybe that's better, Matthew thinks, but his eyes go wide when a familiar frame appears in the back doorway. "Thomas!"

"Hello, Matthew."

He looks strangely somber. Matthew notices that Tamar is doing the same as he, looking beyond Thomas. "Did Ramah return as well?"

John and Nathanael, covered in soot, lug buckets of ash through the front door and smile broadly. "Hey, Thomas!" John shouts. "How did it go?"

Thomas looks downcast. "Uh, it's complicated."

Matthew is stunned when Nathanael blurts, "Did her dad say no or something?" Even he has learned not to be that blunt.

Thomas looks as if he'd rather be anywhere else. "I mean, he didn't say no." He pauses. "Ramah stayed behind in Tel-Dor."

Bless John, Matthew thinks, when the former fisherman tries to cover Thomas's awkwardness by embracing him and saying, "But at least you're back, huh?"

Mary appears from the back door with a cheerful, "Thomas!" But Matthew can tell she's puzzled too. "Is Ramah—?"

Big James enters through the front door, carrying two loads of sulphur on a yoke, as everyone else in the room looks anywhere but at Thomas.

"Ramah stayed behind to work on Kafni," Thomas says. "He is not a believer."

"In Jesus?" Nathanael says. "We knew that."

"In me," Thomas says, forcing a pathetic smile.

"That's disappointing," Nathanael says. "Are you embarrassed?"

"Nathanael!" Big James scolds, smacking him on the shoulder.

"He didn't say no," Thomas says. "He just didn't say yes."

Matthew is dying to pursue this himself, but he can see how Nathanael has already overstepped.

"Ramah is working on him," Thomas adds, clearly trying to sound more upbeat than he feels. "We're hopeful."

It's obvious no one knows what to say. Thomas awkwardly heads out the back door. John goes after him, calling his name.

Matthew continues to silently take in everything as Zee arrives and sets down his sulphur. "So," he says, "the good news is that we got the ash. The bad news is that the townspeople think we followers of Jesus are up to something." After a pregnant pause, he says, "Did I miss something?"

"Thomas is back," Mary says, "and we were just wondering how it went at the market."

Big James speaks up. "We bought more than half of the vendor's supply of sulphur. People are going to think we're building weapons. Preparing for war."

Matthew thinks Zee looks as if he wishes for that very thing.

"Igniting spears isn't the only use for sulphur," Tamar says. "It can get stains out of linens."

"You can make incense with it," Mary says.

"It can purify a room where a sick person has been," Zee says, looking pleasantly surprised when everyone seems startled that he knows that.

Andrew, Philip, and Judas arrive, Philip limping on a walking stick. Andrew asks if Jesus is back.

"He's actually over at our place," Big James says, "talking with Abba about the olive grove."

Philip says, "We need to speak with him immediately."

"Wait, why?" Big James says.

"Philip," Mary says, "what happened to your foot?"

"Were you attacked?" Zee says.

"Nearly," Andrew says.

"We have a big problem in the Decapolis," Philip says.

"But didn't you go back to fix it?"

"We tried. We need Jesus to intervene."

"On behalf of *Gentiles*?" Big James says, looking as if he wants to spit.

"Um, excuse me," Tamar says. "I'm right here."

"You're different," Big James says. "There are hundreds of pilgrims here in Capernaum, our own people, who haven't seen Jesus in weeks, living in squalid conditions in hopes of just one more opportunity to hear his words, like those that captivated them on the mount."

"He didn't promise them more teaching," Andrew says. "They followed us to Capernaum of their own accord."

"The Gentiles are curious now," Philip says. "This was all foretold by Isaiah—'Behold, My servant whom I have chosen, My beloved with whom My soul is well pleased. I will put My Spirit upon him, and he will proclaim justice to the Gentiles, and in his name the Gentiles will hope.'"

Matthew loves when anyone quotes Scripture. "I've been studying the genealogy of Jesus," he says.

"Sounds exciting," Nathanael says, and Matthew struggles to determine whether he's being sarcastic.

Matthew continues, "There appear to be many Gentiles among his own ancestry. Rahab was a prostitute in Jericho who married Salmon, who fathered Boaz—"

"And Boaz married Ruth," Zee breaks in, "who was a Moabite."

"We could let Jesus decide for himself what to do about the Decapolis," Mary says.

"Exactly," Andrew says. "Thank you."

"She's right," Big James says. "Let's go."

All the men but Matthew leave. Tamar rises to tend to the ash and sulphur, looking overwhelmed. Mary approaches and sits across from Matthew. "It smells nice over here."

"Cinnamon," Matthew says. "For the holy anointing oil of the first press." He studies Mary. "Sad news about Thomas and Ramah, huh?"

"It is." She peeks at Tamar as if to be sure she can't hear and leans closer to Matthew. "I have something I wanted to ask you," she whispers.

She has his attention. "You do?"

"Yesterday while I was upstairs, I came across a box with, aah, prayer tassels inside."

Oh, no, Matthew thinks. Now he can't look at her. "What are you going to ask me about them?"

"Why were they hidden away?"

"*Why* is unimportant," he says. "They were hidden for a reason. Did that occur to you?"

She looks alarmed. "I-I put them back, of course! It was an accident. I just wondered—"

Matthew rises abruptly and gathers his bag. "I am glad you're using my old house, but I'd ask you to please not go through my personal belongings." He rushes to the door.

"Matthew, wait—"

But he does not.

Of all the people in the world he'd rather not get sideways with, Mary is at the top of his list.

Chapter 63

CHARLATAN

The Jerusalem temple

Do I finally have him? Shmuel wonders. He's been trying for months to gather enough evidence against Jesus of Nazareth so the Sanhedrin will be forced to take action. The so-called miracle worker should be censured at the very least, but if some of the things Shmuel has heard about him are true—that he actually claims to be the Messiah—he could be sentenced to death.

Shmuel hurries to the Office of Appeals within the great synagogue to meet with an elderly Jew named Harmon, who might just have the final nail for Jesus' coffin. Apparently the old man was bilked out of some money by Jesus. As Shmuel welcomes the man and points him to a chair, Harmon looks irritated. "He said he was sent by God!"

Did he now? Shmuel thinks. "Those were his exact words?"

"Yes!"

"Parentage?"

"He claimed to be of the house and lineage of David."

"No, I mean his father's house. 'Jesus, son of whom?'"

"He didn't say," Harmon says.

"Origin?"

"What do you mean?"

"From whence he hails, man! 'Jesus of what, where?'"

"Oh. I didn't ask."

Shmuel peeks at his notes. "So, you just gave him the money?"

"Yes."

Without knowing anything more about the man? Shmuel wonders. "My sympathy for your loss is dwindling."

"But his preaching was powerful! Like nothing I've heard before."

"Did he perform any signs or miracles?"

"No."

"Was he surrounded by loyal followers?"

"He was alone. He said he was building an army outside Beersheba in the Negev to overthrow Rome. And while he saw that I was too old to fight, he said a fifty-shekel donation would help his troops craft weapons."

Despite his zeal to expose the Nazarene, even Shmuel knows this doesn't sound like him at all. He swiftly stands and gathers his papers. "Thank you for your report."

"You're not going to open a formal inquiry?"

Shmuel sighs. He can't babysit every naïve citizen, old or young. "Harmon, there are countless such conmen swindling people all over Judea, and Jesus is a common name. If we started an inquiry, where would we stop?"

"But you seemed eager to grant me an audience."

"Well, that may be, but your swindler is not the one I'm looking for."

"You make it sound like it's my fault I was defrauded."

Well, if the sandal fits, Shmuel thinks. "I am sorry. You're free to go."

As Harmon trundles out, Shmuel makes his way down the hall to the Beth Midrash, which he finds largely deserted. He reaches his own study partition, the messiest of them all—crammed with scrolls and tablets in heaping piles. He's long been proud to be the most careful student among all the Pharisee rabbis, but this life has become anything but what he envisioned for himself. Bone weary, he drops into his chair and idly riffles through some parchments. He tosses them aside and sighs. Shmuel admits to himself that he's just as eager to make a name for himself among the members of the Sanhedrin as he is to prove that Jesus of Nazareth is a blasphemer. Frustrating as both quests have been, they do go hand in hand.

Chapter 64

ON BUSINESS

The interprovincial livestock market

Atticus loves his work, his position, his very title. To have been chosen by Caesar himself as a *Cohortes Urbana* brought him full circle careerwise, after having served for years in ever-elevating military roles. Now, except for the emperor, of course, he acts as his own boss. He decides where to go, what to do, whom to annoy, whom to expose.

And a day like this one, where he can needle and exasperate the ultimate Jewish arbiters of their own laws, well, except for what he has to walk through and smell, it doesn't get any better than this.

Makeshift pens corralling animals of all types emit moos and bleats that assault the ears, along with unmentionable waste that attacks the nose. Atticus carefully watches where he steps while witnessing this weird theater of the absurd, where garishly robed Pharisees appear fawned over by lowly shepherds. Twelve of the gaudily attired clerics make a show of examining four lambs, while each of the creatures' shepherds seems to nervously watch from a distance. One Pharisee snaps his fingers and says, "Water!" causing two shepherds to trip over each other to rush him a cup.

A third shepherd approaches a dismissive-looking, tall Pharisee. "I think you'll be very pleased—"

"We will make our decisions," Tall Man says.

Atticus can only smile when two other Pharisees press in to hear the tall one's assessment. "Look at the meager chump. Its neck is pathetic."

"But the coat—" another says.

"You could draw spots on it and make it a cow then, yes?" Tall Man says. "This is no lamb suitable for sacrifice."

Atticus, his ubiquitous apple in hand, speaks up. "You guys sure know your stuff. That back part is called a *chump*? Who knew?"

The tall Pharisee approaches, looking Atticus up and down. "Who are you?" Obviously disgusted, he turns to the others. "This is a Gentile!"

"This is," Atticus says, cowed not in the least.

"You are not permitted here! Are you—*eating*?"

"I was going to, but—the smell."

"This is outrageous! These are sacred grounds! Everything must remain kosher. I will have you brought before Caiaphas."

Oh, Atticus thinks, *that would be too fun.* He chews his lip before pulling back his cloak to reveal the credentials emblazoned on his chest. "Don't do that," he coos. "I'm here on Pilate's business. Ooh, I see you're upset. All I want to know is who here is the authority on troublemaking rogue preachers. Specifically in Galilee. Anybody talking about anything unusual?"

"Give us one good reason to tell you," the lead Pharisee says.

Atticus clears his throat, making clear he is about to spit, which would send the Pharisees into a fit. The tall one says, "Yanni! You can ask for Rabbi Yanni!"

Atticus smiles. "Thank you, men." He tosses his apple to the Pharisee, who drops it like a hot potato. Atticus strolls on, passing the disappointed shepherd leading the rejected lamb. "If they don't want it," he tells him, "I'm starving."

Chapter 65

TRESPASSER

Capernaum, Roman quarter

Simon desperately misses being sure of himself. That used to be his entire essence. It isn't that he wasn't often wrong, misguided, or impulsive. He was. And it got him into all manner of trouble. Yet he rarely doubted himself, his feelings, his intentions. Scheming with the Romans, compromising his fellow Jewish fishermen to save his and his brother Andrew's necks … Even initially being so cocksure Andrew had been mad when he claimed to have seen the long-awaited Messiah.

Simon always knows when he's been wrong and is often quick to apologize and try to make things right. But this latest case of having his confidence shattered, his air of surety obliterated, well, it has him rattled to his core. That his offense had to be pointed out by the woman he loves more than anyone on earth makes it all the more painful, obvious, and disconcerting. No, he couldn't have known Eden had been with child, though that is something he wished and prayed for. And no, he had zero way of knowing she had lost the baby—and in such horrendous fashion.

But he *has* been insensitive. He had taken for granted that her thrill matched his over his having been called by the master, and they were both fully cognizant that such a life would cost them dearly. Just how dearly he'd had no idea.

Making it all that much more troubling was that Eden—despite her righteous anger—was quick to forgive. Once she'd said her piece, she was, in a way, maddeningly now willing to keep the peace. In the end, Simon doesn't know what to make of it all. He's been wrong, yes. He's even harbored ill will toward the redeemer of his soul, wondering why Jesus performs miracles for everyone else, it seems—even for Eden's mother, but not for him or Eden herself.

And when he is tormented by all these conflicting thoughts, Simon has to simply leave the house, leave the responsibilities associated with his discipleship, and try to clear his mind. Which is how he now finds himself in a part of town new to him. He can't help but admire the architecture of this wealthy empire. He absently runs his hand over the latticed gates and ornate fences. A woman in a second-floor window glares at him and snaps shut her curtains. A well-dressed couple passes him, and both scowl.

In a strange way, though he's wholly out of his element, Simon feels this stroll is working. His mind is temporarily off himself and his problems. Until he runs into a soldier.

"What're you doing here, Jew?"

"Oh, I—was just walking and ended up—"

"You don't just *end up* in the Roman quarter. How did you get past the guard?"

"I didn't see—"

"You're coming with me."

Gaius approaches. "Canius! What's going on?"

"This Jew somehow got past the gate."

"I'll handle it," Gaius says. "I'll interrogate him myself."

"Are you sure? He's nobody!"

"Go to the entrance," Gaius says, "and make sure Antius is posted there. This never should have happened. I want to know where Antius was."

"Yes, Primi."

Gaius hauls Simon away but soon loosens his grip and whispers, "Don't talk, don't ask questions, don't make a sound until we get inside."

Soon they reach Gaius's home, where he ushers Simon in and latches the door behind them. "You could have been arrested. What possessed you to cross into our quarter?"

"I'd been everywhere else. This was the last part of town I thought would distract me—the novelty of it, you know."

"You couldn't drink yourself into distraction at The Hammer?"

A striking woman in her thirties and a boy of about nine emerge from a side room. Gaius introduces them as his wife, Livia, and their son, Marius.

She narrows her eyes at Simon. "What is this?"

"Nothing to worry about," Gaius says.

"It's the middle of the day and you're not at—"

"I needed a private place to interrogate this Jew who was trespassing."

Livia appears unconvinced.

"I mean no harm," Simon says.

"Are you the doctor?" she says.

"The what?"

"Gaius said there was a Jewish doctor who might—"

"Livia, please," Gaius says, "furnish this man with one of my cloaks. I don't want any more trouble while I see him out of the quarter."

She levels a look at Gaius before leaving the room. "Do you know the Jewish doctor?" Marius says. "Can he help Ivo?"

Gaius says, "Ivo is our, um—"

"Oh, yes, you mentioned him. The son of your servant."

"He's my best friend," Marius says. "He's really sick."

Livia returns with the cloak and says, "All right, Marius, that's enough. Please go to your room."

Livia leans away from Simon and holds out the cloak. Gaius himself looks offended and says, "Jewishness isn't contagious, Livia."

"So, he already knows our whole story," she says.

"Not all of it," Gaius says.

Simon slips into the cloak.

"We'll take the back door into the alley," Gaius says. "This way."

As they pass a bedroom, Simon gets a good look at the dark-complexioned Ivo.

Chapter 66

THE EXPLANATION

Matthew's former home

Mary of Magdala sits on the front stoop, weaving a basket by moonlight and wondering how this new life can be so thrilling and disconcerting at the same time. She wouldn't trade her current station for anything in the world—even though she did temporarily slide back into her old ways, only to be wholly forgiven by Jesus. Learning that being redeemed had not made her perfect proved a hard lesson. She had been so sure she would never go back.

Jesus' understanding and mercy has made her all the more determined to stay on course. Yet now she is out of sorts again. It isn't that she has grievously sinned again, but she has clearly offended precious Matthew—the disciple for whom she has the most empathy. She is not blind to his seeming obsession with her, but she tries to convince herself that it is wholly platonic, as are her feelings for him. Mary simply wants to encourage the young man and assure him of her sisterly affection.

But now she has accidently overstepped her bounds and hurt him—made him angry. She tries to concentrate on her weaving but finds that her angst is making her manipulate the strips too aggressively, pulling them too tight. If only Matthew would let her try to explain.

She looks up at the click of the gate.

"Mary?"

What a relief! It's him. "Matthew," she says quickly, "I'm—please forgive me. It was none of my business and—"

"You aren't the one who needs to apologize," he says, avoiding her eyes. "I am very sorry for my outburst."

"Your feet," she says. "They're covered in mud."

"Oh, yes, it's, um—well, Jesus is always going away to his lonely places, so I thought I would try it."

"Oh," she says, thinking that sounds just like Matthew. "How did it go?"

Mary has to suppress a smile when he tells her exactly what happened. "I barely stepped into the fields before I found myself trudging through mud. I took it as a sign to come back and apologize. May I explain?"

Grateful, Mary nods.

Matthew settles next to her and tells this story …

A few years earlier

Near the end of his workday, with Gaius standing guard a few steps away and looking bored to tears, Matthew sits in his tax booth, meticulously reviewing and recording the day's transactions. Very profitable. He's about to pack up his things and head to the Roman Authority with Gaius when a man, hobbled by age but bearing a dignified air, approaches.

"Just as I planned," the man says. "No line in the late afternoon of the sixth day."

Matthew studies the man quizzically. "You arranged for there to be no line at this time?"

"Oh, someone else did that, long ago."

Matthew senses the man is trying to tell him something, perhaps metaphorically, but he has never been quick to catch such things. "Who?" he says.

"Never mind," the man says. "You've really never noticed? You seem like someone who notices things."

That is a compliment, Matthew is sure. "Thank you," he says. "Traffic *does* slow late in the sixth day."

"Everyone is at home preparing for Shabbat," the man says.

Of course, Matthew thinks. "Shouldn't you be doing that, sir?"

"Shouldn't *you*?" the man says.

Matthew is avoiding the man's gaze but notices Gaius move a step closer to the booth, perhaps expecting trouble. Matthew, however, senses no accusation in the man's tone. "Have you come to satisfy your tax requirement? Why didn't you want there to be a line?"

"Maybe I wanted your complete attention."

Gaius rests a hand on his sword, but Matthew doesn't worry about a man this old and feeble, dignified or not. "Besides," the man continues, "who wants to wait? The name's Yoram, son of Hezron. Tribe of Benjamin."

Matthew riffles through his file. "We require only one name and one ancestor."

"I know. I guess being from the tribe of Benjamin is the last thing I have to be proud of, besides an experience God Himself blessed me with one night some three decades ago. Of what tribe are you?"

Oh, no, Matthew thinks. *He's getting personal.* "I don't discuss those things."

"He was the favorite of Jacob's twelve sons."

That doesn't sound right to Matthew. He's no biblical scholar, but of course he remembers that story. "I thought Joseph was the favorite."

"Aha! So, you *do* discuss these things." Matthew looks up from the man's record as the elder leans on the booth and gazes into the distance. "Well, if not the favorite, he was at least the baby of the family and the only other son born of Jacob's true beloved, Rachel."

Matthew peeks back at the ledger. "Something's not right," he says.

"You might say that," the old man says.

"Your adjusted income from last year is not commensurate with the amount you owe. Did you come into a large sum of money?"

"No."

"Your tax liability is the highest in Capernaum. It does not seem possible to have incurred this much debt, even from a sudden change in fortune."

Yoram smiles like a man with a secret.

Matthew continues, "Wait. What are all these transfers and reassigned figures?"

"Son—" Matthew flinches. How he'd like to still be the son of Alphaeus. "—I don't have many more days on this earth …"

"I can't believe what I'm seeing here."

"Oh, that?" Yoram says casually. "Yes, I bought all the debts of my children and family and put them under my own name."

"I've never seen—it's—this is a staggering achievement of financial acumen. I must say, I am impressed. But why?"

Old Yoram offers what looks like a sad smile. "This world has been wearisome. Living under the yoke for so long … I have seen everything I need to see, and I am ready to meet my maker. Again."

Again? Matthew wonders. *What could he possibly mean?* "Surely with your brilliance, you've also prepared some way to pay this."

"You know," Yoram says, "Benjamin wasn't his original name. Rachel died moments after giving birth to him, and as her soul was departing, she called him Ben-oni, which means 'son of my sorrow.' Jacob changed it to Benjamin, which means 'son of my right hand.' That was kind of him."

But Matthew is stuck on the ledger. "Do you have savings? Land? Assets? Anything you can sell off to fulfill this unthinkable sum?"

"Upon review, it looks like ol' Ima Rachel might have had the right idea. 'Son of my sorrow.'"

"Why would you do this? You will be arrested and sent to a Roman labor camp."

"But they won't be able to come after my children," Yoram says with a smile. "I did it all legally, mind you."

"I know! I'm astonished, but it would be very unpleasant for you—"

"Honestly, how long do you really think I'll last in a labor camp?"

"You are—shrewd."

"And to answer your question, no, I have no assets. I could have kept what little money I do have and made everyone else pay their share. But for what? To watch them suffer as I have my entire life as a shepherd?"

"I thought human sacrifice was against our religion," Matthew says.

"Symbolic self-sacrifice is not. And anyway, I won't be the one running the sword through." The old man gives Gaius a knowing look.

Matthew is in turmoil. "Though I take no pleasure in it," he says, "I have no choice but to have you placed under arrest."

"Thank you," Yoram says. "I understand. May I gift you?"

What in the world is he talking about? Matthew wonders. "Gift?"

"A gratuity," the old man says. "For your wonderful service and kindness in listening to me go on."

Matthew hardly knows what to say. He's about to send this man to a certain—and unpleasant—death, and yet … "It is not customary," Matthew says.

"In truth, I'm offering you the most valuable thing I own."

"An asset?"

"More valuable than gold, more precious than rubies."

Great! Matthew thinks. This might change everything for Yoram. "I may be able to help you liquidate it!" he says. "We could work together! A ledger coming up short on a balance this big reflects poorly on my performance."

The man sets on the counter a pair of prayer tassels of white, with the longest fringe dyed a stunningly beautiful blue-violet, almost turquoise. *Tzitzits?* Matthew is thrown.

"Well," Yoram says, "they are one of a kind. They date back to the time of the first Exile, dyed with the world's most exquisite *tekhelet*."

"There must be a buyer! If the amount settles your debt, you will be spared."

"I don't know," Yoram says. "I encourage you to consider keeping them. For yourself, my son."

"We are not relatives! Please don't use that word."

"I've made my decision. I want you to have them." He leans closer, as if to keep the Roman guard from hearing. "You chose this occupation. I know you don't currently have use for these. But you might need them one day."

Matthew cannot imagine. "That is highly unlikely. I will put these on the market and see what we can do."

Yoram turns to face Gaius and holds out his hands to be cuffed. "Officer," he says, "I confess."

Gaius glances at him but says, "Don't worry, old man. Someone will come to collect you."

"I will look for a buyer," Matthew says.

"When you know their value," Yoram says, "no man will be able to meet their price. Shabbat shalom, young man."

• • •

"More valuable than gold?" Mary says now.

Matthew chuckles. "'And more precious than rubies.' I kept them to respect the genius of that man. I also kept them as a reminder of the sins against my people."

"Why?"

"I want to understand things, Mary," Matthew says as his voice begins to crack. "Especially inscrutable things that unsettle me. And this was the most mysterious of them all. I have so many regrets. If I'd had the tassels appraised and sold, I would incur only more regret, and I couldn't bear it."

"It wasn't about the tassels," Mary says. "They're just a symbol. That man wanted you to have his faith. That was the last thing he had left, his most valuable thing in the world." She can tell Matthew seems to be understanding this, so she continues. "And now you have it! Yoram wanted you to be Jewish again, and you are. It was his dying wish."

"Why would he want that for someone like me?"

"Because sometimes God sends a dove."

"A dove?"

"I've never told you this," Mary says, "but the day I met Jesus, I was ready to end my life."

"What?"

"I was about to leap from a great height when a dove caught my eye. I could not resist following it. It led me to the place where I met Jesus. That old man was your dove."

Matthew appears to be trying to comprehend what she's saying. Mary hugs her knees and gazes at the stars. "Our lives have often been painful, yes?"

"Yes," he says.

"So, we think life is full of scarcity and not abundance. But then there are times when, out of nowhere, the world somehow expresses its longing to be whole. And suddenly, God steps in and we're pulled out of our blindness and invited into redemption. I know I was. I know you were."

Matthew stares at her, his dark eyes shining in the darkness. "I don't know what to say."

"Maybe don't say anything. I know you've felt unworthy, but it's time to add a new accessory—or rather an old one—to your clothes."

He appears puzzled, as if at least thinking about this. He breaks down.

Mary rises and smooths the creases in her garment. "Shalom, shalom, Matthew."

Chapter 67

TASSELS

The Roman quarter, night

When a Roman on horseback clip-clops on the other side of the street, Gaius tells Simon to raise his hood. When the rider is out of earshot, Gaius says, “The next time you need a change of scenery, try a new food. Or teach yourself discus throwing.”

“Discus?” Simon says, still reeling from what he’s just witnessed in Gaius’s home. “Seems like you might be the one who needs a distraction.”

“I’m going out of my way to help you,” the primi says.

“I was a fisherman by trade. I can tell when a ship has run aground. How long has it been like this?”

“I don’t know what you’re talking about,” Gaius says.

“Yes, you do. That boy—”

“It’s none of your business.”

“Your wife asked if I was the Jewish doctor you told her about. You told her about Jesus?”

Gaius appears to stiffen. “The boy’s been sick for almost a month, and he’s getting worse every day.”

"None of your doctors can help?"

"You saw the color of his skin. Most Romans think less of him because he's a servant."

"It's honorable that you kept him on when his mother died."

"He's not—just a servant."

"Your son said they were best friends. Like having a brother."

"They are! Half-brothers."

Simon covers his surprise. "Does Livia know?"

"We don't talk about it. For Roman men, it's a more—common thing."

"That's common for a lot of men—just more accepted in your culture."

"Spare me the sermon, Simon."

"I'm not judging."

"I didn't feel guilty about it at the time. But lately—I do regret my actions. And now he's sick and I can no longer pretend he's not my son. Neither can she." Gaius looks relieved to have it off his chest.

"Silence between a husband and wife," Simon says. "It's poison. And the longer it goes, the worse it gets. Trust me."

"I don't."

"You trust me enough."

"Just stick to your side of the street, Simon."

"Fine. Shalom, shalom."

"Why do you say it twice?"

"Once means peace," Simon says. "Twice means perfect peace. Complete wholeness."

"That'll be the day."

Outside Andrew's flat, same night

Thaddeus can't help it. He likes Matthew and has since he met him. He's fully aware that some of the others still bear animosity toward the eccentric, even idiosyncratic young man. But

Thaddeus numbers himself among those who recognize that all the disciples bring baggage into their new relationship with Jesus. As the master often teaches, it's no longer about the past. Everything has become new. Thaddeus will not judge Matthew by his past any more than he would want anyone to judge him by his.

In the cool of the evening, he has followed Matthew out Andrew's back door onto a modest patch of ground that abuts the alley. He's carrying Matthew's precious tassels, drawn to their ancient beauty but even more enthused about Matthew's plan. "I think it's a great idea!" Thaddeus says. "Especially to have them on before Rabbi arrives."

Matthew seems eager to get on with this, but he also looks frustrated. "Just tell me how to attach them. I mean, I've seen them on others, but—"

"It'd be faster if I just do it for you," Thaddeus says, but as he moves in, Matthew lurches away. "Please don't touch me. I don't like to be touched. Thank you."

Fair enough, Thaddeus thinks. "No problem. So, um, first you have to pull your—it's easiest if you take off your outer tunic first."

"Off?"

"Well, I mean, you have your tallit katan on underneath, right? That's where you'll attach them."

"Could you please turn around?"

Thaddeus is full of warmth and understanding and so fights to suppress a grin at the silliness of Matthew's modesty. Surely Matthew knows that Thaddeus—having been a manual laborer—has seen men in states of undress far more revealing than what he's suggesting. "Sure thing," he says, turning away.

"Why do we wear tassels anyway?" Matthew says.

"God commanded it in the Law of Moses."

"But what do tassels have to do with Torah?"

Thaddeus assumes Matthew should know this, but he's heard the story of how as a boy Matthew leapfrogged Torah memorization to follow his bent toward mathematics and accounting. "The Hebrew letters that spell the word have the numerical value of six hundred, plus there are thirteen knots and threads used to make the tassels."

"And there are six hundred and thirteen commandments in the Law!" Matthew sounds excited.

"See?" Thaddeus says. "You've got it. When we wear these on the four corners of our garments, it's like—"

"It's like being surrounded by God's Word all day."

"You're practically a rabbi already! Okay, so on the bottom right corner of your tallit, there should be a hole. See it? Take three short strings and one long string—"

"The blue one?"

"Yes, which should be the longest."

Matthew, grateful that Thaddeus still has his back turned, pulls his tunic away from his knees and extends the tangled tassels, starting to tie them just as Nathanael appears from the flat. "Jesus is here!" he announces.

Matthew leaps up, snatching his outer garment and holding it in front of him. "We'll be there in a moment, please."

"Okay, but Thaddeus, what are you looking at?"

Matthew detects a hint of humor in Thaddeus's response, but surely not. "I promise we'll be in shortly."

Nathanael slowly closes the door. Thaddeus asks Matthew, "You okay?"

"Yes. He's just so rude sometimes."

Chapter 68

IT HAS TO BE YOU

Andrew's flat

John finds the tiny apartment way too small for all the disciples to be crammed into, but he's also warmed to be surrounded by such friends—especially Jesus, of course. More than once the master has referred to him specifically as a loved one, and naturally this has never been missed. He feels loved. He knows Jesus loves them all, loves the masses, loves even his enemies. But John can't help hoping that he's extra special to Jesus. He's the one the rabbi *really* loves. It's not lost on him, however, that the last two important meetings with the group have been at the homes of the brothers, Simon and Andrew. Well, he won't waste time worrying about that. Jesus has been to his and Big James's house, too.

Among John's favorite experiences with Jesus are meetings just like this one, where the disciples report what has been going on, ask questions, and sit rapt under the advice and counsel of the Messiah himself. Andrew has distributed cups of water and a few meager plates of bread, and he and Philip have quickly filled Jesus in on the predicament in the Decapolis.

"And what was your strategy to clarify it?" Jesus says.

Philip says, "We told, or, we tried to t—"

"We tried to tell one of your parables," Andrew says.

"A parable," Jesus says. "Good. That's what I would have done."

"Which parable?" Thomas says.

"The banquet," Philip says.

"You know," Andrew adds, "the one where the guests give excuses not to come, so everyone else is invited."

John can hardly believe it. "You chose the *banquet*?"

"People get upset by that one," Nathanael says.

"Of course they do," Jesus says.

"Well," Andrew says, "if it makes you feel any better, we first considered the one about the wheat and the tares but thought better of it."

"I already told you that some wouldn't understand that one," Jesus says.

"I'm not even sure I do," Thomas says.

"Give it time," Jesus says.

Philip says, "The problem is that they *did* understand the parable we chose, and it caused a fight in the street."

"Rioting," Andrew says. "Between Jews and Gentiles."

Philip adds, "Leander tells us it gets worse every day. The Hellenist priest who ran the town changed his ways—which is good—but when he abdicated his duties, others wanted to fill the void, projects went undone, everyone got angry and started blaming each other—"

"And it led to stealing," Andrew says, "literal fights. People actually left their homes to wait out the violence."

"*That's* the environment you suggest sending us into?" Big James says.

Jesus pauses. "What part of the parable caused this fight?"

Andrew and Philip look at each other. Philip says, "The part about the people outside the city—the ones in the highways and hedges, the last to be invited and to accept."

"That's what I suspected," Jesus says, sighing.

John has to ask. "Do the people in the highways and hedges really refer to Gentiles?"

"He who has ears to hear," Jesus says, "let him hear." He pauses. "We'll leave in the morning." It appears to John that everyone agrees, despite any misgivings. They trust Jesus, and why shouldn't they? "Everyone go home," Jesus adds. "Gather your things. We take to the highways and hedges before dawn."

As the others leave, Jesus addresses Philip and Andrew. "Boys," he says, "this is part of it. You try to carry heavy things, and sometimes one gets dropped. We pick it up and keep moving."

John is vaguely aware the others are dispersing, but he sits considering the daunting task ahead.

"John," Jesus says, picking up cups and plates and moving to a washing bucket. "May I have a word?"

"Yes, Rabbi." He approaches. *He shouldn't be—* "I can do that," John says.

"This trip is not going to be easy," Jesus says, continuing to wash the cups.

"I'm sorry?"

"The Decapolis will be perilous. The hearts I must reach there are hard, Jew and Gentile alike. Our time there will be fraught."

"We're ready for anything, Master. We have Zee. I can ask my father to come along for extra help. He's good with crowds."

"I want you to stay behind."

What? Have I heard him correctly?

"The rest of us will leave in the morning," Jesus adds. "You will stay and wait."

"But if the situation is fraught, I should be there more than ever."

"For what?" Jesus says. "Strength in numbers? Our challenges there have nothing to do with how many of my followers surround me. This is not about a lack of resources."

"Then what?"

"Hard hearts, John. Cold. Unyielding granite."

"I don't understand."

"You seem to think we needed a full group for this trip. Who wasn't at this meeting?"

John wonders how it has slipped past him that Simon was absent. "Oh."

"You will wait for him and bring him. The success of this trip depends on Simon."

Depends on Simon? John thinks. *What about me?* "Master," he says evenly, desperate to give Jesus no cause to again refer to him as one of the Sons of Thunder, "whatever you need, I can provide."

"Waiting for Simon is what I'm asking you to provide."

"Simon is distracted. He's not himself. Something's off. Maybe it's better if he stays behind."

Jesus dips a cup in the bucket and wipes it with a rag. "John, I love you, but what you're suggesting is not the approach I take with people in pain. You should know that by now."

"Then what about one of the others? Wouldn't it be better if one of them—"

Jesus shakes his head as he rinses and dries the cup. "You've known Simon since childhood."

"What about Matthew? He and Simon were able to work together to find Mary in Jericho."

"Did you think pairing them for that task was a good idea at the time?"

John has no response to that one.

"John, it has to be you. No more questions."

The next morning

Jesus leads Big James, Thomas, Andrew, the still limping Philip using a walking stick, Nathanael, Thaddeus, Judas, Little James, Zee, and Matthew silently across the countryside toward the Decapolis. Andrew notices the blue and white tassels swinging from below Matthew's tunic, brushing his legs.

The mood feels ominous, Andrew thinks. *Like a march to war.*

Nathanael leans into him. "Where's your brother? Is he okay?"

"We've got our hands full without worrying about him for now," Andrew says.

Nathanael seems to accept this and moves on. But Andrew *is* worried about Simon. More than he wants to admit. In his gut, he believes that whatever is wrong at home between Simon and Eden, their love will overcome it. But Simon has always been impetuous. He could just as easily have been called a Son of Thunder as John and Big James were. That is partly what makes him such a strong, natural leader. And it's why they could use him today.

Andrew doesn't know what it means that John has been left behind too. He's ostensibly waiting for Simon, but what then? Will they both catch up with the others, play a role in whatever happens in the Decapolis? Well, there's little use pondering it. Jesus has a plan; he always does. And it will be perfect.

The questions are, what and whom will it entail? Andrew can hardly wait to find out, but he's not necessarily eager to arrive and be in the middle of it. No, this would be almost as exciting if he were just hearing about it after the fact.

Almost.

Chapter 69

THE REBUKE

Matthew's former home

Simon supposes he'd better check in to see what's going on and where Jesus might be. He can't harbor his resentment much longer. He can barely face his own wife, but he must at some point have it out with his master. He is long past any doubt or misgiving about the identity of the Messiah. And he would be an utter fool, despite his pain and anger, to deny the signs and miracles he's seen with his own eyes or the truths he's heard with his own ears.

After his expulsion from the Roman quarter, Simon spent the rest of the night and the wee hours trudging through town, wallowing in his grief and bitterness. Exhausted yet eager to find some closure, he enters the mansion to find Mary and Tamar preparing breakfast. But for whom?

"Shalom, Simon," Mary says.

"What are you doing here?" Tamar says.

"Did you sleep in?" Mary says.

"I didn't sleep at all."

"Why?" Tamar asks.

"Where is everyone?"

Mary says, "They left before dawn for the Decapolis. No one told you?"

Simon shakes his head.

"If you run," Tamar says, "you should be able to catch up with them."

"I'm not much of a runner."

Zebedee enters. "Simon! What are you doing here?"

"Having a cup of water. I'm thirsty."

"Why aren't you with the others? Were you assigned to stay behind and look after the women?"

"I didn't know about the trip. I thought Andrew and Philip went and sorted it out."

Zebedee seems to study him. "You're disconnected, Simon. You don't have a clue what's going on."

Great, Simon thinks. *This is all I need right now.* "You rebuke me, Zebedee?"

John shows up. "Abba?"

But Zebedee remains focused on Simon. "Don't play games with me, kid. Salome and I were at your *bris*."

"Abba!" John shouts.

Zebedee levels a burning stare at Simon and marches out.

"What's gotten into him?" Simon says.

"What's gotten into *him*?" John says. He takes a breath. "Grab your things."

"Fine. I'm ready. I travel light. What are you doing here anyway?"

"Waiting for you."

"Really? Thank you!"

John approaches, his face flushed. "It was not my choice. I would have left you."

"Wow," Simon says. "Did someone eat your breakfast, John? What have I ever done to you?"

"It's what you *haven't* done!"

"Oh, this again."

"You miss meetings! You hang around all night with a Roman official. Your wife doesn't even know where you are!"

"So, leave me behind then! Like chaff in the wind."

"I can't. Jesus says the success of the trip depends on you. You of all people. I don't understand it, and frankly I feel disrespected by it. But what am I going to say to Jesus, no?"

"You could."

"You know I can't." John gathers up his pack. "Let's go."

Simon has never seen John this hot, stomping out to the gate and throwing it open. Finally Simon follows.

Chapter 70

THE THREAT

On the outskirts of the Decapolis

Leander peers over a large outcropping and scans the horizon. Could the tiny dots on the road be Andrew and Philip, coming back to try once again to set things right here? He hopes so, but he also knows they'll be lucky to escape with their lives.

Wait! More men follow. Still, there aren't enough of them, whoever they are, to be able to defend themselves in the city. Leander scoots down the rock and beckons a young boy and a man to follow him into the clearing the group must pass. "Andrew! Philip!" he calls out. "I knew you'd return!"

"Why are you acting like this?" Philip says.

"There is so much unrest and anger, I don't want to draw attention—" Leander gapes. "You—you must be"—he drops to his knees—"the rabbi we've heard so much about."

"More than heard about, as I understand," Jesus says. "Rise. I'm sorry there's been trouble."

"Oh, the strife between Jew and Gentile was there all along in Abila, simmering beneath the surface. It's simply out in the open now. It was bound to happen sooner or later."

"It was bound to happen now," Jesus says, placing a hand gently on his shoulder.

"Rabbi!"

"Telemachus?" Andrew says as the lad approaches.

"Jesus of Nazareth!" Telemachus says. "Your fame has spread throughout Syria, and now your teachings have reached our town."

"So I've heard," Jesus says.

"*He* has not," the boy says, pointing to the man.

"What do you mean?" Andrew asks.

"He's deaf," Leander says, but he had not planned to bother Jesus with this.

"My abba cannot hear," Telemachus says. "His name is Argo, and he can barely speak."

Argo tries but emits only distorted sounds.

"Telemachus," Leander says, "you're out of line. This is not why we need Jesus."

"Why shouldn't it be?" Jesus says.

Philip says, "The problems in Abila are so much greater than one man's—"

"I can think of no better place to start," Jesus says.

"We didn't mean to spring this on you, I promise," Leander says. "I really didn't—"

Jesus silences him with another touch, and Argo kneels before him, still straining to speak. Telemachus tugs at Jesus' tunic. "Please, Rabbi! I mean no disrespect, but—"

"I understand." Jesus kneels before the deaf man, lifts his chin, and looks into his eyes. He puts one hand over Argo's ear and touches his lips with the other. Looking to heaven, he sighs. "*Ephphatha.* Be opened."

Leander has never seen such a look of peace—and amazement—on Argo's face, but soon the man startles, looking terrified as sounds must be invading for the first time.

"Don't be afraid," Jesus says, smiling. "That's what birds sound like. They sing."

"*I* don't even hear it," Big James says.

Telemachus rushes to embrace his father. "Abba! Can you hear me?"

"The sound of your voice," Argo says. "The sound of *my* voice. Telemachus!" He moves his tongue as if discovering it for the first time. "Telemachus. Am I saying that right?"

"Yes, it's perfect."

"How?" he says, sounding overly articulate. "How do I know?"

Leander is more than amazed. Somehow Jesus has healed Argo's hearing and caused him to speak words he's never heard.

They turn to Jesus, and Telemachus says, "How can we ever repay you?"

"I have no money," Argo says. "No way to compensate—"

"Actually, you can by telling no one what happened. I strictly charge you to keep this quiet, which should be easy for you—you've had a lot of practice." Argo laughs, and Jesus continues, "Now is not the time for this word to spread. Do you hear me?"

"*Now* I hear you," Argo says, and they all laugh.

Leander whirls at approaching hoofbeats. *Oh, no!* It's Nashon, a local healer who always charges for his services. He, among many in Abila, became especially incensed at the preaching of Andrew and Philip, whom Nashon now addresses. "You've brought friends? I thought we'd seen the last of you! And consorting with Greeks, I see."

"Nashon," Leander says, "they're here to bring peace."

"That's what they said last time!" Nashon turns to Jesus. "You must be the rabbi everyone's been talking about. Tell me, what sort of a respectable rabbi would be speaking amicably with those who corrupt our Hebrew children by teaching them Greek philosophy?"

Jesus says, "If this so-called corruptor of children were to raise the money for your fee, would you speak to him then?"

"He will never raise the money, I know that. You want to dilute our faith."

"How do you know what he wants?" Argo says, making Nashon gasp.

"What did you say, deaf-mute?"

"He's not a deaf-mute anymore, Nashon," Leander says. "Now go on your way."

"Who did it, Argo? I want to know! Who healed you?"

Leander is proud of Argo for obeying Jesus and simply looking away.

"Your deafness was no doubt punishment for some ghastly sin committed by you or your parents, and I want to know who—"

"It doesn't work that way," Jesus says.

"Oh? Then how *does* it work?"

Andrew is eager to hear Jesus' response to this interloper, but he's also worried about what they'll encounter in Abila itself. He edges away from the others, climbs the rise, and peers beyond the trees. He feels the blood drain from his face. "No!"

Chapter 71

REFUGEES

The Decapolis countryside

Philip rushes to Andrew, and the rest of the disciples join them to see what's going on. Leander takes in the scene. Hundreds and hundreds have made their way to this desolate spot and have erected rickety tents of blankets and tarps. They huddle around small fires they've built all over the landscape.

"What is this?" Big James says.

Leander knows exactly what it is—citizens from Abila and the other cities of the Decapolis seeking refuge from the violence in their neighborhoods.

"Ho-ho!" shouts a man in his thirties leading a handful of others—a couple of women and several men. "What have we here? The Galileans return, this time in droves."

"A drove is a flock or herd of animals," Matthew says.

"Oh, I know," the man says.

Andrew tells Jesus, "They're Syrophoenicians—"

"My friends," Jesus says, "you seem upset. How can I help you?"

"Are you the one they call Jesus of Nazareth?"

"I am."

Leander notices a look of recognition coming over Nashon. His enemy has a name. And this young Syrophoenician continues to press. "They say you do miracles. All we've heard is heresy and rumors from the other side of the Sea of Galilee. Show us proof of who you are."

Leander is surprised to see Nashon gallop away on his horse. What's he up to? Is he not even interested in how Jesus will respond?

The young challenger continues, "Give us a sign or at least food or supplies for all the people displaced from their homes. Otherwise, take yourself and your followers and your monotheism back where you belong!"

Leander turns at the sound of ridiculing laughter and finds five more approaching behind their leader, a woman in her forties. "I'm in awe!" she hollers. "The Jews and their long-awaited Messiah finally arrive to cause even more trouble, and *this* is his army?"

"Nabataeans," Philip says.

"How many are you?" she says. "I have more children than that! Could *I* be your messiah?"

"Blasphemy!" Zee says, looking eager for a fight.

Nathanael says, "Does anyone else think we should move to higher ground?"

"I agree," Judas says.

"Rabbi," Thaddeus says, "tell us what to do."

"Wow," the woman says, "are your followers always this strong and intimidating?" The Nabataeans laugh.

Jesus addresses the disciples. "Everyone stay calm and settle in. Looks like we're going to be here for a while."

Chapter 72

THE TREK

The road to the Decapolis

Simon has to rethink his reckless decision to stay up all night as he trudges along with John. Beyond exhausted, he's as testy as he's ever been. "Just one trip. One errand out of a thousand, and this is the one I can't miss?"

"You said you'd go with him to the ends of the earth."

"That doesn't mean *every* time he goes somewhere. And the Decapolis is hardly the end of the earth."

"He didn't say it was," John says.

"I'm remembering something you told me in Samaria," Simon says.

"I'd rather not talk about Samaria, if that's all right with you."

"The field he tricked you into cultivating for a Samaritan, to correct your prejudice."

"It wasn't a trick, and I'm not particularly fond of that memory, Simon."

"Melech, with the broken leg."

"Agh!"

"You told me in the morning that the man was healed at his home. But we were all at Photina's house. Jesus didn't even have to be present to perform the miracle."

"What's your point?"

"Why can't he just perform a miracle in the Decapolis from Capernaum instead of dragging us all into mostly-Gentile territory where everyone has it out for us?"

"Ask him," John says. "I'm sure he'd be willing to answer your question, since 'success depends' on your being there."

"Oh, come off it. He's nicer with you than with me. I don't hold that against you, do I?"

"How very generous of you," John says. "What other virtues would you like to lord over me? Simon the exceptional. Simon the distinct. Maybe he calls me beloved sometimes because you have Eden. I don't know what you're whining about when you've found someone like her!"

The very mention of her name stops Simon. He knows John hasn't noticed because he continues walking. Twelve paces ahead, John turns. Simon tries to hide his tears, but he can't move.

John turns back. "Look, I'm sorry. I went too far. I wouldn't want someone to resent me for having a wife."

Simon remains rigid.

"Simon! Hey, I didn't mean anything by it. What's going on? What did I—Simon?"

The tears come, and Simon doesn't care. "I trusted Jesus!"

"Of course you do! We all do! Wait, *trusted*?"

"I trusted that Eden would be okay, John …" *I'm going to tell him,* Simon thinks. *I'm actually going to tell John.* "… That she would be safe while we were gone last time."

"What? Wasn't she sa—"

"I didn't know it, John, but before we all left on our missions, she and I conceived a child."

John looks stricken.

"And while we were gone—"

Simon can say no more. John gathers him into his arms. "Oh, no, I'm sorry, brother."

"She almost died along with the baby. There was so much damage, the doctor says she might never be able to—"

"Adonai in heaven," John says as Simon sobs. "Why didn't you tell us?"

"Because I'm furious! I'm so angry—" Simon tries to gather himself. "John, he is who he says he is. I don't just believe that, I *know* it. He is the first and the last. He can do anything. How could he let something like this—"

"Whoa, whoa, whoa, I don't think that's the right—"

"—happen to Eden? To me?" Simon escapes John's embrace. "Let's keep going."

"You're not exempt, Simon. Remember, he said that in this world bones will still break, hearts will still break. But he's making a way for people to access a better kingdom!"

"He heals total strangers! I gave up everything for him ..."

"That doesn't mean your life will now be perfect. In fact, he said the opposite."

"I don't want to talk about this anymore."

They walk in silence, Simon feeling at the end of himself. Finally he says, "Life was a whole lot easier when we fished."

"She still could have lost a baby when you were a fisherman, Simon. You just wouldn't have had anyone to turn to."

Simon stops and faces him. "He could have prevented it. And he did not."

They keep walking, eventually toward raised voices from over the next hill. "Sounds like we're close," John says.

Simon forces himself to keep up with John as they crest the hill, his legs burning. But he puts all that out of his mind when he sees the rest of the disciples gathered around Jesus, as a growing and seemingly hostile mob approaches from all sides. Jesus and the disciples are greatly outnumbered. John turns to Simon with an ominous look as Simon desperately wonders what Jesus meant by "it all depends on Simon."

He searches John's face, turning the words over and over in his mind. John is indeed his brother in the faith, regardless of how they squabble. And Jesus is the Messiah Simon is committed to defending to the end. He leaves John to walk toward the fray and soon breaks into a dead run.

PART 8

Deep Waters

Interlude

990 B.C.

A Psalm of Asaph, a Levite singer and seer commissioned by King David to lead the music in the tabernacle of God:

I cry aloud to God, aloud to God, and He will hear me. In the day of my trouble I seek the Lord; in the night my hand is stretched out without wearying.

My soul refuses to be comforted. When I remember God, I moan; when I meditate, my spirit faints. You hold my eyelids open.

I am so troubled that I cannot speak. I consider the days of old, the years long ago. I said, "Let me remember my song in the night; let me meditate in my heart."

I will appeal to this, to the years of the right hand of the Most High. I will remember the deeds of the Lord. Yes, I will remember Your wonders of old. I will ponder all Your work and meditate on Your mighty deeds. Your way, O God, is holy. What god is great like our God?

You are the God who works wonders; You have made known Your might among the peoples. You with Your arm redeemed Your people, the children of Jacob and Joseph. When the waters saw You, O God, when the waters saw You, they were afraid; indeed the deep trembled.

The clouds poured out water; the skies gave forth thunder; Your arrows flashed on every side. The crash of Your thunder was in the whirlwind; Your lightnings lighted up the world. The earth trembled and shook. Your way was through the sea, Your path through the great waters; yet Your footprints were unseen.

Chapter 73

FAITH

The Decapolis countryside

Local Jewish leaders have joined the small crowd around Jesus, so now he faces them, the Syrophoenicians, and the little band of Nabataeans. The leader of that faction has not yet told Jesus her name, but it's obvious to him she's a force to be reckoned with. "If your followers can't even figure out how best to share or live out your teachings," she says, dripping with sarcasm, "then why should anyone else?"

Jesus is relieved to see Simon running toward them. "Sit down," he says.

"That's your answer?" she says.

"I don't mean you. I mean my students. Sit with me."

"Now?" Andrew says.

"Yes, please. Hello, Simon."

Simon nods sheepishly, trying to catch his breath.

Before anyone sits, Philip says, "Rabbi, we didn't come here to cause trouble."

"It would appear," Jesus says, "that the trouble has found us."

"So, we should address it," Big James says.

"And how do you propose we do that, James?"

The Nabataean woman sneers and turns to her cohorts. "Listen to these characters."

"My friends," Jesus tells his disciples, "sit with me. We cannot go further until we agree on something."

The Gentile crowd looking on murmurs, and the strict Jews appear to whisper conspiratorially—their leader frequently peeking at Jesus. With his back to the others, Jesus speaks loudly enough for them to hear as he addresses his disciples. "I am a rabbi, and as these Jewish brothers behind me will tell you, we like to teach by asking questions. We like to solve problems by talking. It's even better if it starts with disagreement. So, feel free to listen, and if you'd like to argue a bit, that's fine too."

Judas leans in and whispers, "Rabbi, we look weak and defenseless."

"On the way to Jairus's house in Capernaum, what happened when the woman, Veronica, touched me?"

"Power went out from you," Zee says.

"No, I mean what happened to *her*?"

"She was healed," Thaddeus says.

"How?"

Andrew speaks up. "By touching the fringe of your garment."

"No. My friends, you forget so quickly. You are dear to me, but your memories are short."

Matthew's eyes light up. "You said, 'Daughter, go in peace. Your faith has made you well.'"

"Your what?" Jesus says.

Little James and Thaddeus call out, "Faith!"

"Her faith," Jesus says. As the Gentile crowd glowers, Jesus concentrates on his disciples. "Many of you are afraid right now instead of choosing to have faith. In me."

"But Rabbi," Big James says, "you must see what's happening here all around us—"

"Of course he does!" Philip says. "That's the point!"

"Rabbi," Judas says, "increase our faith!"

Jesus speaks quietly. "Judas, if you had faith the size of a grain of mustard seed, you could say to a mulberry tree, 'Be uprooted and planted in the sea,' and it would obey you."

Matthew flinches. "Can a mulberry tree grow in the sea?"

"He's making a point," Thomas mutters.

"Truly," Jesus says, "if you have faith like a grain of mustard seed, you could say to a mountain, 'Move from here to there,' and it would move. Nothing would be impossible for you."

"How?" Nathanael says. "How do we get there?"

"Like Judas said," Philip says, "increase our faith."

"It's not about size, Philip," Jesus says. "It's about in whom you have your faith. If you are secure in your faith in God, trusting in His promises, choosing His will for your life instead of your own"—he pinches his thumb and forefinger together—"this is enough faith. The people we are ministering to are like bees among the flowers, waiting for them to open so they can sip the nectar and spread it to others. But they must see a faith in you that is secure, big or small."

The leader of the Syrophoenicians says, "Looks like you've got your work cut out for you."

Andrew turns to confront the man, but Philip stops him.

"You're right, Teacher," the Nabataean woman says. "Your guys do have short memories."

A huge black man leaning heavily on a crutch hobbles into view. "Excuse me!" he calls out.

"What're you doing?" Simon says. "Step back! We're listening to our teacher."

"So am I," the man says.

"Ignore him, Simon," John says. "This moment is about us and Jesus."

"What is that smell?" the Nabataean woman says.

Simon covers his nose with his forearm. "Rancid!"

The man pulls up the hem of his tunic, revealing the ooze coming through a filthy wrap on his shin. Everyone recoils and turns away from him. "It's an infection, okay?" he says. "My leg is broken and got infected. Mind your own business."

Nathanael says, "You need to get that checked out. It's really bad."

"You're right," the man says.

"Unclean!" the leader of the strict Jews hollers.

"Silence!" Jesus says, rising and approaching the man.

"Look," the man says, "I didn't ask to break my leg."

The Nabataean leader points at Jesus. "And we didn't ask *him* to come into this region and make things worse!"

"I'll talk to you in a moment," Jesus tells her.

The hobbling man says, "I'm here to test what he said about the faith of the bleeding woman."

"I already know, Brother," Jesus says. "I know you." He lays a hand on the man's shoulder.

The infection immediately dissolves, and the leg is made whole. The man drops his crutch and tearfully embraces Jesus as the Nabataeans, the Syrophoenicians, and even the strict Jews stand speechless, jaws dropping. The leader of the Jews rubs his eyes. The formerly menacing Gentiles press in, appearing entranced as the man rips off his bandage and begins to mince step.

"Under normal circumstances," Jesus says, "I would strictly charge you to tell no one. In some regions, and with some people, it's just not my time to be revealed and escalate tension. But it looks like we're past that here."

"It's been a long time since I ran!" the man says. He picks up his crutch and snaps it in two over his knee. "Thank you!" he says. "Thank you!" And he races away through the expanding crowd, still streaming over the hill.

Suddenly the Nabataeans, the Syrophoenicians, and the Jews sit on the ground around Jesus. He notices Simon staring at the remnants of the crutch, sees the contempt on his face, and knows what he's thinking. "I'm glad you came, Simon. It's going to be a long day."

Chapter 74

EDEN

Simon's home

Eden returns from the market, having found herself unable to smile even at friends or acquaintances who greet her. She's still grieving, of course, but that's not it. She's always been able to appreciate kindnesses, even when she herself is troubled. It's Simon. She has forgiven him after having vented and making him feel bad. Maybe he deserved it. Maybe he didn't. But if there's one thing she's sure of, even if she overreacted—and she's pretty sure she didn't—it's that he needs to get over it. Not the loss of their baby, of course. She knows to her core that they'll both carry that grief to their graves. But they need to be together now, to care for each other.

She resonates with his anger, or at least his confusion over Jesus' role in all this. Their faith is rock solid. They know who Jesus is, what he can do, what he does. Did he *choose* to forsake them in the hour of their greatest need? She'll survive this; she knows she will. And she believes, or at least trusts, that Simon will too. But despite her forgiveness and her offer of support, he still seems lost. She rarely knows where he is or what he's doing, and when he's home, he's not really with her either.

If she could only talk to Jesus about all this.

But who's waiting on her doorstep? It's Zebedee, Salome, and Mary. "Oh, my!" Eden says, forcing a smile. She's determined to not let them know what's on her mind. "Shalom!"

"It's good to see you, Eden," Zebedee says, and Salome nods, radiating affection and sympathy, as does Mary.

"What a surprise!" Eden says brightly. "Is everything all right?"

"Could we have a word inside?" Zebedee says.

"Of course." Though Eden doesn't know what to think, she finds herself open to guests—especially these three, though it's clear something is up. She continues to at least pretend to exude sunshine. As she welcomes them in, she goes to the cupboard. "Can I get you anything to—"

"Please, Eden," Salome says. "We're fine."

"Let's sit down," Zebedee says.

Uh-oh. As they sit around the table, they just stare at her, wearing pity-filled smiles.

"Is something wrong?" Eden says.

"You tell us," Zebedee says.

"Zeb!" Salome scolds.

He leans forward. "This morning I ran into Simon at Matthew's old house. He was in a bad way."

Eden affects another smile. "Oh, well, that's his way." She shrugs. "He's all mine."

But her guests are serious.

"I've known him since he was born," Zebedee says. "This wasn't Simon being Simon."

Salome puts a hand on Eden's knee. "We love you like the daughter we never had, you know that, ever since the day you married Simon. A lot has changed in all our lives—especially yours—these past two years. I—we—sense that some part of Simon's distractedness lately has something to do with your marriage."

"We're not saying it *does,*" Zeb says.

"We just want you to know that you can talk to us," Salome says. "We are here for you. No matter what's happening." Eden avoids their eyes, but Salome continues, "Lord knows we're not perfect, but we've been married a long time. And if there's anything we can do to help, we want to."

Eden smooths out her garment and clears her throat, her eyes filling. She hasn't decided how much she'll say. Part of her wants to defend Simon, but she doesn't want everyone to know their business.

Zebedee breaks the silence. "I myself am none too pleased with Simon at the moment. But I know he's a good man. He's learning a completely different way of living that would be bumpy and bewildering for any person. That's not even considering all of Simon's—you know—Simon-ness."

"All I want," Eden says, "is for him to—" She chokes up. Salome touches her shoulder. Eden continues, "—for him to find peace. He's never really had it. His father was difficult—and distant."

Zebedee leans in. "I fished with Jonah for twenty years and never really knew him. I know Simon hasn't had it easy."

"It's not just him," Eden says quickly. "I mean, it's both of us. I thought *I* could be his rock, you know? His home." And she breaks down. "If I'm honest, it started—it started when, um—" She can't bring herself to say it, not in front of Zebedee.

He cocks his head at her. "Are you hurt?"

"No," she says, weeping now, and she can't face him.

To her great relief, Salome senses this. "Zeb," she says, "give Mary and me a moment alone with her."

"Of course," he says, raising a brow, and steps outside.

In spite of herself, Eden is overwhelmed by the love and empathy she feels from Salome and Mary. The story rushes from her and leaves her sobbing as Mary brings her a cup of water.

They sit in silence until Salome says, "How can we help?"

"I don't know! And neither does Simon, which is our problem."

"I'm sorry."

"Eden," Mary says softly, "I haven't known you for very long, and I don't know anything about marriage. In fact, actually as I think about it, I probably should say nothing."

"No," Eden says. "Please …"

Mary hesitates and looks to Salome, who says, "You may not be married, but you have suffered. You have lost family."

"Still, Eden, I am new to all this, so just know that—"

"No, please, Mary."

"Well, you say you completed your ritual purification requirements …"

"Yes. Not in the mikvah because of the broken cistern, but in the sea, yes. And I isolated for the seven days, which wasn't hard since Simon was gone."

"And being cleansed didn't help at all?"

"No, it made it worse, because it didn't bring my baby back. And it didn't help with my marriage. That woman Veronica, whom Jesus healed, when she cleansed in the sea, she had so much joy!"

"She'd just been healed of her malady," Mary says. "Her anguish was over—"

"You're only at the beginning of your grief, child," Salome says. "Have you talked to a rabbi?"

"*The* one I want to talk to is not here. And neither is my husband."

Mary says, "I don't know what it's like to go through what you have, but I've been through enough to know that you need to grieve."

Eden lowers her head and finally sobs. "Jesus gave her healing and joy, but he hasn't given that to me."

"So go to synagogue," Mary says. "It's not about which rabbi is there. It's the words from God he can give us. That's what Jesus gave me."

Chapter 75

SURROUNDED

The Decapolis countryside

Hundreds more arrive by the minute, many joining the tent dwellers over the rise beyond where Jesus and the rest of the disciples face the Nabataeans, the Syrophoenicians, and the Jewish clerics. Soon they come pouring over the hill and begin to press in as Jesus turns to the leader of the Nabataean clan. "Now, what is your name?"

"Fatiyah," she says with slightly less rancor, probably because of having witnessed the miracle firsthand.

"She's Nabataean!" the Jewish leader shouts.

"I didn't ask her ethnicity," Jesus says. "Fatiyah, help us all understand what exactly has happened in this region."

She appears thrilled to have been asked. "Your students preached in Naveh about a kingdom that entranced many in this region visiting the city—including the Augur of Abila, who stopped performing his ceremonial and civic duties upon returning to the Decapolis. Work came to a standstill. Construction was halted. Merchants could not get permits. Wells went undug."

"The region was paralyzed by the absence of one man?" Jesus says.

The head of the Syrophoenicians says, "What Fatiyah is not saying is that the merchants who could not get permits hijacked a caravan of exports from my Syrophoenician brothers."

"We had a deal in place that *you* reneged on!" Fatiyah says.

Jesus spots a Greek near his feet. "What is your name?"

"Eremis. I'm a bronze-caster."

"You appear to be in good health and strength, well-dressed in Athenian blue that matches your eyes. Tell me, Eremis, what is your plight?"

"I bought a plot of land north of here and needed a reading of the auspices to determine the favorability of the gods regarding construction of a new casting facility."

"Hmm," Jesus says. "Sounds so simple."

"But because of what your Jewish missionaries preached—"

The leader of the Jews points at Andrew and Philip and shouts, "Do not associate these people with our order!"

Fatiyah says, "You stood by as their teaching poisoned the minds of—"

"You were not even present, Fatiyah!" the priest says. "We strenuously disavow all of their teachings! We have been punished for crimes we did not commit!"

Jesus raises his arms to calm everyone. "Andrew? Philip? Did you direct your teaching to Jewish citizens?"

"Yes, as you instructed."

Leander says, "But the augur from Abila overheard and was moved."

"Eremis," Jesus says, "what would the augur's reading have told you?"

"Whether there were good or bad omens."

The priest says, "Doesn't that sound absurd?"

"You call *us* absurd, Jew? Your laws about food and purity are laughable!"

John and Big James leap to their feet. "*What?*"

Jesus puts out a hand. "Sit down, brothers. The last thing these people need is thunder."

Eremis says, "How can I build a business without knowing where the gods want me to build?"

The Jewish leader says, "Nazarene, if you are any sort of a self-respecting rabbi, you will not dignify that question with an answer."

Fatiyah scowls at the priests. "Your people's condescension is unending."

"Oh," the Syrophoenician says, "there's never been a note of condescension in your voice, Fatiyah?"

"Let's stay on topic," Jesus says. "So here we have Eremis, paralyzed by fear that his business ambitions might not be sanctioned by the gods of his religion. How could this lead to violence?"

Eremis says, "Because the augur's flagrant rebellion undermined Greek authority."

"And yet the Jewish community was targeted in a wave of brutal attacks!" the priest says.

"My people," Fatiyah says, "were hardest hit for not having our paperwork for Rome."

"So, you turned to crime!" the Syrophoenician leader says.

"Out of desperation!" she says.

Leander tells Jesus, "That's why I invited Philip and Andrew back—to clarify their message."

Jesus smiles. "And how did that work out for you?"

Eremis calls out, "They told a story about hospitality, and for some reason, Jews and Arabs came to blows over it."

The priest says, "The people originally invited to the banquet in your story had perfectly legitimate reasons for not coming."

"Which is another way of saying," Jesus says, "that some people think the old way of doing things is better."

The priest quotes Torah: "'Look to the ancient roads, where the good way is, and walk in it.'"

"You know your prophets," Jesus says.

"Of course I do."

"What about Isaiah?" Jesus says. "'Forget the former things; do not dwell on the past …'"

The priest says, "Do not pit prophets against each other, especially on this issue. So, those people out on the highways and hedges—surely you're not referring to the Gentiles?"

The Syrophoenician leader says, "You sound like you don't *want* us to come to the banquet."

"The meaning of the story," Jesus says, "is that God wants His house full, and everyone who believes in me is invited. Plain and simple."

"Heresy!" the priest shouts.

Fatiyah says, "You know, you sound just like the people at the beginning of the story who declined to come to the banquet."

"I wouldn't be caught dead at a banquet with you. I couldn't stand before God if I did."

"So, you're telling me," Jesus says, "that prior to Andrew and Philip's visit, the Decapolis was a veritable paradise of peace and unity?"

"At least groups kept to themselves," Eremis says.

"Stop it!" Leander says. "The town of Abila has been on edge for decades."

The various leaders seem determined to prove his point, trading insults and charges.

"Aah!" Eremis says, "We've always known the Jews were fractious and divided, but quietly, inside their synagogue."

"At least *we* go to Jerusalem to make our sacrifices," the priest says. "Not like you Greeks who leave your offerings on public altars to rot and stink. Ever ask yourself why Zeus never seems to come down and eat those offerings?"

"Maybe because the wine is spoiled and sour," the Syrophoenician says.

The priest says, "Maybe because there *is* no Zeus."

Fatiyah says, "The augur's apprentice secretly removes the votive offerings under cover of night when the stench becomes unbearable."

"So, basically, your religion is a sham," the priest says.

"Again," Eremis says, "that contemptuous spirit." He turns to Jesus. "Are you proud to belong to this denigrating race?"

"Eremis, please," Leander says. "Jesus, your fame is wide. We've heard that you work wonders and change lives and that you preached a sermon on the Korazim Plateau that some are saying may become the most significant speech the world has ever known."

"I didn't do it to become famous."

"Well, too bad," Fatiyah says, "because you are. And specifically for succeeding in all you set your hand to."

"Looks like you've arrived at your first failure," Eremis says.

Jesus keeps an eye on Big James and John, who look like they're about to explode.

"Jesus of Nazareth," Leander says, "if you are who you say you are, why do you inspire and transform some people but threaten and disgust others?"

"Let me tell you a story," Jesus says, and many groan. "I know, I know, but this is another thing we Jews do, and—come to think of it—so do the Greeks. So just listen up. A sower went out to sow. And as he sowed, some seeds fell along the path—"

"We can't hear you!" someone yells from the crowd expanding by the hundreds in the background. And from the distant expanse of wilderness, other voices cry out that they can't hear.

"Aah," Jesus says. "More have arrived. I'm going to step back so we can welcome as many as possible. Students, please, as I speak, spread out, organize the people, and pass my words along to those too far away."

John looks terrified. "Y-you're sending us out into—"

"Go on," Jesus says.

"We can trust him, John," Andrew says.

Jesus motions for them all to go and notices John fixing Simon with a look, probably wondering if this is the moment where the success of the mission depends on him. But Simon sounds anything but enthusiastic, like anything but a leader: "Zee and Big James, stay here for protection."

Chapter 76

NASHON'S ACCOUNT

The Jordan River

Nashon can't wait to get to Jerusalem and expose the false teachings of Jesus of Nazareth. But he slows his horse as storm clouds gather and thunder rumbles in the distance. He gently rides toward a young shepherdess tending her flock. She calls out, "You've come from Perea?"

"The Decapolis."

"That explains it."

"Explains what?"

"Prayer tassels. You aren't wearing any."

"They're not in style in Hellenistic cities."

"What brings you to Judea?"

"An important errand in Jerusalem."

"You might consider stopping in Jericho to pick up some tassels. If you're not wearing them in the Holy City—"

"Thank you, but I have weightier matters than fashion in mind."

"You'd better hurry," she says. "There's a storm coming."

"There certainly is."

The Decapolis countryside

The disciples fan out in every direction to where they can hear Jesus and repeat his words to the masses. He's flanked by Zee and Big James, and though the colossal crowd vastly outnumbers them, Jesus can't imagine who would dare take on either of these two most-formidable foes. Meanwhile, Simon is wandering, going through the motions of supervising.

Jesus begins, pausing between phrases so the disciples can keep up and repeat them. "This man, Leander, asks how it can be that I inspire and transform some people but seem to threaten and repulse others. And so, I would like to respond with a story. A sower went out to sow. And as he sowed, some seeds fell along the path, and the birds came and devoured them. Other seeds fell on rocky ground, where they did not have much soil, and immediately they sprang up, since they had no depth of soil. But when the sun rose, they were scorched. And since they had no root, they withered away.

"Other seeds fell among thorns, and the thorns grew up and choked them. Other seeds fell on good soil and produced grain, some a hundredfold, some sixty, some thirty.

"He who has ears, let him hear."

John fidgets, warily eying the growing crowd. He notices Simon's eyes are locked on Jesus as if he's searching but also defiant. John nudges him. "Are you seeing this?" He nudges him again. "Simon, this crowd—we're completely surrounded! There have to be thousands."

Jerusalem, that night

Shmuel is startled awake at what sounds like frantic knocking at his door. "What in heaven?" He pulls on a robe and lights an oil lamp as someone shouts for him through the door.

"I'm coming!"

It's a young Pharisee bearing a lantern. "I'm terribly sorry to disturb you, Rabbi, but it's urgent."

Shmuel quickly dresses and follows the young man to the temple and the Office of Appeals. There he finds a stranger. "Rabbi Shmuel, it is a great honor. Forgive the late hour. My name is Nashon, son of Eliab, of Abila."

"You've ridden a great distance," Shmuel says. "Did your tassels fall off along the way?"

The man looks down. "Oh! My goodness, yes, they must have. My apologies. I—"

"Get him a spare," Shmuel tells his young associate. "Please, Nashon, sit down."

"I heard the great Shammai has issued an edict regarding false prophecy," Nashon begins, "to be on guard, alert for anything amiss."

"Yes."

"I have today encountered—"

"What is that vest?"

"Oh, this?" Nashon says, looking pleased and proud. "This was a gift from my wife, Damask, so named for Damascus, where it is made—a silk and linen weave very popular in the Hellenist cities."

"Remove it at once!"

"Excuse me?"

"Take it off!"

"I—"

"According to the Law of Moses, 'You shall not wear a garment of cloth made of two kinds of material.'"

As Nashon removes the vest, he says, "Oh, I thought that was just an old—"

"An old what? Finish that sentence."

"I don't know—something about not imitating Canaanite culture. A prohibition for its time. I didn't think anyone actually—"

"Torah is timeless."

"I understand. Again, my apologies. I did not intend to sin—"

Shmuel sighs. "It is as I expect of the Decapolis. Greek influence has polluted your faith. But apparently not so much that you did not heed Judge Shammai's edict."

"I encountered a rabbi consorting with Gentiles. Multitudes. He even healed a Gentile deaf-mute!"

"Tell me about the preacher."

"Um, okay. Three weeks ago, a pair of students from Capernaum came into Naveh, preaching to a group they didn't realize was both Jew and Gentile. They were repeating the teachings of this rabbi whose name they said was Jesus."

"Of?"

"What do you mean?"

"Jesus from where?"

"A small town called Nazareth, if you can believe—"

Shmuel leaps to his feet. "I require no further information."

"But Rabbi—"

The young Pharisee returns with the tassels, and Shmuel tells him to summon the Temple Guard. "And retrieve Rabbi Yanni. I'll find a representative of Judge Shammai. Meet us at the Herodian staircase."

Mission accomplished, Nashon thinks. But as he exits, passing through the Court of the Priests, he's at a loss. Where has he left his horse? As he desperately looks around, a substantial man emerges from the shadows, leading Nashon's mare. What a relief! And the man is clearly a Roman. In fact, if he's not mistaken, Nashon believes he's dressed as a *Cohortes Urbana.*

"Oh, thank God!"

"Fourteen hands. Athenian blanket. Macedonian bridle leather, Syrophoenician hammer-finished steel shoes—and you left her untethered and untended."

"I was in such a hurry!" Nashon says, fishing a coin from his pocket. "For your trouble. I'm terribly grateful!"

"No, it's my pleasure. But what could be so important that you'd leave such a beauty vulnerable to theft or wandering off?"

"I had important business with Rabbi Shmuel."

The man smiles. "At this time of night? I'm fascinated to know more. You must be very important yourself ..."

Nashon shrugs. "Oh, I don't know. It's just that ..." And he spills the whole story.

Chapter 77

THE DILEMMA

The Decapolis countryside, night

Simon wonders if he is going mad. Part of him relishes being in the middle of the action, seeing Jesus do his thing. But Simon has been itching for a confrontation, a chance to demand how the Messiah could have … well, not necessarily *done* this to him and Eden, but *allowed* it anyway. In his heart of hearts, he knows he's not owed anything by the Creator of the universe, but does nothing qualify him for even a modicum of special treatment?

Normally a spectacle like this one would thrill him, make him lightheaded with anticipation of what Jesus will do next in the middle of this hostile crowd. Simon is doing his duty, trying to manage all the moving parts, but his heart is not in it. Not this time. He's spent beyond reason, his reserves depleted. That's his own fault, he knows. He could have stayed home with his long-suffering wife and not wandered the Roman quarter, and he could have chosen to go home immediately after being escorted out of there, too.

But no, he had to roam the streets of Capernaum with warring thoughts keeping him from rationality. Now he is paying for it. All he wants is to stagger home and collapse, knowing Eden—to whom he has been unconscionably despicable while wallowing in his own self-pity—will be the angel he recognizes that she is. He doesn't deserve her or her selfless kindness, but it's the only balm he can imagine for his tortured soul and body.

In his flesh, Simon wants to stomp and curse at the top of his lungs, forcing Jesus to respond, to give him a private audience. But prudence remains somewhere in the back of his tortured brain, and he clings to it like a drowning man. Jesus wants him here for some reason, and while he's not sure what it is—and wonders if the master really knows what's going on within him—he will do his job. For now, that seems to be half disciple-watching and half crowd control.

The rabbi himself is clearly tired also but continues to power through, preaching and teaching as if his life depends on it. And perhaps it does. Who knows what this crowd, with all its opposing factions, might do when he stops? Zee and Big James remain in place beside him, but as the sun has long since disappeared into blackness, each bears a flaming torch to illuminate him and keep him warm.

Throughout the crowd, the other disciples are still repeating Jesus' words so that all may hear. Simon wonders what the various factions make of his monumental, often paradoxical truths.

"What I'm about to say is for Jews as much as Gentiles! So many cities are missing the need for repentance and righteousness. I have preached and performed miracles in multiple towns, as have my followers, and yet so many still fall short.

"Many of you are from cities such as Tyre and Sidon that have rejected God for centuries. But some cities know who God is and yet reject me when I am in their midst—cities like

Chorazin, Bethsaida, and even Capernaum, where I have spent so much time. If the mighty works done there had been done in Tyre and Sidon or even in Sodom, they would have repented long ago in sackcloth and ashes. But I tell you, it will be more bearable for those cities on the day of judgment than for you.

"So many of you here, listening to me, are eager to be drawn closer to God, to find peace in your souls! In your eagerness, you have more wisdom than most of the religious leaders who refuse to be humble."

Jesus gazes to the stars. "I thank You, Father, Lord of heaven and earth, that You have hidden these things from the wise and revealed them to little children, for such was Your gracious will." He looks back to the crowd. "All things have been handed over to me by my Father, and no one knows the son except the Father, and no one knows the Father except the son and anyone to whom the son chooses to reveal Him. And I am revealing the Father to you now, Jew *and* Gentile! What is stirring in your hearts, in the middle of such division and unrest, is Father God being revealed to you!

"Come to *me,* all who labor and are heavy laden, and I will give you rest. Take my yoke upon you, and learn from me. For I am gentle and lowly in heart, and you will find rest for your souls. For my yoke is easy and my burden is light!"

When Jesus pauses, Simon is struck anew by how the people stare, obviously enraptured.

"Speaking of rest," Jesus continues, "we all need it now, including me. So, wherever you want to lay your head, let's sleep, and I will continue in the morning. Shalom, shalom."

It's not lost on Simon that the leaders of the various blocs of opponents, from Fatiyah to the Jewish priest, nod in seeming approval. Big James and Zee escort Jesus to a small lean-to constructed of sticks and blankets. Simon makes his way to where

Little James and Thaddeus are building a fire. Matthew seems to be staring at the multitudes to the north, while Judas and Thomas approach from the other direction. Matthew asks Judas, "Do you have the count?"

"There are at least one thousand to the south."

"People were still arriving after the sun set," Thomas says.

"Are Andrew and Philip back?" Judas says.

"No," Matthew says. "But before it got dark, both points of the compass looked roughly equal in population."

"So, two thousand?" Thomas says.

"And counting," Judas says.

"I said roughly," Matthew says. "But yes."

Simon is aware of the others' eyes as he walks the perimeter of the camp. His brother, Andrew, and Philip approach him. "We have a situation," Andrew says.

"What situation?"

"The Gentiles have run out of food," Philip says.

"I don't think anyone expected the teaching to last all day," Andrew says.

Why is this our concern? Simon thinks. "No one forced them to stay."

"Simon!" Philip says. "They were hungry for his words!"

"And now they're hungry for food. It's not our problem. Can't they go back to their villages?"

"They were driven out by violence!" Andrew says. "And now it's dark! They need to sleep in these fields."

Philip says, "Simon doesn't know how bad it was when we first came."

"Whatever happened," Simon says, "it wouldn't change anything."

John and Big James approach. "I can see things are going just as well here as out there," John says.

"What do you mean?" Matthew asks.

"Some of these people were driven from their homes more than a week ago," Big James says. "They're hungry and tired."

"Don't trouble Simon with your news," Andrew says. "His mind is anywhere but here."

"Andrew," John says, "be gracious to your brother."

"Gracious? He just said these people's hunger is not our problem—that we should send them away."

"Did you really say that, Simon?" Big James says.

"Who cares?" Philip says. "We just have to solve this one without Simon's help."

"We can't," John says.

"He's not the Messiah, John," Andrew says.

"No argument there," John says. "But Jesus told me that the success of this trip depends on Simon." He levels a look at Simon.

As Simon holds his gaze, Big James says, "Jesus said that?"

"That's why I stayed behind," John says. "The master insisted I wait for Simon and bring him."

"Did he say how it depends on—?"

"No."

Simon shrugs and walks away. Andrew catches up to him. "If it all depends on you, what's the plan?"

"Nothing."

"What?"

"Jesus is capable of doing whatever he wants," Simon says. "In the end, that's what he'll do."

"Brother, you're being very—"

"Look, if Jesus wants to provide a solution for these hungry people, that's what's going to happen. I'm sure of it."

"You don't sound very happy to be sure about it."

You got that right, Simon thinks.

Chapter 78

GOD'S TIME

Judean countryside, pre-dawn

Under darkening skies, Shmuel rides in a horse-drawn carriage with Yanni and Ozem, an older Pharisee from Shammai's staff. Shmuel knows that common non-clerics would likely be aghast if they knew how these holy men bickered like school-age siblings.

Yanni jostles the elder Pharisee who has dozed off on his shoulder. "Ozem! Wake up! You're slobbering on me."

Ozem straightens and rubs his eyes. "How much farther do we have to go?"

Shmuel shakes his head. "You know the distance to the Decapolis, and you know the hour we left."

"An ungodly hour," Ozem says.

Yanni says, "There's no such thing as an ungodly hour, Ozem."

"Tell that to my wife," Ozem says. "We were supposed to take the children to see their grandparents in Gaza today."

"We serve God first," Shmuel says. "Then our families."

"We serve God *by* serving our families," Ozem says. "And you don't have one, so don't preach at me."

Yanni appears to be savoring this. "The only preaching I've heard lately is you repeating Shammai's refrain that fidelity to God's Law *to the letter* is the only thing that matters. And yet here you are complaining about having to actually act upon that conviction."

That's for sure, Shmuel thinks. "While I filed the reports to Shammai about the healings on Shabbat and Jesus commanding his followers to eat heads of grain on Shabbat, he said we should wait to take action until we knew it was God's time."

Ozem yawns. "Wisdom I wish you would have heeded. And who are you to dictate to us what that time is?" Ozem says. "You forget your rank and stature, Shmuel."

How dare he? "To the contrary! Cognizant of my rank and stature, I asked Shammai how we would know it was God's time. His answer? When evidence was abundant. Nashon says the crowds passing him on the road could be described only as multitudes of Gentiles. How's that for evidence?"

"That's the other thing about this," Ozem says. "Gentiles? Why are we meddling in the Decapolis? The Holy City is where things matter."

Yanni responds, "So a sin is a sin only if it happens in or near Jerusalem?"

Sounding annoyed, Ozem says, "No, it's a matter of allocating resources. There's more syncretism and Hellenist influence desecrating our people's practice in the Decapolis than we could ever hope to address in any meaningful way. The hassle of hunting down a single Jew who may be leading a few people astray is myopic and unappealing with all we have on our hands in Jerusalem and throughout Judea. We have to be focused. Our job is to make the Law clear and ensure the people know how to follow it to the letter."

Does he hear himself? Shmuel wonders. "I'm sorry that false teaching is such a burden to you."

"I'm sorry it's such a burden to *you*," Ozem says.

"Enough of all this," Yanni says. "One thing we can all agree on is that if we find this man performing magic tricks or sorcery, we will have to take action."

Ozem sighs. "It's been a long time since I prosecuted a witchcraft case. They can be unwieldy, which I why I let them come to me and don't go looking for them."

Shmuel has had it with the man. He leans out and shouts, "Driver! Is there any way to go faster?"

"I can try."

"You could get out and push, Shmuel," Ozem says. "You summoned a carriage in the middle of the night. Did you expect Caiaphas to handpick your steeds? Just relax."

Atticus follows at a distance on horseback, watching all this from beneath his hood, sipping from a flask to stay warm.

Chapter 79

FIVE LOAVES AND TWO FISH

Decapolis countryside

Andrew can't stay still. From where he sits, he scans the vast crowd as sunrise reveals storm clouds to the west. He wonders how much longer this crowd can endure without something to eat.

Jesus resumes teaching. "Tell me what you think of this!" he says. "A man had two sons. He went to the first and said, 'Go and work in the vineyard today.' The son answered, 'I will not,' but later changed his mind and went."

Andrew rises and marches headlong into the crowd.

Jesus continues, "And he went to the other son and said the same. And he answered, 'I will go, sir,' but he did not go. Which of the two did the will of his father?"

It seems as if everyone shouts, "The first!"

Andrew comes across a man munching on a piece of flatbread. "You! Where did you find that?"

"At the bottom of my bag. I forgot it was in there. A little stale, but—"

"You've been out here this long and just discovered it?"

"I followed some men who told me we were coming to watch a fight."

"A fight?"

"Everyone was just in such a hurry …"

Andrew turns to another cluster of listeners. "Does anyone have food?" They shake their heads, so he moves on.

"You're one of his students, right? Your name is Andrew?" Andrew turns to see Telemachus, the son of the former deaf-mute. The lad says, "I just wanted to thank you again for everything—"

"It wasn't me who healed your father, but I can certainly pass it along."

"You've been asking about food. I want to share what I have." Telemachus unshoulders his basket-style backpack, revealing five loaves of bread and two fish.

"Son, I appreciate the thought, but this would feed maybe one family out of thousands."

"I just wanted to do what I could. Please accept it."

With Zee and Big James still standing guard, Jesus continues teaching, hoping the disciples are still able to hear him and relay his words to the multitudes. "The kingdom of heaven is like treasure hidden in a field, which a man found and covered up. Then in his joy he goes and sells all that he has and buys that field.

"Let me say it another way. It is like a merchant in search of fine pearls, who, on finding one pearl of great value, went and sold all that he had and bought it.

"Listen carefully, because this is accessible to all of you, regardless of race or creed! The kingdom is so valuable that once you have glimpsed it, it's worth parting with everything you have in order to gain it. Even though to others you might look like a fool—throwing away your life savings to buy what would look to others like an unremarkable field—you know about the hidden treasure. And that makes it worth everything."

Thaddeus and Little James emerge from the crowd and appear by Jesus' side. "Have you come closer to hear better?"

Thaddeus shakes his head, and Little James says, "There's an issue."

"My friends," Jesus says to the crowd, "if you'll excuse me one moment, I need to speak with my students."

"The people are all out of food," Thaddeus says.

"Many were already without food for days before we got here," Little James says. "Others have traveled a great distance."

By now the rest of the disciples have gathered around Jesus. "So, give them something to eat," he says.

Nathanael says, "We're out of food. They're out of food. Is it time to send them home?"

"Well," Jesus says, "at this point, they're so hungry and tired, if we send them home, they'll faint along the way."

"You knew they were hungry?" Judas says.

"Yes, Judas," he says, winking. "I can see them while I'm talking. This is a tough one. So, where can we buy some bread for all these people?"

"We came with only a little over two hundred denarii," Judas says.

"Rabbi," Philip says, "that's not enough to buy each of them even a little. I wouldn't even know how to calculate it."

Both Thomas and Matthew raise their hands, but as everyone looks to them, they fall silent.

"Maybe we could go into Abila," Big James says, "and negotiate something on credit."

"That makes sense to me," Judas says.

"Negotiate with whom?" Leander says. "The entire population of Abila is here. The city is nine miles away. Even if we raided every house in town, we'd have to find a way to get it back here, and we'd still be able to feed only a fraction of the masses."

"Could you bring me anything?" Jesus says. "Surely there's some food from someone, even a small amount."

Andrew sets Telemachus's small basket on the ground and opens it as everyone peers in. "Five loaves of bread and two fish," Andrew says. "But what is this for so many?"

"Barley loaves," Telemachus says.

"Oh, two fish and five *barley* loaves," Andrew says with a smirk. "Thanks for clarifying."

John whispers to Simon, "This is humiliating."

"Jesus will take care of it if he wants to."

"You look scared, Simon. What are you afraid of?"

Simon won't meet his eye. "I'm afraid he'll choose them," he says, gesturing to the crowd.

Why could he not have chosen Eden? Chosen me? Simon can't stop thinking it's too much to ask. Here he is, once again a witness to a spectacle he could never have imagined—Jesus, the Messiah himself, preaching the good news of the kingdom of God to races and ethnicities that normally would not even acknowledge each other. Yet here they sit, in clusters of their like-minded friends, just feet from those who have been their enemies for centuries.

Chapter 80

THE MIRACLE

This is wonderful bread, Telemachus," Jesus says, examining a loaf.

"I know it's not enough."

"It's enough for me. I can do a lot with this. Thank you." He gazes into the sky and raises a loaf with both hands. "Blessed are you, Lord our God, ruler of the universe, who brings forth bread from the earth." He breaks the bread in two.

Fatiyah says, "Did they get some bread?"

The strict priest tells his order, "If they've got bread, be ready. We'll probably be first."

As murmurs ripple through the crowd—which has burgeoned to over 5,000 men alone, the disciples push in close around Jesus. "Feed them," he says.

"What has changed?" Thomas says. "Are we—"

"Organize the people into groups of fifty and a hundred, and find twelve baskets to distribute the loaves and fish."

No one moves.

"Was I unclear?" Jesus says.

Thaddeus and Little James head into the crowd, asking for baskets.

Thomas gives Jesus a look. "This feels familiar."

Jesus smirks. "Maybe."

Thomas, Nathanael, Big James, Judas, and Matthew hustle off.

Simon remains. John grabs his arm. "Come on."

Only Andrew, Philip, and Zee remain. Jesus says pointedly, "Feed them."

Andrew and Philip set out as Jesus turns back to the crowd, trailed by Zee. "The kingdom of heaven is like a grain of mustard seed that a man took and sowed in his field!"

Meanwhile, the disciples are returning one by one with empty baskets they have retrieved from the masses. They kneel around Telemachus's open basket with its meager food supply.

"It is the smallest of all seeds," Jesus continues, "but when it has grown, it is larger than all the garden plants and becomes a tree ..."

Andrew takes a loaf and breaks it, putting half in Judas's basket and half in Thaddeus's. Philip cuts a fish in two and gives half to Little James and half to Thomas.

"... so that the birds of the air come and make nests in its branches," Jesus says.

Andrew breaks another loaf, giving half to Big James. Half loaves drop into various baskets, as do pieces of fish. Andrew breaks the last loaf and gives the pieces to Matthew and Philip. He closes Telemachus's basket. "That's the last of it. Telemachus, you can have this back—" But as he grabs it, Andrew finds it heavy. He gapes. The others stare. Without looking back from where he's preaching, Jesus can't resist a smile.

Andrew kneels as the others press in around him. He slowly opens the lid again and gasps. Matthew peeks over his shoulder and breaks into a grin. "What?"

"What just happened?" Thaddeus says, staring into his own basket, which is also now brimming with bread and fish. All around him, the others are finding the same. Most look shocked, some laugh, and Simon glares.

"I have kept you here for all this time," Jesus tells the crowd, "giving you spiritual food! But you clearly need other food right now. Let's eat!"

As the crowd cheers, the disciples move through the various groups of fifty and a hundred, handing out fish and bread from seemingly bottomless baskets. People everywhere are helping each other, feeding each other, assisting the disabled, making sure everyone is fed. Big James lights fires with a torch here and there, and children look delighted with their bites of bread and fish. Matthew appears shaken every time he reaches into his basket and finds it full, despite all the food he distributes everywhere.

Andrew and Philip, with Leander close behind, dispense food to the Greeks, including Eremis. "Maybe now you'll believe us," Andrew says, and Eremis grips Philip's hand with both of his.

Leander approaches one of the cantankerous Greeks and says, "What say you now?"

"I have no words."

But one of his compatriots says, "Yet we all see."

Chapter 81

THE VISIT

The Capernaum synagogue, midday

Yussif is at work in his office when a student interrupts. "Rabbi Yussif, two women are here to see you."

Not wanting to break from his writing, Yussif says, "It's Rabbi Josiah's visiting hours. Is he unable to assist? I'm in the middle of something very important."

"One of the women says to tell you she is the wife of Simon, son of Jonah."

"Oh! One of Jesus'—yes, please send them in."

A few moments later, after Eden and her mother have sat across from Yussif and Eden has told her heartbreaking story, the Pharisee says, "You have my deepest condolences. Torah has very little to say on this specific matter, I'm afraid. But sorrow is sorrow. Especially when your husband is—"

"Gone," Dasha says flatly.

"Perhaps," Yussif says, "but I was going to say distracted. There is much going on with Jesus, and in many ways the world is upending—with Simon in the middle of it. I'm trying to make sense of it myself. Maybe *I've* been too distracted. It's easy to forget there are still matters of great importance to attend to in the home."

It's not lost on Yussif that Eden has pursed her lips and is clearly none too pleased. "Are you angry with him?"

She looks up, appearing to study the rabbi. "Yes," she says at last.

"I understand. You mentioned you did your purification in the sea. Now that some time has passed, what about a new cleansing, but in the mikveh? With a prayerful state of mind, maybe this could be part of a new path forward."

"But the cistern …" Dasha says.

"We received word this morning it will be operational by sundown. And it has been more than just fixed. It has been beautifully appointed. Actually, I believe Simon helped with the speedy repair."

Dasha says, "Perhaps when she is ready. We were hoping today for a reading from Torah."

"Of course." He turns to Eden. "Did you have anything in mind?"

But as Eden appears to consider this, Dasha interrupts again. "Perhaps something uplifting and joyful, Rabbi."

Yussif doesn't take his eyes off Eden. "I'm not sure that would be truthful," he says.

Eden shakes her head.

Yussif stands and approaches the scrolls behind him. "There are many psalms of anguish, even anger, and they are all just as important as the others. In fact, some of the desperate psalms draw us closest to God." He brings a scroll back to his desk. "One of David's chief musicians, Asaph, was inclined to write in this depth. As in this passage. 'In the day of my trouble I seek the Lord; in the night my hand stretches out without wearying.'"

Yussif looks to Eden. "This psalm is desperate, even angry. Do you know who else is undoubtedly desperate and angry?" He pauses. "Simon."

Eden sighs, and her shoulders slump.

"I know him a little," Yussif continues. "And I'm sure he's actually very angry and making that known to others."

Eden seems to fight a knowing smile.

"Perhaps," the rabbi says, "you can pray this with him—and for him." He spreads the scroll anew. 'My soul refuses to be comforted. When I remember God, I moan; when I meditate, my spirit faints. You hold my eyelids open. I am so troubled that I cannot speak. Will the Lord spurn forever, and never again be favorable? Has His steadfast love forever ceased? Are His promises at an end for all time? Has God forgotten to be gracious? Has He in His anger shut up His compassion?'"

Yussif looks up from the scroll, changes his tone from serious to heartbreakingly empathetic, and smiles at Eden. "But that's not the whole psalm, is it?" he says.

Eden shakes her head and closes her eyes.

Yussif continues, "'Then I said, "I will appeal to this, to the years of the right hand of the Most High. I will remember the deeds of the Lord; yes, I will remember Your wonders of old. I will ponder all Your work and meditate on Your mighty deeds. Your way, O God, is holy. What god is great like our God? You are the God who works wonders; You have made known Your might among the peoples. You with Your arm redeemed Your people, the children of Jacob and Joseph."'"

The Decapolis countryside

Just like his fellow disciples, Simon finds himself passing out never-ending bread and fish to the grateful throngs. But unlike them, every time he opens his basket and finds it full, it hits him like a dagger to his heart. *Jesus can do this, just as he can do anything he wants, yet he chooses to leave me—to leave Eden and me—desolate.* The sight of a pregnant woman devastates him anew, and—as if to compound it all—she has a healthy toddler, too, to whom she feeds little pieces of bread.

Not so long ago, Simon knows, he would have been warmed and filled by such a scene. He would have been thrilled that *his* rabbi, yes, *his* master, was responsible for such a touching incident. Ominous clouds gather overhead and mirror his inner gloom.

Simon looks longingly to Jesus, tears streaming.

Little James lugs back one of the larger, taller baskets, full to the brim. Jesus says, "What are you doing with all that bread and fish?"

Looking amazed and joyful, Little James plops the basket on the ground and says, "Everyone ate and was satisfied! No one wanted any more! They were full!"

One by one, the others set down their full baskets.

"You have given us more than we needed," Thomas says.

Matthew tells Judas, "You'll get used to this kind of math."

"I'm in," Judas says.

Philip thanks Jesus.

Andrew says, "I can't believe we ever doubted."

"I'm the one who caused their hunger," Jesus says. "I should be the one to satisfy it, no?"

"I am no longer surprised," Matthew says.

Big James shouts, "You're a new Matthew!" and thumps him on the back, making him stumble. "Oh! Sorry. But I meant it."

"It's always this way," John says. "I don't know why I'm surprised." Sounding wistful, he adds, "It's just like Simon said it would be."

Simon watches Jesus praying, then the master turns and looks directly at him, compassion on his face. Simon holds his gaze as he had when he crested the hill on his way here. What does Jesus want or expect from him? He deliberately drops his basket and walks away, bread and fish spilling.

John moves to go after Simon, but his big brother James holds him back. Jesus looks sorrowful, exhausted, yet patient at the same time. He holds out a hand, palm up, and gentle drops of rain pitter-patter into it.

The crowd seems to rise as one, gathering their children and their belongings and snuffing out fires. The disciples quickly gather their own things as the massive horde begins to disperse.

Chapter 82

LATECOMERS

Shmuel peers out of his carriage, as do his fellow travelers, as the horses slow to a walk near the edge of the bustling crowds. "Nashon wasn't exaggerating," he says.

"He sure wasn't," Yanni says. "This is more than I ever thought—"

Ozem points. "That's a Nabataean robe!"

"That headdress is Arabian," Ozem says.

"We're in a sea of Gentiles," Yanni says.

Shmuel leans out. "Driver! Stop!" He and his fellow Pharisees exit the carriage as people stream past them in droves. He calls out, "What is this? What has been happening?"

"The teacher!" the Syrophoenician leader shouts. "From Nazareth!"

"But—" Yanni says, appearing lost in the rush.

Shmuel grabs a man rushing by. "How long have you been out here listening to the teacher?"

"Two days!"

"But we are miles from any city! How did you eat?"

"He multiplied loaves and fish to feed us. Thousands of us."

"What do you mean, *multiplied*?" Ozem says.

"There just kept being more and more, by his hand! A miracle!"

Yanni says, "We need the testimonies of three witnesses."

The man laughs. "That won't be difficult."

"Did he and his followers also partake?" Shmuel asks.

"Of course."

"He breaks bread with Gentiles?" Ozem says.

The Syrophoenician snorts and turns to go, laughing. "I tell them God performed a miracle, and they say he ate with the wrong people!"

Yanni waves him off. "We already know an Ethiopian woman often travels with him and his students."

"But breaking bread?" Ozem says. "That's worse than I thought. It's forbidden!"

"Again," Shmuel says, "we *need* witnesses!" But he wonders …

Several yards away, amid currents of fleeing pilgrims, Atticus sits astride his horse, listening as Leander approaches the robed clerics. "Pharisees from Judea?" Leander says. "You're a little late. You've missed the show."

"Name the teacher," Ozem says.

"Jesus of Nazareth. A name I'll never forget. A name no one will ever forget."

"What did he preach about?" Shmuel demands. "Did any of it run contrary to Torah?"

"He preached about the kingdom of heaven."

"Which he said was what?" Yanni asks.

"Everything," Leander says. "A mustard seed. A pearl of great price. Treasure hidden in a field. But the best part—"

"I can't wait to hear this," Shmuel says. "What?"

"He said that in the kingdom of heaven, many would come from east and west with Abraham, Isaac, and Jacob. That's all of us—Jew and Gentile together at one table."

"He said what?" Ozem says.

"We need a third witness," Yanni says.

Leander says, "Jesus of Nazareth may be the first Jew to break bread with Gentiles, but he won't be the last. And it will be with *your* patriarchs—Abraham, Isaac, and Jacob."

"Blasphemy!" Ozem shouts, pressing a finger into Leander's chest. "You've hurt our people!"

"We've hurt each other," Leander says. "But he's healing us."

Atticus watches Leander break free and glare at the Pharisees as he presses on to rejoin the crowds.

Ozem spits in his direction. Shmuel looks shocked. Ozem seizes another passerby. "We need three witnesses! What did the teacher say about Gentles reclining at table with the Patriarchs?"

Ozem and Yanni jump into the fray, trying to grab others, only to have them wrench away. But to Atticus, Shmuel appears to have something on his mind. In fact, he looks deeply troubled.

Chapter 83

REST

Decapolis countryside, near the Sea of Galilee

Simon remains puzzled why Jesus thought it was so important he be here for yet another sermon to the masses. He's glad to have another tale to tell for the rest of his life, the feeding of at least five thousand men and their families. But that could have easily occurred without Simon. In fact, he was hardly an enthusiastic participant.

Who knows? Maybe I'm here just for logistics. The disciples need to get back to Capernaum, and he knows the best way. He cajoles Judas out of a few shekels from the treasury bag, assuring him he'll account for it, and heads off alone to the shore of the Galilee. Finding a couple of fishermen he's known all his life, Simon negotiates a fair price for the use of a boat and oars for the night. He bangs on the hull and says, "Okay. Not amazing, but it will do." They load him with ropes and oars and try to talk him into more gear. "No, no, no. No net, no fish, nothing. I just want the boat." He heads back to where the disciples finish cleaning up.

"What do we do now?" Nathanael says.

Thomas says, "It's a thirteen-mile walk to Capernaum, but with this rain coming—"

Thaddeus turns to Little James, clearly concerned about his limitations. "With everything we had to do today, carrying baskets and distributing food—"

"I'll do my best," Little James assures him.

"We would never leave you behind," Big James tells him.

"We're not walking," Simon says. They turn, looking surprised. "I got a boat. We're rowing. It's only eight miles across, and we can row faster than we can walk. C'mon, Big James, you know we're good at this."

The others look dubious, and Simon knows the landlubbers are likely afraid of sailing at night with a bigger storm brewing. But before anyone can say anything, Jesus says, "Simon is right. Everyone get into the boat and row back across to Capernaum before the weather gets any worse."

"What about you?" John asks Jesus.

"It's been a long three days. I need some time alone to pray."

"In this weather?" Matthew says.

"Let me stay with you, Rabbi," Zee says, "to keep watch."

"I'll be fine. All of you go. Hurry. Follow Simon. You all did so well today. Shalom, shalom."

Simon is as mystified as the others look when Jesus sets out alone in the gathering darkness. Maybe Simon shouldn't care, but he does.

John sidles next to Simon. "I stayed behind and brought you so you could get us a boat?"

"I won't be in your way for long, John."

"Simon, have faith."

"Faith isn't my problem. In fact, I think I was a mistake. Even God must make mistakes, right?" Simon knows as well as

John does that this was a stupid thing to say, but he looks directly into his eyes and arches his back, wordlessly telling John to move along before this escalates. As John moves on, Simon tells the others, "You heard Jesus. Let's go."

Atticus continues to watch from a distance.

Meanwhile, Shmuel finds himself in a daze, aimlessly wandering the Decapolis countryside as Gentiles pass him in the growing darkness. For the moment he neither knows nor cares where his fellow clerics have gotten to. He climbs a hill, his mind racing, as the crowds around him thin and he's able to take in the vastness of the area. Down below, Jesus seems to materialize out of the crowd.

As the Nazarene ascends the incline, Shmuel doesn't know whether to keep moving or stand and face him. He freezes. Their eyes meet, and it's as if they're regarding each other.

"You look familiar," Jesus says, sounding weary but friendly.

Shmuel doesn't know how to respond. "I—"

"I'm sorry," Jesus says. "I mean no offense. More specifically, you look troubled."

I look *troubled? I* am *troubled, but how would he know that?* Still, Shmuel feels compelled to be transparent. "I am."

"I'm going up this hill to pray," Jesus says. "Would you like to join me? We don't have to talk about anything if you don't want. I know sometimes people who are troubled just need someone to sit with them in silence."

In truth, nothing sounds better to Shmuel. But he wonders what others would make of his sitting with, perhaps chatting or even praying with, the man who has become the enemy and the target of the Sanhedrin. As for troubled people needing someone to sit with them in silence, he knows exactly whom Jesus is referring to. "Like Job," he says.

"That bad, huh?" Jesus says.

"Not quite. More like David."

"Aah, do share."

"'How long must I take counsel in my soul and have sorrow in my heart all the day? How long shall my enemy be exalted over me?'"

"You're losing something," Jesus says, looking suddenly sad. "I know what that's like."

"What are you losing?" Shmuel asks.

"Time."

Shmuel is profoundly confused.

"Come," Jesus says. "Join me in prayer for a little while."

"Will you speak with me after?"

"I will—if you still want to question me after we pray."

Jesus heads up the hill, and the Pharisee follows, no longer caring who sees or what they think.

The Sea of Galilee

With the four former fishermen—Simon, Andrew, Big James, and John—leading the way, the twelve disciples quickly fill the boat and find themselves in deep waters. But several hours later, the black sky is alive with lightning, the water is roiling, and the other disciples look terrified, especially Matthew and the smaller men. Zee appears to be doing his best holding down the cargo, but even Simon realizes how long he and the other three have been rowing against a vicious wind.

Big James shouts, "We're not getting anywhere!"

"The winds are too strong!" Zee says. "We should turn back!"

"We can get there!" Simon hollers, sounding more confident than he feels. "Just keep pulling!"

"Simon!" John yells, "It's the fourth watch of the night, and we've been stuck in one place for hours!"

I don't care if it is *after three a.m.,* Simon thinks. *We're not quitting.*

An enormous wave crashes over the hull and slams Little James to the deck. Thaddeus rushes to him.

"I'm all right!"

"We can't take much more water!" Nathanael says.

"We'll founder!" Big James says.

"Let's go back!" Thomas shouts.

"We're better off wet and cold on land," Andrew says, "than drowned out here!"

Lightning illuminates their petrified faces, and Simon is mesmerized by John's look of shock. What is he staring at?

Atticus moves to the edge of the water, his cloak billowing in the wind and rain. He can't have seen what he thinks he just saw, silhouetted against the horizon in a flash of lightning. But when he squints into the distance, whatever it was has disappeared. He wonders why he stayed out here watching in the first place and determines to get back to his horse and find a cozy inn somewhere. He stomps across the laden sand and mounts, but before he can ride off, he sees something again. *What could that be?*

In the boat, Simon bellows to John, "Keep rowing! What are you doing?"

"Did anyone else just see that?" John says.

"What?" Philip says.

"Over there!" he says, pointing.

"I don't see anything!" Judas says.

"Me either!" Zee says. "What are we looking for?"

With the next flash of lightning, Simon makes out the faintest apparition—that has to be what it is. A figure, on the water, in the distance.

"A ghost!" Andrew shrieks. "It's a ghost!"

"A what?" Matthew says.

"It can't be," Big James says.

"We have to get out of here!" Andrew says. "Everyone row! Row faster! Go!"

But in a grave, calm tone, Simon says, "No! Nobody move!"

"Simon!" Andrew says. "What?"

"I said everybody stop! Hold this position." Simon remains focused on the very place he last saw the specter, and when lightning strikes again, he sees Jesus amid the waves.

As the others scream, Zee says, "That's not a ghost!"

Andrew says, "Are you crazy?"

"Trust me," Zee says. "I know what a ghost looks like, and that's not one!"

"Do not be afraid!" Jesus says. "It's me!"

The men begin hollering. "Jesus!"

"How—what are you doing?"

"You're scaring us!"

"Impossible!"

Thomas says, "How is this the second-most-incredible thing I've seen today?"

Simon stands, fighting to keep his balance in the rocking craft, boring into Jesus with his eyes. *It's him. It has to be him. But—*

Jesus' eyes are locked on Simon. "This surprises you? Did you learn nothing from today?"

"If it *is* you," Simon says, "command me to come to you."

"Simon, no!" Andrew says.

"Are you out of your mind?" Big James says.

"If you are who you say you are, bid me step out of this boat!"

A wave slaps Jesus' face as he holds Simon's gaze. "You have faith to walk on this water?"

"Absolutely! You can do whatever you command, and if you command the water to hold me, I will walk on it!"

"If I call you to me, you will step out in faith?"

"Yes!"

"Then why are you upset?"

"Why are you chasing after Gentiles when your own people have problems right here? When your own *person*—me—has problems? I've been right here in front of you, believing in you, and you're breaking up fights in the Decapolis!"

Jesus simply stares at him. "Then come to me. You, weary and heavy-laden. I will give you rest."

Simon takes off his sandals.

"Simon?" Andrew says. "No!"

Matthew stares.

As the others shout in fear, confusion, and excitement, Simon grabs the edge of the boat. He swings a leg over the side and inches his foot toward the water. He stands, unsteadily, on the surface, then steps out of the boat, strangely full of bravado but also rage. Jesus reaches out to him. "Do you still have faith?"

"Faith hasn't been my problem! I gave up everything to follow you, but you're healing total strangers!"

Jesus looks steadier on the water than Simon feels. "Why do you think I allow trials, Simon?"

"I don't know!"

"They prove the genuineness of your faith! They strengthen you! *This* is strengthening you! And Eden! Keep your eyes on me!"

A wave crashes into Simon, and the disciples cry out. He takes his eyes off Jesus and considers the waves—huge, merciless, churning. Everywhere he looks, the sea is scarier, fiercer. Fear overtakes him. "I'm sinking! Help!" Suddenly he's in the water up to his chest. "Lord, please! Save me!" Jesus moves toward him, and as the water reaches Simon's chin, he lets out a primal scream. "Save me! I'm dr—"

As he goes under, he reaches desperately, and Jesus grabs his forearm and lifts him out. Trembling, Simon is pierced by the look of compassionate disappointment on Jesus' face. "Oh, you of little faith. Why did you doubt?"

Ashamed and humiliated, Simon says, "Please don't let me go. I'm sorry. I can't do this on my own. Don't let me go. Please!"

"I've got you. I have so much planned for you, Simon, including hard things. Just keep your eyes on me. I promise." He helps Simon into the boat.

"Don't let me go."

"I've got you." Jesus turns to the raging sea. "Peace!" he shouts. "Be still!"

Immediately the rain stops, the wind ceases, the waves settle. Simon continues to cling to Jesus. "Don't let me go. I'm sorry! Please. Don't let me go." He weeps softly, aware the others are soaked, exhausted, spellbound.

Jesus strokes Simon's matted hair. "I'm here. I'm always here. I let people get hungry, but I feed them."

Simon continues to repeat, "Please! Please, don't let me go."

Postlude

Capernaum mikvah

Surrounded by candlelight, wrapped in beige linen and with arms outstretched—Dasha holding her hand on one side and Salome holding the other—Eden steps into the ornate purification bath. They guide her step by step down the stairs.

The three women recite together, "Blessed are You, Lord our God, King of the universe, Who gives and takes away." Now, as they release her to step deeper into the water until it's up to her neck, they recite, "Who comforts us in our grief, and binds the wounds of the brokenhearted? Who mourns with us for the life that could not be?" Now up to her chin, "In the shadow of Your wings do we take refuge."

Eden tips her head back and closes her eyes, going under. She emerges with an exhale, her body and soul ritually cleansed. She is moved to pray for Simon. "Don't let him go. Please, don't let him go." And she remembers the end of the psalm of Asaph:

"I will appeal to this: to the years of the right hand of the Most High. I will remember the deeds of the Lord; yes, I will remember Your wonders of old. I will ponder all Your work and meditate on Your mighty deeds. Your way, O God, is holy. What god is great like our God?

"You are the God who works wonders; You have made known Your might among the peoples. You with Your arm redeemed Your people, the children of Jacob and Joseph. When the waters saw You, O God, when the waters saw You, they were afraid; indeed the deep trembled.

"The clouds poured out water; the skies gave forth thunder; Your arrows flashed on every side. The crash of Your thunder was in the whirlwind; Your lightnings lighted up the world. The earth trembled and shook. Your way was through the sea, Your path through the great waters; yet Your footprints were unseen."

Late the next morning, Simon finally reaches home to find Eden in the doorway. He reaches for her as it seems everything, everything rolls off his back. Their foreheads touch, and he gathers her to himself.

THE END

Acknowledgments

Thanks to:
My assistant, Sarah Helus
My agent, Alex Field
My editors, Larry Weeden and Leilani Squires
The Focus on the Family team
Carlton Garborg and BroadStreet
And my heart, Dianna